TIDES *of* FATE
BOOK TWO

THESE
HOLLOW
SHORES

A.P. WALSTON

First published in the United States by Alexandria Walston.

ISBN 978-1-7373891-6-3 (hardcover)

ISBN 978-1-7373891-5-6 (softcover)

ISBN 978-1-7373891-4-9 (ebook)

First U.S. Edition: August 2022

Alexandria Walston

For my papa, who has a drawer full of all my old writing.

EARLIER

He stood over the Old Crow, glad to be bloody well rid of the bastard.

William Stedd had been responsible for all the bloodiest acts to befall the sea the last twenty years. Fucker was likely the reason they were considered pirates now instead of what they'd been before—lost and wandering people of the sea, all their glory and gold stripped from them for a single gods-damned mistake.

The wet wheezing of Stedd's quartermaster drew his gaze. The male sat propped against the cliff face, blood dribbling down his weak chin. A spider's web tattoo stood out starkly against the pale flesh of his chest, a bloody compliment to the spider on his captain's fucking throat.

"Something funny?" Trevor asked, fists clenching as a phantom breeze ripped past them.

"Aye, aye." He nodded his head, hand pressed against the torn flesh at his side. "Captain said if ye killed him, to ask ye a question."

"Oh, and what be that?" Tate asked, steps quietly trailing behind Trevor's as they stepped forward in unison.

The male grinned, his teeth stained red. "How is that wee sister of yours, Lovelace?"

"I wouldn't know. She's no' here, last I heard she was on Aidanburgh, visiting our auntie."

"That's no' what the captain said." Something sunk into Trevor's gut at the prick's words, a knowing that was cold and cruel. "Said he had a real nice talk with her while ye were out spelunking for a fucking *cup*," the quartermaster spat, chest lowering slowly. "Said she looked real right and pretty in black...mourning colors, them, but they've always looked nice on a fem."

Trevor turned to Tate, remembering what Taylee'd been wearing that morning when they'd each dropped a kiss to her brow. His brother's throat bobbed, and a wild look slowly crept into his gaze.

Fuck.

Trevor wouldn't remember the sprint through the forest back to the *God's Beau,* but he'd hear the bloody slam of his door against the wall for years.

He'd remember the sound of Carsyn screaming, his face pressed against Taylee's neck as he held her.

He'd even remember the strange quiet that overtook the ship as that stone cup rolled against the cherry red planks of the *Beau.*

Trevor did no' want to remember any of it.

But he would.

CHAPTER ONE

Trevor'd been sixteen years old when these fucking tattoos sank into his skin layer by bloody layer.

At first, they'd been a dead grey color, looking more like a bruise. He'd thought naught about them, the things no more than a blur on his sun-tanned skin. Maybe he should have, because day by day, they'd sharpened into something he did no' understand.

He'd hidden the lines crawling on his palms and the symbols trailing to the middle of his knuckle, the whorls that stretched to his wrists. More than once, he tried covering them in ink that wouldn't wink, in something that would bloody well hold still, but it always leaked from his skin.

Trevor'd worn gloves at first, and long-sleeved shirts later when the tattoos grew. Oh, those marks he could no' explain grew like any babe would. They started on his hands and crawled up his arm wi' every adventure he lived through until they wrapped around his throat. They were no' just bonnie shadows on his skin. He'd learned what the matching sets of ink on his hands could do.

'Tis when the song of *more, more, more,* first started singing in his blood.

Wi' a pair of damned hands like these, Trevor could do anything —*be* anything.

And he'd wanted all those bastards surrounding him to know his bloody name.

To fear it.

He looked at his hands now, covered in blood and bruises, but neither were dark enough to hide the ink on his skin. He remembered what they looked like clean and free of gloves, his thumb brushing a strand of hair behind the lass's ear wi' a backdrop of stars behind her. Trevor'd rather think of his hands like that than what they were now.

What they'd have to be before this whole fucking mess was done and over wi'.

Gone and fucked this one up right and true—could no' have fucked it up worse if he tried. If Tate were here, he'd be bloody disappointed between his fits of laughter. Swallowing past the anger that threatened to bubble up, he scrubbed at his scalp and the knotted strands of hair tickling his ears.

Bloody embarrassing being trapped behind bars like this, and to make matters worse, Trevor'd lost the map. Cunningham had every intention of following it to its bloody end, order-following prick that he was. Trevor'd checked their course every hour, his heart sinking a wee farther each time.

Fucking hell, he didn't want to go to Calaveras.

No' like this.

Trevor scanned their small cell again.

Naught had changed.

Anna laid unconscious on a wee cot. A line of latticed metal kept them contained on three sides. The hull of the ship pressed against his back, rocking wi' the tides and cool to the touch. The lass's prick brother leaned against the bars across the way, staring at him wi' eyes so like the ones Anna had.

He looked like he was feeling as well as any of them could. At least he had his boots, that was more than Anna could say. She'd left her heels at her da's estate, instead choosing to run through snow and ice wi' naught to protect her wee feet.

Bloody hell, the lass was absolutely daft, but he was here for it, for every second she would allow him to be.

"Can I fucking help ye?" Trevor finally asked, tired of feeling the weight of Markus's gaze.

Shite, there were other things in the gods-damned cell to look at.

Markus shrugged, rubbing his hands up and down his legs before leaning forward to rest his elbows on his bloody knees. They both turned, staring at where the lass was unconscious on the cot. Her cheeks were flushed wi' fever, the rise and fall of her chest slow. Blood matted the hair along her temple, smearing the blonde wi' pink.

A gods-damned marshal had cracked her wi' the hilt of his rapier, and she'd dropped like a rock, lovely eyes rolling back into her skull. He didn't remember much after that, after that red haze had veiled his vision. Some screams and the breaking of bones, but naught else.

Trevor's stomach churned, and he kissed his middle knuckle before pressing it to his forehead.

Please, he thought, the sound quiet even in his head.

His mum had wasted away in their room above the brothel. She'd gone slowly, cough racking her wee frame, a fever always wetting her brow. His auntie had caught a fever too, it had burned her from the inside out. Trevor hadn't been there to see that; he'd been on the Old Crow's ship by then.

Now his lass had a fever, cheeks rosy and skin like milk. Her eyes had been glassy whenever she'd been awake enough to vomit into a bucket. Trevor'd held her wee hand and her hair while Markus paced across the cell. Bloody hell, he hated fevers—they reminded him of too many of his ghosts, and he'd fight like hell to keep her from becoming one too.

Anna coughed, and Trevor clenched his jaw.

"I'm worried," he admitted in a whisper, glancing at her brother.

He nodded, staring at her form. "Me too."

Dropping his hands into his lap, Trevor tipped his head back and stared at the planks above their heads. Fuck, how did he get them out of this one? He wasn't strong enough for a full jail break at current, and he might have exaggerated a wee bit when he'd told the lass he'd be fine. Infection wouldn't kill him, nay, but it would slow him down.

Even now, sleep pulled at him, trying to force him under so the bloody wound would mend.

The hair prickled along his arms and the back of his neck. Markus was fucking staring at him again. Trevor glanced from where Anna slept like a princess in one of Taylee's books to her brother. There wasn't any anger in his gaze. Where had all his fury gone?

Trevor shifted.

Bloody hell, why was Markus staring at him like that?

He knew what to do wi' anger. But curiosity? Fuck if he knew. Trevor liked Anna's quiet wonderings and the way his skin warmed when she trailed him wi' her gaze. He liked that he held her attention by just being—he liked it even more that it was because of who he was and no' what.

But her brother?

Trevor wanted no part of his curious stare. He didn't fancy males, no' like that at least. Pressing his lips into a thin line, he breathed deep. Should probably tell the prick, lest he get any bloody ideas. A brig could be a cold, lonely, place and Trevor had no intention of keeping Markus warm.

Markus's left cheek hollowed. Trevor'd noticed him gnawing away at his cheeks more since yesterday. Wouldn't be surprised if he'd chewed them raw by now.

The blond finally opened his mouth, voice cracking from disuse. "Why did you tell me where that blasted map leads and what sleeps there?"

Ah, shite, that's what his staring was about.

He nodded slowly, turning to his hands as all the years he'd lived and all those he'd yet to fucking see sat on his chest like an anchor. "Because..." he started on a breath, picking at one of his nails. "I needed ye to understand why the Coalition and the Senate can't have the damn thing. Someone else on this bloody ship needs to understand what's what and the lass is..."

A smile split Markus's face, but it was no' a happy thing. "I understand. And I'll help. But let's get one thing absolutely clear," Markus said sternly, leveling Trevor wi' a fucking glare. "My sister is my first priority. If what you say is true, going to that island could end in catastrophe. But...if Anna isn't here, it's not a world I want to live in, and it can burn."

What the fuck was this shite?

If things weren't so serious, he'd tell Markus he looked just like his bloody da when Anna'd told the old bastard she was carrying his child. Something in his chest twitched, a wee flex of muscle and feeling that had him looking toward the lass.

She might have used it to stoke her da's temper, but wee ones wi' her didn't sound like such a terrible fate.

"Aye, mate. We have an accord on that."

If Tate could see him now, putting a single fem before the safety of every male or female who found a livelihood on the sea, he'd probably shite himself. Oh, aye, he'd burn the bloody map to keep the seas safe, but any feelings of warmth the lass held for him were going to burn right along wi' it.

Markus cleared his throat. "Are the stories true?"

Trevor flexed his fingers, watching Markus's blond curls bob on a made breeze. Shrugging, he twirled his fingers, following the wind as it stirred the collar of his coat against Anna's cheek. "Depends on which ones ye be asking about, mate."

"Any of them—*all* of them." He stopped, a deep breath leaving his lungs. "The hurricanes, being unable to die? That you defeated sea monsters and sunk islands? Or...or the cursed black blades?"

"Blades are Tate's thing, but aye, the stories are true," he said quietly. "Truer than I'd like."

Markus laughed, the sound a wee like breaking glass, sudden and broken, meant to turn away the eye. "What about taking tithes?"

"No' this again." Trevor rolled his eyes, turning back to the prick. "I told ye, I've never taken a tithe. What use would I have for bonnie lasses out past the Black Line? Especially ones wi' soft hands that've never seen a day of hard work?"

"We were always told you sold them to the slave trade."

"I've never had anything to do wi' that fucking trade," he snapped, gaze narrowing at the male.

5

"I've always guessed as much," Markus said wi' a wee grin, dropping his attention to the floorboards. "I studied you, you know. Looked at credible accounts and their ship's manifests. You have an eye for pretty things, king."

Trevor's cheeks warmed as he glanced at Anna.

"I'll stop you right there," Markus snapped. "You keep my sister out of your thoughts."

"Ye said it, no' me, mate. 'Tis no' my fault I fancy lovely things."

"You're insufferable," he said quietly, gaze looking far off.

Was he thinking about all the whispers he'd heard about the Pirate King over the years? Or what all those gods-damned whispers meant about the ocean blue?

It was a sea of myth and monsters, fucking full of stories waiting to be told.

"I suppose it's rather good fortune." Markus sighed. "We're going to need more than a little luck to get out of this blasted mess."

Shite, they'd need more than luck.

Trevor shook his head, mostly to himself. They'd need one of Fate's tides to bend, to pull them along a different path. Fucking unlikely, that. The gods might be willing to bend their knees and change course every now and then, but Fate was no' such a fickle creature.

When Fate made a decision, she stuck wi' it, no matter the consequences.

He turned to Anna. She and Fate had that in common.

Bloody hell, his chest tightened at seeing her tucked away in his coat. It dwarfed her, covering what was left of her dress. The damn thing was caked in grime and dirt, keeping it from glittering like starlight. Even wi' it torn and wrapped around her legs, Anna was still the loveliest female he'd ever seen.

To hell wi' the black spot on her hand, the Senate, and being dragged back to Calaveras, cursed as it was. If none of that killed him, it'd be the lass that finally did him in.

Markus shifted. "Do you...have some kind of plan, then?"

A plan?

Fuck, he never had one of those.

And if he did, it was always bloody terrible.

"No." Trevor shook his head, looking to the male. "No' one you'll like, anyway."

"Anna always has a plan; I've never liked hers either." Markus licked his lips, gaze moving to rest on the lass. When he spoke, it was fast and quiet. "I don't have to like you—and I don't. But all I can think of when I see you is her blood on my hands. I can't do that again, Lovelace...I *can't.*"

Bloody hell, Markus wasn't the only one haunted by that night. He remembered her skin cleaving open like butter beneath a warm knife and her blood spilling between his fingers as he did all he could to save her. Worst of all, he remembered how cold his arms had felt after they tore her from him, how his chest had hollowed out at seeing her settled in Markus's quarters.

"It won't," he swore. "Ye aren't the only one wi' her blood on your hands, mate...and I reckon I have more of it."

He wouldn't let the lass get hurt, no' if he could help it. Trevor'd reveal who he was and chase every gods-damned demon from her door even if it meant she'd treat him like one in the end. They'd grown too close, and he wanted too much. Trevor rubbed the back of his neck, wondering how he had room for anything past his wants and desires.

"It might not seem like much," Markus whispered slowly, "but I *am* sorry. She's going to hate you when she finds out who you are."

Trevor's throat bobbed. "Aye, I know."

Markus laughed, head shaking a wee from side to side. He waggled a finger at Trevor like he was a gods-damned child. "I don't think you understand, wretch. This is going to hurt her just as much as it hurts you, and Anna gets her temper from—"

Steps cascaded down the stairs.

He looked up as Anna stirred briefly, her wee fist clenching. Trevor assumed they were here for him and forced himself to stand. Even if they weren't, he had plans to make sure he was the one they left wi'.

7

The lass'd be worried out of her bloody mind if she woke up and Markus was no' there.

Better that he went.

And he did no' mind torture so much.

Four marshals stopped in front of him, the only thing separating them being the lattice work of metal. Keys jangled on a ring as one stepped forward, and then Bryce fucking Cunningham stood in front of him as well, all shiny black boots and a perfect marshal uniform trimmed in gold.

Ah, so the bastard was in charge now, was he?

He had to dip his chin to look the prick in the eyes. They were light brown and shaped a wee like someone from Xing. The lass had allowed herself to be courted by this male for years—how the hell had she managed it?

Trevor knew why the cunt had panted after Anna; he knew all too well what she brought to the table. Anna was worth a hundred of him and deserved a male of similar worth. 'Tis a terrible thing that Trevor was no' worth even ten men. He had stains on his soul and painting his skin that proved just how unworthy of her he was. But he could protect her, and she could hate him, and one day he might be all right wi' how things shook out.

"I have some questions for you," Cunningham said.

Fucking fantastic, that.

Trevor leaned forward, gaze narrowing down at the wee male. "Oh, no, bucko. I'm the one that has questions for ye."

CHAPTER TWO

"Is he awake?"

"Yes, captain."

"Excellent."

Trevor almost rolled his whole bloody head. What the fuck did they think he was doing? Knitting? Sleeping the day away? The pricks had obviously never tried sleeping wi' their hands manacled and bolted to the floor. If they wanted him to sleep, they should have thrown him a gods-damn goose-down comforter and a pillow to match.

A shiver worked its way up his spine, a thing made of waiting and chill. He'd lost his shirt earlier, soaked it completely wi' blood. Bastards hadn't gotten another as of yet, but Trevor didn't think they were worried about him catching a bloody cold. Wasn't so worried about that himself. Nay, he was a wee more concerned wi' the bastards noticing how quickly he healed after he fell asleep.

That, or they'd see one of the sirens on his skin moving; the wenches liked flirting a wee much.

It was only a matter of time.

Trevor chewed away at his lip, focusing on the whorls on the planks and counting every line from one side of a board to the next.

9

The silence was stiff. A soft wind blew outside the bulkhead. Still had to get Anna out of this wi'out her getting hurt. Shite, *and* her brother. The gods knew the lass wouldn't leave the prick behind.

It'd be rather endearing if it was no' so frustrating.

The captain of the ship slid a chair in front of Trevor and sat down, crossing an ankle over his knee. Boots were still polished to perfection, shiny enough that he could nearly see his reflection. Shite, did he look like hell.

Lass might no' fancy him so much after this.

A lamp swayed on a large swell just behind the bastard's head. Ignoring the shadow it cast, he felt a wee nostalgic about being chained to the floor. He'd spent many a night aboard the Old Crow's flagship as such for one bloody reason or another, usually after a brief lashing.

"So," Cunningham started, thumb tapping against one of his rapiers.

Trevor looked up, breathing despite his tensing shoulders. He'd like it best if they just got on wi' it, no sense waiting for the inevitable. Wasn't like he didn't know what the hell would happen next—get the shite beat out of him, poke at Cunningham's temper, get the shite beat out of him some more, repeat.

"So," he replied, nodding his head, staring into the prick's eyes.

Fucker did no' even blink.

"You've been hesitant to talk," Cunningham mused.

"Nay, I've been talking quite a lot. Ye just don't like what I bloody well have to say."

Cunningham's gaze narrowed like he was thinking—no good would come of that, he was calling that shite now.

"I can't help but wonder if it's the content of my questions. *I* wouldn't want to discuss my personal history as a criminal, nor my connections to an allegedly cursed pirate map. That would be rather incriminating." He paused, staring at Trevor. "No, I think I would rather talk about Miss Savage, if given the chance."

Like hell they were discussing the lass.

"I'm sure ye would." Trevor grinned. "Ye and she have a history, aye?"

"Oh, yes, we do." Cunningham smiled, and a flare of anger lit beneath Trevor's skin. "But I'm more interested in *your* history. How did Miss Savage find herself in your company? Given her past with pirates, I have a hard time believing she sought you out."

Was it Cunningham that wanted to know—or her fucking da?

"Have ye seen me? Fems seek me out all the bloody time for one reason or another."

Cunningham snapped.

Bloody hell, Trevor hated the sound of that snap.

He closed his eyes and breathed deep as the first marshal's fist glanced off his body. The beating was short and sweet, leaving him gasping for breath and cradling the fucking wound at his side. Coughing, Trevor pulled himself to his knees, blood trickling from the corner of his mouth.

"We met on the road, like she told her da."

"And you just...stuck around?"

"The lass landing in my lap just happened to be bloody good luck —I was looking for her brother," he said, spitting a wad of blood from his mouth. "Ye worried she might fancy me?"

Cunningham arched a brow, dragging his gaze from Trevor's knees and up his chest. The prick sighed, leaning back in his chair. "Speaking of Miss Savage's poor decisions and pirates she's had an unspeakable interest in, perhaps you can tell me where Trevor Lovelace has run off to."

Interesting thing, that.

'Tis the first Cunningham had mentioned the Pirate King.

Had they finally beat around enough of the gods-damned bull-shite that he was ready to ask the real questions? A vein throbbed at the surface of the male's temple despite his calm exterior. Most felt at least a wee bit of anger for the Pirate King, but this was more than that.

"What did the king do to piss ye off?"

"What hasn't the Pirate King done?"

"'Tis easy to blame a male you've never even met, 'tis even easier to swallow what you're fed wi'out looking at it," Trevor growled, glancing toward the bulkhead.

A storm was working its way in this direction; he felt it in the pressure around him and in how the wind pressed against the hull. Wi' that black spot on the lass's wee hand, 'tis no' all that surprising. He rolled his shoulder, flexing his fingers as he stared outside.

Bloody hell, even if he got Anna off this gods-damned ship, what was he going to do about that storm?

The hit came unbidden from behind, leaving Trevor wheezing as he held the festering wound on his fucking side. Swallowing stiffly, he grinned down at his manacled hands. Fuck, he wanted to tell them who he was just so he could hear them whisper his gods-damned name. So he could see the fear in their eyes at what they'd forced onto their ship.

It was a pull, a tide all its own, trying to drown him in his own angry desires. He opened his mouth to do just that, meeting Cunningham's cruel brown eyes, but something warm unfurled gently in him. Trevor pressed his lips into a thin line, teeth grinding together.

He had more to think about than himself.

"If you won't answer questions about the king, perhaps you'll answer some questions about the map?"

About bloody time the prick mentioned the map.

It always came back to that scrap of leather—the fucker was cursed.

'Tis why he'd set out to find it to begin wi'. It needed to be locked away to keep those who would seek it out safe. Naught but pain and trouble came from following it, Trevor could attest to that.

Cunningham threw the map down in front of him. With a scowl, Trevor stared down at Calaveras, settled far behind the Black Line. Sea monsters peppered the water, and a hideous fog hid most of the fucking island. The edges of the map were scrawled in letters and words he couldn't read, pressed into the corners and empty spaces.

Bloody hell, he'd never wanted to see this shite ever again, and yet here it was.

He looked away from the red x; 'tis rather fitting it looked like a bloody sore on a male's skin, a bleeding red thing against the white of pus and bone. Should have fucking burned the damn thing when he had the chance instead of agreeing to take the lass wherever she wanted to go.

Bloody hell, Anna walking on those hollow shores fucking terrified him.

Calaveras had a price, one soaked in blood.

"Let's start with something relatively safe." Cunningham leaned forward. "Do you know who first scribed it? I can't find a signature anywhere."

"You'll have to be a wee more sparing wi' your words, bucko. I'm an unsavory sort, no' a scholar."

Cunningham's nostrils flared as he breathed deep. "Who. Penned. It?"

"I don't know," Trevor said truthfully. "I don't know if anyone does."

There were some questions he did no' mind answering, simple ones that wouldn't lead Cunningham any closer to the beastie sleeping beneath Calaveras's shores or to the guardians patrolling between the trees. If he was better wi' his words, he might have tried to throw the bastard off, to buy them time.

But he was no' one for words and wasn't about to try to be now.

"Do you know what is on that island? What everyone so desperately wants?"

Bloody fucking hell, the prick didn't know.

"Aye." He sighed. "Death and madness."

Cunningham's lips pressed into a thin line, thumb doing that bloody tapping against his rapier. He motioned to the map wi' his foot. Arrogant prick. "What language is this?"

"A fucking dead one."

Might no' be able to read the damn thing, but at least no one else could read it either.

The blow to the back of his head blurred his vision. Gods-damn them all to hell, soon as he slipped these bloody manacles—

Trevor swallowed hard, glaring over his shoulder at the marshals in their pressed black uniforms as they sneered something ugly at him.

"I thought as much," Cunningham said.

Something in his tone made Trevor sit up a wee straighter. "Good luck finding anyone who can read that shite."

The captain's gaze shifted from the map to Trevor, a grin twitching against his lips. Leaning forward, he put himself wi'in reaching distance. All Trevor had to do was lunge forward and he could wrap his hands around the male's gods-damned throat.

"Luckily for you and I," he whispered, words and breath soaked wi' wine, "I happen to have a woman aboard who prides herself in completing such tasks."

Fucking hell, he wanted to snatch every one of his bloody words back.

Fear dug deep into his chest, bottomless as the ocean he loved. Why did he put that bloody idea in Cunningham's head? He didn't want the male anywhere near Anna. Opening his mouth on the matter might damn her further, but—

"Ye leave the lass out of this," the words spilled from his mouth in a harsh growl, skin feeling too tight. "Ye put a single fucking hand—"

"I have no intention of laying a hand on Miss Savage. You've spent enough time with her to know that I do not have to touch her to break her." Cunningham stood, smoothing out the front of his jacket. If there had been any bloody wrinkles, Trevor hadn't seen the fuckers. "At least, not when her brother is so readily at my disposal."

Shoulders slumping, the breath whooshed out of him, drawing a stiff cough. Bloody hell, he had no' thought of that. Aye, the lass would do anything for her brother—including letting the devil straight out of hell.

Cunningham's boots barely made a sound as they passed him on the way to the door.

"You have a few hours with him," he said. "Make sure that when

14

you return him to Miss Savage, she sees what can be done. Hopefully, the display coaxes forth an ounce of good-will from her."

Trevor clenched his fists and glared at the ground.

Shite.

CHAPTER THREE

Anna's brows pinched together as she tried to swallow. Her tongue felt closer in kin to a caterpillar than any muscle in her mouth should. Instead of swallowing, she coughed and gagged, quickly turning to her side. Pinching her eyes shut, she prayed to every god and goddess —one of them was bound to relieve her of this headache. Her stomach twisted, and whatever she laid upon swayed.

Bugger—she was going to vomit.

Vomit all over herself and wherever she laid.

Anna almost laughed. If she didn't know any better, she'd say she was on a—

"Anna, are you all right, old girl?" Markus screamed, voice bouncing off the inside of her cranium.

She pressed the heel of her hand into her eyes with a groan, swallowing back the bile attempting to make its way up her esophagus. There had to be a bucket here somewhere, a bowl, a container—something. Anna opened her eyes and stared at a wall with boards running its length horizontally. Her gaze narrowed at it.

Was that shiplap?

Turning over, she found her brother's gaze from across the enclosed space. Oh good; apparently, he wasn't screaming, her hearing was simply sensitive. Splendid, utterly and absolutely splendid. Had

16

they gone drinking again? Had Markus convinced her to attempt the Cordelaine Crawl in Bellcaster again?

Her brother sat on the floor with his knees drawn up to his chest, and he leaned back against metal work. Frowning, she saw he was bruised, a nasty gash burrowed deep into his hairline.

She squinted at the metal filigree behind his head.

Were they in *jail*?

Her gaze traveled to the gate, focusing on the lock.

"Bugger."

"Right-o, Anna."

Must have been quite the crawl, she mused as her stomach twisted painfully.

Anna lurched on the small cot, hand over her mouth. A bucket sat on the ground in front of her, cracked and already soiled. She reached for it greedily, skin heated even as her fingers wrapped around its edges, and she emptied the remains of her last supper into it. Spitting into the bucket, she set it down and leaned her elbows on her knees, dropping her forehead into her hands.

"How are you feeling?"

Did he really have to ask?

Anna grunted her response, wiping her mouth with the back of her sleeve.

"That...*well*, I see."

She squinted down at the fabric, specifically at how large the sleeve was around her hand. Whose coat was this? It certainly was far too large to be hers. Anna glanced back at her brother and the casual clothes he wore.

Everything came back to her like dominos cascading down—Mihk with a cup of tea, the pirate sitting across from her on the train. Markus firing a pistol atop a train car. Watching the pirate unbutton his shirt, and then another flash of him wading across the hot springs. That image dissolved into the feeling of his lips and teeth on her throat.

And—and then Bryce walking through the metal shack's door.

Hello, little bird.

Groaning, she dropped her head into her hands. "*Well* is not the term I would have used," she muttered more to herself than to her brother. "At least we're not dead, that's rather promising."

Head pounding in time to whatever this damn rocking was, she remembered fighting and then...*running?* She shook her head. That was absurd. She had run from very few men in her life, but—

But this was Bryce, and Anna knew well what he could do in a fight, especially when armed with a blade.

"How are you feeling now?"

"Splendid, absolutely splendid." She cleared her throat and clapped her hands together before turning to her brother. "Or...I will be once we get ourselves out of this mess."

Markus winced, pulling at the thick scab at his hairline. "That'll be a tall order."

"Why is that?"

"Aside from being on a blasted ship with a heading in one of the circles of hell?" he asked dryly, though it was more of a statement. "There is the matter of retrieving the map. The *captain*," Markus said begrudgingly, "has the damn thing. He's quite set on finding whatever there is to find in the name of the Briland Senate. We're simply here to ensure he can do that."

"Is that so?"

Snorting, he crossed his arms against his chest. "Apparently, his schooling didn't include dead languages and lost nautical paraphernalia. Honestly, Anna, I expected more from the Cunninghams."

Bugger.

What a mess.

Anna closed her eyes tight, pressing the back of her hand to her mouth. Frustration bubbled and melded with the nausea, and she couldn't quite find it in herself to remain calm. They were on her arrogant ex-suitor's ship, sailing out to God-only-knew—

"We're on a ship?"

"Yes," Markus answered, a bone-deep wariness coating his tone.

"A *ship*," she said again, flipping her palm over to view that damnable smudge. She glanced back around their confinement. Good God, that meant they were holed up in the brig of a ship.

Bryce's ship.

Her brother eyed her carefully. "Just how hard did Cunningham hit you?"

"How long?"

"Two days," he replied without missing a beat.

Losing all breath in her lungs, she turned toward Markus with wide eyes. "What? That—that can't be right."

"You hit your head again," Markus explained quietly. "Terrible fevers...I—*we've* been really worried, old girl."

She'd thought she'd lost half a day, maybe—an entire day at most. But *two* days? As if there were not enough things to worry about... splendid. She had five days to plant her feet back on land before the unexplainable started.

Anna smoothed her hands down her thighs and looked around. They had to escape the brig before they did anything else. Her brows drew together at the itty space; it was little more than a ten-by-ten-foot box. How had the pirate and Markus gotten along without the threat of her wrath looming over their—

The pirate.

"Where is he?"

Panic climbed its way up her throat as she met her brother's bright blue gaze. He dropped his attention to his hands, picking at his cuticles. His voice lowered as a small amount of reluctant admiration crept into it. "Cunningham needs the pirate for information. The wretch hasn't said anything as far as I can tell. The captain is in as good of a mood as he's ever been in."

Information?

That meant Bryce was...

Her gaze dropped to Markus's wrists where she knew the scars would be beneath his sleeves. Anger, hot and visceral, burned its way through her veins. Anna swung her legs over the side of the cot, stomach twisting with the sudden movement. There was plotting to be done, an escape plan to be hatched, and neither of those things would see fruition with her lounging about in a sick bed while her pirate was—

Anna cut herself off as a gust of doubt ripped through her.

It was one thing to escape from a cell in the capital, another to pry themselves from the maw of Chesterhale and the vigilant gaze of Bryce's sister. But it was entirely something else to escape marshals while in the middle of a damn sea.

Oh, yes.

This was going to be quite a tall order, indeed.

Stiff boots descended the stairs one grueling step at a time. The cadence was slow and confident—arrogant, even.

She would have known the gait of his walk anywhere after spending two years nearly keeping stride with it. He had always needed to be a step ahead of her, a boot in front of hers, the one walking first into a room.

Anna had let him then.

Now she wished she had tripped him.

Boots dipped below the ceiling line, taking their sweet time on the stairs. Another few steps revealed dark, stiff trousers, and then Bryce Cunningham, as she knew it would. A black matte lion winked at her from his throat, boots shined to absurdity and not a single hair out of place. He wore a marshal's uniform, stitched with gold to show his rank.

Splendid, the rat had seen a promotion.

He approached with one hand resting on his rapiers, the other tucked away in a pocket. Her mother had always told her that if something looked too good to be true, it often was, and Bryce Cunningham was the prime example of that.

Perfect, all the women had whispered behind their hands or fans.

Perfect, the men had grinned as they watched Bryce's form in the training yards.

Perfect, Senator Chelsea Cunningham had said beneath his breath, *but still nothing like Hadley.*

Anna walked slowly to the thinly pounded iron lattice until she was close enough to see the gold flecks in his brown eyes. Without shoes, they were nearly the same height, standing eye to eye. Bryce had short thick eyelashes that fluttered briefly, his gaze dropping before meeting hers once more.

"How are you finding your accommodations, Miss Savage?" he asked quietly.

Scorn burned her throat. "Where is he?"

"There is some business we must square away," he continued, ignoring her question. Anna's fingers slowly curled into fists. "I find myself in need of your expertise with dead languages. There is writing scribbled all over the map. I need to know what it says."

"Piss off," she growled. "Where is he?"

One of Bryce's finely manicured eyebrows raised. He leaned forward, tilting his head to the side. "Whoever are you looking for, little bird?"

"Do not play games with me, Bryce."

"Then don't play them with me." He glanced to his shoulder, wiping something invisible from his coat. His gaze slid back to her, and Markus shifted on the ground at her side. "Your full cooperation with this will go a long way in showing the Briland Senate whose side you're on. It very well could be the thing that keeps your brother from Chesterhale and you from that splendid convent in Xing."

A shiver prickled between her shoulder blades.

If she didn't help, she would go to a quaint convent where the weather was more agreeable.

If she didn't help, Markus would check in for an extended stay at Chesterhale.

And if she did help, the pirate would be blamed, and her father would likely arrange for him to swing from the gallows in the Bellcaster harbor. The panic crawled back up her throat at the thought of his boots swinging against the backdrop of the horizon.

No, she wouldn't—it couldn't happen.

Not like that, not to him.

"Where is my pirate?" Anna said, seeing every crack in his façade.

He might be able to hide the fractures from his crew, but he couldn't hide them from her.

Anna would pry them open if she needed to, put enough pressure on every single crack until he shattered.

Bryce's jaw ticked. "You want that wretch? Let's see how you feel when I'm through with him."

Anna grasped the bars in front of her as he turned away, steps growing distant. "Trust me when I say this is not the path you want to venture down."

"It is the only path you've left me."

Anna shook her head, voice rising as the captain climbed the stairs. "Not if you're willing to do the hard work and forge your own path." She smiled up at him savagely when he came to a standstill, looking over his shoulder at her. "But we both know you loathe getting your hands dirty."

Cunningham frowned and stomped his way back up the stairs.

"You hurt him—" she stopped, hearing the door at the top of the stairs slam shut.

Bugger.

CHAPTER FOUR

Markus's lips drew into a thin line.

Cunningham had taken him on a tour of his ship before Anna regained consciousness. The *Contessa* was a splendid girl, made from a rich mahogany with cream-colored sails, flying Bellcaster's evergreen flag. Markus had tipped his nose up at the time; Bryce's vessel was bare of any of the subtle adornments of his own, missing the small details that made the *King's Ransom* so spectacular.

Surprise was not a strong enough word to describe what Markus had felt at seeing that they were sailing in a cluster of three ships. They had been plain as day, flanking the *Contessa* on either side. He'd recognized the *Oceana's Ire* captained by Lucas Walker, but not the other. On all the decks, he'd spied men busying about in uniforms of black or green. Bryce had wanted him to know who held all the cards; that was the entire point of the walk. Well, he held all except for one.

Bryce Cunningham did not have Anna on his side, and that was a rather precarious place to situate oneself.

If only Cunningham knew the prize he sought was trussed up in that dark room with him. He scrubbed both palms against his face before lacing his fingers behind his neck. The room had smelled of blood and metal, the floor freshly scrubbed. Chains dangled from an anchor in the ceiling, and a set of manacles had been bolted to the floor. Lovelace hadn't looked worse for wear at the time, but Markus also hadn't been given the opportunity to ask how he enjoyed Cunningham's hospitality.

A begrudging admiration had sprouted for the pirate against Markus's best intentions. Lovelace had occupied Cunningham well enough that he hadn't come back for Anna, and he would always remain grateful and cooperative with anyone who kept his sister from harm. He'd even sell his soul to the very devil he'd championed against all those years out at sea.

"*Anna,*" he muttered, dragging his hands down his neck.

She ignored him, pacing the small length of their cell with wild eyes. Good God, she reminded him more of a blasted animal than his brilliant sister. Whatever logic she normally operated with had flown the coop; even her dress had transformed into something full of spite as it whipped around her legs.

Markus watched his sister carefully. For a woman who had been unconscious for two days, she seemed to be in rather brilliant health. Then again, since her last brush with death, Anna had always seemed a little more than human to him.

Anna stumbled at the first audible grunt from the pirate, using the bars to catch herself, fingers tightening around them until her knuckles paled. Shaking her head, she muttered something beneath her breath. Markus's brows drew together as her gaze darted from the lock to the frame of the iron gate of their cell, and then to the staircase across the way.

Bollocks, what plan was she turning over in her head?

"Anna," he murmured a little louder.

How was he supposed to approach her while she remained in this damnable mood?

Everyone had always believed Markus had inherited their father's temper simply because of their uncanny resemblance. He was reminded of this common fallacy as he watched his sister walk back and forth, wearing a track into the smooth planks of the brig.

No, those who knew his sister well knew that if Anna strove for peace, it was only so she would not pursue war.

Fortunately for him (and the rest of the world), his sweet sister's blasted temper only reared its god-awful head on rare occasions—when she did not get her way or when she felt backed into a corner with no way out. Both were certainly pressing in on her now, wrapping her in a suffocating embrace of what-ifs and hows.

Anna jerked her head, physically turning away from the pirate's next grunt. A loud thump followed the sound, not of flesh being tenderized, but of a body hitting the floorboards. Markus turned curiously as the pirate's voice trickled back into his ears.

Oh, splendid, now the wretch was laughing, the sound strained and hoarse.

And then...gone entirely.

Anna stopped.

Her head slowly turned to the stairs across the way—it was a preternatural stillness, one their ancestors had likely utilized as predators. From where he sat on the ground, he saw her throat bob, fingers twitching at her side. She leaned toward the bars of their cell, feet planted firmly on the ground.

The brig had gone quiet; nothing but the sound of their breathing and the endless drone of waves against the hull filled the space. He wasn't entirely sure if he should be glad for it or terrified by the implications. Anna sniffled, wiping her nose on the pirate's coat sleeve, but otherwise retained her fury.

Blast it all to hell, he couldn't imagine what thoughts ran rampant in her head. If their roles had been reversed, if it had been that golden-green gaze he couldn't escape trapped in that room with Cunningham and all the other marshals...Markus shook his head.

He couldn't even entertain the idea, let alone how it gutted him.

"Anna, I'm sure—"

Anna growled low and feral, kicking her handy vomit bucket. Sailing across their cell, it slammed against the hull wall and splattered its contents with a sickening slap.

He frowned at the mess—they were going to have to clean that up. And by *they*, Markus of course meant *she*. But his gaze softened as he turned back to his sister, the fingers of one hand pinching the bridge of her nose while her other hand rested on her hip.

"Not one word," she whispered, voice breaking as she resumed her pacing. "I need to think."

Markus stood, bones creaking and muscles aching. He turned to the cot, frowning at the sad, lumpy contraption. It was too short for him to lay down on, his legs would hang off at the knees, but it would be kinder on his rump than the brig floors.

The silence in the cell stretched on for what felt like forever, punctuated only by Anna's incessant half-muttered thoughts, until, finally, her shoulders lowered, and she stilled. Leaning forward, Markus rested his elbows on his knees and waited until Anna sighed softly.

He cleared his throat. "Careful, if you keep pacing like that, the crew might mistake you for our sire."

"Good. Perhaps they'll fear me like him too," she said, turning to face him.

Dark circles plagued the spaces beneath her eyes like bruises, which wasn't uncommon for Anna. She had spent plenty of her nights illuminated by gaslight with a book or charcoal rubbings cracked open in front of her. But the look in her eyes? Anna had always been his mirror, an echo of what he was feeling, a reflection of who he was.

Never had her eyes looked so distant and different than how he felt.

Good God, she cared deeply about the pirate, and she didn't even know who the blasted man was. Catastrophic did not adequately describe the events that would follow her realization. But he would deal with that when they got there.

First, he needed his sister sharp with her wits about her.

Suppose that meant he'd have to comfort her about Lovelace.

Markus scowled, swallowing past his own disappointment at the prospect of it all. He glanced at her again, at the bitter fury swirling in her gaze. It was so at odds with the potential devastation in every line of her frame, like she was preparing herself for a blow.

Was he really going to console his sister about the Pirate King?

At this rate, he'd throw an entire soiree in the name of the wretch if it brought a smile to her face.

"He's going to be fine, Anna," Markus whispered sometime later, the words tasting foul in his mouth.

Anna's breath hitched, and he knew he'd hit the mark.

Come on, old girl, he thought as he patted the mattress in invitation.

She slumped onto it within seconds, lip wobbling as she picked at the grime and bits of forest still embedded in her gown. The dress was more than a lost cause, but he didn't have the heart to tell her that.

"How do you know?" she asked quietly, looking up to meet his gaze. "How do you know Bryce won't outright kill him?"

He shrugged. "Cunningham hasn't gotten what he wants yet, and you know how he is…"

Anna nodded. The anger still sizzled in her gaze, so he continued carefully, slowly, like one might approach a rabid dog. "Well…he isn't cheering, so the scoundrel must not have died yet. I think that's rather promising, don't you?"

For whatever reason, that drew a brief laugh from her. "No, he's not the kind of man to be killed so easily."

Licking her lips, she leaned her head against Markus's shoulder, and her greasy curls tickled his nose. He imagined his hair fared no better, probably limp and tinted brown with filth. He'd trade his left arm for a hot bath and soaps at this point, and that wasn't an exaggeration.

Breathing out, he glanced down to his hands before looking back to the latticework of irons that caged them. Now that Anna was conscious and *calm*, they could begin the work on whatever brilliant escape plan she had marinating in the back of her mind.

"What else is bothering you, old girl?" he asked, keeping the grim anticipation from his tone.

"Nothing." She swallowed. "Everything."

He nodded. "Sounds rather accurate, actually. I promise you, Anna, we'll find a way out of this. Together. Even that damnable pirate," he said, bumping Anna with his shoulder, the words tasting like a lie on his tongue. "Imagine what Father will do when he hears you've wedded a pirate. If his hair hasn't started thinning yet, it will when he finds out about your impromptu nuptials."

Anna's gaze snapped up toward his. Her eyes were wide and panicked, and a flush quickly colored her cheeks. "We're not—it's not like that," she said, clearing her throat and returning her attention back to picking the dirt from beneath her nails. "I think...I think we might be *friends,* though. Or we were, I'm not so sure about now."

Friends?

Is that all she thought this was?

Leave it to his stubborn sister to absolutely refuse to label anything, to give it meaning when she was not ready for it. Markus wanted to ask her, to prod her forward, but if she didn't see what he did, then he'd leave it be. Hopefully, Lovelace's betrayal would wither it away before she realized what stood between them.

"...and what about now?" he asked gently.

"He's going to hate me."

"Anna..." Markus sighed, tucking her beneath his arm. "I don't think it's possible for anyone to hate you, least of all the pirate."

"I should have put a bullet through Bryce's eyes, and—and I didn't. I just stupidly clubbed him over his fat head." Anna swallowed hard.

"It is not your fault," he interrupted. "If we're assigning blame, we can lay it at Bryce's feet because it is *his,* Anna. Not yours. I don't know what nefarious plan our sire has concocted or how all these blasted pieces fit together, but—"

A door slammed, followed by the heavy sound of something hitting the stairs.

The noise was timed, rhythmic—just off beat with whoever marched down the steps.

Anna shot to her feet, attention anchored to the top of the stairs. A set of marshals descended the steep planks, the pirate in tow between them. Lovelace's head was slumped forward, his feet trailing behind him as blood dripped from his nose. Turning to Anna,

Markus reached out and gripped her bicep at the first sign of forward momentum.

She would lunge.

She would fight them, tooth and nail.

Markus saw it play out in his head as easily as he might imagine cuffing Cunningham. Anna glared down at him, gaze narrowing on his fingers before her jaw ticked, and she returned her gaze to Lovelace.

The heavy key turned in the lock.

Anna stared at the metal gate as it creaked open.

For the love of God, just stay still, he thought.

Her bicep jumped beneath his hold, and Markus tightened his grip further, watching the marshals drag the pirate into their small cell and dump him unceremoniously at their feet. Lovelace's head cracked against the planks, and he rolled to his side, head lulling and body limp. He felt Anna's indecision as if it lived in him too; he knew she was weighing the pros and the cons of lunging at the marshals and beating them to death before going after Cunningham and doing so much worse.

I should have let you drown, she had coughed, pulling him through the shallows.

Blast it all to hell, it's what Markus would have done if their roles were reversed.

Turning away from the marshals in their disgustingly clean uniforms, Anna's gaze dropped to the ground where Lovelace lay unconscious. The poor bastard looked more like a recently tenderized slab of meat than the most fearsome pirate the seas had seen in decades.

Markus stood, keeping an eye on the marshals as they stepped through the gate. It clanged shut behind them, the metallic ring echoing about the brig. Anna dropped to her knees, hands hovering over Lovelace's bare chest. Her gaze skipped back and forth from one injury to the next—good God, Markus wasn't even sure where she should begin.

"Can I request medical supplies?" she asked quietly, gently

touching the pirate's split lip. "And an additional bucket for washing?"

"What's the magic word, girl?" The marshal on the left grinned.

Anna looked up, throat bobbing. Markus clenched his jaw, certain one of his teeth would break from the pressure. Exhaling, she let her hands relax until one laid in her lap and the other rested against his chest. Markus stared at the touch, chest tightening.

"*Please.*"

Markus twitched. Instinct that had laid dormant for a very long time roared to the surface at her hollow tone. Hands clenching into fists, he turned a wicked glare on the marshals. If this blasted cell had not been between them, he would have killed them for making his sister feel small.

The marshal on the right cocked a brow, grin pulling against his lips as he looked down at her, gaze trailing her length, clearly enjoying the view of Anna begging on her knees. Markus shook his head. The only thing keeping his mouth shut was the wrath she would rain down on his head if he buggered her chances at obtaining the blasted supplies.

"Of course, Miss Savage," one of the pricks said.

The marshals left, their steps careful and quiet.

Good riddance.

With a sigh, he looked toward his sister, stepping backward until the cot hit the backs of his legs. Sitting quietly, he watched as she examined another one of Lovelace's wounds. Her touch was gentle—reverent, even—and surprisingly clinical as she scanned the pirate's body. Her fingers traced a minor cut to the hem of his trousers before peeling the blood-soaked material back.

Markus slumped back against the wall and pulled his hair.

This was going to be a very long voyage.

CHAPTER FIVE

This had to be punishment from some petty god or goddess.

The pirate laid on the floor before her, his chest rising and falling with slow, shallow breaths. If she hadn't been watching the uneven movements, she would have missed them altogether. Anna ran her tongue over her teeth, tracing the tattoos that poured over his pecs with her eyes. The ink spilled down onto his sternum, forming a loose point.

"Still asleep?" Markus asked, stirring across the cell.

Anna made some noise that must have passed as an affirmation, as he closed his eyes once more and curled onto his side. She returned to staring at the pirate again, brows drawing together. Bryce had never known how to apply the right kind pressure; it seemed her father had taught him a new trick or two.

The pirate's ribcage was nearly one giant bruise; the discoloring wrapped around his torso before meeting at his spine. The lacerations circling his wrists like bracelets weren't nearly as raw as her brother's had been, but the implications of them twisted her stomach all the same. None of what Bryce had inflicted compared to the wound on his side, the one he had likely acquired at her father's estate.

The wound had grown green and yellow, pus collecting just beneath the scab. The bruising around the damn thing was vicious, and heat rolled off it in thick waves. She had hardly looked anywhere else, too busy plotting how she could treat an infection like that with the limited supplies the marshals had dropped off.

Sucking on her teeth, she let her gaze slip to the patches of filth still plaguing his skin. Anna dunked a strip of cloth she had torn form Markus's shirt into a bucket of water and wrung it out. The pirate wouldn't get completely clean without the proper soaps, but she needed something to do with her hands while she pondered that infection.

Dirt and grime had collected in every ridge the pirate had, the peaks and valleys of abdominal muscles, the hollows of his throat, and between every dip of his ribs. Even the fine hair that grew on his arms and trailed below his bellybutton had been gritty to the touch. Four loose sponge baths later, and the pirate wasn't in much better shape.

The only saving grace of this entire endeavor had been finding those four precarious freckles in the dip of muscle at his left hip, each one dropping lower like a falling star.

Her hand stilled along his pec, staring down at the nautical lines and sea beasts cresting the water. It was another odd bit of silver lining that she now had an unobstructed view of the pirate's skin and the rare opportunity to study it without judgment. It was such a shame only pirates had tattoos. She had never gotten around to asking anyone why that was.

Anna glanced at the eleven or so freckles on the pirate's face.

She'd have to fix that as soon as he woke up—because he would wake up, he had no other alternative.

His skin was soft beneath her finger as she trailed it down the swell of his bicep, following the outline of a mermaid's tail. The tattoos made it difficult to find the grime and dirt by sight. It was a rather serendipitous occurrence that she could feel the grit just fine.

"Could you stop with that nonsense?" Markus droned, clearly very annoyed with her proximity to the pirate.

Anna shrugged, unable to find a single apologetic bone in her body. His dislike of the pirate was rather ridiculous at this point, and she planned on telling him so as soon as she felt up for the ensuing argument. Instead, she remained quiet, index finger following the prow of a ship on the inside of his bicep as she looked for more filth.

The ship rolled violently, and bile burned its way up her throat and coated her tongue. Her throat bobbed, swallowing the evidence of her weak tolerance of the ocean back down. The nausea wasn't as pronounced as it had been, especially with the rather splendid task before her. But that did little to distract from the knowledge of the growing swells and what likely came next.

Anna lowered her hand, turning it over to see the darkening spot on her palm. Nearly the size of a large coin, it consumed the center of her hand.

"Mmm," the pirate moaned sleepily. "Don't stop, luv."

Cheeks heating, warmth traveled down her chest and then lower still. Anna sat up, leaning away from the pirate. Maybe putting some distance between them would pull her thoughts back together, pull them away from the mortifying embarrassment of being caught *touching* him.

Good God, this was worse than when she'd been caught staring on the train.

"I'm afraid I don't know what you're talking about," she said, tucking a stray curl behind her ear.

"The touching, lass. It felt nice," he said, voice hoarse. Even though his eyes remained shut, the rake's mouth pulled into a knowing grin.

Maybe Markus was right.

Maybe the pirate didn't hate her.

"If ye want to continue, I'll no' be opposed to it."

A grin grew on her face, mirroring the one on his. "Must be the fever."

"Aye, of course." He nodded his head softly, cheeks flushed. "Could no' possibly be because I like it when ye touch me, Anna."

Markus choked in the corner, and Anna had to smother her smile. Her efforts were in vain, though; the smile forced itself back onto her face when she caught her brother's scowl out of the corner of her eye.

Anna licked her lips and turned her attention back to the pirate. "How long have you been awake?"

"Long enough."

Swallowing hard, she thought back to the rough sponge bath she and Markus had engaged in only an hour ago. Her brother's hulking form had been enough to hide most of Anna from the lurking gazes of Cunningham's crew, but judging from the pink dusting the pirate's pale cheeks, he likely had gotten more than a glimpse of her skin.

"I hope you enjoyed yourself."

"Lovely as always," the pirate commented off-handedly, finally opening his beautiful, dark eyes.

"I'm impeccable, what did you expect?"

"I'll no' argue that, but ye missed a spot. I'd be happy to help next time, beastie. Reckon I could reach all those hard-to-reach places on your back and..." The pirate twitched, smile dipping into a grimace as he tried to sit up.

Markus sighed dramatically from his corner. "So it begins."

"Don't worry, mate," the pirate said, movements stiff and strained as he pulled himself toward the hull wall. "I'll save ye from the chore."

The redhead made it to the wall and all the way upright before resting his elbows on his knees across from her. He dropped his head down into his hands, scrubbing at his face before running his fingers through his hair. Tipping his head back, the pirate rested it against the hull, exposing the column of his throat. He must be exhausted; Anna wasn't sure how he was awake with the abuse his body had sustained.

She squinted at him, gaze drawing up from his toes to his face—he looked a teensy better now. Which was to say that he didn't look quite like the corpse he had when the marshals had unceremoniously dropped him into the cell like a sack of potatoes.

"I'm sorry," she said suddenly, the words rushed.

The pirate cleared his throat, a soft grin gracing his lips. "'Tis no' your fault, lass."

"I'm still sorry."

"If ye insist on being sorry, I may have to insist on a kiss." He winked. "Appears you've already undressed me, seems only right."

She raised a brow, sneaking a look at her brother. "How do you know it wasn't Markus?"

Markus gagged, clearly distraught with the idea of undressing the pirate.

Well, that made one of them.

"That's how, luv," he said, chuckling softly.

Her grim mood broke with the sound of the pirate's laughter, throaty and hoarse. It even brought a smile to her brother's face, though the sound also caught the attention of the surrounding sailors and marshals rooting around the brig, moving various crates and barrels. The pirate glanced between her and the sailors on the other side of the cage.

Bugger, he missed nothing.

"Ye might want to change your bloody heading," he called, voice dark and deep, full of promises that only the reaper normally made.

"Shut your fucking mouth," a sailor called from beyond the cell.

"Never mind, mate." The pirate shrugged. "Just thought I'd try to help the lot of ye from drowning, but shite, if ye insist, go right ahead."

"Oh, 'tis that so?"

"Aye. Reckon there's at least one gods-damned hurricane brewing."

"Bloody daft." Another sailor laughed.

"That's no' what your sister said." The pirate grinned, successfully blanketing himself in attention. He used the hull to steady himself, fingers outstretched. "Lass told me I fucked about as rough as a hurri—"

"The hell did you say?"

"Ye heard me! And if ye have a fucking problem wi' it, ye can climb in here wi' me and see for yourself, bucko."

Anna kicked his leg, drawing a stiff hiss from the pirate. If he kept this up, they'd come in here and try to beat him to death. She'd be forced to defend him then, and as she hadn't quite figured out how they were going to get themselves out of this mess, she couldn't have any of that alpha male peacocking yet.

She squinted at him. Had he thought this through at all?

The pirate rubbed his shin, frowning at her.

Of course, he hadn't.

Anna raised her brow at him, tempted to cross her arms against her chest as well. "Rough as a hurricane, you say?"

A quick blush dusted his cheeks, but he leaned into the devilish grin, and her heart thundered wildly behind her ribcage. "Aye, luv. I can be as gentle as a summer breeze too. I can be whatever ye ask of me, and we've all the time in the world to figure out what ye like best."

"Good God, man, quit while you're ahead," Markus groaned, disgust clear in his tone.

Anna smiled, feeling the ghost of the pirate's weight upon her like it had been at her father's estate—of the scrape of his teeth and the warmth of his lips on her skin. Bugger, she was certain the temperature had risen considerably. Her cheeks warmed as the pirate's grin widened, a rakish knowing glimmered in his dark gaze, like a secret shared between lovers.

She remembered exactly what the pirate felt like pressed tight against her and, bugger, he *knew* it.

The ghost of a breeze brushed against her rump, drawing her attention to their surroundings. She turned back to the pirate. How had he known a hurricane was forming on the seas? She had suspected as much with the darkening mark on her palm, but how had he? Anna ran her tongue over her teeth, ignoring the heat in her cheeks as the pirate winked at her.

"How do you know a storm is brewing?" she asked, each word like a pulled tooth as it left her mouth.

"I'm partial to the pressure changes."

Markus scoffed. "You've never been in a hurricane and lived."

"Have so," the pirate said, sliding down the wall. "Four bloody times now, and each one was worse than the last."

"That's unfeasible. I wasn't born yesterday."

"Thank the fucking gods for that," the pirate exclaimed, kissing his index finger's middle knuckle and touching it to his forehead quickly. "Otherwise, your sister'd be way too bloody young for me."

Markus ground his teeth as Anna pinched the bridge of her nose. How long would it take Markus to pounce upon the pirate this time? Running a hand down her face, she turned an unamused stare on the pirate. Despite enjoying his comments and how they melted the chill of dread in her limbs, she'd rather he didn't antagonize her brother.

"How old are ye, anyway?"

"Twenty-five," Markus said, an edge of suspicion in his voice. "We turn twenty-six in the spring."

Anna turned away from them. She didn't have time for their shenanigans. Someone had to rip them from the jaws of defeat. She squinted at the lock on the gate—picking it would be easy enough. A few of her lock picks and her hammer had remained tangled in her hair. Sneaking off the ship wouldn't be overly difficult.

The rub lied in finding the map.

Her father had revealed his hand at dinner.

If he wanted the map this badly, she wanted it more.

"And you?" Markus asked in the background, their voices fading to a dull drone.

That cursed bit of leather was likely with Bryce.

"Twenty-eight...ish."

At least that's where she would keep something valuable.

"*Truly?*" The surprise in Markus's voice was sincere enough that it drew her attention. Bugger, perhaps Bryce had hit her harder than she remembered. "I could have sworn you were older."

"You're in good company then, mate."

"She's still too young for you, *wretch.*"

The pirate snorted, a smile on his lips. "We'll let the wee beastie be the judge of that."

"You jest." Markus huffed a brief laugh. "My sister is a terrible judge of character."

"I claim you, don't I?" she said, glaring at her brother.

"I do believe you are only proving my point, old girl." Markus smiled, elbows rested on his knees.

Anna rolled her eyes as she stood, attention returning to the overlapping metal bars. Honestly, they looked more decorative than anything. If she applied the right amount of leverage, this entire side would likely lift right off.

It would make a ridiculous amount of noise, though.

No, best to pick it.

Slow, confident steps echoed into the brig, sending a chill up Anna's spine. She froze, blood freezing in her veins as a fire lit in her belly. Looking at her brother, his stone-cold façade confirmed what she already knew. They would recognize that calculated walk anywhere. They had grown up with it, had sparred with it.

Good God, she had even slept with it.

A sour taste made itself home in her mouth at remembering she had once been intimate with the owner of that walk. The pirate stood, leaning back against the hull as Bryce came into view, flanked by two marshals and a sailor. His smile reminded her more of a shark, with fathomless black eyes to match.

Without thought, she placed herself between the pirate and Bryce.

"How are you finding your accommodations now?" Bryce asked, coming to stand right in front of the bars once more.

"Ample," she replied, lifting a shoulder. "If anything, I'm a bit parched."

"*Parched?*"

Anna nodded slowly but it was the pirate who laughed, drawing the attention to himself. Bryce's gaze narrowed at him, cheek hollowing briefly before the wine-haired man spoke. "What else could the lass possibly want, ye wee bastard? She's got her brother for conversation and me for if she grows...hungry."

Bryce's lips thinned, his throat bobbing. "Shall we speak in private, Miss Savage? Perhaps over a glass of wine since you are *so* terribly thirsty?"

She didn't want to go with Bryce. But Anna thought of the bruises on the pirate, of the lethargic ebb his pulse had been beneath her finger earlier. She thought of her brother too, of the scars hiding beneath his clothing, of what he had looked like strung up like a piece of meat in that train car.

At this rate she'd follow Bryce straight into hell if it meant her pirate and brother would remain untouched.

Anna sized Cunningham up—surely, he knew she wouldn't be joining his company for the sheer fun of it. Taking her to his quarters would provide her with a splendid opportunity to locate the map. Glancing over her shoulder, she met her brother's gaze. He nodded slowly, keeping Bryce within his sight, understanding and warmth bleeding into his icy blue eyes.

The pirate, though?

Understanding and warmth were nowhere to be found in his dark depths. A shiver rippled up her spine at the look on his face and the open anger in his eyes. They were dark, only made darker by the bruises marring his skin.

In the background, the gate creaked, swinging open with a light cry, but here and now, it was only Anna and the pirate. She gave a light shake of her head. Splendid scoundrel that he was, the pirate ignored it, pushing off the wall and stepping forward until he stood just behind her. His knuckles brushed her ribs, the hard planes of his face angled down to her.

"Worried?" she asked, trying to coax something less reckless from him.

"About ye?" he murmured, leaning down so his lips nearly brushed her ear. "Always, luv. In my defense, you're always doing something bloody reckless. I'd feel better if I could at least see ye."

In some strange roundabout way, she would feel better too.

Not because he would be watching her, but because she would be able to see him.

"Today, Miss Savage," Bryce said impatiently.

Nodding her head, Anna started to turn back to the captain and then stopped. Her gaze locked with the pirate's. Good God, she was so certain he could hear her heart beating furiously behind her ribs. Anna lifted her hand and placed it on his chest, leaning up onto her toes until her lips brushed the scuff on the underside of his jaw. He exhaled hard, muscles tensing beneath her palm.

"Please, don't do anything stupid," she whispered, stepping away from him.

Her fingers slowly slid from his chest and then she crossed the threshold of the cell, easing a deep breath into her lungs. She hadn't thought the pirate's gaze could get any darker, that the handsome planes of his face could become any harder, and yet they had. That thing that slept beneath his skin was yawning awake behind her.

Do not do anything stupid, she thought repeatedly.

Anna pulled the pirate's jacket tighter around her shoulders, letting his scent soothe her nerves. The darkly spiced smell seemed to reach out and hold her. It was a poor alternative to the real thing, but it would have to do. She would wear the pirate's coat like an armor, wrapping herself in his scent until she could believe he stood right behind her.

True to form, Bryce placed his hand at the small of her back, warm and familiar but altogether wrong. Anna flinched away from his touch and forced the scowl from her face. This was an opportunity to find that damnable map, and if she had to wine and dine Bryce to get it, then so be it.

"Ay, prick!" the pirate said, bringing Bryce to a standstill.

Stupid, hulking, idjit of a man, Anna growled inwardly.

She closed her eyes tight before turning to look over her shoulder. The pirate stood with his arms hanging between the spaces of the lattice. Here, in the shifting dark of the brig, there was no mistaking the redhead as a pirate, not with his tattoos flowing down his arms and chest like spilled ink, and certainly not with the glimmer of retribution in his gaze.

Bryce's fingers twitched along her back as he shivered. If not for his close proximity, if not for his disgusting hands on her body, she never would have known. His face remained a calm, if annoyed, façade.

The pirate's attention fell on her like a brand.

Unlike Cunningham, it wasn't fear she felt as he stared at her—no, it was desire burning her alive.

Rather brilliant timing, really.

Anna glanced up at the captain, watching as one of his brows cocked in question.

"I expect my lass returned in the same gods-damned condition she be leaving in," the pirate said, his voice composed of gravel and death. Anna shivered—*his lass*. "Do we have a fucking accord?"

"Your lass?"

"Aye." He leaned his head back, exhaling. Despite the distance, her hair fluttered, stray strands tickling her ears. "I don't see anyone arguing it, no' even Anna."

Grinning down at the floorboards, she felt the acidic heat of Bryce's attention on the side of her face. His fingers tightened around her waist as he pulled her in close to his side. The captain made short work of the stairs, and soon she felt the absence of the pirate's gaze like the sun disappearing behind the clouds.

"I expect you to be on your best behavior," Bryce murmured, opening the door and crossing the threshold to the main deck.

CHAPTER SIX

Markus tracked Anna with his gaze. Every step away from him echoed like a death knell, pulling a piece of his soul farther and farther away. Based on the tension in the pirate's shoulders, he assumed Lovelace felt the same. It inexplicably warmed something in his chest, prickling at his skin and pulling a grimace onto his face.

Good God, why did he find it comforting that the wretch shared his sentiments?

As the Pirate King, he supposedly had a hand in all nefarious business at sea, knee deep in the slave trade, up to his blasted eyes in stolen goods and illegal ware. But Lovelace had claimed otherwise and, unfortunately, the fresh bastard had been anything but dishonest with them thus far.

Are you Trevor Lovelace? Markus had asked as soon as they awoke in the brig.

He hadn't even hesitated before replying, *Aye*.

Markus sat on the cot with a huff, the damn thing creaking beneath his weight. The pirate leaned his forehead against the bars. Tapping his fingers against his thighs, he stared at Lovelace's back and the tattoos displayed on his skin. He hadn't lied about studying the ships the Pirate King targeted—all merchant vessels with priceless cargo.

If the man in front of him wasn't responsible for the slave trade, who was?

"Is it the Coalition, then?" Markus asked absently.

Lovelace looked over his shoulder, cheeks already dark with new growth. "What?"

"Is the Coalition orchestrating the slave trade?"

"Truthfully, I don't know." The pirate turned, sliding down the bars until he sat on his rump. A moment later, he reached up and rubbed the back of his neck, frustration forcing the worry from his features. "Been a wee busy wi' fighting off Briland ships and keeping the Coalition in line. I've been burning slave ships and doing what I bloody well can, but..."

Markus saw the answer in the pirate's gaze as clear as day.

It wasn't enough.

"It's hard"—Lovelace swallowed, staring at his hands—"when the crew slits their own throats or dives into the bloody water before I can say a single gods-damn word."

"I...I understand," he said quietly.

And Markus did.

Hunting the Pirate King might have consumed most of his time at sea, but when his ship came across slavers, Markus never hesitated to run them down. As soon as the men on board realized they were caught, the result was always the same—slit throats or bailing into shark-infested waters.

Lovelace lowered his gaze to the floorboards in front of him, brows drawn together. He chewed on his lip, and for a second, Markus understood his sister's infatuation with the blasted man. He was easy enough to look at, the brogue was rather brilliant, and worst of all, he appeared genuine.

"Ye ever come across anyone wi' snake bite tattoos?" Lovelace asked, looking up.

"Like...puncture marks?"

The pirate nodded stiffly.

Half a hundred tattoos flashed through Markus's head, each one associated with a different captain. There were spider webs on John

Black's men, and the *Plight's* crew wore matches and burning trees. Every captain had a unique shadow on their skin that marked and identified them as pirates.

Lovelace's crew had one, a crown at the base of the neck between the shoulder blades.

"The bloody pricks that tried taking Anna had them," Lovelace growled, gaze darkening like clouds before a storm.

"And you think that means they're involved with the trade?"

"I don't know, 'tis the first lead I've had in a long bloody while. Suppose I'll start stripping the fuckers and looking for snake bites here on out."

Markus frowned at the prospect, and the look was mirrored on Trevor's face. Dealing with slavers was one thing, cleaning up after them another. Stripping them naked and taking a good long look at their corpses was an unfortunate fate he didn't want to contemplate.

But it was a damn good idea.

"You'll probably have to scrub them, as covered in grime and grease as they are." He grinned softly, imagining the Pirate King taking a rough wired brush to dead, grimy scoundrels.

"*Me?* Shite, no. Tate'll be the one wi' the bucket and soaps."

"Not...not the Man-Eater?" Markus cleared his throat, thinking of the small crown tattoo he'd kissed.

Trevor laughed, wincing as he placed a hand over the festering wound at his side. Markus had pretended he couldn't smell the thing from here, but the stench wafted over occasionally, turning his stomach. That was the first thing that would need treatment, and with how often he had caught Anna staring at it or prodding its swollen edges, his sister knew that too.

"Jules doesn't listen to anyone—she never has," Lovelace said fondly, lighting a small fire of jealousy in Markus's veins. "She's kind of like a cat, mate, wi' bringing ye bloody dead things and sleeping in the sun."

He wasn't wrong. Markus had learned rather quickly that Juliana Gray did not listen to requests or instructions. He had a plethora of strategies and ways of convincing someone to do something in a roundabout way—he had to with a sister like Anna—but none of them had worked on Juliana.

Where his sister refused to do things based on principle, the Man-Eater simply couldn't be bothered and therefore could not be convinced otherwise.

Markus scrubbed his fingers against his scalp. He could still picture that damnable stretch of land perfectly. They had only been marooned a week, and with its small cluster of trees and well of fresh water, it hadn't been nearly large enough to qualify as an island. Markus picked at his cuticles, remembering its crescent shape and fine sandy beaches.

He remembered Juliana Gray lying on the beach half-shrouded in shadows from the tropical trees, her arms tucked beneath her head. She had been perfectly at home naked on the sand in front of someone who should have been her enemy.

Lovelace cocked a brow, a sly grin growing on his blasted face. "But ye knew that already, didn't ye?"

"I..." Markus's cheeks heated as he chewed on the inside of his cheek. He cleared his throat, forcing his voice to be smooth and collected as he spoke. "I don't know her as well as you think I do."

It was the truth.

Markus likely didn't know the master gunner as well as Lovelace currently believed. He certainly didn't know her as well as he'd like. Sometimes he wished he had asked her more questions during their forced tropical vacation—questions about her family and upbringing, about the tattoos that lined her body and what he had seen that first night during the storm.

He had never been one to hold his tongue or hide behind words, but he had cared about what Juliana Gray thought and what she would think about him if he asked the wrong thing or dug a little too deeply into her life.

"'Tis fine. If ye want to talk, talk. If no', I am perfectly fine no' knowing the wee details of Jules's life."

He didn't want to talk about it, and even if he did, Trevor Lovelace ranked rather low on the list of individuals he would willingly confide in. Shrugging, Markus looked for anything else to talk about, anything else to fill the space between them while they waited for his sister to return.

Because that is what they were doing, using words to make up for her absence and distract them from thinking about where she was and who she was with.

"That's too bad about the tithes," he said a few minutes later.

"You're like a gods-damn mutt wi' a bone," the Pirate King groaned.

Markus grinned, glad to be putting some distance between him and Lovelace's possible inspection about what had transpired between him and Juliana. "We always believed if the worse came to worst and we offered up the prettiest man aboard, you might be more lenient in your dealings."

"The prettiest *male?*"

"We didn't have any women on the ship. Bad luck." Markus grimaced. "It's the best we would have been able to do at the time."

"They were going to offer up ye, weren't they?"

"It would have been a mutiny."

The pirate laughed, shaking his head as he laced his fingers in his lap and glanced up at the ceiling. "Who do ye think started that bloody rumor?"

"Does it matter?" Markus asked, looking up as well. Anna was up there in the confines of the captain's quarters. "I...I heard it from my father, I think."

"No surprise there; your da' is a bastard."

"On that, we agree." Markus sighed.

A weariness overtook him as if all the exhaustion he should have felt the past week finally weighed down his shoulders. He laid down on the cot, dropping his forearm over his forehead as he kept his attention fixed on the ceiling. His stomach twisted in on itself, dread and something worse making themselves home in his heart.

"She'll be fine," he told himself and the pirate. "Anna is always fine."

CHAPTER SEVEN

Anna stared at the door to the captain's quarters apprehensively, a strange sense of déjà vu overtaking her. Never in a thousand years would she have guessed she'd be standing in front of Bryce's door again, especially not after she had rejected his proposal.

Bugger, she had a terrible feeling about this.

Maybe it was because of the ease with which Bryce strode into his quarters or the expectancy in his gaze as he turned to her. Closing her eyes, she breathed deep, filling her lungs. The brine on the wind felt splendid against her cheeks. It ran through her hair and skimmed her lower lip playfully before tangling itself between her fingers. The phantom breeze dissipated just as curiously as it had appeared, taking any sense of relief she had felt with it.

Bryce stood just to her right as she took everything in. Nothing had changed, not a single detail—at least none that pertained to Captain Bryce Cunningham and him alone. Everything in his private quarters had a place, and there was a sparseness to his belongings that Anna hadn't missed.

A desk fit for a giant kneeled before the bay of windows at the back. Great grey clouds swirled behind the glass, and the ocean water was nearly black with the coming storm. A large, sturdy chair lingered behind the cherry wood desk, two smaller stools sitting in front. The walls on either side contained a handful of books, limited to the topics he believed useful.

No fantasy, no romance—none of the finer things life had to offer.

His books were sorted by topic, bundled together by likeness on varying shelves. Staring at one of the rows, Anna stepped forward. She didn't recognize any of those old, leather-bound books. Bryce must have acquired them after she had dismissed his proposal. Turning, her gaze dropped to the floor. Trunks were tucked tight against the same wall, just next to an itty breakfast nook. Cunningham's bed had been built into the wall on her right, opposite the nook and his trunks.

She sighed. The only thing that had truly changed was the evidence of her frequent visits. Bryce had done away with the ornate carpets and had likely shredded the goose-down comforter she'd left behind. There was a single pillow on his bed, for him and no one else. It sat rigid like a soldier against the wall, lonely and cold.

How could so much change and yet nothing at all?

Anna's stomach rolled, and she gripped the fabric of the pirate's jacket as she tried settling the traitorous thing. Looking down on her, a bit of concern bled into Bryce's brown eyes before it evaporated completely. "Would you like some ginger tea to help with your nausea?"

Even though she wanted it terribly, she shook her head. "Give it a few days, it'll settle down."

If all went according to plan, she'd be vomiting over the edge of a long boat on the open ocean by then.

Turning, he walked toward a cabinet. It squawked, and Anna knew exactly which cabinet it was when glasses clinked. She busied herself glancing at the various lanterns in the room. It was warm and bright in here, warmer than it had been walking along the deck, but she would much rather be out in the cool breeze.

"Would you like a blanket?" he asked from behind her.

Anna shook her head again, walking forward to sit on one of the small stools in front of his desk. She figured the only blanket he had to spare was the threadbare quilt folded at the foot of his bed. For as someone as ambitious and cognizant of status as Bryce, she had always been surprised at the décor of his quarters. Even his desk was starved for something to sit atop it—there were no pencils or scraps of paper, no readily available weapons, and certainly no maps.

Although that could have been intentional.

Bryce's heat enveloped her back, causing a creeping feeling to tingle between her shoulder blades. Reaching over, one of his long arms set an uncorked bottle of red wine on the desk, quickly followed by two long-stemmed crystal glasses. They had belonged to his mother, and he rarely broke them out. He would have expected her to know that.

Anna squinted up at him. What game was he playing at?

Nostalgic reunion?

"Ask your questions, Captain."

"Bryce," he corrected, voice soft.

Anna snorted. "I'm afraid, as my captor, familiarity is no longer open to you."

"Captor? That's an interesting perspective."

"Is it?" she asked.

"It is." His steps traveled to her right before quieting. "The story Senator John Savage has created is that I'm rescuing you from a hoard of pirates. Apparently, I snatched you from their clutches on some pirate-infested isle no one has come back from. We're to return together with whatever great prize we discovered there in tow."

Rolling her eyes, she tilted her head to face him. "My father wouldn't know a good story if it bit him on the ass."

Bryce loomed with a hand resting on his rapier. It wasn't a threat, he had always stood like that—always at attention, always ready for the next brawl, always something to prove. His deep brown gaze fixated on her blue one before dropping to her bruised and scraped feet. Throat bobbing, his gaze traveled up her legs, lingering briefly on her torso before finally resting on her face once more.

"I could offer you the use of my bath away from the rest of the men."

"Don't bother. They've already seen everything there is to see."

He raised a brow, lips pressing into a thin line. "Can't say I'm surprised."

With quick, delicate movements, he poured the wine. Anna's stomach ached at the sight of anything fresh. A salmon bathed in lemon and butter or a roasted chicken sounded absolutely divine right now. Sitting across from her, he pushed one of the glasses forward. Anna glanced at it dismissively, turning back to him and watching as he tilted his head back and drank deep.

The ease with which he ingested his wine was rather concerning.

"How have you been?" he asked, swirling his glass.

Anna sat up straighter, motioning to the room around them. The pirate's jacket slipped open, allowing a cool draft across her skin. "Aside from this debacle, not half bad."

"Still looking for the khan?"

She nodded. "Bugger is as elusive as ever."

It was Bryce's turn to nod, the complete picture of perfect understanding. But then his attention lowered, snagging on something on her chest. Anna tried to still her breathing, tried not to stiffen or flinch beneath his careful scrutiny. She knew well what caught his interest. It was that damn scar on her chest—the one that ran from the side of her neck and through her clavicle before carving its way between her breasts.

"I heard about that—quite a few times, actually," he said, tipping his glass in reference to her chest. "All conflicting accounts, but I knew they couldn't be true. Thrown from a horse? Unlikely, you could ride before you could walk. An accident on an expedition? While probable, you would have bragged up and down the coastline about it. One man even suggested you'd been mugged." Bryce sipped his wine, his gaze lingering on her scar over the rim of his glass. "I laughed at that one. Annaleigh Rae Savage, *mugged?* Never in a thousand years. Tens of stories circulated high society about your precious flesh."

"That's not entirely surprising; all they have left to do is gossip about their betters."

"I've heard the real story. Your father can't keep all the sailors from talking. He even confirmed it when he requested my aid. You're damaged goods now, aren't you, Miss Savage?"

Anna's stomach churned, bile creeping its way up her throat. Despite her discomfort, she rolled her shoulders back, further exposing the low cut of her dress. She glanced down at the ugly mark that marred her skin.

"I don't know," she mused, thinking of the pirate. "Some have used it as a trail of sorts—a path that might lead to sweeter places. Now, where's the map?"

Bryce's lips pressed into a thin line before he raised a hand and rifled through his jacket. After a moment, he flicked his wrist, and the Pirate King's map slapped onto the desk unceremoniously. "Can you read it, Miss Savage?"

Leaning forward, she prodded it open with her index finger. The images were crude and roughly scratched, but it was a map. There were bodies of water and masses of land peppered throughout, most of which she recognized at first glance, especially the continent. But there were islands that had not been penned on any map she knew of.

Ah, that was why—they were east of the Black Line.

Anna scowled at the looping script tucked into every odd and end place—there was a familiarity to it, a knowing she couldn't quite shake. Her finger traced some of the loops and letters, searching her memory for its source.

"Well?"

"Well, what?" she asked absently, rolling the dialect over her tongue.

It was so splendidly old, but she'd seen it before, this language that held the beginnings of many within it. Where, though? It had obviously been recent; she hadn't needed to stare at it for hours before something sparked. From the corner of her eye, she noticed Bryce make some annoyed gesture toward the map.

"No."

"No?" he asked, disbelief coloring his voice as Anna's jaw slackened.

Aepith.

It was *Aepith?*

The Pirate King's map had been crafted by the ancient seafarers?

The stone jaguar floated up from the recesses of her mind, bubbling forth until it was nearly front and center. If not for the trouble they were in, the jaguar might have succeeded in stealing her attention away completely.

Anna supposed the chance of the Pirate King possessing an Aepith map wasn't entirely out of the question. If the legends were to be believed, most pirates were remnants of the very last Aepith sailors —the lawless and reckless ones, those who sought treasure and renown above all else. Too bad the valiant and the noble had all drowned.

Or at least, that's what the mythos surrounding the Aepith had always claimed.

"No, I can't read it," she said, leaning away.

At least not yet, she thought.

"You're...absolutely sure?" he asked, leaning toward her on his forearms.

Her throat bobbed, and she glanced back toward the map. Tracing another line, she tried to find a bridge to their meaning, a quicker way to understand. But this was not quick work. It was not work for those with little patience. She shook her head, gaze lingering on a symbol that looked familiar.

Hello, she thought, staring down at it.

"That's rather disappointing. You're supposed to be the best, Miss Savage."

"Don't let the Board of Antiquity hear you say that," she murmured. "They'd be quite distraught with having to confront the truth after all these years denying it."

Following the symbol, she found another and stilled.

Not-dead? Not alive?

Anna inhaled deeply. That wasn't quite right...undead, perhaps? Squinting, she leaned forward to another, tracing the curves of what appeared to be a sentence. Undead wouldn't do either; it presumed actual death had occurred, and this connotated differently. She skipped to another sentence.

Maybe it translated to something more along the lines of not-killed or un-killed?

Unable to die?

Without death?

Scratching at a splotch of dirt, she narrowed her gaze at another symbol. The damnable stone jaguar with those judgmental golden eyes flashed before her mind. At the chilling quiet in the room, she glanced up from the map and met Bryce's hard stare. An intensity burned behind his eyes, one that she hadn't seen before.

The hair on the back of her neck prickled.

"Come now, Miss Savage. I was really hoping you wouldn't need...encouragement."

Encouragement.

"I'm trying," she told him quietly.

"I suppose you need a reason to *try harder.*"

Anna watched in horror as Bryce stood from the table and crossed his quarters to the door. She glared at his back as he requested the pirate's presence from whoever lingered outside, her jaw nearly dropping at the implications of it all. With a click, the door closed again, and Bryce faced her, his gaze immediately meeting hers. To his credit, he didn't flinch, simply tucked his hands into his pockets and returned to his chair.

He poured more wine, and Anna's eyes burned.

"What is wrong with you?" she hissed, voice sharp as a blade.

"Nothing, I assure you, Miss Savage," he said. "Now, are you helping or not?"

"You aren't giving me much of a choice."

Bryce drained his glass and then tsked. "Of course, I am," he said, leaning back in his chair. "Will it be your brother or the pirate, Miss Savage? Which one will I break first?"

Anna pulled the map closer, lowering her head to the task at hand. Bugger, this was nearly impossible. She wasn't sure if she wanted to laugh or cry. Her brother or the pirate? The choice had been so easy once, but the pirate had grown on her like a prolific fungus. She didn't want her brother harmed, but the thought of Bryce cutting ribbons from the pirate's flesh made her nauseous.

"Excellent choice," he praised, setting his glass down.

Anna's glass remained untouched. Good God, this was difficult enough without the added difficulty of intoxication. She had to keep her brother alive, keep the pirate alive and whole, and keep Bryce from doing anything stupid in his clearly intoxicated state. Oh, and decipher an impossibly old language that hadn't been spoken in God only knows how long.

The list did not end there, and she was rather annoyed by that.

Bryce cleared his throat, drawing Anna's attention. Had he said something? He waited until she had blinked several times, until she narrowed her eyes in annoyance. "What?"

"I have more questions."

Anna nearly pulled her hair. Bryce needed to make up his damn mind—did he wish to catch up over dinner or did he want to know where the Pirate King's map led?

She couldn't do both at once.

Anna was good, but she wasn't that good.

"What's his name?"

Anna dropped her gaze back to the map. "You'll have to be more specific."

Sliding her tongue over her teeth, she tapped a symbol. It stood for an item or a thing—a bowl, perhaps? No, that wasn't quite right —a cup?

Undying Cup?

Goblet of Undeath?

"The *pirate*," he said as if it were obvious.

"No, I don't know his name," she said, glaring at the symbol that very well could hold the pirate's life in the balance. "And even if I did, I wouldn't tell you."

None of her guesses were right, not exactly.

Death, not-death.

Undeath.

54

"It never came up?"

"What never came up?"

Bryce made an agitated noise in the back of his throat. "The pirate's *name*."

"No, it never—" She stopped, the Aepith name that had been chiseled onto the stone jaguar flashing against her eyelids.

Eero.

Eero's Chalice.

The color drained from her face, stomach curling in excitement and dread.

"Miss Savage?" Bryce began, voice far off.

The Immortal Cup was supposed to be a myth.

"I don't know." She finally looked up, meeting his gaze. "I truly don't know his name."

He appraised her, probably looking for the honesty in her eyes. Bryce must have found it because he turned away, leaning back in his chair as he drained another glass of wine. Anna didn't give much credence to legends and myths, but what if they were true?

Or at least based on more truth than she gave them credit for?

"How fitting," Bryce snapped suddenly, irritation seeping through his cool façade. "Does Markus know the pirate's name?"

Anna opened her mouth to answer when the air caught in her lungs. She found herself in a singular moment, one that cleaved the time between what came before and what came after. Markus had known who the pirate was, and he'd likely known for some time.

She laughed quietly, shaping it into something else—something she did not feel, could not feel right now. It was something armored and confident, something that could be convincing and sly. "Markus isn't nearly as pretty as me. If I couldn't coax it from the pirate, what makes you think my brother could?"

Bryce's jaw ticked.

Splendid, that apparently was not the right thing to say.

He leaned forward, smile crooked and cruel. "You're protecting the pirate, Miss Savage, and I would like to know why."

"He hardly requires my protection."

"What, pray tell, has he done to covet such favor from you?" Bryce finally laughed, disbelief and scorn laced throughout his voice. "I cannot comprehend it. Did you fuck him too, is that it? I wouldn't be surprised, you seem primed to open your legs for filth like them—the Pirate King couldn't possibly be the only one."

Anna reeled back as if she'd been smacked. She ran her tongue over her teeth as she stood, leaning over the table and glaring down at him. "*That's* what this is about? You petty, self-righteous—"

"Of course, that's what this is about!" he screamed, slamming his hands on the desk. Bryce lurched as he came to his feet, using the table to stand. "I wanted to marry you! To have a family with you, one where we would grow old together and watch any children we might be blessed with thrive! And instead, you go and whore yourself out to the Pirate King! Was being with me really such a miserable existence that you'd rather have a blasted pirate as the father of your child?"

The father of her—

Good God, Chelsea Cunningham must have told his son about what she'd said at her father's dinner, that she had emptied her savings and bought a quaint cottage on the Aidanburgh coast because she thought the sea air would do wonders for a baby—her baby with the pirate.

"Bryce, that's not—"

"Was I not good enough?"

"—if you would just listen—"

He laughed. "Do you know how many women would have killed to be you? To live in comfort with a man—"

"That's not what I wanted!" she roared, slamming both palms on the desk, chest heaving. "*You* are *not* what *I* wanted!"

"No." Bryce sneered, looking down his nose at her. He quieted, mouth bracketing with rage. "You wanted to spread your legs and fuck a crim—"

The echo of the slap filled the space between them in a way anger and hurt had not been able to.

Anna remained stunned for a five count, not quite remembering when she struck him. She looked from her stinging palm to the clear print of it on his cheek—she could count her fingers. Bugger, she'd mucked this one up right and true.

Fingers fluttering to his cheek, Bryce's gaze locked on Anna's hand.

She shuffled back a step, throat bobbing and attention sinking to the rapiers he wore at his waist. The pirate's jacket slipped from her shoulders, and it wasn't until that exact moment, with Bryce staring at her with such grief and fury, that she realized she might not be as indispensable as she originally thought. If push came to shove, Markus could read the map. It would take him longer, but it was entirely possible, and Bryce knew that too.

His gaze dropped from her face to the skin left exposed by the cut of her gown. He shook his head, lunging forward. Anna ducked beneath his fist, the desk acting as a natural barrier. She needed to gain distance—any distance. Staying out of his reach was all she could think about as she twisted to the side to avoid his next attempt at grabbing her.

Bryce, true to form and regardless of his befuddled state, hurdled the desk with ease. The wine bottle broke against the floor, and Anna cursed herself for not picking the damn thing up—it would have made for an excellent weapon.

Stay out of his reach, the words pounded with each footfall.

Her hand wrapped around the door knob, and she tried to wrench the thing from the wall. It opened a fraction before Bryce's body slammed into hers. Crying out, her teeth clenched in frustration and the sharp pain of the collision. He forced her to the right of the door where she couldn't reach the knob. Anna tried turning, twisting so she could face him, but her body was wedged tight.

Something changed in the air. The skin along the back of her neck prickled.

Bugger.

She threw her elbow back once, twice. He grunted, fisting her hair and ripping her head backward. His breath was hot on her neck as he spoke, but she couldn't hear it, not out of her right ear. Bryce's free hand wrapped around her waist, pulling her closer with fingers that bruised. Cringing, she pushed one shoulder up to block his mouth from her throat. From the corner of her eye, she saw the hilts of his rapiers.

"—little bird," he cooed.

His breath smelled of wine.

Anna pulled one of his rapiers from his belt and aimed it downward, hoping to catch his foot and immobilize him. All she needed was a second of reprieve, a moment to think.

But the blade planted firmly in the floor, oscillating slowly. Bryce stepped into her, pinning her to the wall with his hips. In the background, she was vaguely aware of the screaming, a warning of some kind, but she couldn't find it in herself to care. No, she did not have an ounce of concern for men who could listen to this and not send aid.

Let them drown.

Let the sea reach from the deep below and pluck every single one of them from the ship.

His hand followed the curve of her waist, hips pressing into her backside, and then his lips were on the sensitive skin under her ear.

The door blew open, splintering against the wall.

Bryce hastily stepped away, nose bloodied. Leaning into the wall for support, Anna heaved a breath in and out. She could just see the outline of whoever had broken the door. They were massive, shoulders stretching the breadth of the frame.

Anna blinked. It was...it was the pirate.

A preternatural stillness overtook him, and then he moved, strides devouring the space between them. She watched with wide eyes as the pirate wrenched the rapier from the floor and flew at Bryce in one fluid motion. There was a shriek of steel on steel, then another and another.

"What are you doing?" she screamed, worry shredding her insides.

"I want my gods-damned bragging rights," he called back over his shoulder.

Their movements were a blur. At first, Bryce set the pace, driving the pirate back. Then the captain faltered, eyes growing wide. His arm buckled beneath the weight of the pirate's swings, and he danced backward. Grinning, the pirate spun and slashed downward again and again as sparks jumped from the connections of their blades.

Anna blinked.

Bryce's rapier launched across the room, imbedding itself in the wall of the breakfast nook. The pirate's laugh boomed through the captain's quarters, taunting and wicked. Good God, the pirate had Bryce stepping backward, had him retreating and reaching for the knife in his boot.

Anna shifted forward as sailors and marshals flooded into the room in a sea of black and evergreen uniforms, shouting orders as the desk slid back against the floor. She caught glimpses of the pirate and Bryce between the natural curves of bodies—the pirate was beating Bryce into the floorboards. Blood had spattered on either side of the captain's head, and the pirate's knuckles had ripped open. Blood ran down the pirate's face from a cut between his eyebrows.

It wasn't until Bryce landed a well-aimed punch to the festering wound at the pirate's side that he growled, lips thinning as his swing stopped and then started again. Bryce had always possessed an excellent attention to detail—he missed almost nothing—so he hit the pirate there again.

It mattered little.

Her pirate was brilliant. Even with Bryce brutalizing his side, it took four men to pull him away. A sailor helped Bryce to his feet, his brown gaze centering on the pirate as he fought those trying to contain him.

He killed one, then another. Three more appeared, then a knife kissed his throat, close enough that one wrong move could tear it open. Stomach fluttering and skin heating at the sight, Anna screamed. She wasn't even sure what, maybe something about leaving him alone, about protecting him.

Whatever it was, it got Bryce's attention.

They made eye contact through the crowd.

Bryce yelled some order, and the men swarmed Anna—grasping at her arms and holding her still. The pirate froze, gaze skipping to hers wildly. Throat bobbing, he settled down, blood meandering down either side of his nose and catching in the stubble above his lip. He spat a wad of blood from his mouth, and the glob landed soundly on Bryce's boot.

A slow smile curled the captain's lips as he stared down at her pirate.

"Let her be."

"Oh." Bryce clucked his tongue. "I do believe I have figured out how to make you talk, wretch."

Anna looked from the color draining the pirate's face to the triumphant smile on Bryce's.

"Take him below deck," Bryce said, attention flickering between Anna and the door that no longer sat on its hinges—it hung, looking as drunk as Bryce probably felt. "Anthony, would you mind sitting with Miss Savage?"

Anna caught the pirate's gaze before the marshals forced him from the room, his neck craning all the way around so he could see her. Something agonized and guilt-ridden stared back at her, but beneath that was leagues of self-loathing.

He blamed himself.

"Not at all, Captain," Anthony said, rolling up his sleeves with a wicked, knowing look.

"Give me ten minutes. If you don't hear from me, begin."

Oh, bugger.

CHAPTER EIGHT

Trevor coughed, another shite-eating grin on his face as he stared up at the fucking captain. Hit his female? Force her up against a fucking wall? Trevor reckoned no'. Soon as he slipped these manacles, he'd crush the shite's windpipe and watch him suffocate, eyes bulging and beet red. His grin widened as he thought of the wheezing the male would do. Probably beg something fierce too.

His head ripped to the side, the back of some marshal's hand connecting wi' his cheek.

"Well, wretch?" Cunningham drawled from a chair. He sat wi' his elbows propped on the back, looking like some gods-damned king. "Are you going to tell me what I want to know now?"

Trevor shook his head. "Ye drunk fucking cunt. Did ye think to take her against the wall?"

The wee shite smirked; the sight boiled the blood in his veins. "Why? Do you know from experience that she likes that? Rough against the wall with her fingers in your hair to keep your mouth at her neck?"

Trevor fought the heat that damned his cheeks—he'd certainly thought about it more times than he could bloody count. He'd had a lot of time to think about when and where he might have her if only things were different. The gods-damned wall remained in his top five fantasies.

The prick waved him off, the motion lazy. "No need to answer. If you have, then you're in excellent company." His lip twitched as he rolled his neck, something dark and jealous seeping into his voice. "I hear she even fucked the Pirate King."

Trevor's teeth nearly broke from the fucking strain. Oh, aye, the lass had tumbled him once before. But she'd also tried killing him too, so it evened out in his head. He watched the captain across from him carefully, gaze narrowing at the frown bracketing the male's mouth.

The fucker was jealous.

Throwing his head back, Trevor laughed. "You're jealous! Ye are bloody well jealous of the Pirate King for tumbling the lass!"

Cunningham's cheeks reddened a wee bit, but 'twas enough for Trevor to keep prodding. Maybe if he kept the captain's attention, he could save Anna from further pain, and this seemed a touchy enough subject. Throat bobbing, he called up a wee bit of what he remembered from that night.

'Twas easy enough; it'd been a cherished thing before he'd found Anna again.

"Tell me, lad," he said, cocking his head as wee guffaws broke through his breath. "Was it before or after she left your worthless ass? Were ye the laughingstock of Briland when they found out your ex—whatever the hell the lass was—fucked the king? Oh...what a sorry state ye must have been in, knowing the king's cock had been in her. Is that what ye think about when ye see her? Do ye picture it—how the wee bonnie lass might have stepped from her dress, wearing naught but a dark, lacy thong, and led him to bed?"

The prick looked about ready to fly at him, knuckles bleeding white.

Fucking good.

Trevor leaned forward, looking from one sailor to the next like he was sharing a secret wi' them. "The way I hear it, the lass kept him up all bloody night. He had scratches on his back and bruises at his neck for fucking *weeks*. Kept the crew up too wi' all her moaning while he stretched and filled her tight—"

The next hit knocked the breath from his lungs.

"Tell me, what's worse?" Trevor coughed, licking the new split in his lip. Bloody hell, he was getting tired of being hit on the fucking face. "That ye loved her then, or that ye still do now?"

Another hit, this one straight to the gods-damned festering wound.

At least it was no' his face.

Trevor wheezed, looking up. "That all ye got, bucko? 'Cause I can sit here all bloody day."

Cunningham stood over him, lording a wee bit. A bright lantern swung just behind the prick's head as he turned and slumped back into the chair. Whatever rage the male'd been feeling was gone now, replaced wi' an eerie calm that Trevor did no' have a good feeling about.

"For you?" he finally asked. "Yes."

Looking from one marshal to the next, his gaze skipped over the sailors in their evergreen uniforms entirely. They were no' the ones he needed to worry about. The bloody fools could hardly follow orders when presented wi' a monster like him. His brows twitched. No' a single one of the bastards moved. He looked from left to right again before settling his gaze on Cunningham.

"Such a shame I didn't know you had a soft spot for women sooner," he said, looking above.

Trevor didn't answer.

"Or is it only for one woman specifically?" he asked as the boards above their heads creaked. "I, more than anyone, understand your sentiments toward Miss Savage. Careful with that one, though, wretch. She'll tear your heart out the first chance she gets."

He heard the slap through the floorboards, clapping like thunder to his ears.

Growling, Trevor glared at the ceiling as he heard Anna swear and grunt, fighting back. He tried lunging upward, but the gods-damn shackles anchoring him to the floor held true. His stomach tumbled through the fucking floor.

Trapped.

Trapped like a bloody mouse, unable to do a thing to help the lass.

"Leave her be!" he snarled at Cunningham, planting his foot and pulling against the shackles for all he was bloody well worth.

A bit of dust rained down on him as a body hit the boards.

He couldn't do it.

He couldn't listen to Anna and no' do anything about it.

"You know what I want."

Even Cunningham winced at the next stiff slap.

Bloody hell, he was going to kill them—he was going to kill them all. Clenching his fists, he felt the whistle of the wind around the ship like it was the breath in his own lungs. Oh, aye, he'd slaughter every last one of these fucks if it was the last thing he did.

Cunningham leaned forward, dirty brown gaze narrowing. "Now, tell me, Tate. Where is your brother?"

A low laugh left his lips, straining the cuts in Trevor's mouth.

Tate?

The boards above groaned, and a male coughed, swearing something vicious at the lass. Anna spat at him, the sound quickly followed by another clap. Something broke against a wall and clattered to the floor—was the lass throwing shite?

Feet shuffled along the floor above, and wi' each step Trevor grew stiffer and stiffer. The male above grunted again. Red crept into his vision—they were dead, they just didn't bloody well know it yet. The wee captain played wi' a fire he did no' understand, could never hope to understand. No' if he was willing to do that to her.

'Twas fine, really.

If the prick wanted the king, then it was the king he would get.

His gaze remained on the boards above even after the male screamed. A thump like a gods-damned body hitting the floor followed, then silence. Such stiff, terrible silence. Trevor's gaze was trained above. He needed something, some sign she was okay, or he was going to lose his fucking—

"Come get your damn pig!" she screamed down at them.

Trevor breathed deep, turning from the ceiling and back to Cunningham, a smirk twitching at his lips. It was bloody hard to turn away from where his female was, especially wi' knowing she'd look at him like he was a gods-damned demon after this.

Falling back into his role as the bloody Pirate King felt a lot like shedding a second skin—or donning one he had no' worn in some time. Bryce fucking Cunningham saw the change, stilling wi' wide eyes. The crew behind him saw it too, stepping back and gasping—their reactions encouraged a wee chuckle.

Trevor grinned, a row of knives in his mouth.

"Ye wanted to know where the Pirate King is, bucko?" He spat, forcing himself to his full height.

The chains groaned and snapped, floorboards creaking from the sudden strain. Real thunder boomed in the distance, accenting his words. Many of the males jumped at the weather's punctuation as the wind ripped around them in a vicious circle.

"Well here I fuckin' be."

Oh, aye, the king had returned.

Gods help whoever had disrespected his queen.

CHAPTER NINE

Good God, Anthony hit like he had anvils for hands.

Anna wiped her bleeding nose against her arm, bracing a hand against Bryce's desk as the room lurched to the side. Anthony's boots were just visible from the other side, sticking out like a sore thumb. She shook her head at him; both he and Bryce were fools. Fools for thinking it would take one man to cow her—and a mediocre one at that.

Dropping to her knees softly, she pressed her ear to the floorboards.

"Well, here I fuckin' be," the pirate snarled, voice crackling with threats.

Chaos reigned, chains rattled, and orders were screamed. A wind ripped around the space hard enough to force its way between the boards. It brushed against her gently as men shrieked and...and cried. Anna was on her feet, stumbling to the door. The pirate would need her help, and she would need Markus's. If not for the locked door, she would have ripped it from its hinges. Glaring down at the brass knob in her fingers, she knelt in front of it, inspecting it.

Jerimiah Hearthall?

That was new—the *Contessa* originally had locks by Christopher Satin.

Perhaps some things did change. Her stomach rolled with the next climb and fall of a wave, her fingers fumbling for the few remaining lockpicks threaded in her hair. Anna hummed the pirate's shanty beneath her breath as she worked, a bead of sweat dripping from her brow.

The lock clicked.

Anna shoved her picks into her hair and peeked out the door.

It was nearly full dark, the sun just a sliver of light setting in the west, illuminating the amassing thunderheads above. The wind tore up from the glittering waters, cold and crisp. Bugger, she could smell the pirate in that breeze. His scent was layered beneath the cold brine, something dark and spiced.

She crept behind barrels and crates, hiding behind anything that would keep her out of sight. Luckily, the crew was more concerned with the approaching storm than looking for a woman they believed to be locked within the captain's quarters.

Her bare feet were light on the steps as she tiptoed down them. She slipped in something warm and wet at the first landing before slamming into a rather large, masculine frame. Anna's fist connected with the man's throat; a grin broke across her face as he recoiled into a wheezing mess. Lunging, she looked for a way to get under his guard or onto his back so she could twist his fat head from his damn—

"Shh—" he hissed as Anna's knee missed its intended target and slammed into his thigh. "It's *me*, damn it!"

Anna abruptly stopped, stumbling forward from the momentum. She could hardly see her brother in this murky dark. The shadows sharpened the hard planes of his face and darkened his eyes to a near indigo blue. Launching forward, she wrapped her arms around his torso. Good God, she was so relieved to see him. But how had he escaped the brig?

"Markus," she whispered, drawing away from him. "What happened?"

"I don't know, Anna. They came for the pirate, but as they dragged him out, he said to be ready and to find you and escape. He said he'd worry about the map and catch up." He laughed then, the sound almost bitter. "I should have believed him when he said he could get you out and distract the lot of them."

The pirate wanted them to leave...*without* him?

Anger curled hot in her gut—like hell she'd be doing that.

"We can't leave him. You know we can't."

Markus vigorously scratched his scalp with both hands. His hair stood straight up, springy curls pointed in every direction. "He created an opportunity for us; he's making a sacrifice. Now honor it, Anna."

His eyes were hard and bloodshot, his stance stiff. Anna dragged her gaze from his boots to the tips of his hair again. This was hard for him; she saw the guilt in the lines of his face and in the tension of his shoulders. She hadn't expected it would be difficult for her brother to leave the pirate behind. She doubted Markus had expected to feel this way as well.

"I have developed a small amount of respect for him," Markus croaked, looking completely uncomfortable with the admission. "And I promised him I would get you out. Do not make a liar of me."

His hand wrapped around her bicep and he pulled her forward. Anna stumbled, unable to take a single step in the direction she'd just come from. It was like her legs had turned to stone, intending to root her to these steps. Looking over her shoulder, she gazed into the descending dark.

"I can't," she said, eyes stinging.

"Anna—"

"No. You don't understand. I *can't*, Markus." She stared at the ground, furious with the idea of leaving the pirate.

Good God, it was a despicable feeling.

"Anna..."

She shook her head. They weren't leaving the pirate on some tropical island. Bugger, they'd be abandoning him to Bryce's ministrations. The captain was furious and cruel as it was, she could only imagine how that would escalate when Anna and Markus disappeared into thin air.

"It's not right, and I know I shouldn't care about him because he's a damn pirate, but I can't leave him—not to entertain Bryce while we run away with our tail between our legs. You get the boat, and I'll get the pirate."

Markus sighed miserably.

"Don't worry, I'll be in and out with none the wiser."

"When has that ever worked?"

"Never. But there's a first time for everything," she said, smiling softly.

Her brother looked up and closed his eyes. Rolling his sleeves up, he shook his head at her. "I'll meet you on deck. Please, for the love of God, be careful. If anything happened to you because I let you—" he stopped, sniffling once before turning. "Just—I love you, Anna. Be careful."

"I love you too," she whispered, watching her brother take the stairs two at a time.

She counted to ten, then descended into the bowels of the *Contessa*. The run down was a haze, nothing but the creak of the ship as it listed one way and tossed her into the wall before groaning as it righted itself. Anna shook her head, feet pounding against the boards. She followed the sound of screaming marshals and fearful sailors like breadcrumbs until she stood in front of a door.

Throwing the door open, she saw the pirate standing over a floor covered in corpses—none of which belonged to Bryce.

Bugger, where had he run off to?

"What the hell are ye doing here, lass?" he asked, stepping around the bloodied, misshapen bodies.

"It isn't obvious?"

"You're supposed to be wi' Markus getting off this bloody ship," he told her, rubbing at one of his wrists, a manacle still locked around it.

Anna squinted at the iron cuff and followed the short length of chain as it swung lightly with his movements. A stream of blood flowed down the band, weaving through the links until it fell to the ground.

Swallowing hard, she looked away from the pirate. She needed something to distract her before she marched back up those stairs on a suicide mission to gut Bryce Cunningham. Anna had every intention of being the last thing that man saw some day, but fortunately for the captain, she was more concerned with getting her brother and pirate off the *Contessa* in one piece.

Anger simmered in her veins as she picked a saber from the planks. Its grip was coated in blood and warm to the touch. She wiped it off on the pirate's coat before giving it a deft twirl and turned back to the pirate. "When have you ever known me to do as I'm told?"

He put distance between them, jaw ticking as he flicked a saber into his waiting hand with his foot. "Travel south by southeast until you reach Bellena. Tell them you're looking for Tate."

"I came back for you and don't have any intention of leaving without you," she said stiffly, fingers tightening around the grip. "What part of that is so hard for you to understand?"

"Why the hell would ye do that, lass?" he breathed out.

Vulnerability shattered the tough expression he'd been wearing. It made him nearly unrecognizable, and despite the blood and bruises that covered his face, he looked younger. The saber slackened in her hand—bugger, her answer mattered to the pirate.

"I'm not..." She cleared her throat, at a loss for words. "You're my friend, I think, and you don't deserve to be abandoned. You shouldn't be abandoned, not by someone who cares about you."

"Your friend?" he questioned, face unreadable.

Anna didn't know what to say.

Floundering, her mouth opened and closed several times. *Friend.* Was that even the right word for how she felt about the man standing in front of her? Probably not. She certainly didn't think about kissing any of her other friends. But friends also exchanged names and had every intention of staying in each other's lives. They had never had the chance to build that foundation of trust and understanding, but that didn't mean they couldn't.

They just had to survive this first.

He must have seen something in her gaze because his jaw ticked. "Ye don't even know me, luv. Ye don't know who I am. If ye did"—he paused, voice breaking—"if ye did, you'd leave me to whichever one of Fate's tides I'd found myself wading through. Just like most."

Frustration roared through her as she took a step closer, closing the distance he had tried to put between them. Consequences be damned, let the whole crew hear what she had to say, let them come running. But they were having this conversation here. They were having it now.

"Tell me and let's be done with this. Good God, I *know* you're a high-ranking pirate in the Coalition. I *know* you don't think highly of them, which means you probably side with the Pirate King. I *know* you're a captain, but I cannot bring myself to contemplate which ship and who might hold your leash."

The pirate looked away from her, something like shame rippling across his features. His lips pressed into a thin line, and he scrubbed at the back of his neck. She saw the sadness in his gaze then, the deep, cool ache as it glimmered from his eyes.

Anna stiffened the tremble beginning in her lip and tried to blink away the stinging in her eyes. His jaw loosened, eyes closing as he struggled with something internally. Finally, he opened them, gaze dropping to the puddles of blood on the floor as he spoke.

"I...shite. I'm the Pirate King, luv."

The—*what?*

"There's no way. He has to be my father's age." Anna couldn't help it, she laughed outright at the absurdity of it all. "*You?* The Pirate King?"

He nodded his head, seeming to deflate.

"Trevor Lovelace?"

"Aye. 'Tis my name, been so since birth."

She snorted, rolling her eyes. "Scourge of the Seas?"

"I'm bloody serious, Anna."

She counted the eleven or so freckles on his face, letting her gaze bounce from his shoulders to his hands. Every line of him was strung tight as if waiting for a blow. It was the stiff line of his full lips coupled with his newly shuttered gaze that did it, though.

Oh, bugger.

CHAPTER TEN

Get the blasted boat?

Markus shook his head, creeping up the stairs on the balls of his feet. The notion sounded simple enough until one considered they sailed through shark-infested waters with a storm brewing at their back. That, of course, did not include Cunningham's sailors or the marshals that patrolled the ship.

And that was all without taking *Anna* into account.

Leaning against the wall, he pinched the bridge of his nose and closed his eyes. He should have expected this, he should have known trying to leave without the blasted Pirate King would not have gone over well with his sister. He honestly had been tempted to tell her who the damn man was just to see her reaction, to coax a harrowing escape out of her.

But the old girl likely would have gallivanted off to find Lovelace anyway, if for no other reason than to confront him. Telling her and not telling her were two very different paths to the same destination. One way or another, Anna would have gone after him. Hopefully, withholding the identity of her pirate would keep her levelheaded. At the very least, her temper wouldn't be stoked and driving her every action.

Maybe that cool focus would keep her alive.

Markus smoothed back his hair and adjusted how his shirt sat on his shoulders before peeking onto the deck. Bollocks, he couldn't remember the last time stress had plagued him quite like this—heart thumping in his chest and nausea churning his stomach. His booted feet were near silent on the deck, not that there was anyone to listen for his steps.

There wasn't a single blasted sailor or marshal on deck, not that he could see.

He turned his attention upward, squinting into the light mist falling from the sky as he searched the crow's nest for activity. None. Despite the inactivity on deck, he was careful to remain in the shadows.

Looking left and right, he noticed the few lanterns that had been lit swinging back and forth lazily with the rock of the sea. The waves brushing against the hull and the general creak of the ship were the only sounds from above deck, but they did little to muffle the screaming that echoed out portholes.

His hand passed over a crate not far from where a cluster of small wherries waited for him. Of course, Anna had failed to mention what he was supposed to do after he secured a boat. Markus glanced over his shoulder. It appeared the distraction Lovelace had planned was going according to plan.

He had grown up on stories of the Pirate King—of the Old Crow and the Baron that came before him. But those surrounding Trevor Lovelace had always been the worst. His father always took liberties when he told the stories, diving deeply into his treachery at sea and the various atrocities he had committed.

Trevor Lovelace had become something of a legend over the years, saturated in fantastical mystery and intrigue. But if the stories were true, Cunningham's men would have their hands full trying to contain the Pirate King. If not for the reckless abandon with which Anna operated, he might have been comforted by that.

Lovelace would keep Anna alive.

Markus had never been more certain of anything in his life.

He didn't know the extent of the pirate's feelings, but the wretch felt enough that he had chosen to protect her at every blasted turn. He hadn't even tried to hinder or curb her tenacious tendencies. Lovelace had simply waited on standby in case she needed him.

He hated it, but the pirate might have been good for his sister.

At the very least, he was better than anyone Bellcaster had to offer.

He crouched behind the crate and sighed. It was rather fitting that the man who suited his sister best was the one she'd spent the last three years running from. Perhaps it was more ironic than anything. Markus grinned and stood, gaze anchored on the wherry only feet away.

Rounding the corner quickly, he froze at the thump against his stomach.

Markus frowned—had he been punched?

The muscles of his abdomen spasmed, and then the pain started. Looking down, his brows furrowed at the band of metal protruding from his stomach. He followed the blade to a familiar guard—he'd know the blasted thing anywhere. Every captain in the Briland Navy had a rapier with that specific guard; Markus had always joked that it made identifying bodies easier.

Bollocks.

He followed the guard to a hand and then to the cool appraisal on Bryce Cunningham's face. The rapier ripped free of his gut, pulling a grunt from his lips. Markus swallowed past the scream stuck in his throat, gaze narrowing down at Cunningham. His knees cracked against the deck as his hands went to the bleeding wound—he had to staunch the bleeding, but it found a way between his fingers anyway.

Blast it all to hell. Despite all he had lived through, Markus had never been stabbed—he had never suffered a wound that could turn fatal in the blink of an eye.

He stared down at his hands, almost surprised to see how thoroughly stained in red they were.

The world tilted on its axis and his eyes drooped closed as the sound of steps came from either side of him. He looked up; Bryce was nothing more than a blurry spot of black against the dark of the night as he cleaned his rapier with a handkerchief.

"Bring them up. I have a question for Miss Savage."

Markus was vaguely aware of the hands banding around his biceps and the dragging sensation against his knees and the tops of his boots. The alarm didn't set in until he realized Cunningham's men were dragging him to the taffrail. This conversation would not be taking place from the relative safety of the captain's quarters, where a surgeon might be present.

A question, Cunningham had said.

What could the bastard possibly want to ask?

CHAPTER ELEVEN

Her pirate...

He was Trevor Lovelace.

She blinked several times, looking at the pirate seemingly for the first time.

That meant—that meant they...good God.

Her gaze dropped to his booted feet. Working up, she traced the line of his tattoos before settling her gaze on his eyes, where conflict roared like a heavy storm. He stood with his legs slightly apart, his shoulders relaxed. Blood dripped from his nose, and sailors and marshals in their death pallor covered the floor between them, but not an ounce of the man standing before her looked like the Pirate King.

How could her pirate be Trevor Lovelace?

Anna laughed, unsure of what else she was supposed to do. Embarrassment heated her cheeks and clouded her head. He knew how she felt about the Pirate King; was he telling the truth, or was he trying to force her away to protect her?

She shook her head at him. If he thought he could manipulate her into leaving...

Good God, she saw red.

Anna opened her mouth to yell at him as something solid collided with her back, reminding her there was a time and a place for

76

confrontation, and the middle of a jailbreak was not one of them. She'd smack his fat head off his shoulders when they were safe.

She turned with the momentum, ducking beneath a marshal's fist and blocking the next sweep of his blade with her saber. Their swords met with a sharp clang that rattled her arm and hurt her ears. Anna flinched as a revolver fired, dancing around her opponent. He brought his steel down again and again until her arm ached from the effort or parrying and blocking.

Somewhere between one blink and the next, blood sprayed her face, a knife protruding from the sailor's throat. The dying marshal's knees buckled, revealing the pirate just behind him. Wasting no time, he laced his blood-soaked fingers with hers. Her chest tightened, skin warming beneath his touch as they ran.

"Come on, lass. Ye can hate me when you're off this boat."

"I don't—"

Did she hate him?

No…Anna felt something rather distant from hate for the pirate. Her foot slipped in a slick pool of blood, and his hand tightened around hers for a moment. Her heart stumbled right along with her, and if not for the security of his grip, she would have hit the ground.

"'Tis fine, luv. I hate myself sometimes too," he said as they cleared the room and ran straight into another contingent of sailors and marshals at the bottom of the stairs.

Anna thumped against the pirate's back as he stopped. His muscles coiled beneath his skin, making him look larger than a moment before. Bugger, she would never say it out loud, but the pirate was a specimen among men.

Hand still in his, she leaned around the pirate's shoulder and stared up at Bryce's crew. It was a sea of critical gazes staring down at her—at them. They weren't judging the pirate, though; he had acted exactly as a scoundrel of the sea was expected to. It was Anna who had gone against the grain, who had chosen to help the criminal instead of adhering to the wishes of the captain.

A gust tore down the stairs with enough force to cause the men to stumble forward. It broke around the pirate, just barely brushing her cheek and shoulder, the visible skin of her thigh and calf. No one moved as the wind came in soft starts and stops. Anna glanced at the pirate; it almost looked as if he'd timed his breathing to it.

A marshal descended slowly, one step at a time, as a hand wrapped around her wrist as tight as a shackle. Her arm was wrenched over her head. She screamed as more hands curled around her arms and the sailors lifted her off the ground. The sea of marshals and sailors flooded down the steps in one vicious tide. Claustrophobia was not a fear that normally lived beneath her skin, but the press of bodies against her was near suffocating.

Craning her head, she tried catching the pirate's gaze, but there were too many men on him for her to find his dark eyes. She heard him struggling somewhere behind her as the crew dragged her forward, ascending one step at a time.

"Anna!" he screamed.

The door in front of them blew open on a wicked gust. Anna blinked into the thick mist falling from the sky as they forced her through the frame and onto the deck where Bryce Cunningham waited in the distance. She jerked backward, bare feet sliding against the deck at the vicious victory in his eyes.

A way out. She needed to find a way—

Markus.

Her brother sat bent over on his knees, face turned to the deck. From the pull of his shoulders, she suspected his hands might be bound behind his back. Bugger, she knew where this was going. Something dark and twisted hollowed her out, running ice through her veins. The sailors continued dragging her forward, farther from the pirate but closer to her brother.

Panic crawled up her throat. There was a growing puddle of blood around his legs, and his skin had a waxy quality to it that made her heart race. She found the wound almost instantly; his dark shirt had slicked to the skin against his stomach, soaked completely with blood.

"Markus!" she screamed but he shook his head at her.

No.

No—no—no—

Anna choked on an uncomfortable laugh.

How the hell was she supposed to get her brother and the pirate out of this in one piece?

So much for the frying pan or the fire—she had done a nosedive straight into one of the deeper pits of hell, where there was nothing but brimstone and ash with no way out. Tears ran a hot track down her cheeks as she continued to laugh.

They weren't getting off this ship—not alive.

Anna breathed deep. It was time to adjust. There had to be something she could offer Bryce, something to lessen the severity of the consequences for their short-lived rebellion. There was one thing she could offer, one bribe he might be interested in taking—but it would infuriate her brother and the pirate.

Anna swallowed hard. They could be furious with her as long as they were alive.

The pirate laughed, drawing her attention to where he now lay face down on the deck. One marshal wrestled with his arm, trying to pin it behind his back. Despite the hold, the pirate fought his way back up. She looked between her brother, pale and bleeding out, and her pirate, full of rage and energy.

The entire ship listed drastically to the side as the pirate grinned and thrashed beneath the hold of Cunningham's crew. Panic flared in her chest as the men holding her slid toward the taffrail, toward the damn ocean. She pressed the balls of her feet against the deck—falling into the sea wouldn't seem so bad if she could swim. She screamed as the taffrail approached, and then the pirate's gaze fell on her like a spot of warmth and the ship righted itself.

Anna took gasping breaths—what the hell was that?

"Little bird," Bryce said as he stepped into her line of sight, gaze roving the *Contessa* curiously.

His lip was swollen and bloodied, his left eye blackened from his scuffle with her pirate. Looking down, she saw both rapiers had been returned to his side. She glanced from the captain to the rest of the main deck, gaze ravenous.

Anna was a master of her own fate, of the world around her.

If she wanted an opportunity or a miracle, she would force one into existence by sheer will alone.

Her hands trembled at her sides as the marshals forced the pirate to his knees, hands wrenched behind his back. It seemed to take half the crew, but they managed it. Bryce raised a brow at her before striding toward the pirate, his hands clasped behind his back. He was the spitting image of his father.

I want to be like him, Bryce had whispered when they were children.

The pirate grinned up at Bryce, teeth stained pink. His breaths were deep and slow, his chest rattling when he exhaled. Fear curdled the blood in her veins as she searched for that splendid opportunity, that miraculous event that would tip the scales. But they were surrounded by water on Bryce's God-forsaken ship, and the hands holding her were firm, bruising the skin beneath their grasp.

Lightning flashed from above them like a fine spider web.

She made eye contact with the pirate, something zinging between them with the weight and intensity of his stare. Leaning forward against the press of iron fingers, she shook her head—whatever he was planning, she wanted him to stop.

Bugger, why did the pirate have such a strong urge to knock on death's door?

The crew stepped away from the pirate, coaxing an even larger smile from him.

"What to do with you?" Bryce mused, walking in a circle around the redhead.

Panic set in, true panic that froze every muscle in her body before she started thrashing. Her elbows connected with flesh, as did the back of her head—she didn't care.

"Leave him be!" she snarled, kicking the nearest sailor as she seethed. "I said, *leave him be*, Bryce!"

Bryce stopped at hearing his name pass through her lips.

It was not a sweet caress of the five letters, it was not a breathy sigh.

It was a *killing*.

A strangling of every sound, a promise to bury his name where no one would ever find it.

Only the glassiness of his gaze revealed his earlier wine-fueled rage. Gaze glittering darkly at her, the slight slant from his Xing heritage made him look all the more menacing. She'd found it endearing once. Now, she hated all that he was and had ever been—she hated all he would ever be for as long as he had left to live.

Which, if she had anything to say about it, would not be much longer.

"Did you say something, little bird?" he asked.

Anna tried lunging forward, but the hands around tightened. "I'll stay in your quarters, and you can keep them below deck," she argued. "I'll listen. I'll be good. I'll solve that map. Please, leave him be. Leave Markus be. Chain them, gag them, I do not care, as long as you leave them be."

"It's too late for that," he stated quickly. "*Choose.*"

"What?" Anna asked in disbelief, looking from the pirate to her brother.

He wanted her to—

"The pirate or your brother. You do not require both."

Once upon a time, the choice would have been easy. Her brother's name would have left her lips with the same unconscious automaticity as breathing. Markus—of course, she would always choose Markus. But his name found itself forced behind her teeth, unable to break free. Anna laughed hoarsely, chest tight and throat feeling as if it might close entirely.

Bugger. She couldn't utter Markus's name, not with the fear of what would happen to her pirate keeping it caged behind her teeth.

The pirate thought she hated him?

Hate is not what kept her brother's name tethered to her tongue.

"'Course she picks her brother," the pirate scoffed, drawing everyone's attention to him.

Anna shook her head furiously. He needed to shut his damn mouth! She could figure this out still, she just needed time. He ignored her, sitting back on his heels, arms in chains behind him and a smile on his face.

Could the man be any more confident in the face of potential doom?

Bryce walked a circle around the pirate, touching a finger to his lips in thought. "Now, I do seem to recall you have a nasty habit of coming back from the dead. But I wonder how long it will take you to find your way back from the bottom of the ocean."

Lightning cracked against the dark clouds before striking the ocean by the *Contessa* with a stiff hiss. Anna winced from the light, just able to see what looked like a ship trailing them in the distance. She couldn't make out the flags or sails; it was just a speck on the horizon. Her brows drew together curiously. Was it another of Bryce's ships, or were they being followed?

The sailors hauled her pirate to his feet and marched him to the taffrail. Glancing from the darkly churning waters surrounding them, Anna turned back to her pirate. He might have fooled Cunningham, but she refused to believe he was the Pirate King—he couldn't be the Pirate King. He was too kind. Too considerate. Too gallant.

Good God, he was too *young* to be that God-awful wretch.

The pirate's grin sharpened as they strapped the cannonballs to his boots. "'Tis a bloody good thing I'm a strong swimmer, ain't it?"

Anna stilled, watching as Bryce cocked his head and stepped closer to the pirate. "Bryce, I am begging you—"

"Trust me when I say you have not even begun to beg yet, Miss Savage," he said, gaze focused on the pirate. "Now...you are entirely too calm, wretch."

She nearly laughed, surprised she and Bryce agreed on anything right now.

"I disagree. I have naught to fear from ye."

Bryce reached forward, hands digging around in the pirate's trouser pockets. Her brows pulled together—what the hell was he looking for in the pirate's trousers? She doubted the captain had any interest in what his pants contained. The pirate's face hardened, though, his muscles tightening as Bryce leaned away. Something wet left his pocket with a snap.

Anna squinted. Was that the map?

Despite the vicious glare on his face, the pirate's grin held firm.

When had he lifted that off of Bryce?

"Curious," Bryce said. Anna found herself in full agreement once more. "How did this happen?"

"Before I was a pirate, I was a cutpurse in Aidanburgh," he said smugly, a short scoff leaving his lips. "It helped put food on the table when picking through the bloody garbage did no'."

Bryce sighed in a withering sort of way that spoke to his annoyance with this entire affair. Turning, he looked at Anna, and her stomach plummeted—she'd seen that look on his face before the last time they'd walked through a market together.

The pirate winked, a genuine smile curling at the corner of his lips. Her mouth dried at seeing it—despite the blood and their current circumstances, she easily recognized the handsome mischievousness to his grin. But then he dipped his head lightly, a farewell of sorts, and bile climbed up her throat.

Bryce pressed a finger to the pirate's chest, and he fell overboard.

The splash echoed even above the thunder.

Anna blinked.

Her head shook of its own accord, the soft murmur of *no* repeating over and over. A sob ripped itself from her chest, and she swallowed hard, vision blurred by tears. She was only vaguely aware of her feet scraping against the boards as they led her back down below deck.

"Someone clean up this mess," Bryce barked in the background. He could have been miles away for all it mattered.

Anna had thought she knew what heartbreak was—how it could curdle a person's insides. She hadn't. She had been so incredibly foolish. Now, she wondered if someone could die from such a thing, if she already stood with one foot in the grave.

CHAPTER TWELVE

Everything was dark and muffled.

Why was it so dark?

(Had there ever been any light?)

"That was stupid of you," a deep voice murmured seriously.

It *was* stupid of him.

He should have known better—he should have known letting his sister gallivant off into the sunset in search of the Pirate King would only end in ruin. There had never been a tale about Trevor Lovelace that ended in anything but death or destruction.

(But what was death to a living legend?)

If Trevor Lovelace was a living legend, Markus was a living contradiction, filled to the brim with hollow feelings and wants, always chasing after that next thing that might create the sensation of space inside him

(Hollow men make for hollow dreams.)

A younger man scoffed. His voice sounded more familiar to Markus's ears. "I don't think the ship's surgeon is in a position to make such accusations."

"A ship's surgeon might not be, but I reckon a close friend of your father is."

His father didn't have friends, not truly.

Everything comes down to investments and alliances, Markus.
(Everything?)

"You shouldn't have thrown Lovelace overboard, and you sure as hell shouldn't have run Savage's son through," the older man continued. The more he spoke, the more his voice tugged at Markus's memories like a loose thread in a sweater. "There are consequences to actions, boy. It's best you start remembering that."

Consequences were the small suns congregating behind the skin of his abdomen, burning him slowly from the inside out, reducing everything he was to a fine ash. If he had teeth, he would have gritted them; if he had muscles, they would have been clenched.

(Did he have substance if he could not see it?)

(Did this pain really exist at all?)

"God-damnit," the old man growled as sunbursts lit behind Markus's eyes. "Hadley wouldn't have buggered this up this bad."

Silence.

Silence like the dead of night.

Vacant like the look in her eyes when Markus had left.

"Will he live?" the younger man asked, his voice like razors and fetid rot.

"Time will tell." The older man sighed, and—and Markus thought he *felt* something move inside him.

(Termites burrowing deep, maggots filling a corpse.)

Time.

Time was only seconds and minutes and hours racing toward the end.

(Was this his end?)

He would have rather drowned.

CHAPTER THIRTEEN

It had been four days.

Anna spent the first two crying until her eyes had nearly swollen shut and she thought she would drown in heartache. On the third day, she hadn't possessed any more tears to cry, but found she had anger in spades. She had spent her time screaming obscenities at Bryce and anyone else who dared walk the floors around or above her. Today, she was neither sad nor angry, but quietly resigned to the two possibilities of her fate. Anna was a rat trapped beneath a heated bucket with a choice to make.

Stay put and die.

Or chew her way out.

Growling, she twisted the sliver of metal between her fingers, ignoring the way beads of blood slicked the lockpick as it bit into her flesh. Bryce had taken her pirate. He wasn't about to take her brother—not today, not any day of the damn week. Oh no, Anna would take his ship. She would take his crew. And then she would take his pitiful life.

Hearing footsteps, she went limp.

Something clattered against the boards, swiftly followed by swearing. Anna waited twenty seconds; the *Contessa* groaned its discomfort at battling the storm-churned waters in the background. Was this the pirate's doing? All his rage and anger at drowning made a physical thing? It was easier to believe he might be manipulating the waters from beyond the grave than acknowledging it might have something to do with the pesky spot on her hand.

That, and she rather liked the idea of Bryce being struck by a lightning bolt.

When the bilge remained quiet, she surged back to work. Her arms twisted and fingers rotated this way and that as she tried to pick the manacle's lock without seeing it. Anna itched her scalp on the floor and tried not to acknowledge how slicked with grime it was from the moist air.

Once she sprung the lock, she had to find Markus. She hadn't seen him since—

Since then.

Anna threw the image of the pirate falling over the taffrail from her mind with a swift push. Instead, she focused on the dark, dank underbelly of the ship. Bryce had made the same mistake as most. He had tried to contain her, and she was going to make him regret it even if it was the last thing she did—and it very well might be. Chained aboard a ship sailing into a hurricane in the middle of the ocean was not the ideal place to be when one couldn't swim.

The ship lurched precariously sideways, and her stomach rolled right along with it. Careening to the side, she slid through the bilge water. Her stomach flipped, and she fought the urge to vomit, wanting nothing to do with that in her hair. It already looked a ratty mess, tangled and unkept. She wasn't going to be able to save its length and would have to lob it off. While the loss was unbelievably miniscule considering what else had occurred in the last seventy-two hours, it still stung.

It was the emotional equivalent of a papercut on an amputated limb.

Anna worked at the lock furiously, fueled by frustration and a strange sense of revenge. It was different, this feeling. She'd never been one for vengeance, but it ran hot through her veins now. Clenching her jaw, she tried feeling for the tumblers, using her imagination to paint a picture of each twist and turn, of what its equal and opposite reaction might look like inside.

A relieved grin twitched at her lips at the faint click. It was hardly audible above the commotion above deck. She blew a stray knot of hair from her eyes and eased her arms forward, shoulders aching and arms stiff—even her elbows pained her.

Narrowing her gaze on the stairs, Anna dragged herself to her feet. She stumbled to the thin bit of wood keeping her from her brother and potential freedom. A challenge loomed above her head, but this was no different than any other situation she and Markus had found themselves in over the years. Just pick the lock, find a weapon and a change of clothes, and sail away with Markus and that damn map.

The door's lock gave rather quickly, as if it couldn't be bothered to keep her contained—as if it did not dare keep her from her brother or the tasks laid out before her like stepping stones. Anna stood, wincing as the hunger pains ran rampant. Bugger, her body weighed a thousand pounds; even keeping her head up was an effort that threatened to topple her.

Anna wandered the hull, crouching and sneaking about in the shadows as she itched at her scalp, fingers catching in her tangled, dirty curls. Normally, her hair shone a bright ashy blonde with honey and sand-colored strands threaded throughout. Anna didn't have to look to know her hair had been reduced to a grimy, greasy mess.

The poor lighting cast dark shadows over crates and barrels, full of anything the sailors could possibly need while at sea. She found one such barrel full of oranges and grabbed two, eating them as she looked for the crew's quarters, where hammocks likely swung back and forth in time with the turbulent swells.

Hopefully, they would be bare of any slumbering sailors.

Anna needed a change of clothes like she needed her next breath. Her dress had been regrettably unfit for a rescue mission *before* leaving her father's estate out the window. As it was now, her poor gown of spilled starlight was hardly fit for a jaunt around the main streets of Bellcaster, let alone what she had planned.

Stubbing her toe on a crate, she inhaled harshly to keep from making any noise.

God-damn—

Anna closed her eyes and breathed deep, waiting several seconds before looking down at her weensiest toe. It wasn't broken, but it was already well on its blasted way to bruising.

She would have liked to add shoes to her list of items to acquire, but the likelihood of finding a pair in her size was slim—and even if there was a magical pair of boots in her size lurking somewhere on this ship, she simply didn't have the time to find them. She didn't even have time to nurser her poor little toe.

Anna ran her tongue over her teeth and crept forward through the bowels of the ship.

The ship listed to the side, and she caught herself on the door-frame to what looked like some of the crew's quarters. Bugger, she could investigate her feet later; right now, she needed to procure a change of clothes, steal back the map, find her brother, and get off this damn ship.

As much as she wanted to plant a bit of steel in Bryce's gut, she knew a losing battle when she saw one. Anna had never been one to entertain or engage with any idea that ended in less than absolute victory, which was why she would accomplish what she could and let this vicious storm take Bryce and all he held dear.

Most hands were above deck, securing lines and preparing to meet the storm head-on. They were all fools, the king of which was Bryce for believing they could sail through this—for believing he could take what he wanted without any consequence. Though she was loath to think about or admit to them, Anna knew there were consequences to her actions.

He was a consequence, after all.

She should have just helped Bryce.

A board creaked on her next step, drawing a sharp inhale from Anna. She counted to sixty, waiting to see if any of the shadows in the swinging hammocks would shift to life and catch her sneaking about.

None of the inky masses shifted; if there were any souls within the cabins, none of them stirred at her entrance.

Breathing a sigh of relief, she stepped into the cabin. Lightning flashed through the portholes, brightening the space for a brief second before shrouding her in darkness once more. Anna tentatively let go of the door frame and entered the crew's quarters, stomach rolling with each rise and fall of the sea's swells until she pressed her knuckles to her mouth.

Anna lowered herself to the ground, lifting a trunk's heavy top. It swung back on well-oiled hinges. As she picked her way through it, she hummed the pirate's shanty, focusing on the familiar cadence instead of the way her stomach twisted in on itself.

Right on top of the stack of clothing, she saw an evergreen long-sleeved shirt and a pair of dark brown, cotton trousers. She lifted the shirt and squinted at it—the sleeves were long, but she could roll them. Despite the breadth of her hips and thighs, the pants would require a belt or suspenders.

She shrugged out of the pirate's jacket as she moved to the next trunk, finding a pair of old cracked suspenders within. Dressing didn't take long; her dress had been reduced to cobwebs that barely clung to her body, it was simply the matter of stepping out of them. The hackles on the back of her neck raised for the half second she stood only in her thong.

The trousers scratched at her legs and the shirt was terribly long, but it was better than traipsing around Bryce's ship in her under-things. Anna grinned; that would have been a splendid distraction if Markus hadn't already been stabbed. Seeing his sister traipse about in her underthings would likely push him straight into an early grave.

She made it to the door before her steps slowed and she turned around, gaze settling on the pirate's jacket. She reached for it and wrapped it tightly around herself, breathing deep. His scent had faded a little more with each day. Inhaling what was left of it, she moved back to the door and peeked around the corner.

It wasn't long before she found herself creeping down the hall that housed the kitchens. At the very least, she'd find some manner of defense—she didn't care what the kitchens would provide, only that she'd have something sturdy in her hands.

It could be a damn cast iron pan for all that she cared.

Humming the pirate's shanty beneath her breath, her lips moved soundlessly with the few words she could remember, something about stranger tides and salted fair ladies. Could he sing? She should have asked when she had the chance.

The kitchens were dark; only one lamp lit the space within. It swung back and forth soundlessly, following the eerie creaks of the ship as it fought the ocean's pull. She turned away from the swinging lantern, mouth souring. A butcher block full of wooden handles sat on the counter across from her.

And just in front of it laid an unsuspecting loaf of bread.

Anna grinned. Surely, it was stale, but it was something. Anna tore into the loaf's hard exterior, savoring the mere feeling of something edible in her mouth. She took another bite, staring down at her stomach.

Good God, she hoped it would sit well.

Markus would never let her live it down if she vomited on him.

A massive wave rocked the ship, surprising her. Anna shot forward, face connecting with the cupboards. Her arms windmilled as she tried to catch her balance, hands scrabbling for a hold as the ship rocked again. Landing hard on her back, she grunted and slid toward the door and out into the corridor. The ship righted itself, rolling her right back into the kitchen.

Anna fisted the fabric above her stomach as she pulled her legs underneath her, groaning at the tumbling sensation that still ran rampant in her stomach. Bugger, should she leave her brother behind? The storm would follow her; he'd only be caught up in it if he went with her. Safe was a relative term, though, wasn't it? He would be safer from the storm, but certainly not from Cunningham's machinations. Anna would rather a freakish weather pattern over Bryce Cunningham any day and she knew Markus would too.

Looking up, she narrowed her gaze on the butcher block. If the pirate was watching this debacle from far above—or the more likely scenario, from a watery grave below—she was certain he was laughing.

Chest tightening and eyes stinging, she crawled forward on all fours. Damn him—damn him and his ridiculous mouth. She shook her head, continuing forward. She was rather unconcerned with how much noise she made currently—if it killed her, so be it. Judging the size of the swells and with how the wind howled outside, she likely didn't have much longer to live, anyway.

Anna dragged herself to her feet and ripped a knife from the block, stumbling as she went. Picking up the bread from the floor, she jogged out of the kitchen, tearing another chunk from the bread. She glanced down at the knife as she chewed. The cleaver would be an excellent resource for dismembering whichever marshal or sailor planted themselves in her path.

Tearing another chunk of bread with her teeth, her feet slapped loudly against the planks as she climbed the stairs. Even from the depth of the stairwell, she heard the storm roaring around them, drowning out the calls of the crew. Anna slammed into the wall, dropping the bread as the ship listed once more.

"Bugger it all to hell," she growled, storming up the stairs.

This storm couldn't kill her.

Anna would row her merry way away from Bryce Cunningham with her brother and that would be that. She sprinted up the last flight, gasping for breath and narrowly avoided the backswing of the door after launching onto the deck. The air was biting cold, pulling every one of her muscles taut and ripping at her clothing, causing it to billow and snap the pirate's coat. The damn gusts even found a way into her trousers, ballooning them.

It was dark—so unfathomably dark.

Anna couldn't remember the last time she had been surrounded by a night as thick as this. Not a single star winked above, and the moon was nowhere to be seen. The clouds had blackened into charred ethereal things. Squinting up into the storm, she stumbled back as lightning struck the ocean only thirty feet away. She clasped her hands over her ears at the resounding crash of thunder, staring at the funnel the lightning had revealed.

Anna swallowed hard, fixated on the churning clouds that were revealed with each lightning strike. The hurricanes that had chased her from the dig site in the Emerald Isles hadn't been this monstrous. They had been smaller, whip-like things that sunk ships in their path. The vessel Anna had been on was lighter, less encumbered by archaeological findings than the others. That was likely the only reason she had escaped.

Frowning, she looked down at the damn smudge on her palm. It had blackened nearly the entire surface, and small bubbling masses had appeared this morning, oozing quietly. They didn't hurt; if anything, her palm had ceased feeling anything.

The crew called back and forth, a mere whisper compared to the roar of the storm. Their voices drew her attention all the same. Brows furrowing, she looked around. Why were they still sailing in the direction of the hurricane? Who in their ever-loving mind would willingly sail toward that behemoth? It had clearly been made to pull ships apart plank by plank and had every intention of doing so to the *Contessa*.

Anna pulled the pirate's jacket tight around herself. There had to be a reason. Bryce might be an idjit, but he was a good captain; he wouldn't sail toward that unless he thought he had to.

Lightning continued to strike with increased fervor. The clouds lit up with crackling light as bolt after bolt was thrown at the ocean. She leaned over the taffrail, squinting into the distance—were they running from something or someone?

The sky lit up once more and Anna stumbled backwards, shaking her head.

Good God, the hurricane was the safer option, indeed.

She needed to get off this damn boat.

Behind them, a vessel sailed, cutting through the water like hell sat at its heels, heedless of the monstrous swells and damnable black waters. The ship was bone white with black sails and no jolly roger in sight, but this vessel didn't need one for identification—or to strike fear into the sailors.

Everyone knew the *Pale Queen* when they saw her.

Anna's thoughts whizzed by, each one incomplete and frantic, a snapshot of a plan that disintegrated upon conception. She shook her head, pacing a step to the left and then to the right, gnawing on her lips. Every idea of an action she might take was dismantled, pulled apart piece by piece by the dredges of stories she'd heard about encounters with the *Pale Queen*. Every story ended the same, every telling a reminder of what would happen to those who crossed Trevor Lovelace and his cursed crew.

A fate sealed away in a very dark, watery tomb.

An end at the bottom of the seas.

"Oh no," she growled, brows bunching together. "No—no, no."

She'd been successful in outrunning the Pirate King this long; there wasn't a chance in hell she'd allow the monster to catch her now. Not here, not like this. Anna had a brother to save, a map to steal, and a pirate to hopefully avenge.

A calloused laugh croaked from her chest. Anna was splendidly and irrevocably daft. She had never let something like that stop her before, and she wasn't about to let something silly like the stability of her mental faculties get in her way now. She needed every crazy idea, every inconceivable act, to force a miracle from the heavens.

Stepping back into a pocket of shadows, she ran her hands down her face and closed her eyes. She only needed five more minutes to think, to plan contingencies. The crew and Cunningham had more to worry about than whether she stayed locked down below. She snorted; they likely wouldn't notice her absence unless she paraded on deck in her knickers.

"What are you doing above deck?" a man growled from next to her.

Eyes widening, she grabbed the front of his shirt and spun, slamming him into the wall with one forearm pressed against his chest. The cleaver she held to his neck flashed with the next bout of lightning, her breaths heaved in time with each strike. A light mist swirled down from above, growing heavier and colder with each passing second. Anna breathed slowly, muscles trembling from the effort of moving with such haste.

When she spoke, her voice came low through chattering teeth. "Where is my brother?"

He glanced behind her, motioning overboard with a tilt of his head. Anna turned slowly, forcing him to move as well, shifting her gaze to the sea as lighting illuminated another ship.

The *Independence*.

Bugger.

Getting him off Bryce's flag ship was enough of a task but finding her way to the *Independence* was another thing entirely. Running her tongue over her teeth, she turned back to the sailor. His uniform had turned nearly black with how saturated it was with water—sea water or rainwater, she couldn't be sure.

"Why was he moved?"

The man's throat bobbed, and a bead of blood welled briefly on her cleaver before being drowned out by rainwater. "Captain thought it bad luck to keep you two on the same ship."

Anna nodded before spinning her cleaver and striking the sailor with the back of the blade. He dropped to the ground like a sack of potatoes, the sound barely a whisper over the growl of the storm and the panicked calls of the crew.

Rolling her shoulders back, she looked from one part of the ship to the next, a plan slowly forming in her mind. The mist turned into a strong drizzle as a particularly strong gust snapped a few ropes above her head. She narrowed her gaze at them—it could work. Good God, it was reckless, but she wasn't entirely convinced there was a course of action that wouldn't be.

Anna tracked a path from the ropes of the *Contessa* to where her brother might be on the other vessel. Bugger, she couldn't be sure if the sailor had told the truth, but she didn't have time to doubt his words. Searching the *Contessa* would take too long, especially if her brother wasn't on it.

Her gaze narrowed on the stairs leading to the helm. If her plan was going to work, the ships needed to be closer; landing in the sea between would only serve in drowning her. She crept forward and around the corner before running to the stairs. The next angry swell caught Bryce's ship at an angle, forcing water over the taffrails and across the deck in a violent torrent, dragging four men overboard.

Her arms shook as she climbed the stairs, using the railing to pull herself along. A man stood between her and the helm. Glancing between the cleaver in her hands and the back of the sailor's neck, she steeled herself. Something such as discovery seemed trivial now, unworthy of her remaining patience and energy—but altogether something she could not afford.

Any noises she might have made crossing the planks between her and the sailor at the helm were smothered by the progressing chaos of the storm. The sails above snapped and tore, unfurling in tattered strands. The sailors, dark blurs against a blacker sky, held fast to the rigging as the storm tried to pry them from their posts above.

Anna walked across the deck, moving quickly on the balls of her feet, her cleaver gripped tightly in her hand. The act itself was quick and bloody, something she would have to process later. Her stomach rolled with the ease of her actions, at how quickly the flesh and bone of the sailor's neck gave way beneath her cleaver. This wasn't her or the sailor, or the sailor or Markus, in some dastardly brawl. This was convenience, this was hoping violence now might not lead to greater violence later.

Gritting her teeth, she moved to the helm, ignoring the way warm liquid squished between her toes. The rain was a torrential force, but it wasn't strong enough to completely clear the deck of the man's blood by the time she strode through it. Anna swiped the back of her hand against her forehead and squinted into the murky shadows of the storm.

Where was the *Independence*?

"Bugger," she growled as the next wave rocked the Bryce's ship.

The force of it sent her stumbling to the side and into the railing. The wheel whirred, clicking as the entire ship rejoiced its freedom. Anna lunged forward, growling as handles cracked against her fingers.

The wheel nearly dragged her down once she held the smooth wooden handles.

Anna's gaze wandered from left to right, forward and backward as she searched for that blasted ship. She found it, off the port side —but not before spying the *Pale Queen*. The ghostly vessel was close enough that she glimpsed the crew readying for battle. At its prow stood a dark figure, their black captain's coat snapping in the wind.

The Pirate King.

God-damnit.

Breathing deep, Anna hurriedly set a course that would run Bryce's ship parallel to the one that allegedly held her brother. As she turned and ran for the main deck, she swiped the sailor's sopping hat and pulled it down over her head, stuffing her curls up beneath its sticky brim as she went.

No one noticed the change in course; every man aboard held more concern with keeping themselves from being swept out to sea. Anna held the hat tight against her brow, keeping her eyes downcast as she threaded her way through the gathered sailors. With her hat, trousers, and bare feet, no one would suspect a woman hid beneath the pirate's jacket.

The ship shuddered violently as the *Pale Queen's* cannons trumpeting like a warning before war. The ship shivered again, listing to the side—her gaze shot between the *Independence* and the one she stood on. Anna grinned, bright and fierce, before laughing. The distance between Bryce's ship and the one holding her brother had just shortened considerably.

Shoving her way past the press of bodies, she ran toward the mainmast. Another boom sounded, followed by the scream of men and the spray of wood. Fingers digging into the rigging, she started climbing *up* when every other sailor and marshal wanted nothing more than to get *down*.

Anna looked over her shoulder as she climbed; the *Contessa's* mizzenmast had cracked and fallen. It dragged behind them like a lame limb. The crew pointed frantically ahead. Her stomach hollowed, and her foot slipped on the rope as she faced the source of their panic.

Good God, a maelstrom had formed.

"Oh, luv," she mocked in the pirate's accent, climbing the rigging with her teeth clenched. "Would ye look at that? 'Tis a bloody swirling puddle of death!" Anna snorted and dropped the pirate's playful brogue. "Oh, when I get Markus out of this..."

Her teeth banged against each other as the ship lurched once more, the screams of faceless men echoing in her ears. With a quick swing of her leg, Anna pulled herself into the crow's nest, hips slamming into the opposite side painfully.

The ship tipped, caught in the outer ring of the maelstrom.

She swallowed her scream, staring down at the mouth of the churning vortex. Anna felt each fire of the *Pale Queen's* cannons in her soul, every impact swaying the crow's nest. A glimmer of gold caught her attention, drawing her gaze. The next flash of lightning revealed the Man-Eater from across the maelstrom, one hand on her hips as she pointed and screamed. The *Pale Queen* wasn't close enough for her to see the woman's mad grin, but it came to Anna's mind.

It wasn't long before Bryce's ship broke with a deafening crack, slumping like a dying man. The crow's nest reeled in response, catapulting Anna over the edge and into the air between the ships. Anna saw the *Pale Queen's* figurehead from the corner of her eye—a woman, a goddess of the sea, though her name suggested a mere queen. Her gown billowed behind her, and an elegant crown of coral sat regally at her brow. She felt watched, the skin of her arms prickling even as she plummeted downward.

At least someone would witness what happened next.

Anna reached in every direction until she felt the rough prickle of rope in her hands. Gripping it tight, she cried out at the hot burn in her palms. She came to an abrupt halt that nearly pulled her shoulders from their sockets and the rope snapped, then instead of plummeting downward, she was soaring through the air and across the gap between ships. The wind shifted around her; if not for the strange warmth of the gust, she wouldn't have noticed the caress at all.

Tears stung her eyes and burned tracks down her cheeks as the sails of the *Independence* approached. Anna swallowed hard and let go, hitting the sails. She held on as they tore in one long strip. It would be fine—this would be fine. Humans were only as strong as they believed themselves to be—Anna would not break upon the deck like a damn egg.

She didn't break.

She saw stars.

Every bone in her body protested and groaned at the impact. At first, she couldn't move—couldn't even breathe. Maybe this was death. At the very least it was limbo. Nothing but darkness before her and nothing but ringing behind her.

Bugger, were they death knells?

Sound crept back painfully slow, like an animal dragging a carcass behind it. First, she tasted blood and then she inhaled ash. Splendid, she had lived. Pulling her legs beneath her, Anna pressed up on her hands, a foreign sense of urgency calling her to her feet. Her head swam, and both arms slid out from under her. Anna turned her hand over, examining the deep slits on her palms and the blood flowing from them.

Her brows drew together, gaze narrowing at her left hand and the damnable black spot that sat untouched. The rope left bleeding wounds on the insides of her fingers as well as above and below the spot, but the dark mass itself remained untouched—not even a fragment of rope had embedded itself in her skin.

Anna licked her lips, squinting at the bugger.

Could she cut her hand off and throw that overboard?

Shaking her head, she rolled to her side with a wet gasp. As strange and slightly horrific as her palm was with that dark splotch resting atop it, she didn't have time to ponder how to get rid of the damn thing. Nothing short of a vile sense of stubborn pride forced Anna to her feet. Everything in her seemingly grinded together like stones in a crumbling tomb.

Anna wrapped her arms around her ribcage, wincing into the glare of the fire. It had completely consumed the foremast and most of the mainmast. Fire ran down the ropes, leaping in glee. She shook her head, watching as the *Independence* slowly caught fire. As if things weren't problematic enough...

Her foot paused in its step.

How many days had it been?

Anna glanced at the sky, scouring the horizons. They could have breached the seventh day. No, of course, they had passed into the realm of the seventh day at sea, how else could fire burn in the face of a hurricane? She stared down at the blasphemous spot on her hand once more.

If not for needing both hands for what came next, she might have actually considered cutting her hand off then and there.

Lightning crackled through the clouds, illuminating the *Pale Queen* and her ethereal figurehead. Her porcelain features were cracked, the paint flaking endlessly into the sea. Anna thought it looked a little like ash on skin. There were rings on the figurehead's fingers and gems in her coral crown. Even the lace of her dress seemed to billow behind her.

Anna shook her head.

Could absolutely nothing go in her favor?

Two men stood just behind the figurehead, and her stomach knotted at the sight of them—the Pirate King and his quartermaster, conveniently accounted for. Her gaze caught on the broader one; all she could make out was his red hair, slicked black from the rain, and a cream shirt. He wore a splendid charcoal coat, edged in silver.

Time slowed as if she had stepped into a stream with a current that ebbed calmly instead of barreling onward. Anna shivered, feeling his gaze on her with an intensity she rarely experienced. It was warm and inviting, not at all the intrusive repulsion she had expected to feel.

There was something about this, about him...

"Anna! Watch out!"

The spell broke, and time rushed forward with a ferocity that unmoored her.

"Markus?" she asked

It hadn't sounded quite like her brother, but no one else would call for her like that. No one else cared enough for her for that twang of absolute panic to enter their voice.

She whirled around, expecting to see the massive frame of her idjit of a brother. What she was met with was the flash of a rapier raised high above her head. Ducking to the side, she watched the blade bite into the already-splintered wood of the taffrail.

Anna dodged and danced away from the sailor, trying her best to keep his rapier in her sight. Each movement was agony. The handle of her cleaver was slick with her blood. He stumbled, and her cleaver found its way to his clavicle, biting straight through bone and into the plump veins of his neck. Anna closed her eyes and turned away from the spray of blood.

The man fell to his knees, the cleaver stuck in him.

She met his gaze, so terrified and incredibly young, before he fell face forward onto the deck. Blinking the rain from her eyes, she stared down at the sailor. For a moment, he had looked like Griff with those wide green eyes.

"Markus," she whispered hoarsely, hands trembling at her sides. She shook them out and cupped them around her mouth. *"Markus!"*

Anna headed for the only opening she knew would lead below deck. If the crew hadn't been washed over the taffrail in these monstrous waves, they'd be below. Bugger, she must have been hearing things earlier. There wasn't any way her brother could be on the damn deck with whatever injury he had sustained.

Anna gripped the knob in both hands and pulled.

It didn't budge an inch.

She banged her fist against it and screamed her brother's name. Lightning brightened the sky, revealing the mess around her. Smoldering bits of sail and rope fell from above in dense smoking clumps and fire had nearly consumed the main mast.

Anna swallowed hard, pressing her forehead to the door, biting back every emotion threatening to unravel her. Turning, she leaned back and laughed, though it sounded closer in kin to a choked sob. The powers that be had worked against her and Markus from the start, through every arduous step of this journey and there was little anyone would be able to do to convince her otherwise.

Markus probably wasn't on this damn ship.

In the distance, Anna saw a lone ship sailing away—*Oceana's Ire* was painted brightly against its hull.

He was probably on that one.

The *Independence* shuddered and tilted on its axis. From this vantage, she stared down into the maelstrom once more. It was a foreboding, dark vortex—as good as any coffin. Better, even, if she were honest. How many could claim an entire maelstrom as their resting place? It was an ending fit for a pale queen, a twist in the tides of Fate that she could never guess at.

Anna stepped into a solid chest. She closed her eyes and exhaled sharply through her teeth. Apparently not all the crew had spilled over the sides or hidden beneath the deck. She would have thought it admirable if not for the arm slipping around her waist.

She felt the rain acutely on her face and watched the lightning reveal the next swell. Anna struggled against the man, gaze fixated on the incoming wave, but exhaustion stiffened her veins and weighted her eyelids. A frustrated noise slipped from her lips, high-pitched and desperate, as her nails dug into his skin. He noticed the wave too late. Just like that, it was before them, an epitome of the storm's rage.

Or perhaps it was the pirate's revenge made real.

Did he blame Anna for what happened like she did?

There wasn't any time to find something to hold onto, not that it would have mattered in the end.

CHAPTER FOURTEEN

It was dark,
  (So dark.)
  like floating in ink.
  (Like a pair of eyes.)
  Anna stared down at a pool, bubbling and fetid. Her lips curled back at the chill wafting off of it and she leaned forward, hair rising along her arms like she was being watched. Her lungs hurt, aching with a ferocity she had never experienced before. Worse than the dark was the cold, numbing and burning at the same time.
  How was that?
  (Was she a fallen star?)
  Stepping away from the ominous pool, she slipped, and everything became inexplicably darker. She felt it then, the rush, the pull—that thing of warmth that had always bloomed beneath her skin when he was near. She glanced from the pool to the shadows that shrouded the space.
  (Were the stars hiding beneath his skin or hers?)
  Anna was furious because it was a lie.
  (A lie, a lie, a lie, like so many things were.)
  She may sleep beneath the sea now, but he had been lost days ago.

(lostlostlost)

Her chest burned, a line of fire running from her neck and ending between her breasts.

(Could she be lost if she'd been here before?)

CHAPTER FIFTEEN

Anna was nothing, and then she was everything.

Coughing and sputtering, she gasped for breath. Even with its dull echo, the sound was horrendous to her ears, like she heard it from a distance. The pain, the aches, the uncertainty, Anna felt it all in such dense waves that she was sure it would smother her.

Anna moved her head to the side, wincing at the strangely smooth surface pressed against her cheek. Coughing, she cleared her throat and pinched her eyes shut. What had led her to this moment? Why was she lying face down on—she peeked her eyes open.

Bone-white planks?

The last thing she remembered was a cell, something about Markus, and...she had lost something. Anna swallowed past a knot of grief, unsure of where it came from and even more fearful of when she might remember. Scrubbing her face against her forearm, she pulled herself to her elbows. Rain pelted her back.

"Well, well, well..." a masculine voice purred, his soft brogue pooling in her ears. Anna's brows furrowed at the familiarity of the cadence. "I'll have to ask my brother what he baited his fucking hook wi' to catch a lass like ye."

Her head ticked to the side, fixated on the man's voice. It took her a full minute to register the lilt, how the words tumbled from his

105

tongue and the shape of his mouth when he said them. Surprise and then something worse jolted her upright.

But then as he spoke again, she noticed his voice wasn't quite as deep as her pirate's had been. It was a little rougher around the edges as well. When it all came back, pain ripped through her soul, and unwanted tears gathered in her eyes. Clenching her jaw, she forced them back and breathed deep.

The map.

The storm.

Her pirate.

lostlostlost

Something thumped against the deck, startling her.

"This is the tithe you offer?" another man spoke slowly.

"I—I—surely the Pirate King would find her suitable!" another man called. Anna cracked an eye open in their direction, spying the sailor who had dragged them both into the ocean with his stupidity. "Look at her, she's fair beyond reason. She should buy my safe passage! And if that isn't enough, she's a Savage. The senator will offer trunks of gold for her safe return."

She laughed then, a high-pitched hiccup.

Her father would do nothing of the sort.

The air tightened around her like a held breath, warming her skin as many pairs of eyes turned to her. She opened her eyes fully and stared at the pale boards beneath her. Anna pushed to her elbows as a pair of dark boots planted themselves next to her head. She could barely see them in her periphery, her heart thundering in her chest.

"Might as well just throw me back in," she croaked, throat stinging. "My father won't pay a copper for me."

"Ye can't swim, luv, and I just fished ye out," another purred quietly from in front of her.

Keeping her gaze down, she was nauseous at hearing the moniker in that handsome brogue. Anna curled her fingers into fists to hide their shaking, pushing every thought she had about her pirate from her mind. A small seedling of hope unfurled deep in her soul before she squashed it—even if her pirate was the Pirate King, that would complicate things she'd rather not complicate.

Anna had slept with, poisoned, and then promptly stolen from the *Pale Queen's* captain. She doubted her pirate would have tolerated even half of her shenanigans if he were truly Trevor Lovelace.

"Captain, we can handle this here," a woman said.

Anna fixed her attention on a swirl in the wood in front of her; it looked like a woman's face with large, curling eyebrows. She listened to someone walk toward her—only it wasn't boots, it was the wet slap of feet against the pale boards. Anna dragged her forearm against her eyes and forced her knees beneath her, head bowed and back hunched.

The Pirate King might want her dead, but she wouldn't die lying down.

Their knees popped as they crouched in front of her. They wore dark trousers, slicked tight to their skin and sopping wet. And—and they were...male. He wore no shirt; she could just see his torso with her head bent as it was and her hair working as a curtain.

Outside of death, she wasn't entirely sure what to expect.

There wasn't any getting out of this. Even if she could abscond from the *Pale Queen's* crew, there would be no true escape other than the sweet reprieve of lost life. Anna sat on a vessel in the middle of a turbulent sea, hunted by hurricanes and plagued by unfathomable guilt. The knowledge clamped down like a vice on any calm she had.

"Now," he whispered, the warmth of a finger pressed against her chin in a demand to look up. "What is a lovely, no'-dead thing like ye doing drowning out here? There are easier ways to die, lass."

Anna's entire body shook, eyes snapping open and lips parting in surprise. Her pirate was alive and whole—albeit soaked to the bone and shirtless. Tears stung her eyes as he offered her a small, shy smile and his thumb brushed her cheek, the line of her jaw. Anna leaned into the touch, ready to lunge forward and throw her arms around his neck.

One tear fell, then another.

He was alive. He was alive. He was—

She jerked back out of his hold.

He was the Pirate King.

"You weren't—" Anna nearly choked, tears running down her face. "You weren't lying."

"Afraid no'," he murmured, smiling dropping from his face. The pirate—Trevor Lovelace—rocked back onto his heels and stood.

"I don't—even if—" Anna stopped, trying to collect her thoughts. "You're supposed to be dead," she whispered on a croak, caught somewhere between surprise, relief, and utter dread at the implications. "I watched you fall overboard. They tied a cannonball to your boots. That storm—"

The crew laughed around her, and Anna suddenly felt so incredibly small.

"Ye would no' believe how many times I've heard that, lass."

Trevor Lovelace stepped back, his bare feet dragging on the ground. The wind tousled his sopping hair, and water meandered its way down his bare torso. So the scoundrel really had gone in after her. Why would he do that? More than that, why would he offer her his hand? She glared at the outstretched offering, gaze fixating on the black of the tattoos and the honey gold of his fingers. When Anna turned back to his face, the Pirate King was no longer smiling. He cleared his throat, hand dropping to his side awkwardly.

"How did you survive?" she asked blatantly, ignoring how the question soured her tongue.

Lovelace shrugged one massive shoulder. "Ye act like I know how any of this shite works."

The *Pale Queen* rocked and her captain looked toward the sky before his gaze settled on the horizon. The clouds were the blackish blue of a new bruise and lightning bolts lit up their innards almost constantly.

Anna looked left and then right. Something close to unease was building in her gut—a forlorn sense of apprehension, maybe. She had asked how the Pirate King had survived, but maybe she should have asked him how she had.

He raised his voice, the lilt familiar and endearing despite her best judgment. "Take her to my quarters, we've a fucking hurricane to outrun."

The crew became a blur of motion; some scuttled up the rigging while others made their way below deck. Their calls carried easily enough over the loose exhale of wind and dainty rain drizzle. A hand wrapped around her bicep, gently pulling Anna to her feet. Her knees knocked together, and her hands shot out to the side for balance.

"What about him?" one of the pirates called over the soft wind.

"Gut him. The lass is no' a tithe, she's no' a thing to be traded or whatever else he was trying to do." Trevor Lovelace paused mid-stride, his back to her. "Keep the fucker's head, though."

"His...head?" a different pirate asked.

Based on his wine-red hair and the resemblance to the Pirate King, it was Tate Lovelace, the quartermaster of the *Pale Queen*.

"Aye. Did I fucking stutter, boyo?"

Anna blinked, attention shifting back to the man who had pulled her overboard. He stepped back and away from the crew until he bumped against the taffrail. Tate Lovelace slid the cutlass from his belt with a sigh. It made a scathing, eerie noise, one at such pitch that it cut through the wind as easily as it might flesh.

The pirate holding her upright led her away as the sailor pleaded for his life. Anna stared at the approaching door, the nervous energy clawing at her insides only made worse by the man's fervent pleas. Something about being in Lovelace's quarters didn't sit well with her —was this a courtesy, or another empty gesture like holding out his hand? Did he have his crew deposit every half-drowned woman they came across in his private quarters? One would think he'd shove them below deck until they reached the markets.

The sailor's body hit the deck with a stale thump, then the door closed behind her.

Anna stood awkwardly in the center of the room, hugging herself with her shoulders hunched. Her inhales were shaky as she finally wiped at the tears running down her cheeks. She scrubbed at them and sniffed, gaze traveling about the Pirate King's quarters as the crew yelled back and forth outside the room.

It wasn't at all what she had expected.

Where Bryce Cunningham's quarters were bare and included only what was necessary, Trevor Lovelace's were meant for a king. It was fitting, she supposed. The room wasn't terribly big, but it was filled and lived in, a place someone spent a great deal of time with the ones they cared about.

A large ornate rug covered most of the floor, thick and soft beneath her feet. Two deep chairs in a pale eggshell color stood guard just in front of Lovelace's desk, and behind that were tall windows overlooking the ocean and—

The *Oceana's Ire* was sailing away.

Chest tightening, Anna busied herself with memorizing where everything else was in the room—one never knew when they might need to throw a vase in self-defense.

A crystal chandelier hung above her head, swaying gently with the motion of the ship. On her left sat a cutout with a breakfast nook, and bookcases lined the entire wall. On her right, a bed hid within a matching cutout, and pillows covered the entire space against the wall. Anna stared long and hard at the thick comforter before glancing at the closed doors and drawers lining the right wall—they were likely clothes and bedding.

It was cozy, close, and it smelled like him.

She hated it.

Unsure of what else to do, she sat on one of the velvet chairs in front of his desk and twisted her mother's ring around her finger while she waited. Looking left, Anna's gaze immediately wandered to the books stacked on the shelves. Most were made of leather with gold foil adornments, but none of them had titles on their spines. Anna shook her head, sinking deeper into the chair. As much as she wanted to know what kind of books were on his shelves, she would only find more questions by thumbing through them.

She shivered again, despicably aware of how sopping wet she was.

The door behind her opened and closed, whisper soft. Anna turned and stared at the Pirate King, not at all surprised to see him. These were his damn quarters after all. Instead of meeting her gaze, he immediately turned and opened a door on the right side of the room.

Shirts.

Staring, she let her attention trail his naked torso and the tattoos spilling over his shoulders. He snagged a long-sleeved blue shirt with leather ties at the chest.

"Are ye okay?" he asked, arms threading through the sleeves.

Anna remained quiet.

Okay was a relative term.

Lovelace nodded, pulling the shirt over his head. He shook out the bottom half of it and opened another drawer. This time, he snatched a dry set of trousers and undershorts. Oh—*oh*. Flushing, Anna looked away as he turned from her. His wet trousers hit the floor, quickly followed by a smaller slap of fabric. Anna swallowed, face warm, and hugged herself tighter.

She would not look—she wouldn't.

"I'm cold," she murmured, picturing the plethora of shirts and shorts contained within the cabinets. "Cold and tired and hungry."

And livid, but she didn't say that.

Lovelace sighed. "Soup is being warmed for ye. It should be ready soon, and ye can sleep in my bed." He swallowed loud enough that even Anna heard it. "And I don't have clothes for a lady—for *ye*. I have dresses, but I don't think ye want to wear...shite. Ye can wear some of my clothes for now, lass. It'll be better than sitting in those wet things."

Her pirate had been many things, but he had never been this hopelessly awkward.

Anna nodded curtly as his steps trailed around her. Tilting her head to the side, she just caught Lovelace from the corner of her eye. He had a pair of boots in one hand and a knot of socks in the other. He approached her slowly, head lowered and hesitant, before sitting in the matching chair next to her.

She shied away, something in her chest aching at having him this close and yet so far away.

His jaw ticked.

Anna pretended not to notice.

"How long until we catch Cunningham?" she asked, keeping her eyes on him instead of the windows where a ship sailed away.

Lovelace's brows furrowed as he laced his boots. She squinted at him, at the tense line of his shoulders and the way he meticulously looped and pulled the laces of his boots.

They weren't going after Markus.

"You have to help me," she said in a whisper, afraid of shattering the hollow calm in the room. Tears stung at her eyes, and she hugged her knees to her chest. "I lost him."

lostlostlost

"I lost Markus. I need to get him back."

"Again?" Lovelace asked gently. "It's a wonder the prick still breathes."

"*How long?*"

Sitting up, he rubbed the back of his neck. "We'll catch up wi' him later, luv. We've a wee bit of business to square away first."

"But my brother—" she started, arms tightening around her legs.

"Will have to wait."

Anna shook her head. "You don't understand. He needs me. He could die and I wouldn't be there—" She stopped, swallowing hard. "We are going after him first. Everything else can wait. Turn this ship around now, Lovelace."

He leaned forward and tapped the inside of his palm. Anna turned her left hand over and stared at it. The damnable smudge had swallowed the skin of her palm, and the veins of her wrist were blackening. Bloody rope burns lined her fingers and the flesh the spot hadn't consumed yet.

"We can't sail much of anywhere wi' that fucking thing; have to get it removed first, and there's only one male I know who can do that."

Disbelief coated her tongue like oil, cool and slippery.

"You're the blasted Pirate King! Why the hell can't *you* fix it?"

"If I could fix it, I would have done it by now," he said, rising to his feet. "As it bloody well is, it'll be hard enough to stay ahead of this fucking storm on our way to the bastard."

Dread settled in her core. "Where are we going?"

"Tiburon."

Anna barked out a rough laugh and turned to glare at his back as he walked to the door. "What ever happened to never taking me places I do not wish to go?"

His shoulders raised and his fists clenched at his sides. The Pirate King was clearly uncomfortable with the words she had hurled at him like knives. Good, she had been aiming to maim. The silence between them said more than anything he could have, and it was likely more honest too.

The door closed behind him.

"Tiburon," she said, wiping furiously at her stinging eyes.

Not if Anna had anything to say about it.

CHAPTER SIXTEEN

Shite.

Trevor did no' think it would be this bloody hard.

His hands tightened around the taffrail and he leaned forward, gazing at the fog collecting below. His head felt like a stone bell, heavy and hollow. He couldn't remember the last time he'd slept more than ten bloody minutes. Oh, nay, wi' all his cat naps, Tate had started meowing every time they crossed paths.

Wee shite, he thought, rubbing the back of his neck.

Pressing his lips into a thin line, Trevor let his head tip forward.

The cool breeze on his face was nice.

If only it was just the sleepless nights eating away at his bones—no, it was the lass too. He'd wanted her on his ship and in his life, aye, but now that the wee fem was aboard the *Pale Queen* and in front of his crew, he wasn't sure what to do wi' her. Shite, he wasn't even sure what to do wi' himself. Cat was out of the gods-damned bag, and he could no' be just a male anymore.

No' when he was supposed to be the king.

Trevor looked up toward the sky one last time before heading to the stairs and taking the fuckers two at a time. He needed a hot meal and something that would burn on the way down. It was late, the wee hours of the night when the stars twinkled against a blanket of glimmering blue. Off in the distance, the sun inched up over the horizon, bathing the sky above and the ocean below in oranges and yellows. Fuck, it was prettier than what chased them—clouds blacker than the ink on his skin.

Promises in front of him and death behind.

Some things never changed.

A second set of steps echoed Trevor's. He glanced to the side and nearly groaned. Tate'd snuck up on him, dropping down the stairs stride for bloody stride. Based on the smug look on his brother's face, this talk would require a pint of grog—maybe two.

Trevor sighed.

It'd likely warrant *three* bloody pints.

Tate said naught, simply following Trevor like a lost duckling. The bench groaned as he sat down and propped his elbows on the table. Trevor ran his hands over his face and shot his brother a look. Tate did no' take it very bloody seriously. He sat next to Trevor, straddling the bench and tapping his fingers on the tabletop.

Their mum would've been appalled wi' their table manners.

"Is there a reason you're here, or do ye just enjoy my suffering?" he grumbled from under his hands. A pint slid across the table, and Trevor tipped his head in thanks before pinning Tate down wi' a suspicious glare.

"'Tis what keeps me young, Trev," Tate said wi' a smile. "Atlas sent me to ask about the course...and the lass."

Trevor took several long pulls of his grog before setting it back down and wiping his mouth wi' the back of his hand. Of course, the bloody lass was involved. Bloody hell, she'd been causing naught but trouble since he'd fished her out of the gods-damned sea. He'd talk wi' her about it, but last time he'd entered his quarters, the lass had thrown shite at him.

Shite, shite, shite, he'd thought, hands raised to avoid the bloody vases, *abort, abort, abort.*

She was a wee angry wi' him.

If it wasn't causing so much trouble, it would have been adorable.

Finishing his pint, he stood. Fucking hell, the weight of all the years he'd lived pressed down on him. Should probably go check in wi' Atlas about what Anna'd done. If there was a male aboard who loved the *Queen* as much as Trevor did, it was Atlas. Trevor paused at seeing Tate lean his head onto his fists wi' a gods-damn grin. Glaring, he leaned his hand against the tabletop and waited. Shite, whatever it was, it couldn't be good. Trevor quickly recalled what else the lass could have destroyed in his quarters and swallowed hard.

If it was his good bedding, gods help him, he'd lose his fucking shite.

"What about the lass?"

The bastard's lips twitched into a bigger smile as he shrugged. "She's gone."

The whole world shifted.

Anna was...she was *gone*?

"Gone?" he echoed, staring at a point just over Tate's shoulder.

"Like the wind," he confirmed, voice sounding like it came from a distance. "Sabotaged our steering too, but I've Silas looking into it. Ye realize she does no' need the picks to get out of the bloody room, aye? Fuck me, Trev, the lass used *forks* to scale the side of the *Queen* and then lowered a boat all by her lonesome."

Trevor blinked.

Closed his eyes.

A deep growl rumbled up from his chest before he scrubbed at his scalp wi' his fingers. "Forks, ye say?"

"Aye, forks. Resourceful one, that."

Trevor's feet pounded hard against the bone-white planks of *Pale Queen*. He cleared the main deck in moments, the door to his cabin in sight. He'd suggested taking up residence in his quarters that first night—thought it might make her feel safer, and it was the only quiet place on the bloody ship.

Shite, he might have given her too much room, too much time to herself—made it too easy for her to think it was her *or* them instead of her *and* them.

One of the double doors banged against the wall as he threw them open, panting. Sweat dripped from his brow, and he sucked in a tight breath, searching the room. Tate was no' blind, but the wee shite had a habit of missing whatever he was bloody well looking for even if it was in front of his gods-damned face.

Everything looked as it should.

Gaze narrowing at the bed, he noticed a wee lump underneath the blankets. Trevor knew the lass would no' be under them, but a male could hope. He ripped them off, revealing an arrangement of his pillows. Striding to the bay windows, he threw them open and looked out. As his gaze wandered up, his fingers dug into the frame of the window.

Up the side of his fucking ship were wee indentations.

Tate's even steps sounded behind him, and Trevor turned to face him. His brother leaned against the door frame of his quarters, looking at his nails.

"I told ye so," he said, and it took all Trevor had no' to throw the smug prick out the bloody window.

"Fuck off, Tate," he snapped.

Glaring down at the blackened lines on his palms, he tried to figure out where in the gods-damned world the wee fem had run off to. Tilting his hands to the side, he looked back out the window and to the darkening clouds wi' a vicious smile.

Try to run from him?

He thought no'.

CHAPTER SEVENTEEN

Anna screeched all her frustration at the ocean, reaching for the small pail at her side. Water was quickly flooding her get-away boat. It was an itty thing, more of a canoe, really. The poor wherry wasn't meant for rough voyages on the open seas with its single mast, but it had been the only boat she could get into the water herself without alerting the crew or king. She choked back a laugh.

It had seemed like a *splendid* idea at the time.

Now the little boat might end up as her casket.

"Bugger," she hissed as she pitched water from the boat.

The icy water had climbed above her ankles, numbing her feet. If her boat went down, she was going down with it. Dying would be a rather large set back. Nostrils flaring, she paused and stared down at the rising water. The list of tasks she needed to complete was concise. Father would have been proud of her for narrowing her focus to a select few objectives.

Escape the Pirate King.

Rescue Markus.

And kill Cunningham, if the bastard still breathed.

Anna hadn't planned on her wherry sinking in the middle of the ocean, though. Who would plan for a ridiculous, unfortunate circumstance? Anna shook her head, glaring down at the rising water in the wherry. She tossed her curls over her shoulder, pulling strands from her mouth before settling her hands on her hips.

Lovelace had something to do with this, nothing would convince her otherwise.

A quick movement along the horizon caught her attention. Anna squinted at the harsh glare of sunlight reflecting off the ocean, white bubbles frothing just out of reach. Dark shadows moved gracefully just beneath the surface. Anna blinked several times, praying to every ancient deity she could name that she was hallucinating. Good God, that had better not be—

Something smooth and gleaming like liquid smoke broke the surface of the water.

"So," Anna said, looking up at the darkening clouds. "Sharks? *That's* how it's going to be?"

Her scowl deepened as more dorsal fins cut the water like blades. Small striations along their sides gave away their breed—tiger sharks. Anna cursed her despicable luck; those buggers ate damn near anything. When had her luck become so foul?

Did it coincide with crossing Lovelace's path the first time?

Perhaps tumbling the Pirate King was akin to breaking a mirror—the only reward being living to tell the tale and seven years of bad luck.

Anna cocked her head to the side, noticing a change in the air.

Everything was still, and the natural maritime sounds had disappeared. She leaned forward, her wherry no longer rocking, and squinted at the waves. A small bit of fear diffused into her bloodstream at seeing the ocean as smooth as glass before darkening to a blue so deep it must have resembled the night sky in hell.

The discoloration spread like spilled ink, clouds blooming outward from under the wherry—from *behind* the wherry. A shadow fell over her as a gust of icy air caught the sail and snapped it open. Anna dared not turn around, not even as thick fog flowed around her small vessel and chased the tiger sharks away.

Anna knew what she would find without looking to investigate.

"Lovely!" a boorishly handsome voice called.

The wherry rocked and her stomach flipped; the response had

absolutely nothing to do with the ocean and everything to do with the brogue that chased her even in her sleep. Breathing deep, she glanced back up at the sky and muttered, "I would have preferred the sharks."

"It would appear your wee ship is sinking, lass."

The smile was evident in his tone as the words tumbled from his mouth. There was something else beneath the playful purr—relief, perhaps? Anna shook her head. She was reaching, looking for something that would never and could never be. Even if he had cared for her once, there wasn't any way he still did.

"Piss off, Lovelace!" she screamed, throwing her middle finger in the air.

The echo of his laugh trickled down from far above. Two individuals looked over the taffrail from just behind the figurehead. Anna had to squint just to see them. One was a woman, a study in sepia with golden skin and honey-brown hair—the *Pale Queen's* master gunner, Juliana Gray.

The scoundrel next to her did not need an introduction.

The *Pale Queen* continued at a slow, leisurely pace, like she had all the time in the world. Anna hadn't realized his ship was capable of such a crawl, not when all the legends spoke of how quickly the *Pale Queen* covered leagues.

Her attention slowly turned to the figurehead; she was an ethereal, devastating beauty. The lovely woman glowed faintly as dainty fingers of fog slid around her lovingly, curling between the crown of coral upon her brow. Weathering bloomed across her features like fine spiderwebbing, but it made her no less eye-catching. Every fold of lace stood out against the woman's body and flowed behind her, rippling against the hull.

No one had ever wondered at the origins of the *Pale Queen;* most believed she was born of the nightmares rumored to sleep at the bottom of the ocean. Seeing the quality of craftsmanship, Anna disagreed. The Pirate King's flagship hadn't risen from the depths of some hellish sea, she'd likely been painstakingly crafted in the Emerald Isles by a master shipwright.

A loud splash accompanied by something dense landing in her

sinking vessel startled her. The poor wherry lurched to the side. Stepping forward, she caught her balance and reached for an oar. She swallowed stiffly, listening as whoever landed in the wherry waded closer, water sloshing around their legs noisily.

Bugger.

"'Ello, beastie," he said quietly.

Gritting her teeth, she turned enough to catch a glimpse of his predatory grin and the stubble darkening his jaw. Good God, the man was handsome, but that knowledge did little to keep her from swinging the oar at his fat head.

If anything, it only encouraged her to swing it harder.

The Pirate King's eyes widened, arm raising to block the wood from hitting his perfect face. The oar cracked against his forearm with a thunderous snap, breaking the paddle clean off. Looking to the splintered end, she nearly rolled her entire head in exasperation.

Of course, his arm broke the damn oar.

"Bloody hell, Anna!" he said as Anna hurdled the remaining piece at his head like a javelin. Lovelace ducked it, the broken oar bouncing harmlessly off the hull of the *Pale Queen*. He stared at the hull before slowly turning his attention back to her. "Are ye done?"

Shifting her weight, she angled her head up and stared into the redhead's eyes. Anna wasn't petite—her legs told the truth of her eating habits with the way they eroded her breeches at the thighs. But the Pirate King was a hulking being—the epitome of why might so often won over right.

Lovelace held out his hand, callused and covered in tattoos until his middle knuckle. She hadn't decided if it was a lifeline or a noose. Blowing a wisp of sun-bleached hair from her face, Anna glared down at his hand. He cleared his throat and tipped his head toward her almost nervously, nose slightly scrunched.

"Do ye have anything else you're going to try to fucking hit me wi', luv? Or can we..." he trailed off, gesturing vaguely with his head toward the *Pale Queen*.

Anna narrowed her gaze at him skeptically as questions tried to claw their way up her throat.

How did he know where to find her?

Why would he try to find her at all?

"There's sharks in these waters," he said tightly, attention dropping to the water. "Man eaters..."

Anna ran her tongue over her teeth, refusing to break eye contact.

"I know you're stubborn, but ye can't swim, and in case ye did no' notice, your wherry is sinking."

The taffrail was only a few inches above the water. She shifted uncomfortably, opening her mouth to say something, but a bubbling gurgle belched between them and the wherry angled downward.

Bugger.

His hand remained stretched between them. A tattooed eye in the center of his wrist stared at her from a mass of tentacles. It blinked— or at least she thought it had blinked. Anna stared down at it with wide eyes. The wherry gurgled again, slipping farther beneath the water. Anna reached forward at the sudden lurch and grasped the pirate's hand in hers. It was warm, his calluses rough against her skin.

If he had been any other man, she might have enjoyed having her hand in his, but as it was—

Lovelace's fingers tightened, pulling her gaze back to his. He grinned down at her, brushing his bangs back with his free hand before scrubbing the stubble along his jaw.

As it was, she did not enjoy it.

"Captain? Are you planning on swimming to Tiburon?" Juliana Gray called down.

"No, Jules," he replied quietly, holding Anna's gaze.

He tugged her forward, a mere suggestion. Anna stiffened as his grin widened. What was he planning? The Pirate King stepped forward, so she leaned away, gaze running from his trousers to his eyes once more. She looked behind him at the thick rope hanging from the main deck of the *Pale Queen*. She couldn't hold on to that; she could hardly grip her pail with the thick burns on her hands.

Oh.

Anna turned back to him, mouth already open in protest. "If you think—"

In one swift movement, he hefted her up into one arm and grasped the rope dangling from the taffrail. Nostrils flaring, she glared down at the Pirate King. His grin softened as he shifted, grip tight but not uncomfortable. Winding the rope around his arm, he placed a boot against the ship, likely to keep the barnacles from flaying them as they steadily rose.

"I could have done it myself," she lied through her teeth.

He nodded his head, arm raising as the crew pulled the rope up. Anna slid her arms around his neck and tried to ignore their proximity —his arm beneath her rump and his mouth near her throat. It was entirely too easy for her to think of another time she'd been in his arms with his teeth and tongue in that very same spot.

Warmth grew in her cheeks, and she looked away. His shirt snapped open in a soft breeze, the collar waving almost in signal. Leaning forward, she inspected the tattoos along the back of his neck and shoulders. She hadn't had many opportunities to see the shadows along his back. A beautiful imperial crown stared up at her from between his shoulder blades at the base of his neck, weathered and inked with thin intricate lines.

One day she'd ask why only pirates wore their stories on their skin. But she'd be damned if it was today.

"Wi' the clouds, ye were easy enough to track...and between us, I broke all the bloody boats," Lovelace said into her neck, his nose brushing along her jawline as he looked up. "I figured ye were wondering—just don't tell Jules."

"All of them?" she asked incredulously, meeting his gaze for a second before looking up to where Juliana Gray lorded over their ascension. He was entirely too close to maintain eye contact. "That seems rather wasteful."

"I knew you'd try to wander off the first bloody chance that presented itself. Ye do everything fast, lass, but three days seems a wee quick even for ye."

"It was five days," Anna corrected.

She'd done nothing but eat, sleep, and stretch for those five days. She might have even done some light lifting using her body weight to test her muscles. Anna had been surprised at her own strength, at how quickly her tender flesh lost its bruises, especially with what her body had sustained the past few weeks. Between rescuing Markus from the claws of the Senate, obtaining the map at their childhood estate, and being swept over the railing—

Closing her eyes, she swallowed hard past the growing knot of unease in her throat and tried to fight the chill threatening to reach up from her soul. Her body might be on its way to well and good in a remarkable amount of time, but she wasn't entirely sure how long it would take for her mental and emotional faculties to right themselves.

The nightmares had started last night, which was how Anna had found herself awake in the dead of the night with the visceral compulsion to leave.

"I'll see this through to the bloody end, no matter how bitter it may be," he said quietly, and based on the prickling sensation along her jaw, the Pirate King was staring at her. "I got shite to deal wi' on Tiburon first is all. Won't take long, lass, I promise."

"Oh?"

"Aye, *oh*," he huffed. "Coalition needs some fucking reminders, for one."

Anna frowned.

Those cutthroats, the five chiefs in the Coalition of Pirates, wanted her dead. She hadn't decided yet if the scoundrel whom she clung to also wanted her in such an irrevocable state. Anna had done nothing to encourage otherwise, except for maybe pushing him against a wall and kissing him.

Embarrassment and frustration warmed her skin. She turned to look down at him, nearly nose to nose. "And that's more important than my brother."

"Aye," he said, throat bobbing. "Can't sail after the prick if you've still got that gods-damned spot. That requires dealing wi' the Coalition's shite, and while I'm there, might as well remind them who the fuck I am and how I feel about the trade."

It seemed noble enough.

Bugger, it even seemed *reasonable* enough.

"I've heard the *Pale Queen* is fast enough to stay ahead of whatever pirate lore nonsense this is."

He nodded. "'Tis true, aye. But it's no' a pace I can keep, and it's no wi'out consequence."

Not for the first time, Anna noticed the heavy shadows beneath his eyes.

Mythical mumbo-jumbo aside, she couldn't go to Tiburon. She didn't like the idea of confronting the Coalition, and she liked the idea of the Pirate King doing so on her behalf even less.

"As soon as you show them the mark, they'll know who I am and what I did," she said quietly. "And they *will* try to kill me."

Something feral and dangerous stirred in his dark gaze, making his irises nearly swirl. Lovelace clenched his jaw, his voice rough when he spoke. "They'd have to get close enough first. I can keep ye safe, Anna; ye don't even have to get off the *Queen*."

Such promises...

Looking away, she felt the weight of his words like chains wrapping around her ankles, dragging her down. Lovelace shifted as they reached the taffrail. A small cluster of pirates looked down at them over the edge as rope burned into the pale railing.

As soon as the damn taffrail was in reach, she grabbed on and pulled herself over, straddling it and breathing deep. Like everything else aboard the *Pale Queen*, the taffrail was made of bone-white wood and intricately carved. Throwing her leg over the side, she slid onto the deck and scanned her surroundings.

Juliana Gray stood to the side in a sleeveless cotton shirt, the laces along her chest undone. When she spoke, her voice was cold and even. "Captain, it's about gods-damned time."

"Aye, captain," another mocked with a chuckle. "We were getting worried, we were."

Tracking the sound and the light brogue that roughed its edges, she found Tate Lovelace leaning against the taffrail not far from her.

Good God, the Pirate King and his quartermaster were cut from the same cloth.

Tate Lovelace tucked a stray lock of wine-red hair behind his ears;

the rest of it fell haphazardly to his clavicles in splendidly tangled strands. Because the quartermaster refused to don a shirt, Anna could see wings of bone connecting his sternum to his shoulders.

In the five days Anna had been aboard the *Pale Queen*, Tate Lovelace had worn a shirt for none of them.

Crossing his arms against his chest, the quartermaster invited her gaze to drop to the agonizingly beautiful tattoos decorating his skin. A pair of cutlasses sat at each hip, their hilts poking above his trousers like a real pair might. All manner and sizes of blades kissed his arms from wrist to shoulder, inside and out. Every piece on Tate appeared to match, black-bladed and intricate.

It was a stark comparison to the quilt of ink the Pirate King had wrapped himself in.

As if feeling her stare, he turned and grinned, one brow arching.

Good God—caught staring like a juvenile again.

Anna pulled her boots off one by one, dumped the water out onto the *Pale Queen's* deck, and tossed them over her shoulder. Trevor Lovelace sighed behind her, but she was already well on her way to his quarters. She needed to think, needed some distance between them. His heavier steps kept time with hers, but she ignored them—ignored him.

Had anyone ever ignored the Pirate King before?

The deck was smooth beneath her feet, an obvious sign it was well taken care of. Even now, there was a dark-haired pirate across the way with a brush and a bucket. The man himself was stark against the bone-white planks of the deck, a bandana around his forehead, and dressed in only a pair of cotton trousers. Leaning back on his heels, he rested his hands on his hips and breathed deep. A crooked smile grew on his face as he held his hand up to the sun and waved at her, his glorious abdominals on display.

Was *every* member of the Pirate King's crew stunning?

Anna swallowed hard and glared at the ground, jaw ticking.

Good God, she needed off this damn ship.

"Wait," Lovelace said quietly from behind her.

Anna snorted. There wasn't a chance in hell she was waiting.

Space—she needed space.

"Anna," he said, voice shaded with annoyance.

Shaking her head, she anchored her gaze on the set of double doors marking his quarters.

Lovelace had said he would keep her safe, but Anna had never wanted such a thing for herself.

The Coalition of Pirates were a dangerous sort, steeped in honest cruelty and backhanded promises. The island they inhabited sat in front of the Black Line, the last bastion of civilization before the black waters. She didn't know much about Tiburon except that it had an idyllic coastline and housed the secret sanctum of the pirates.

Anna doubted anyone else knew much more—plenty of good men had been sent to Tiburon to find out and report back, but none had been successful in divulging any useful information.

Tiburon was precarious enough to find one's way to, especially unshackled, but the meeting place of the Coalition was supposedly in the middle of a theoretically cursed strip of jungle, one that was said to be impossible to navigate unless you'd been through its shadows before.

Honestly, its secrecy sounded more dramatic than anything the khan had scribed.

What could they possibly be hiding there? More importantly, what didn't they want anyone to attempt to find?

Lip twitching nearly into a smile, Anna tried to smother the familiar feeling building in her gut and wrapping itself around her heart. She had wondered about their council in the past, at its shroud of secrecy and death—and at the trove of treasure that slept at its center.

She caught sight of wine-red hair out of the corner of her eye. Glancing, she took in the hard, handsome planes of the Pirate King's face and the curve of his jaw. A plan unfurled in her mind like a flower reaching toward a rare band of sunlight.

An opportunity sat in front of her despite how furious she was with him.

Anger is the emotion best welded into steel and slipped between ribs, her mother had told her once.

Could she get into that treasure trove and explore the inner workings of the Coalition?

The Pirate King lingered behind her, hands hanging at his sides. She turned away from him, not at all comforted by his presence—he had become difficult to look at, completely the same and yet entirely different. This man was harder, grittier, the circles beneath his eyes were darker, and he always seemed to be far fiercer than he needed to be.

Yet, Lovelace had been kind and gentle to her, especially when he thought no one was looking.

"Luv...I..."

Anna's throat bobbed, and she turned away from him.

She needed to think, and she wouldn't be able to do that with him in the room.

Lovelace closed the door softly, but it did little to hide the vicious curse that left his lips.

CHAPTER EIGHTEEN

Markus's eyelashes fluttered against his cheek, tickling his skin.

"Good God," he growled, clenching his eyelids shut against the pounding in his skull.

What pub crawl had he participated in to summon such a hellish consequence? There was no doubt in his mind that the blasted thing had been born in some circle of hell. He'd sworn off the Cordelaine Crawl after his and Anna's last birthday, but he'd deny his sister no—

His brows pinched together, eyes still closed.

That wasn't right.

Markus's fingers splayed against the cotton sheets beneath him. His brows furrowed—he kept silk sheets on his bed at his father's estate and flannel on the *King's Ransom.* As accustomed to living on a ship as Markus was, it took him a moment to recognize the gentle rock and sway as he laid there.

Bollocks, if he wasn't on his blasted ship, then whose ship was he on?

He started to raise his hand to his pounding head and stopped. Pain erupted in his abdomen, pulling a stiff growl from his lips. Markus stared at the ceiling for a moment, hesitant to investigate the latest consequence of his actions.

Slowly, his chin dipped, and his gaze lowered.

Someone had draped a quilt over him; it covered his legs and most of his torso. Markus sighed; he'd lost his shirt somewhere along the line again. Maybe he was simply destined to remain half-clothed. A strange scent wafted up from beneath the thick quilt; it was something between potential infection and antiseptics—joy. Disregarding the acute pain in his torso, he propped himself up on his elbows and lifted the quilt.

Trousers.

Excellent.

Bandages covered the lower half of his stomach in thick layers.

Oh, that's right—the bastard had stabbed him.

Cunningham had stabbed him, thrown Lovelace overboard, and—

Anna.

Panic surged through him, tunneling into his marrow like a maggot would rot. Markus's lips pinched into a line as he forced himself upright, wincing at how tender the muscles of his stomach were, before he remembered Cunningham had tossed her below deck.

He stared down at the red blooming across the bandages and sighed before letting his gaze rove over the room. Ribbons of light shone through a porthole, illuminating motes of dust. Markus breathed deep, gaze narrowing on the spot of blood that grew against his bandages, nose twitching.

Was it infected?

He wouldn't know unless he undressed it...but remaining blissfully ignorant sounded rather splendid right now. Someone hummed beneath their breath, and the sound raised the hairs along the back of Markus's neck. He turned. Surprise and dread filled him before it hardened into something closer to loathing.

Bryce Cunningham sat in a chair against the wall, turning one of Markus's blasted boots, of all things, around in his hand.

Markus's gaze narrowed before his stomach rolled nervously.

It was his left boot.

"Your sister used to keep things in the hollowed-out heels of her shoes," Cunningham said by way of greeting. "It reminded me of a magpie."

The man was surprisingly relaxed, his feet stretched out and crossed at the ankles on a circular threadbare rug. His sleeves were rolled to his elbows, and the top buttons of his uniform were undone, showing off the skin at his throat and the dip between his clavicles. Ignoring his pale, unmarked flesh, Markus's attention fixed on two very small black marks along the inside of Cunningham's forearm.

"Lock picks, small packs of poison..." Bryce sighed, dropping the boot to the floor as his gaze slowly met Markus's. "But never notes."

"My sister has never been much of a romantic. Are you truly surprised she didn't keep your love letters?"

"No." He shook his head, a strand of dark brown hair cutting across his forehead. "I'm not surprised by that, though with your reputation and whatnot, I'm surprised *you* do."

"Everyone is bound to fall in love eventually, including me," Markus said quietly.

"'I should have let you drown.' That doesn't sound like love. Man or woman?"

Markus remained quiet, watching as Cunningham's dark gaze dropped downward, stilling on his chest for a moment before he straightened and unrolled his sleeves. Smoothing out the fabric, Cunningham set to buttoning the cuffs at his wrists.

"Does it matter?" Markus asked despite knowing the answer.

"Bellcaster would say it does."

"Well, it's a good thing I've never given a rat's ass what Bellcaster thinks, isn't it?"

Cunningham scoffed. "A trait you and your sister both seem to have inherited from your mother."

If there ever had been a man that knew better than to insult one's mother, it should have been the one in front of him.

Biting the inside of his cheek, he inhaled slowly, aware of how every breath and twitch of muscle sent liquid agony to his core. "Speaking of my delightfully delinquent sister, where is she?"

"Below deck, where she will remain for the rest of our journey."

He nearly laughed, imagining the angry creature his sister had likely transformed into—fueled by rage and the intrinsic need to rebel against captivity. "I imagine that is going over well."

"She's drowning in her ire, I assure you," he said, looking just over Markus's shoulder.

Markus eyed the brunette as he stood and strode over to a dresser. A platter occupied its top with a decanter and plate of bread. He poured himself a glass of wine, drained it, then poured another. Something was off about his posture and the calm that smoothed his features, but Markus couldn't quite put his blasted finger on it.

"Wine?" he offered, turning to glance over his shoulder.

Markus shook his head.

Good God, under no circumstance would he be wined and dined by Bryce Cunningham.

"Are you feeling all right?" the brunette asked, eyebrow arched as he turned. "I've never known you to turn away from a drink."

He'd been *stabbed*.

What did Bryce expect?

His gaze narrowed at the brunette. He did know alcohol did not get along with one's clotting factor, didn't he? Markus also maintained a strict rule that he did not drink unless it was somewhere his grievous mistakes could be well documented and ferreted back to his father on a large scale. He could not be an embarrassment if there was no one to see it or sing of it to the high heavens.

And an audience of one did not qualify for such a showing.

"That just goes to show that you don't really know me at all."

Cunningham pressed his lips into a thin line, cocking his head to the side. Despite the hesitancy with which he held his words in, an amusement danced in his eyes like a secret shared between friends. "We've known each other since we were children, our fathers are best friends. I might know you better than you think."

John Savage didn't have friends.

Again, Markus shook his head. "You could know someone your entire life without truly understanding them, Bryce. You might believe you know their heart and their mind and find out later that you never really did...but you already have some experience with that, don't you?"

Bryce drained the glass of wine. "Now that you're awake, you can get to work."

"Doing what?"

Cunningham threw something onto the bed; it landed on Markus's lap. He blinked down at it for several seconds as the door creaked open on old hinges.

The Pirate King's map?

What the hell was he supposed to do with this?

"You and Anna had the same schooling—the same obtuse, theatrical upbringing," Bryce said, as if he saw the questions lingering in Markus's gaze. "If she could read it, you can too."

The laugh erupted from his chest in a rough bark, rocketing pain through his stomach. Doubling over, his hand hovered above the reddening bandages, brows furrowed and lips pulled tight. "Me? You are sorely mistaken, old chap, if you think anyone can do what Anna does."

At the sound of timed steps, Markus glanced back to where Cunningham stood by the door. A line of Briland sailors in their ever-green uniforms marched single file into the small quarters. Each man had a stack of four or five leather-bound books in their hands. They were old, though they'd clearly seen recent use.

In minutes, he felt like he'd stepped into any space Anna had inhabited. Columns of books had been laid about the room in haphazard piles without any rhyme or reason. His chest tightened and he swallowed past an uncomfortable lump of nervous energy.

Bollocks—this would need immediate cleaning.

His gaze skipped about the room once more, from the meager porthole to the small dresser and desk next to it. "This is going to take me a long time, I am not the linguistic wizard my sister is," he said, recognizing the quarters for what they were. "If you want this done expediently, I would bring the journals to her."

"As I've said, Miss Savage is below deck, steeping in her anger. I doubt she's in the mood to receive guests."

"She'll *receive* me, I'm her brother and I will come bearing the gift of books."

"No."

Markus's gaze trailed from Cunningham's boots to his face, brows furrowing at his sudden stillness. He was lying—though Markus couldn't quite tell about what. Breathing deep, he searched for any other viable reason as to why he shouldn't be returned to his sister.

"I'm sure your quartermaster opposes this arrangement."

"I don't have one," Bryce said dryly.

Markus snorted, completely unsurprised. "Of course, you don't."

The bastard likely had no need for one with how efficient and organized he was.

"I don't have one," he elaborated quietly, "because your sister killed him."

Ah.

That would do it.

The door swung shut and locked from the outside. Markus looked from one stack of books to the next and huffed a small chuckle. Anna would have been in heaven had their positions been reversed, but as it was, this was closer to hell for him. Frowning, he laid back and ran his hands over his face.

Maybe he had died.

It would explain Cunningham's presence.

CHAPTER NINETEEN

Two days?

Anna thought she had more fortitude than that.

She leaned back against Lovelace's desk and stared at the double doors leading to the main deck. Sucking on her teeth, she sized up the door like it wanted to tussle. Out—she needed out of this room that so clearly belonged to the Pirate King, from the smell to the way he had arranged his bedding and breakfast nook.

Anna glared at the ceiling and pinched the bridge of her nose before striding across the bone-white flooring and tightening her fingers around one of the intricate brass knobs. Wincing at how the action pulled at her healing hand, she inhaled and opened the door. It made no noise as it slid open, the hinges clearly well oiled. Peeking through the slit, she squinted into the light and onto the main deck.

Bugger, it would have been a splendid day for sunbathing if not for the mess she was in.

Her gaze scanned from one side of the near-empty deck to the other before trailing the stairs that curved up either side of the captain's quarters to the helm. Well, she supposed this was rather serendipitous. A breeze tousled her hair as she leaned forward, cracking the door wide enough that she could slip from the room unnoticed.

"Lovely day for a stroll, wouldn't ye agree?"

She glanced up and found the dirty undersides of a pair of feet dangling above her head. "Just out for a bit of fresh air, quartermaster."

Anna stepped completely from the safety of the Pirate King's quarters and raised her hand to blot out the sun. One foot disappeared, quickly followed by the other. A moment later, the quartermaster leaned over the railing with a grin that could break a maiden's heart.

She lowered her hand now that Tate Lovelace blocked the sun with his body. The top layer of his hair was knotted at the back of his head, leaving the rest of his wine-red locks free to cascade over his shoulders as he peered down at her.

True to form, he wore nothing but cotton trousers, a thick belt circling his hips and hiding a teensy more of the inked cutlasses at his side. The muscles of his abdomen flickered and came to life as he stretched his arms above his head.

Did he expect her to find anything about him remarkable?

Anna had seen the Pirate King nearly naked in the hot spring; there was little that could impress her after that.

"Call me Tate," he said, lowering his arms.

"Tate," she echoed, testing the name.

It fit the quartermaster—he was handsome and tall, angular with broad shoulders that tapered into a narrow waist. Tate was nowhere near the behemoth his brother was, not even close to being made of the same brute muscle and strength, but he certainly wasn't lacking.

Waving a hand over her shoulder, she started off in the direction of the galley, stomach rumbling. If the quartermaster wished to follow her, she had no qualms with it. He'd likely been assigned the tedious task of keeping her on the ship after her last stunt.

A seagull squawked in the distance and then another call came from overhead, this one decidedly more human. Her gaze shot upward as she walked, squinting into the glare of the sun. A dark splotch hurdled toward her, all its angles cast in shadow. Her gaze narrowed further at realizing not what it was, but *who*.

The loud crack of something against the deck sounded from behind her.

"You're awake," he said on a breath, barely audible.

"I am," Anna answered as something dark and spiced hit her nose. She ignored the shadow—*his* shadow—as it fell over her shoulder. Bare feet struck the planks behind her, following at a long-legged, leisurely pace. Anna sucked on her teeth, shoulders stiffening.

"Can we—" Lovelace stopped, clearing his throat.

No, they could not.

Keeping her sight trained on the staircase leading below deck, she inhaled slowly and relaxed her hands from the fists they had formed. She couldn't think straight with him so near, couldn't get past the anger that boiled in her veins or the way he made her heart thunder in her ears.

The Pirate King's presence only served as a reminder of her brother's absence.

"Anna," he murmured just loud enough for her to hear. Hearing her name fall from his lips like a plea pulled her to an immediate stop. "As soon as we do the things that need doing, I promise we'll rescue that bloody damsel in distress ye have for a brother."

She turned to meet his stare, and her breath hitched.

When was the last time he'd slept?

Looking from the mottled blue bruising beneath his eyes, she glanced at the rest of him. He wore a simple wide-necked shirt with short sleeves and trousers that ended at his knees. The stubble she'd seen two days ago had thickened, and his eleven or so freckles were stark against his pallid skin. His hands clenched and unclenched at his sides.

Anna swallowed every bit of sympathy that had bubbled up from its cage as he dipped his chin toward her. Was it a motion of apology or recognition? Did she care why he leaned toward her, gaze deepening?

Maybe once—but not today.

She tipped her chin up in challenge. "Markus needs my help *now*."

"Aye, lass," he said, running his lip through his teeth. Clearly, the

Pirate King was tired of arguing the same points with her. If he wanted agreeable, perhaps he should simply do what she wanted. "It's no' just the Coalition and your wee spot we're stopping for. We need to restock, and the *Queen* needs some work. I won't march my crew to their deaths—at least no' wi'out the proper supplies."

The crew chuckled briefly around her.

Anna snorted. "What kind of captain lets the ship's supplies run this low?"

Lovelace turned toward his brother and crossed his arms, feet planted like an old oak ready to endure a storm. "Oh, I don't know. Tate, why don't ye tell the fem who let the supplies get this fucking low? Gods know ye passed eight ports on your way to fish me out."

The quartermaster shuffled behind her as a second set of steps tapped down the stairs from the helm. Every head aboard slowly turned as if pulled by the same unseen hand and focused on the lithe figure. Off in the distance, lightning crackled, and a disgustingly warm breeze brushed her cheek.

"The captain doesn't owe you any answers," Juliana Gray said flatly.

Anna glanced at the thunderheads rolling across the sky in their direction—it certainly seemed like a warning from the powers that may be. Disregarding it entirely, she anchored her gaze to the master gunner of the *Pale Queen*.

Juliana Gray lounged against the bottom rail, one hand on her hip—she was a petite thing, lithe but well-muscled. Her honey-brown skin glowed in the remaining light and matched her loose wavy hair. The golden-green eyes that Markus had spoken so fondly of had narrowed into golden slits as she stared at Anna.

"He wouldn't owe me any answers if he would let me off his damn ship or go after Cunningham."

The Man-Eater's gaze shifted until she stared at the Pirate King, one thin eyebrow arching upward. "I've said as much to the captain, but for whatever reason—"

Anna turned to Lovelace as Juliana closed her mouth. Wind whipped around the deck as he breathed deep, his chest expanding and throat bobbing. His gaze was steady and calm as he stared at Juliana, a bottomless abyss any woman would willingly fall into. The Man-Eater's nostrils flared briefly. Anna glanced between the two repeatedly—they apparently didn't need words to have a conversation.

Her skin heated as something in her core tightened uncomfortably with that knowledge.

She knew the name of what boiled her veins now, and it wasn't anger, but a close cousin.

Lovelace's attention hadn't left her; she could tell he stared at her by the warmth his attention created. Never had Anna hated biology as much as she did at that moment. How could one be so aware of the presence of another without any choice in the matter?

It was as if the very fibers of her being reached out for his, looking for connection.

If she could cut them out, she would have.

"Juliana," he said gently, "mind the helm."

"Aye, captain," she growled, letting her gaze slide to Anna.

Her leaving did nothing to dissuade the boiling beneath Anna's skin; if anything, it only fanned the flames of her ire. Jaw clenching tight, she tried to wrap her head around why he consistently attempted to dissolve her troubles before she had the chance to do so herself.

It was something a suitor might do and most definitely something a husband would do.

But he'd never been either and he never would be.

Trevor Lovelace was the Pirate King and Anna was only an heiress. A bitterness she had never known crept up her throat; this was likely the first and only time she would ever be considered below someone's station.

Anna rounded on him, a haughty chuckle threaded with her words. "I don't need your damn help."

Cocking a brow, Lovelace shifted his weight as they made eye contact. Anna felt the spark like lightning in her soul as his lips twitched into a brief smile. His face softened and—bugger, she turned away from the truth that reflected back at her.

I'm right here, lass, she imagined his soul saying to her through his eyes.

That was part of the problem.

"And while we're on the topic of me *not* needing you," she swallowed, settling her sights on the stairs leading to the galley, "I'd rather you just drop me off where my brother is. You don't need to bother with this whole"—she waved her hand over her shoulder, searching for words—"black spot business. I'll be fine—I'm always fine. I can rescue my brother, get in and out with none the wiser."

It was both true and not true. She did not need the Pirate King's help to rescue Markus, but she did need his aid in reaching the island.

Anna needed his ship and his well-seasoned crew—she did not need him.

Chewing on the inside her of lip, she wrapped her arms around herself. All this atrocious luck for a map which had been endorsed as impossible to acquire. She had suspected for a long time that the Pirate King's map wasn't at all mythical or cursed, but it had enough of a reputation that it might as well have been.

Sequestered away on the *Pale Queen,* the dreaded bone-white vessel of the Pirate King.

Guarded by a cut-throat crew and blood-thirsty captain.

Some even believed the entire crew had been cursed. Anna hardly believed in fairy tales as a child, and the years hadn't changed her opinion on the matter. The Pirate King was...she didn't know what he was, but she had yet to find evidence of some curse or mythical power, no moonlit transformations, no scaled skin. His accent and appearance were enough for her to suspect some supernatural deal, though.

No one was as brilliantly handsome as he was without paying some kind of price.

Anna placed her hand on the railing down into the galley; it was smooth beneath her touch. The Pirate King's hulking form appeared in her periphery. "No can do, lass. That bloody spot will get us fucking killed long before we get to that island. Between the slavers, the Coalition, the bloody Senate, and any of the other beasties sleeping in that wicked deep—"

"The *Pale Queen* can outrun any vessel, let them try and take us," she interrupted.

Lovelace stepped around her, stopping on the stairs so they were eye to eye. Anna leaned away from him. She couldn't breathe, let alone think, with him in such proximity. Gaze narrowing, his attention dropped to her lips before lifting back to her eyes. Anna's heart thundered behind her ribs loud enough that she was certain he could hear it too.

God knew he was close enough.

"I'm the king, lass; I don't run from fights."

Anna laughed. "No, if this conversation is any indication, you only run toward them."

Holding his gaze, she inhaled slowly, waiting for his face to relax the way it always did after he and Markus got into a scuffle. There was always that dark simmer in his eyes, a cunning that had been born of the cold, and a grin that was sharper than any blade. It had never taken long for that serious facet of him to melt into something less—only Anna wasn't prepared for it this time.

"Maybe I'm only running toward ye."

Anna held her breath, unsure of what else to do. How was she supposed to react to something like that, especially when he stared at her with a gaze as bold and dark as the mantle he wore? She almost opened her mouth, but logic took hold of her thoughts and ripped them from the cruel fingers of emotion. Swallowing past it all, she bit back the words pressing against her teeth.

Anna wasn't entirely sure where they stood, or if they were even standing on the same side of the line.

Shrugging a shoulder, she stepped around him, leaving the Pirate King to catch up. "How long?"

The sooner she was rid of him, the better.

"Week, tops," Lovelace said, stepping in turn with her once more. He dragged his hand against the back of his neck, chin tipping toward her. "Less if all goes well wi' the chiefs."

"A *week?*"

He stared down at her as she stopped, gaze whipping wildly to his.

"*Queen* has to be careened, that'll take some time, but cleaning all the shite at her will double our—"

"That's seven *days*—"

"—speed, and supplies have to be gathered,—"

"—one hundred and sixty-eight *hours*—"

"—and then there's that wee spot," he said almost cheerfully.

Anna blinked slowly, using the hand railing to keep herself upright. "A week."

"Aye." The rakish sparkle returned to his eyes, just a glimpse of her pirate as a small grin appeared like a ribbon of light on a cloudy day. "Can sunbathe all ye like."

Her throat bobbed as she turned away. Bugger, the man was tragically attractive even when armed with a snarl; when he smiled, something lit up inside her.

"Can one sunbathe from the bowels of Tiburon?" she asked absently, thinking of all the other splendidly secret places she could be exploring while they were on that damn island.

"What are ye planning, beastie?" he asked, the intensity of his stare warming her back.

Anna padded across the galley to the nearest table and sat. The wood was smooth beneath her hands. It was a stark contrast to the planks that adorned the rest of the *Pale Queen*. Squinting down at it, she picked at the finishing with a nail—most likely stained teak. Anna drummed her fingers against the table once, then Lovelace was standing across from her, hands flat as he leaned forward.

"What are ye planning, beastie?" he asked, brogue deepening.

One of the crew dropped a pair of pints at the side of the table and kept moving—rather brilliant plan, really. Anna wrapped her hands around the cool glass, ignoring how the galley quieted to hushed tones. Sniffing, she brought the pint to her nose and chuckled.

Good God, whatever it was, it burned her nostrils.

What would Markus do? she mused morbidly, staring into the dark liquid.

"*Anna*," Lovelace said, fingers splaying and stretching against the table.

She took a mouthful of whatever hellish liquid they had served her and winced. "I plan nothing."

The Pirate King gave her a look that tightened her chest.

"Nothing that wasn't on the docket already, at least."

His lips pressed together as he leaned closer, close enough that he towered over her. Anna closed the distance between them, pressing her hands against the table and rising from her seat. She stopped when they were a breath away, staring into his fathomless eyes and pushing away the knowledge that heat flared against her cheeks and trickled down her chest.

"I'm going with you."

And she would.

Anna did not need a champion; she did not need a man to fight her battles. If the Pirate King wanted this blasted mark off her palm, so be it. But while he was busy playing politician, she would be listening for information and looting the Coalition of any treasure that wasn't bolted to the floor.

Anna grinned, smiling straight up at Lovelace.

His gaze lowered to her lips. "I thought ye said ye didn't want to go to Tiburon because the Coalition wants ye dead."

"And you said you could keep me safe," she shot back. Some distant part of her glowed at the idea of his attention remaining on her lips. "You're the Pirate King, aren't you? Won that title fair and square? I don't need protecting, but if I did, I imagine you would do a splendid job."

Trevor Lovelace stared hard at her, irises swirling like clouds in a dark storm. Lifting his chin, he scoffed and turned away, feet marching him back toward the stairs. Staring at his back, her jaw slackened and her eyes widened.

He thought he could walk away from her in the middle of a conversation?

The roaring in her veins came back with a vengeance, the rhythmic thumps pounding like a war drum. Anna downed another mouthful of whatever spiteful drink they had served her and stormed after him.

"For as much as I would love to sit and sunbathe, I'd rather not be killed by some two-bit Coalition assassin while I'm wearing nothing but my skin on the beach!" Anna said adamantly.

Stumbling, he turned a surprised look on her.

That's right, scoundrel, Annaleigh Rae Savage sunbathed *naked*.

Anna grinned up at him. "What, you thought I wore a bathing suit?"

Lovelace opened his mouth and then snapped it closed, cheeks pinkening. He shook his head and plowed ahead toward the stairs. "Ye will be surrounded by my crew, as safe as can be in your gods-damned skin."

"Do you honestly believe that? You think one of the chiefs can't find a way to supplant an assassin in our midst? Maybe they already have." Anna dropped her voice to a whisper, glancing over her shoulder at the crew in the galley. "Do you really trust everyone on this ship?"

"I trust my crew wi' my life *and* wi' yours." He frowned slightly. "Reckon I trust them more wi' ye, actually."

Anna ran up the steps after him, reaching for something—anything—that would get her on that island. If the Pirate King planned on voyaging to Tiburon for supplies and to remove the spot, she was going with him. All that knowledge was ripe for the taking; the island held answers to questions she hadn't even asked yet.

"I want to go with you."

He stopped, shoulders rising. "Ye did no' want to go before. Why the hell do ye want on Tiburon so badly now, lass?"

"Why?" She laughed, hating the words before they even poured from her mouth. "Because I don't trust you!"

"Ye—ye don't trust me?"

"No," she snapped. "*You* say you're getting this damn spot removed, but how do I know that's actually what you plan on doing? For all I know, you'll be selling the *wee Savage female* to the highest bidder—a brilliant plan, really."

Anna clenched her jaw, watching as her words hit their mark. She held the man's dark gaze, refusing to acknowledge the slimy feeling dripping between her ribs. When he had been her pirate, he had always denied the Pirate King's involvement in the slave trade.

Bugger, she'd been bold.

Maybe too bold.

Lovelace threw his hands up as he climbed the stairs to the main deck. "Bloody hell, fem! Fine! In my cabin, ye should find a fucking dress or two. You'll be on your best gods-damned behavior on Tiburon—seen and no' heard. Understand, Miss Savage?"

Anna recoiled. "Excuse me?"

He stuffed his hands into his trouser pockets and started toward the helm, powerful shoulders hunched. The wind ruffled the tail of his shirt, pulling it tight against his back and torso. Anna clenched her fists at her side, staring at his retreating form once more—and to think the Pirate King claimed he didn't run from fights.

"I'm not wearing a dress," Anna told him, voice rising over the wind.

Lovelace stopped and looked over his shoulder. "If ye plan on coming wi', ye sure as hell are. Hopefully, if ye look docile enough, they'll bloody well forget who ye are and what ye did."

"It was a few ships."

"Ye burned them to fucking tinder, lass."

"They were slave ships!" she yelled, pointing at him. "*You* would have burned them too!"

"That is neither here nor there," he said with the finality of a reaper. His eyes darkened, any emotion he might have felt smoothed into nothing as he shifted to face her completely. "I expect a dainty fem next I see ye, one dressed in the finest bloody silks the Pirate King has to offer."

Her breath shallowed, and for a moment, Anna forgot that the man standing before her was the Pirate King. Blinking, she saw *her* pirate—a brilliantly wicked rake who always looked out for her and had only ever put her first.

Me first, luv, the pirate had said, standing slowly.

Anna had never feared the pirate and likely never would.

Lovelace puffed out his chest, looking down at her. His eyelashes were thick and dark against the tanned skin of his face, his freckles casting him in an oddly innocent glow. Jaw ticking, Anna jabbed him hard on the chest, finger digging deep into his pec.

Surprise flashed across his face as the whole crew held a collective breath.

Even the cool breeze stilled.

"Listen here, you ass!" She poked him again, stepping closer. "You may be the Scourge of the Seas, a king among criminals, but no one orders me around. No one ever has! I am not your personal doll to dress and pamper as you will. And if ye want me in a dress, *lad*," Anna spat mockingly, "you're going to have to put me in the damn thing yourself."

The quartermaster whistled low, pure delight etched into every line on his face as he leaned against the mainmast. Gaze darting between his brother and her, his head shook faintly. It was a fascinated kind of astonishment that shaped his features, and based on the mischievous glimmer in his eyes, it had nothing to do with yelling at the Pirate King and everything to do with embarrassing his brother.

Trevor Lovelace cocked a brow, jaw clenching as a flush pinkened his cheeks. His chest expanded beneath the thin cotton shirt on a deep breath. As it hissed back through his lips, the wind snapped the sails open, and his infernal gaze met hers.

"All right, lass," he bit out, promptly throwing her over his shoulder. "Ye want to play this game, I'll fucking play."

"Wh—*put me down!*" she screamed, looking down at his rump.

"We'll be there by day's end, and when we step onto Tiburon tomorrow, things are going to be different," he growled. She felt his voice rumble up through his chest as he stomped toward a set of stairs that led deep into the hull. "I have a gods-damned reputation to uphold, ye won't be fucking wi' it."

One of the Pirate King's arms banded around her waist as the other pressed against her legs, hand wrapping around her thigh. Anna kicked her legs and pounded her fists against his back, but Lovelace didn't pay her thrashing any mind. It was like hitting a brick wall with a stick. Instead, his bicep flexed, holding her tightly against him. Her face grew hot before the fierce heat traveled down her neck and chest.

Anna was—good God, she didn't want to put words to what she was.

"I need ye to act like a lady," he said, softer this time. "Or ye stay with the crew."

A bitter laugh broke from her chest. "So I have to be a pretty little doll on your arm in front of all your friends, hm?"

"They're no' my mates, and ye didn't have a bloody problem wi' it at your da's party."

"*You* were the pretty thing on *my* arm, not the other way around," Anna growled in his ear, trying to push up off his shoulder.

"I have Tate," Lovelace announced loudly as his foot hit the first step. "Do no' test me."

Eyes widening in surprise, her gaze darted to the man in question. Anna didn't trust the wolfish grin on his face—and she certainly didn't trust it after his thumbs sank into his trousers, intentionally revealing the deep v of muscle.

Sucking on her teeth, she looked away as the quartermaster waggled his eyebrows at her. The Pirate King wasn't the only one with a reputation, but his brother's was just as atrocious—no, Tate's was worse. At least the Pirate King had never been accused of more than trafficking women or killing them. Tate Lovelace had entire ballads written about him—about his smile and about the words he might whisper in a woman's ear.

"I'm not scared of him," she ground out, glaring at the side of the Pirate King's head.

He snorted. "I would be."

Her ribs ached with the furious pace he descended the steps. She bobbed up and down, jostled as he nearly jogged into what she suspected were the bowels of the ship. Was he honestly taking her to the brig? As Anna fisted his shirt for stability, he came to an abrupt halt, sliding her down his body.

His hands scalded her hips, fingertips lingering before he stepped back.

A metal gate clanged shut between them.

He wouldn't meet her gaze, and every step away from her seemed forced.

Anna crossed her arms, seething as she scoured the small cell. "You think *this* can hold me?"

"No," he answered matter-of-factly. "But it'll be good practice. All the locks on Tiburon and every gods-damned Coalition flagship were made by the same fucking smith."

CHAPTER TWENTY

Throwing the door of his quarters open, Trevor stomped inside and slammed it behind him. A picture to his left rattled against the wall. Shite, he needed somewhere he could be alone wi' his thoughts, somewhere to try and get the lass out of his gods-damn head. Even when she was stubborn as hell, she made him feel a wee like he was dying inside.

He let his shoulders relax and scrubbed at the back of his neck. His gaze traveled from the clothes strewn about the bloody floor to the sheets in tangles at the foot of his bed. It was a fucking mess, but the sight of it warmed his chest.

Shite, should he clean the place up a wee bit?

Or would the lass think he was poking his head into her things?

Trevor frowned.

These were his blood quarters, he could do wi' them as he liked. He bent, fingers brushing one of his favorite shirts. As he straightened, he smelled Anna. Couldn't be the lass, though, she was still in the brig. He glanced down at the dark blue long-sleeved shirt in his hands—no bloody way. Raising the cotton shirt to his face, he breathed deep.

Oh, aye, the shirt smelled like her all right—like citrus and silk on a warm summer day.

His gaze slowly moved to the bed—that fucker likely smelled of the lass too. Staring at the wrinkled sheets and tousled covers, Trevor imagined her laying in it—he imagined what wee bit he remembered of the time they'd laid in it together. He shifted on his feet, fingers tightening around the cotton shirt in his hands—

Trevor glanced down.

What the hell did his cock think it was doing?

Bloody thing had a mind of its own.

Shaking his head, he sighed as he tossed the shirt to the ground. Shite. Fucking shite. Could no' even be in his quarters wi'out a gods-damned erection roaring to the bloody surface. Padding across his quarters, he opened the bay windows at the back. Hopefully, the breeze would carry some of that lovely silk and citrus out to sea.

Bloody hell, the lass had ruined him for any other female.

He didn't remember much about their tumble, definitely no' as much as he would have liked. But that kiss in her da's estate had struck a deep chord in him. Whenever Anna neared, that bloody chord plucked, reviving the ghost of her nails at his back and running through his hair until they were a living thing on his skin once more.

He flexed his hands; they needed something to do that wasn't pretending they were the lass's.

Trevor paced out of his quarters—he couldn't stay in there.

He needed to see the horizon, the place where the sun met the bloody water. Breathing in the brine of the sea, he focused on the pull of the ocean and the breeze whirring through his hair and against his clothes. He unfurled his fingers, letting the wind weave over and through them playfully on the way to the helm.

"I like her, Trev," Tate said wi' a quiet laugh.

'Course the wee shite was waiting for him.

Was no' like anything else had gone according to plan today.

"Anna is easy to like," he said over his shoulder.

He hadn't met a lass as easy to be around as Anna; something about her just...calmed him. Which was rather bloody surprising considering all the trouble she found herself in. Calm was the last gods-damned word he'd ever use to describe any situation they'd found themselves in, but it was the truth.

His brother pushed off the taffrail, following him up. "Soon as she isn't pissed as hell, the fem and I are going to get along swimmingly."

Jaw ticking, Trevor nearly missed the next step. Shite, he could no' deal wi' that. He could put up wi' one or the other, no' both. If anything dragged him to an early grave, it would be those two chuckleheads teaming up on some bloody project.

"What's bothering ye? Is it the lass, or the meeting we'll be having wi' the Coalition?

"Can we talk about something else?" he snapped back, reaching the top of the stairs.

Couldn't see Tate's gods-damn grin, but he felt it. Tate hummed something beneath his breath before chuckling. "Oh, aye. So would ye rather talk about the lass or the Coalition *first?*"

Trevor groaned. "Fucking drop it, Tate."

"The Coalition, then," he said, sounding rather pleased.

Bloody hell, it should no' be allowed for someone to be so cheerful all the time.

He dragged his hands across his face before leveling his brother wi' a glare. "I don't have much to say—"

"You've never been one for words—"

"—but I'm making a fucking point about the trafficking. Ye still have that head?"

"Aye, 'tis hanging outside Jules's porthole." Tate grinned.

"Ye leave the Man-Eater be, Tate, ye got enough scars on your face from her. If you're not bloody careful, she'll take something that really matters to ye."

"Oh, like what? My cock?" Tate laughed. "She's no' a fan of monsters, remember? The fem wouldn't come near it."

Trevor snorted. "Nah, something like your tongue."

Tate's smile faltered, and a wee bit of panic entered his eyes. "Jules —Jules wouldn't do that."

"She's bloody good at figuring out what matters most to a male. I'd be careful if I were ye."

Fucking hell, she was like a gods-damned scent dog when it came to finding all the tender spots a male might have. The Man-Eater had figured out exactly what he held close as soon as he dove into that bloody maelstrom.

Trevor could no' remember feeling that kind of pure panic run through his veins, no' since Taylee died, and the lass had caused it twice now.

"Have ye seen any slavers wi' snake bites?" he asked, remembering the males who'd tried stealing his lass away.

"Most we run down have them, aye." Tate sighed, shoulders pulling up. "I thought maybe it had something to do wi' the Viper at first but...but Abu Shazar has been hit hardest, and she's fierce about her people. For as much of a fucking cunt as she is, she wouldn't sell them away."

Trevor nodded his head. "Aye, blaming the Viper would be too bloody easy."

"What do ye think a male would get out of that? She's got a longer list of enemies than ye do."

"Fuck if I know, but I want ye to look around Corazon."

"What for?"

"Anything. Everything." Trevor ran his lip through his teeth, crossing his arms against his chest. "Maybe snakes or—shite, I don't know."

And he bloody well didn't.

Trevor hated knowing there was a threat out there to anyone the slavers might like. It was like a gods-damned onion, though. He was getting all the fucking blame for the slave trade—Anna had made that clear to him whenever she opened that lovely mouth of hers to talk about him. But once someone got past pointing fingers at the Pirate King, they shifted their sights to the Viper because of those gods-damned snake bites.

How many different directions would he have to fucking sail in to figure out whose bloody idea it was to start the slave trade?

Trevor leaned back against the taffrail, dragging his hand across the back of his neck. Sure, the trade had been around for centuries—

some piece of shite had always thought selling people like meats was a profitable enough business. But bloody hell, it had never been organized like this, like they'd banded together under one flag.

He'd find the fucker eventually—no one had time like Trevor did.

"I do no' like snakes, Trev. They're fucking angry noodles that could kill ye."

"Such a wee babe." He sighed, shaking his head. "I'd rather be looking about than dealing wi' the Viper and the Coalition. Bunch of gods-damned toddlers, all of them."

Tate didn't answer.

Fucking suspicious, that.

When Trevor turned to look at his brother, the shite had a bloody grin on his face again. "What about the lass, what are ye doing wi' her?"

Sighing, he laced his fingers behind his head. "I don't know. I wanted to keep her on the *Queen*—she seemed like she wanted that too, but..."

Tate hopped onto the taffrail, leaning forward until his elbows were on his thighs. "Out wi' it, it does ye no good in *here*," he said, tapping his chest.

"She wants to go now, and I don't know why."

"Anna yelled it at ye, Trev. The whole crew heard—she doesn't trust ye."

Trevor shook his head, joining his brother on the taffrail. "I reckon trust has never stopped that fem in her life. There's another reason she wants to go; I feel it in my bones, Tate."

"Ye sure 'tis no' in *one* bone?"

Cheeks heating, he glared at his brother.

He'd seen the look in her eyes, just a flash—like catching the sun's glare off a mirror before all went dark. The lass wanted to go wi', and now he had to figure out why, and maybe a way to keep her on the *Pale Queen*. Whatever real reason she had for joining him would do naught but cause trouble.

"Should have kept your damn mouth shut." Tate chuckled, bumping him wi' his shoulder.

Trevor stared down at his hands. "I just...she's no' like us, Tate. How am I supposed to keep the lass safe when she's so bloody fragile?"

"Naught will happen, ye said it yourself."

He looked from his hands to the white planks of his ship. What wee light broke through the clouds made them glow—his ship was a ghostly beauty; he'd never seen one that was lovelier. The breeze was cool, and the seas grew rougher as they neared Tiburon, but he funneled all that gods-damned wind straight into the sails.

No matter how much he dreaded it, the faster they got to Tiburon, the better.

The door to his quarters opened and closed, echoing up through the window he'd cracked. A moment later, her voice drifted up to him on a made breeze. He smiled softly at the lullaby she hummed—it was the same one he'd heard on the train, the one that had whispered to him who she was.

Had her mum hummed it to her?

Trevor didn't know much about Sara Sommers, but he'd heard the female'd serenaded the Viper wi' a lovely, mournful song.

"Did she drink from the cup? I feel like that would solve some of your bloody problems," Tate murmured.

"I don't know."

"When I found ye, it was half full of rum. Back then, ye never left the rum unfinished—and ye'd never filled that bloody cup to drink before."

Trevor frowned, mouth souring. Bloody hell, there had been plenty of things to drown himself in then. The light at the end of his tunnel had been too far to see. Shite, maybe if he hadn't been three gods-damned sheets to the wind that night, he'd be able to remember more of what happened.

Maybe he'd know if she drank from it or no'.

Maybe he'd have fucking asked her to and saved himself all the trouble.

"A male might ask his female to drink from the cup," Tate

continued quietly. "Especially if it keeps some of those bloody worries from his mind."

That would solve a great many of his fears. Trevor was terrified about the lass falling in the bloody ocean and drowning, about catching a stray knife meant for him. Drinking from that cursed cup would calm most of the turbulent energy that ate at him like acid.

It would even soothe the fact that she'd grow old one day and he'd be left wi' naught but ash and the abyss.

"She's no' my fem." Trevor murmured. The words twisted him up inside. "'Tis her choice, I'll no' make it for her. Forever is a long time, Tate."

"No' as long as you'd think. When you're wi' the people who make ye happy, Trevor, no' even forever is enough," he said quietly, pausing a few seconds before laughing. "Still can't believe ye threw her in the bloody brig."

Trevor shrugged. There wasn't a cage that could hold the lass. "How long did it take?"

"Forty-two seconds."

Bloody hell.

The lass was a witch wi' her lock picks.

Shaking his head, the good-natured fun slipped from Tate's face. "How many times do ye think?"

Trevor raised a brow in question.

"How many times," he started, throat bobbing, "do ye think she's been locked behind a door?"

Something black bubbled up in Trevor's veins. He'd never considered she'd learned to pick a lock out of defiance or need.

"Too many," he growled. "But Anna likely learned how to pick a lock after just one."

He shook his head, fucking furious for the wee lass Anna must have been. He couldn't imagine putting his babe behind a locked door —he'd kill anyone who fucking tried. Chest aching wi' the thought of wee red-headed lasses and lads wi' bright blue eyes, he slid from the taffrail. He turned and propped his elbows on it after a pause, sighing as he stared out into the glittering blue sea.

Trevor closed his eyes and listened to her hum. He didn't know if Sara Sommers hummed the lullaby to her babes, but he knew wi'out a doubt that Anna would. He could see it playing behind his closed eyes —the lass swaying back and forth wi' a wee bundle, humming quietly.

Ruined.

She'd ruined him, and Trevor could no' find it in himself to care.

CHAPTER TWENTY-ONE

Anna frowned at her reflection.

She had been right when she had believed the length of her hair couldn't be saved. Where her hair had hung around her breasts in long curls before, it now bounced around her shoulders in an erratic multitude of blonde corkscrews. It hadn't been this short since she was a small girl running around her mother's work sites with Markus.

Scowling, she leaned toward the mirror.

She looked like a boy.

Anna sucked on her teeth, fingers tapping against the most pitiful, spur of the moment vanity she had ever had the displeasure of utilizing. Her gaze hopped from one insignificant item in the room to the next, doing everything in her power to avoid meeting the gaze of the woman behind her.

Doing so would only provoke conversation, and Anna had no intentions of entertaining small talk.

The thin copper tub in the corner caught her attention first; she held it within her sight for as long as she could stomach, heart rate steadily rising with each passing second. The water had surely gone cold by now. Anna had refused to climb beneath its still, steaming waters when it had been brought in. Instead, she'd quickly washed herself off with a washcloth and nearly drowned herself in floral perfume.

Anna had just finished dressing when this woman threw the door open and invited herself in. The woman, with a tray in hand, had happily disclosed that her name was Zarya, and she was one of the cooks aboard the *Pale Queen*. Anna had prayed she was the one responsible for the delicious soups and pastries and not the monstrosity the Pirate King tried passing off as tea.

If she hadn't known any better, Anna would have guessed Lovelace was trying to poison her.

It would have been poetic justice if it was true.

Glancing back to Zarya, she sighed quietly. The woman had long, dark hair plaited back into a singular braid that was tied off with a red ribbon. Her eyes were a striking emerald color framed in long dark lashes—not unlike Hadley's, which might have been what raised her hackles to begin with.

Anna gnawed on her lip.

Zarya was beautiful and proportioned in a way she never would be.

Her splendid hourglass frame was more than a contrast to that of Anna's pear shape. She'd never cared about her body's shape before; if anything, Anna had flaunted it and used it to her advantage. She was an heiress with the resources to acquire brilliant gowns and the confidence to fill them. But Anna *had* found the dresses the Pirate King had spoken of.

Those dresses would have been terribly loose on Anna's bust and incredibly tight on her hips and thighs.

But, good God, they would have fit Zarya splendidly.

Anna hadn't planned on entertaining the Pirate King's daft idea of dressing her like a doll. She'd been *curious*. Once she had been filled to the brim with disappointment and had cursed her curiosity, Anna had dressed in something more practical, something she could fight and run in—because she expected to have to do those by night's end.

Cream cotton breeches fit her like a second skin, and dark, supple boots reached her knees. The sapphire shirt she wore was short-sleeved and fit snugly in the waist. The buttons on the shirt were brass, and she'd left a scandalizing number of them undone.

If Markus had been here, he would have—

Clenching her jaw, she traced her scar in the mirror.

He would be fine. He would be fine. He would be—

"Finished."

Good God, she hoped not.

Glancing over her shoulder and into the mirror, Anna was reminded that every single one of the dresses would have fit Zarya splendidly.

Perhaps the Pirate King had a type.

Not that she cared.

It would certainly explain the complete abandon with which Zarya had opened the door and her ease within these quarters. Anna sucked on her teeth. She would not care—she wouldn't. She *didn't*. It was none of her concern and even less of her business which women Lovelace fancied, no matter how much it hollowed her traitorous insides.

They'd kissed once, that was all.

Except it wasn't all, and she desperately tried forcing that knowledge from her mind as Zarya stepped back and admired her handiwork. If not for the woman's careful, patient fingers, Anna likely would have had to cut her hair even shorter. Her gaze dropped to those fingers now, expecting long, elegant instruments, and paused.

Zarya's fingers were long and narrow like a pianist's might be—like Anna had expected them to be—but they were horrifically scarred.

Good God, what had happened?

Zarya clasped her hands in front of her body. A rush of heat flooded her cheeks at being caught staring and met her own icy blue gaze in the mirror. Just over her shoulder, Zarya leaned forward, arms crossed beneath her bust. She smiled softly, lips full against bright, white teeth.

"You are lovely," she said quietly. "When you are in that place, remember you're seeing the captain through his eyes."

Anna's gaze darted to meet the bright green of Zarya's. "What do you mean?"

She opened her mouth, but a knock on the door pulled their attention to the back of the room.

Using the mirror, Anna looked toward the noise and found Lovelace leaning against the frame. There was a frown etched upon his face, and his eyebrows were pinched together as he fussed with the lapels of his captain's coat. His hair was wet, and it wasn't until she cleared her throat that his gaze raised from his fingers.

They made eye contact through the mirror, and something warm zinged through her chest.

Good God.

If not for watching her squeeze past the Pirate King, Anna never would have noticed Zarya's absence. Sweat dripped down her spine as she stared at him in disbelief. Out of all the ways she had imagined the Pirate King meeting his demise, heat stroke was not one of them.

A pair of dark trousers clung to his legs, dropping from his waist into well-loved boots that ended at his calves. A wide belt enveloped his hips and stomach, and a blue sash stuck out the top and bottom. Lovelace had hardly laced the top of his off-white shirt, showing off the hard muscles of his chest and the tattoos covering his skin. Then, of course, was the gaudy captain's coat. Made from a thick, inky material and trimmed in silver, it billowed softly behind him on the warm breeze.

For their plan to visit an island supposedly rife with danger, the Pirate King had a surprising lack of weapons. His lips twitched into a small smile at her slow examination. Warmth prickled at her cheeks as his gaze lowered, chin dipping.

Am I to your liking? she wanted to ask.

Instead, she said, "Are you finished staring?"

"Are ye finished wi' being angry?"

Anna's gaze narrowed at him. No, she was not.

Lovelace nodded his head, not quite in defeat but something that may have been cousins with it. He pushed off the wall, hands hanging at his sides. His slow steps were soft against the pale planks despite his boots.

"So...you're mad *and* ye do no' trust me."

"Have you given me any reasons to?"

"You're alive, aye?" he murmured, taking another leisurely step.

"Setting the bar a bit low, are we?"

The Pirate King sighed through his nose, clearly aggravated. "Does a name really matter that bloody much to ye, lass?"

Anna nearly laughed; a name had never meant anything to her.

In Briland, a name was the trumpet signaling one's status, it was a placeholder given to one on a silver spoon. A name didn't tell her if an individual was fair or hardworking, it didn't tell her if they were honest. But a name was composed of letters, every one of them a vessel for meaning and power if she allowed them to hold it.

It just so happened that most of the names Anna had allowed an ounce of influence and grandeur belonged to members of Lovelace's crew—and it was *his* name that mattered most.

"Not usually," she said, her voice quieting. "But you know why yours did."

She might not have been able to admit it if she had to really look him in the eye instead of meeting his gaze through the mirror.

"Because we fu—" He looked away, a flush high on his cheeks and pinkening his ears.

Anna laughed, using the vanity to push into a standing position as she faced him.

"Anna, I—"

"I don't trust most of the men I fuck," she said crassly, cheeks burning. "Is that why you're here? To remind me of the consequences of my actions? Because if you are, let me assure you I am well aware that you are one of them."

Lovelace's throat bobbed, and he stopped in his tracks. "No, lass. We've reached Tiburon, 'tis time to go ashore. If you're ready, that is."

"Splendid." She clapped her hands, stalking forward. As she passed the Pirate King, he latched onto her bicep, anchoring her in place. The heat of his hand burned through her thin cotton shirt, leaving the impression of his palm on her arm. Anna glanced up at him, brow raised.

"'Tis going to be dangerous," he murmured, closing the distance between them. "The Coalition will challenge me, and I'll have to be fucking ruthless, and..."

"And yet I don't see a single weapon on you."

"I can kill every gods-damned prick in that room before most even have the chance to stand," he growled. "I can protect ye, Anna; ye have naught to worry about."

"Confident."

"Skills like mine do wonders to a male's confidence," he said quietly, leaning closer.

Gaze narrowing, she dropped her voice to a near whisper. "Why are you telling me this?"

"Ye deserve to know what you're walking into. I've always been honest, and I know what kind of trouble ye chase, but I'm the gods-damn king for a reason, and you're going to see why if ye come wi', lass. Really *see* it. I can no' be what I have been."

The last sentence broke from his mouth in a pained whisper.

His fingers slipped from her arm as he stepped away. Anna felt the loss of his hand as if his fingers had laid roots and grown into her skin. His foot slid back, boot dragging against the floorboards. As the Pirate King stared down at her, his jaw clenched, and his fingers twitched at his side.

Clearly, unspoken words wanted out.

"I'm worried they'll see it," he finally whispered, voice nearly inaudible.

Anna wasn't entirely sure what he meant by *it*, but she had the sense that it was heavy—like a noose around one's neck or a cannon-ball tied to laces.

Clearing his throat, he held out his arm. Anna glanced at his peace offering before looking back into his dark gaze. Emotion rolled through his eyes like the storm clouds that chased them. "I swear to every god that swims in these seas, Anna, I'll help ye find that brother of yours. Just...fuck, do no' do anything daft. Or at least bloody well warn me first. *Please*."

"I promise nothing," she said, tentatively threading her arm through his.

Lovelace leaned toward her, something warmer than amusement flooding his features.

A man cleared his throat.

Her gaze flicked toward the door—how long had Tate been standing there?

"We're just waiting on ye, Trev," Tate said, a small chuckle leaving his lips.

He'd pulled his hair into a bun. The sunlight spilling from the open double doors only served to highlight the beautiful bronze and gold beads woven through his wine-red locks.

Whatever heat that had built up beneath her skin fizzled into warm embarrassment. Tate's eyebrow raised as he stared at them, another god-awful grin appearing on his face. Anna glanced from the quartermaster to his brother, unease tightening in her gut as her cheeks grew warmer.

Bugger, they hadn't done anything that warranted Tate's teasing gaze.

"Aye, here I come," Trevor Lovelace said, pulling away from her and shoving his hands into his pockets.

The quartermaster's grin widened until it was a crooked, devious thing. "Don't rush on my account; I'm in no bloody hurry."

Grunting his response, the Pirate King stormed forward, leaving Anna to stare at his back as she followed him. Tate nodded his head at his brother, but grinned wickedly down at her as she passed.

Nothing happened, she wanted to growl at him, and yet threading her arm through the Pirate King's had felt as scandalous as running through the Bellcaster harbor naked.

Anna ignored the quartermaster as she passed him—if he wanted to believe in some ridiculous shenanigans, she'd let him. Tate Lovelace wouldn't be the first man to make assumptions and he certainly wouldn't be the last.

It was warm outside, the sun painfully bright. Anna held up a hand to blot it out and trailed after the large, looming shadow Trevor Lovelace left in his wake. His steps were long but lazy, the epitome of a man who did not want to appear in a hurry despite the ground he covered with each step.

A warm breeze rolled off the island, bringing with it the brilliant scents one expected from tropical islands—albeit a tropical island at the forefront of supposedly cursed waters, but a tropical island, nonetheless.

Lovelace slowed, gaze on the contrasting greens of large trees and the white sandy beaches. Tropical birds of every color and design called back and forth, their brightly colored feathers soaring above and lingering in the jungle. Nearly hidden from view and cast in the shadows of great palms were bits and pieces of ships. Some were brightly colored, others old and weathered.

Anna leaned against the taffrail and looked down into the crystal-clear shallows of Tiburon. Just below the *Pale Queen*, hammerheads swam back and forth, their elongated heads carving through the water with ease. Farther out were the remains of ships that had tried to sail the southeastern tip and failed.

The sunken vessels were brilliantly clear beneath the water. If she had wanted, Anna could have counted each plank or starfish upon their hulls. Some sported figureheads of ancient gods or voluptuous sirens, but none were as ethereal or full of grace as the *Pale Queen*. Colorful fish darted in and around the ships, and the seagrass floated off the hull like mermaid hair, ebbing with the tide.

Tiburon might look positively idyllic, but it was easy to hide something monstrous beneath a pretty veneer.

Stomach twisting, Anna turned her attention to the hustle and bustle on the main deck. The crew was busy at work, loading and unloading various crates into small boats. Lovelace had said they needed to restock supplies, but it looked like the crew intended to take everything that wasn't bolted down ashore.

Her gaze wandered the deck until it landed on the *Pale Queen's* captain not five feet from her. Leaning with his back to the taffrail,

Lovelace slouched with his arms crossed against his chest, seemingly unbothered by the sun or warm kiss of the wind. He had to be sweating near to death in that damn coat—not that she cared. As if feeling the weight of her gaze, his shoulders stiffened, and his thumb started tapping against his arm.

"The *Queen* needs to be careened," he finally said without turning to her. "Means we've to unload everything and beach her. Works best if we let the tide do most of the work."

"Seems tedious."

"It might to some," he agreed. "But I like the work, it suits me."

Anna snorted—of course a man with a physique like the Pirate King found honest, hard work enjoyable. Across the deck, Tate motioned for one thing or another. The quartermaster was shirtless yet again, showing off the muscles of his torso and arms.

Good God, was it genetics?

Were Lovelaces simply predisposed to be pleasing to the eye?

"Well?"

"Well, *what?*" she asked, slowly turning to face him.

A handsome grin already pulled at his lips. "Is it to your liking?"

Am I to your liking? echoed softly in the recesses of her mind.

Anna looked over her shoulder, attention shifting from the warm, crystalline waters to the white sandy beaches before scanning the tropical jungle peppered with pastel-colored structures. Bugger, the island would have been perfect if not for the Pirate King's claim to it. Something about the sway of the trees and how the sunlight glinted off the water called to her. There were secrets and stories beneath the surface of Tiburon, too—a monstrous spirit beneath an idyllic face.

Bugger, that might be what excited her most.

"I suppose..." She trailed off as she tracked another shirtless crew member as he strutted past.

A layer of sweat glittered against his skin. Anna squinted at him. Had she seen him before? A small grin twitched at her lips; it was the same man as before, the one who had been scrubbing the deck.

From the corner of her eye, she watched Lovelace trace the path of her gaze. At finding the object of her interest, his throat bobbed, and he turned away from her. His smoldering eyes were rife with unsaid words. He couldn't be jealous, could he? Well, if the Pirate King didn't know he was much prettier than the man walking across the deck, Anna wasn't going to be the one to tell him.

Crossing her arms beneath her breasts, she raised a brow. "The view is surprisingly delightful."

"The bloody *island,* lass."

Dragging her attention from his boots to his face, she leaned back against the taffrail. "Oh...*that.* Bugger, I hadn't noticed the thing. I suppose Tiburon wouldn't be such a terrible place to be marooned. Likely full of secrets just waiting to be uncovered."

Trevor snorted and pushed off the taffrail. "Every shore past the Black Line has been hollowed out by bloody secrets. Tiburon just happens to have the fewest—and it's the loveliest."

"All the islands?" she asked, steps falling against the pale planks in time with his.

"Oh, aye."

"And here I thought all the islands past the Black Line held *treasure* of epic"—Anna stopped, eyes widening at the small symbol from the map as the jaguar floated back to the forefront of her mind—"The Immortal Cup, Eero's Chalice."

"Ye read the map?"

"Of course, I read the map. Eero's Chalice is a myth, though," Anna said, frowning. "What could my father possibly want with a *myth?*"

"One might say I'm a bloody myth," he muttered, making a beeline for his brother. Trevor Lovelace cleared his throat, soft brogue raising above the commotion of the crew. "Aside from the gods-damned immortality? Fuck if I know, but the bastard is going to have a hell of a time finding it. I reckon your da's more interested in what sleeps there, anyway—few years ago, there was word of a bloody senator asking about it."

Her father desired what supposedly slept on the island?

What had been scrawled into the corner of the damn map?

Staring hard at the ground, she tried to dredge up the rough impressions of the map that had remained with her, but it was just out of reach. Most of that night was a blur of sensations at best and a slurry of nightmares at worst. But even if she could recall the finer points of the Pirate King's map, she had no way of investigating them. No Bellcaster Grand Library, no sneaking into the bowels of the university or bribing the Board of Antiquity's pages to bring her certain scrolls and texts from the archives.

She had *nothing,* not even Mihk to volunteer his services as a sounding board.

Good God, she'd give her left leg for Mihkel Tamm and his prudish wit right about now.

Lovelace whistled, loud and shrill. A chorus of responses echoed back, layered with the calls of gulls and tropical birds. Beneath it all, the tide lapped at the *Pale Queen's* hull, rocking them softly. Markus required saving yet again, and the Pirate King was the only resource she possessed.

It's for Markus, she told herself, *you do not have a single book—you do not even have Mihk.*

"And *what,*" she asked pointedly, "sleeps there?"

"Look at ye asking a question," the Pirate King said, turning his head to grin at her. "The Kraken, for one."

Was she supposed to believe her father was after some creature of the deep, all tentacles and terror, beak and blood, and as large as a ship? Anna had read old accounts while studying as a child; they had all seemed impossible then, and her opinion on the matter hadn't changed.

"The Kraken is an old story to explain why ships have gone missing at sea, there's no way...it can't...it's not real. I'm not some child that believes in old Aepith stories. They were nothing but Neolithic man's way of explaining what was considered incomprehensible at the—"

"Have ye seen your hand, lass?" Lovelace said, placing his foot against the taffrail.

"*What are you—*" Anna started, heart thundering as he climbed up.

"Ye might want to reconsider believing in Aepith stories," he said, stepping into the open air.

A scream formed in her throat at watching him drop over the taffrail and toward the ocean for the second time in as many weeks. Lunging forward, she looked over the edge wildly, waiting to see bubbles frothing up or to watch his body sink to the ocean floor. She couldn't swim—she wouldn't be able to dive in after him.

The echo of a phantom storm and her own cries filled her ears.

"—ready, Anna?" he asked, hand outstretched.

Lovelace stood in a longboat, brows furrowed as he stared back up at her.

"What?" she asked, feeling the warmth of the sun on her skin.

"Are ye ready?"

Nodding her head, she placed her hand in his and allowed the Pirate King to help her into the longboat. His fingers were warm and rough against hers, the flesh of a man in his prime, not of one who had been drowned and brought back to life.

He was alive.

He was alive.

He was alive, and she wanted to strangle him for that stunt. She glanced at the strong column of his throat before noticing three others in the longboat with them. Anna wasn't entirely surprised to see Juliana Gray and Tate Lovelace, but she didn't recognize the dark-skinned man already seated amongst crates and burlap sacks with them.

Sighing, she pressed close to the Pirate King on the opposite bench.

It seemed the safest place to sit, considering Juliana looked ready to bite and the obnoxious grin remained on the quartermaster's face. The third pirate appeared nice enough—he had pleasant features and an easy smile. It was a stark contrast to the Man-Eater's pinched brow and deep scowl, or the way she sat with her hands fisted in her lap.

The longboat lurched as they were lowered into the waiting grasp of the sea, souring her veins with fear. Tate and the unnamed pirate each grabbed an oar and started rowing. The paddles cut into the water's surface like a hot knife through butter. The despicable rocking tied her stomach into painful knots. Normally, she would anchor her attention on the horizon, on a space far off that didn't move, but she couldn't bring herself to look away from the matching pale planks of the longboat.

Anna hadn't been able to stare into her bathwater, she wasn't entirely sure how she would tackle the ocean.

A curious dark sack laid at their feet, and the smell wafting off the bugger scrunched her nose. Good God, it was an awful stench— rotten and decayed. She breathed deep despite the burning in her nostrils—something about it was familiar, but she couldn't quite put her finger on it.

Anna kept her eyes down; it was better than meeting Tate's inquisitive gaze or the Man-Eater's golden-green stare with its feral gleam. The Pirate King bumped her once with his shoulder and then again with his elbow.

"Docile as a wee doe," he whispered down to her.

"Keep reminding me and that's the last thing you're going to get."

With every pass of an oar, Tiburon grew closer; once the water shallowed, Tate and the dark-skinned pirate jumped from the side. The echo of the splash raised the hair along her arms, but a quick glance revealed the water was no deeper than their knees. Neither man seemed to mind their trousers and boots getting soaked.

They started pushing the boat, muscles along their arms straining. Tate's jaw ticked from the effort as the longboat scraped against the sandy shallows. Fifty paces to their right, a contingent of the Pirate King's crew stood, most with long ropes in their hands.

Anna squinted at the froth along the beach and the crystal-clear waters that hid nothing. Most islands had some sharp drops and inclines, a rocky jut just waiting to tear holes in a hull. This portion of Tiburon didn't, though, it was gently sloped with soft beaches the whole way down.

Juliana Gray and Trevor Lovelace jumped from the longboat and onto soggy sand as Anna scanned the rest of the beach. The master gunner stalked off, screaming something at the men holding ropes.

She called again, and the crew started to pull, some singing and others bellowing out the chorus as they stepped backward in unison.

Lovelace waited next to the longboat, water lapping at his boots as he held out his hand in offering. Ignoring it, she clenched the side of the boat and propelled herself over edge and into the soupy sand. Anna retreated inland quickly; the gentle brush of the tide against her boots was all the incentive she needed.

Wrapping her arms around herself, Anna's gaze slid from the expanse of white sand to the greenery of the jungle. It seemed to stretch onward forever. When they had been standing on the *Queen's* deck, she had seen old bits of ship and colorful wooden structures, but from here on the beach, all she saw was the mist weaving through the tropical jungle and shadows reaching between the trees.

Anna turned at the sound of rustling clothes and blinked.

Apparently, Tate and the nameless pirate *had* minded soaking their boots and trousers.

Her lips pressed into a thin line at seeing the tanned skin of Tate's rump and the thick muscle of the other pirate's thighs. She cleared her throat as the dark-skinned pirate dragged a new pair of trousers up his legs. Loud and carefree, Tate laughed and bent to grab his trousers and shake the sand from them. Anna immediately turned around, biting her tongue to hide her smile.

"Bloody hell, Tate, cover your ass!" The Pirate King growled, annoyance and embarrassment woven delicately into his tone. His eyes darted to her. "We've a *lady* present, shite-head."

Looking over her shoulder, she caught Tate mocking his brother beneath his breath. The nameless pirate stood with an awkward smile as he tied the misshapen sack to his belt.

Bugger, why were they bringing the smelly sack?

"I can't stand wet clothes, and ye know we've to keep the poor bastard dry," Tate said, grinning. He cocked his head suddenly as he tightened his belt. "Miss Savage, ye haven't been introduced yet, have ye? Bodhi here is the surgeon on the *Pale Queen*."

"Salutations," Anna said, glancing curiously at the burlap that swung at Bodhi's side. "And you believe our confrontation with the Coalition chiefs will require a surgeon?"

Tate chuckled. "Oh, lassie, *we* won't need one, but *they* bloody well might."

"Splendid," she said, squinting at their surroundings once more.

There truly wasn't a single soul on the beach except for those belonging to the Pirate King. If not for the prospect of unearthing delicious secrets at the Coalition meeting, she might have taken Lovelace up on his offer of sunbathing.

"This beach is only used for careening."

"For everyone?" she asked, turning to look at Trevor.

"Not for everyone, no," he said, walking toward the treeline. Tate and Bodhi were several feet in front of him. For a moment, Lovelace's face grew stern, brows pinched and nose curled as he turned to Bodhi. "Sorry about that, mate."

Bodhi shrugged, an easy grin back on his face. When he spoke, it was soft and sincere, "Not a problem, Captain."

There were stories hidden in his voice, Anna was certain of it.

A literal line had been drawn in the sand between the beach and the jungle. The trees closest to the beach were smaller with long, thin leaves. Small trails of sand bled into the shroud of the canopy, and sweet floral scents carried on the breeze. It was a much-needed reprieve from the rancid sack at the surgeon's side.

As they passed under the blanket of thick shadows, Anna glanced upward. The trees stretched toward the sky, branches reaching for the sun. The tree trunks were a multitude of browns and tans, creating a collage of varying color.

Soon, the soft sand turned into springy loam, and little bushes sprung up on either side of the meandering path. Vibrant flowers sprouted from the ground in dense patches, their stems and leaves the color of emeralds. The sun broke through the canopy in small patches along the jungle floor in patterns that reminded her of the print on a leopard's coat.

The hair on the back of her neck raised once more, pulling her gaze upward. Anna couldn't see the canopy completely, a fine mist kept it enshrouded, but she felt watched. With the intrigue and mystery surrounding Tiburon, she half-expected to see glowing red eyes peering down at her from above. Every time she turned upward, though, she only caught the quick flutter of wings or a falling feather.

For an allegedly haunted jungle, it was surprisingly quiet—though she had never put much stock in the mad ravings of men who had returned with less of their mind than they'd set out with.

All that lies past the Black Line is madness, her mother had told her once, head bent over a worn journal.

And Tiburon? Anna had asked as she leaned her chin against her mother's desk.

I imagine that's where it starts.

"Don't worry, lass." Tate chuckled, ruffling her hair as they stepped onto a fine carpet of moss. "I'll protect ye."

Anna shucked his hand from her head and glared at him. "What gave you the impression I was worried?"

"You're a wee fem, of course, you'd be terrified of traipsing through a cursed jungle. Naught to be ashamed of, lass."

"I hold very few fears," she told him. "Trees and shadows are not amongst them."

"Oh? What do ye fear, then?" Tate grinned up at the canopy as he walked next to her. "My brother told me his lass was fucking daft, but he did no' say she was so brave."

His.

Anna might have ignored the quartermaster's wording if not for how Trevor Lovelace stiffened ahead of them. He had rolled the sleeves of his captain's coat up at some point and his hands were pressed deeply into his pockets. Tracing the tattoos along his forearms with her eyes, she considered every possible fear she could share with Tate Lovelace if she wished. She didn't need to say anything, and yet she found herself opening her mouth and turning to look up at him.

"Losing my brother," she said honestly.

It was an old fear, one she had lived with for as long as she could remember. Anna had grown accustomed to its weight, to that prickle in her veins. Maybe if she focused on an old fear, the cold press of dark tides wouldn't haunt her quite so terribly.

Anna had forgotten what fresh fear was like.

Tate nodded his head, smile falling from his face like a petal drifting to the ground—slow and sad, elegant in a way she didn't think it should be. "Ye might have more in common wi' my brother than ye think."

"What do you mean?"

"You're no' the only one who'd do anything for the ones they love, Anna." He paused, tucking a stray strand of hair behind his ear. His sleeve fell with the action, revealing the wicked-looking blades tattooed along his forearm. "Reckon even ye would sell your soul to the bloody devil if it meant keeping your brother safe."

Anna snorted; he wasn't wrong.

She would go past the ends of the earth for Markus, but a crippling fear slept beneath her bravado and anger for the Pirate King; it danced hand-in-hand with her worry over her brother. He was positively brilliant when he needed to be, but that atrocious map had been scribed in blood in a language that had given Anna difficulty when deciphering it.

Markus could do it—*eventually*.

But of all the things Bryce had been, patient was not one of them.

Shaking her head, she returned her focus to the narrow, beaten path.

The pirates knew exactly where they ventured, leaving Anna to amble along after them, gaze scouring their surroundings for clues or threats. She didn't know these trees or the trails that wove between them, but that didn't mean she wouldn't by the trail's end. If she could find her way through Heylik Toyer with relative ease, she could find her way out of a jungle on Tiburon.

The treeline on her right thinned, revealing glimpses of what lay behind the sweltering heat and sticky jungle air—buildings painted in pastel colors, narrow paths edged in tall seagrass, and bright flowers. The small voices and laughter of children followed the briny sea breeze through the trees.

But it was just a glimpse, there and then gone.

"Keep your eyes down, Miss Savage," Bodhi whispered from behind, voice like mahogany and mist. "Don't look too close at the shadows."

Anna nearly laughed.

Of course, he wanted to avert her attention from the treeline.

She wouldn't be able to find her way if she'd never seen it before.

"If..." she started, mouth slowly closing as a chill crept up her spine.

A sudden wrongness struck her; that was the only way to describe the immediate stiffening of her muscles and the plummeting temperature. Gnawing on her lip, she crept forward with her gaze centered on the Pirate King's back. His shoulders had stiffened, and his shadow grew darker as it trailed after him.

How strange that she could see its outline so clearly beneath the shadow of the canopy.

The scent in the air clung to her, it was oily and almost metallic like—*blood*. Anna scowled as the atrocious smell slid against her flesh, creating a film against her skin. Rubbing her arms, she kept her gaze on the impressions the Pirate King left behind in the loamy soil.

Every step forward pulled at her bones as if her very soul protested the prospect of venturing further beneath the darkening canopy. The path widened, flanked by misshapen rocks and crumbling tree trunks covered in moss.

Anna spun her mother's ring with her thumb at a furious pace, forcing deep, even breaths into her lungs. Whatever laid ahead would be fine, it would be explainable. The damn pirates might not be invested in a logical answer, but she was a scholar—if there was an answer to be had, she would find it.

Steps slowing, she squinted down at a particularly large rock, smoothed from time and weather. A pictograph stared up at her from beneath clumps of tangled moss. It had been etched first and then painted a rusty red that blended in rather well with the weathering on the rock.

Hello, there, she cooed to herself, gaze devouring every detail. Her brows furrowed, and something cousins to annoyance settled deep in her gut. *Why is it always Aepith?*

Whoever had scribbled over the rocks did not want anyone stumbling this way into the jungle. She had never feared a place rumored as cursed, had never shied away from an adventure that promised something unearthly. Those outings had never been anything more than the sleight of an ancient hand or smoke and mirrors, though.

But that didn't mean the warnings here were unwarranted.

Another shiver crept up her spine. Something was terribly wrong here.

She might not ascribe to the same mythic mumbo-jumbo as the Pirate King, but that didn't mean Anna ignored the apprehension making itself home in her gut. Running her tongue over her teeth, she stared down at another lumpy rock with the same symbol scrawled into it—*danger*. Most of the khan's temples had elicited a similar response from her bones.

What could have possibly caused it?

Better yet, what was it hiding?

That had been the rub of all the khan's sacred places and temples: more often not, the path of most resistance held the greatest reward at its center. Anna watched the Pirate King belligerently step over a line of painted rocks and into a dense jungle thicket.

Should she warn him about potential booby traps?

She shook her head. The pirates knew where they were going; they picked their path with scrutiny.

The shadows off the beaten path grew darker, but she could still see the outline of the Pirate King's shadow against them, twice as dark as any shroud spilled from the trees. The air bit her lungs, and her breath fanned in front of her face in thick clouds. The skin along Anna's arms prickled, the cool touch of darkness dragging her back beneath the sea.

Anna leaned into the heat radiating off the Pirate King's back. The least the scoundrel could have done was warn her about the drastic changes in Tiburon's microclimates. If not him, anyone on his damn crew could have suggested—

Her head turned as quick as a whip to the right.

Pins and needles raised along her skin and dragged their cool fingers up her spine, forming an uncomfortable point between her shoulders. She'd been watched all her life; she knew what it felt like to be caught between someone's crosshairs.

Anna turned her head to the right. If she was being watched, where were they hiding?

Tate and Bodhi walked two paces behind her. The disgusting sack hanging from Bodhi's belt swung with his steps like a pendulum on a clock. Tate raised a brow at her, his own gaze sliding to her left and right. Shaking her head, he faced forward once more, letting her attention settle on the canopy.

"Do not look," Bodhi warned again in a murmur, his voice carrying on some frozen breeze. "No one likes what they see."

Her brows pulled together.

What more was there to see than shadows and trees? They'd long since passed any buildings masquerading as civilized establishments with their laughing children. Is that what he meant? That Anna wouldn't like the pastel-colored buildings and the quaint families that inhabited them? Well, he was right—it clashed terribly with what she could remember of her last visit to Tiburon.

Nothing quite says "idyllic destination" like rusty cages and rubbish.

The bushes rustled to her left, leaves shivering and shaking. Delicate petals of little flowers drifted downward as another set of saplings trembled. Anna turned, tracking the fast movement in a patch of ferns. It ended at a tree, its base spanning at least fifty feet. The trunk climbed high, its top hidden in the haze above. Knobby roots like the knuckles on a crone's fingers stretched up from the ground.

She noticed the quiet then, how the jungle held its breath. The hum of insects had silenced, and a bird's wings ruffled one last time before the jungle descended into stiff silence. Anna lifted her foot to take another step, her gaze straying to a strange shine on the shadows. Cocking her head, she squinted at them.

How curious, they looked more like obsidian mirrors or still pools of ink.

Like his—

Do not look.

Her pulse hammered in her ears, and everything slowed. From the corner of her eye, she saw Lovelace's coat blow back on a breeze, its movements akin to molasses in winter. It wasn't possible to tear her attention away from the trees and their dark reflection. Then from out of the quiet, the rushing of waves and wailing of wind grew until she heard nothing else.

And a voice, wretched and hoarse.

In her periphery, she saw herself staring with eyes like an abyss. Not like the Pirate King's—no, this other Anna's eyes were black with no trace of white. She stepped forward, flora disintegrating into black dust as she passed. A grin split her face, and her head cocked to the side with a crack like thunder.

No one likes what they see.

Shadows spilled forward from the darkness between the trees. Reaching forward, they consumed the not-Anna as they barreled onward with edges like torn paper. Anna couldn't move, but her mouth and tongue burned with the taste of rum.

Goosebumps raised along her arms, her foot finally falling. She was going to be sick; nausea churned in her gut and broke a light sweat upon her skin. The wretched voice from earlier grew from a whisper into a scream, hoarse and cracking. Her eyes widened, and a tremor of fear ripped through her.

It was Lovelace's—*Trevor's*—voice shouting across the void.

Everything blurred together into a collage of shapes and colors except for those blasted shadows, and still he screamed, mournful and devastated, but Anna couldn't see him. She couldn't even turn her damn head away from the veil in front of her. Panic seared her veins, making it nearly impossible to think past the emotion thickening his voice and catching in his throat.

Anna hadn't been able to leave him on Cunningham's ship and she wouldn't be able to do so now.

Nothing had changed.

He was her friend even if the word didn't sit right on her tongue or in her head.

His voice cracked, a choked sob echoing forth, and she could feel it, feel the visceral heartbreak and hopelessness.

Her foot was so close to the jungle floor but not quite there. Anna blinked, closing her eyes against the wind that raged and tore at her like nails. And then she screamed—or at least tried to. The pain in her stomach nearly crippled her as something warm and wet ran like a river down her stomach. Bugger—that was blood. She was bleeding—bleeding out. Her chest tightened and breathing became an effort as the chill set in, as the dread and knowing settled deep in her bones like a seedling taking root.

And still, Trevor screamed.

Anna's boot scuffed against the ground.

The shadows shrank back, and she felt the sun warm on her face as every sound disappeared.

CHAPTER TWENTY-TWO

In his dream he stood in front of a mirror, a boy of eleven staring back up at him. It wasn't another version of himself, not another Markus in another place, the difference of a single choice separating them. No, this was a memory—this *was* him. He knew by his hands at his sides and the red coloring of his cheeks.

By the stinging he felt in his eyes even now, a ghost of what it had been at eleven.

He remembered picking a fight with one of the other senator's sons; that's where the dirt on his coat had come from, why his white button-up was untucked and peppered with dust. Drops of blood had fallen onto the front of the monstrosity, part of the uniform of the boarding school his father had carted them off to at the time.

Markus couldn't recall which boy he'd fought, but he remembered all too well why he'd slugged the prick in the first place.

He had spoken poorly of Anna.

Markus stood up for his sister all the time; the boys and girls at the boarding school always had something to say about her. They whispered near open windows and behind cracked doors.

Did you know Anna was caught kissing Bryce Cunningham behind the old oak in the courtyard?

I did!

My daddy told me they're sending her to a special boarding school for feral little girls.

But that wasn't what had bothered him.

It was the conversation with their father afterward, when John Savage had asked why Markus was picking so many fights over words —*words are worthless, fickle things,* his father had said in that stern bored way of his. *Why do you let them bother you?*

"Because," Markus told himself now in the mirror, "words are meaningful. If you're told something over and over again, eventually, it'll be true."

Like the tide eating away the beach, his mother had chided one day after he called his sister something rude, *everything falls to the subtlety of consistent erosion—even people.*

A hand landed on his shoulder.

Markus glanced at the mirror, recognizing the snake scale cufflinks and his father's ring on his right hand. There had been a time when he hadn't hated the sight of that blasted ring and all it meant.

Today marked the day between before and after, caught in limbo.

Before today, Markus had marveled at the solid gold ring, a serpent with glittering green eyes winding its way around his father's finger. After today, Markus would grow irate at seeing the damn thing. Over time, it would look more like a noose poised to tighten around his neck.

He didn't want to inherit his father's acquisitions nor the means with which he had obtained them.

New money, they had called Markus before he knew what that meant.

His father sighed behind him. "We've been over this, Markus. I built bridges so you could walk across them, not use them as tinder."

"I don't need your bridges; I'll swim."

His father stared down at him, disappointment clear on his face. Markus hadn't understood it at the time; Anna's marks had always been better than his and she handled Bellcaster with far more grace than he could ever stomach. Or at least she had until they were seventeen or eighteen. She had decided then that catering to the needs of Bellcaster high society was a waste of her time.

Markus had never understood why anyone would make themselves smaller to please another, and he'd thanked every god his mother had taught him about when Anna realized the same.

"Markus," she whispered in his ear now.

He turned his head, following the halo of her curls, springy and nearly white like when they were children. Blinking awake, he rubbed his eyes and stared into the darkness. A minute passed in silence, followed by her quiet giggle.

Did she think she was a schoolgirl again?

Good God, he'd have to remind his sister she was nearly an old maid.

But then her laugh deepened into something other; something that could never belong to his sister. It was husky and dark, curling his toes and pulling him upright on the bed. Markus squinted into the dark, running his gaze along the orderly stacks of books and old leather-bound journals. His heart clenched at the sight of them standing sentinel over him, like some part of his mother that had been left behind to guard him in his sleep.

Because that's what the blasted books were.

His *mother's* journals and the dusty tomes he remembered her poring over late at night.

"I should have let you drown," the woman whispered, a chuckle chasing her words.

The sound drew his attention to a pair of golden-green eyes hanging in the air near the doorway. They were loosely almond shaped and narrowed into a sharp glare, the whites nearly luminescent.

Markus would know that gaze anywhere.

He would know it in his sleep and in his death.

That's how he knew it was not Juliana Gray.

"Who are you?" he asked quietly, leaning onto his elbows.

Her sparkling white smile cracked against the darkness, crooked and full of too many canines.

"I should have let you drown," she whispered hoarsely. "Won't you come and drown?"

It was the kind of whisper he wanted to hear from a woman late at night, wrapped in nothing but silk or his arms. The tip of one of her fingers beckoned him forth. Markus's legs slid over the edge of the bed, feet slapping against the cool planks of their own accord.

The wound at his stomach pulled angrily, drenching his back and chest in sweat nearly immediately. Swallowing past a knot of pain, he placed a hand over the injury and marveled at the heat wafting from it. One of his feet slid forward and then he braced his hands at the edge of the bed. His brows furrowed and he prepared for the sharp pain that would erupt in his gut as soon as he stood.

The door cracked against the frame with a loud clap.

The golden-green gaze disappeared, and the room suddenly filled with light and the calls of the crew. Cunningham stumbled in, leaning against the door frame as he took deep, heaving breaths. His feet were bare, and his long-sleeved shirt hung from his shoulder.

Markus's gaze narrowed at the sudden brightness. His surprise at the captain's rather rude introduction was smothered by his confusion at Cunningham's erratic state.

Were those scars?

Anna had never mentioned the small, shiny white scars along the swell of Bryce's pec.

"Do not," he heaved, throat bobbing as he glanced over his shoulder wildly, hair in disarray. "Do not leave this room."

"May I ask why?"

A splash echoed in the distance.

Cunningham sighed, his profile haloed by light. "Myths, monsters, and men with no real sense of conviction."

"I find men lose what little loyalty they might have when faced with the unknown or certain death," Markus said off-handedly, head pounding with his lack of sleep.

He couldn't have been asleep for long, certainly not long enough to deter the stinging in his eyes. Markus pinched the bridge of his nose and closed his eyes tight. It could not have been a coincidence that his headache always worsened with the appearance of Bryce Cunningham.

Another splash sounded, drawing Bryce's frame tighter. He pulled his shirt back over his shoulder and turned to Markus expectantly, smoothing his hair back with both hands. "How much longer?"

"I don't think you understand what you're asking of me," he said quietly, attention falling back to the stacks of his mother's journals and books.

They looked more like tomb stones and less like sentinels.

"If Miss Savage could—"

"My sister is a linguistic genius."

"Your sister is likely dead and of no further use to anyone," he snapped back, a raw quality to his voice that Markus hadn't expected.

He stilled, gaze slowly meeting Bryce's. "I—I thought you said she's—"

"I lied," Cunningham bit out. "She fell over the edge in the storm —joined Trevor Lovelace at the bottom of the blasted ocean. If you don't want to join her, you will give me what I want."

"You're wrong." Markus grinned, something cruel and wounded. If his sister had expired, he would have felt it, something would have been intrinsically wrong with the universe. "If there is anyone who could survive that, it's Anna. She could argue her way from death's door, and let us not forget Lovelace's fondness for her. She's likely eating grapes from his hand while being fanned by his brother."

Cunningham's jaw tightened, lips pulling into a thin, pale line. "Alive. Dead. She's still not enough; she's still useless to me."

"I understand it hurt, Bryce," Markus said quietly. "I know you were in love with her before you even started courting her. I can only imagine how it felt asking for her hand only for her to reject you. But this is not the way to get back at her."

"You don't know anything."

"I know releasing the blasted Kraken is a daft idea at best. I—"

"The Kraken?"

Bollocks.

He shouldn't have said that.

"I don't know what my father said or did to convince you that this is the path to walk, but you need to stop and think. How could this possibly be a good idea? We don't know what will happen, I hardly understand any of my mother's gibberish or the language the damn map is written—"

A man screamed in the distance, cutting the words from Markus's mouth.

Cunningham turned, fingers white-knuckled around the brass knob. "You've got a very short time to figure this out, Savage. We've crossed the Black Line."

And then he slammed the door.

A picture fell from the wall, glass breaking.

Markus was left in silence, surrounded by his dead mother's journals.

"Blast it all to hell," he hissed, forcing himself to stand. Gritting his teeth, he hobbled to the small chair and table in the corner and sat down in front of his notes. "I should have paid more attention to Mother's lessons."

He ran his hands through his hair before pulling on the strands and closing his stinging eyes tight. He had made a real mess of this. Good God, he would never poke fun at Anna again for her prowess with language. Markus dropped his chin onto his hand and selected one of his pencils from a small cup on his right, twiddling it back and forth before opening a notebook.

Luck had not been in his favor; the only thing he had been able to discern thus far was where the Kraken was on Calaveras. That, and they'd need some ridiculous King of Kings to help them raise the bugger—or at least, that's what he thought this passage denoted.

He tapped his eraser against his notes and turned a page of his mother's journal with his other hand. In front of him, a rather large book sat open, its pages turned to a roughly scrawled jaguar in a dramatic crown. Beneath the regal big cat sat five other symbols, almost like a coat of arms from old Bellcaster lineages. Markus looked at each of them carefully, attention slowly shifting between them before centering on the spider.

Markus snorted.

One man overseeing a collective.

Honestly, it sounded like—

His gaze dropped back to the jaguar wearing the crown, jaw tightening. It sounded suspiciously reminiscent of the Coalition of Pirates; five splendidly murderous men overseen by the demon king himself. Was there a connection there? If the Pirate King was somehow related to this ridiculous King of Kings, did that mean Lovelace was somehow tied to the Kraken?

Was the Pirate King some bastardized version of the Aepith King of Kings?

Markus wasn't sure, but there was really only one way to find out.

Too bad that meant he had to decipher some of his mother's notes and the rest of a book written in Aepith. The language of the ancient seafarers was not one he even remotely recognized, though there were threads or symbols that did feel familiar, like seeing an old friend.

How did Cunningham expect him to read this?

And on such short notice?

He sighed, shaking his head with a chuckle.

Anna likely spoke it fluently.

CHAPTER TWENTY-THREE

"Do we have to do this every fucking time?" Tate exhaled, his voice sounding more akin to an echo in a cavern.

"You know the rules, boyo."

Anna's breath came in quick stops and starts.

Don't look, no one likes what they see.

Glancing to the side, she caught Bodhi's knowing gaze.

One of his thick brows arched as if to say, *I tried to warn you.*

Anna looked away, embarrassed for a reason she couldn't identify, and noticed they were no longer on the dark path that promised secrets and shadows. She stood in a circular clearing, the sun beating down on her back. Sweat accumulated in the waistband of her breeches and behind her knees. Bugger, she had never lost time before. But that was the least of her worries.

She looked left and then right. Where was the Pirate King?

Panic roared through her as his scream echoed in her ears unbidden. She found Bodhi where he had been before, standing just off to the side, arms crossed against his chest. Unfortunately, that damn bag still clung to the belt around his hips, and flies had started buzzing around it. Tate cackled something sharp and fierce from in front of Anna, pulling her attention straight to him.

Where was Trevor?

"Drake, if I didn't know any better, I'd say ye like seeing me naked, ye piece of shite," Tate grumbled beneath his breath.

She had never lost time before, but that was the least of what was missing. Her gaze skittered from the thick tree trunks to the flowered tendrils of moss that hung from the canopy. Two men she didn't recognize leered in front of the quartermaster. Behind them, Trevor leaned against the doorframe.

Relief.

Anna felt unbridled relief of the likes she had never known before —and a little bit of betrayal and guilt. Reassurance had not felt like this when she had found Markus chained on the train. What did that say about her? Her anger at the Pirate King wasn't supposed to know bounds until they were sailing for her brother. Bugger, it stung. Everything about this pricked at her pride, and a new kind of embarrassment lined her skin and heated her cheeks.

Anger is a fickle thing; it can run as hot as flame or chill one to the bones.

But it is always honest, and it cannot be tricked.

Anna's teeth ground together.

She wasn't angry with Trevor.

She was angry with *herself*.

The warm, languid breeze ruffled Trevor's shirt, displaying the ink that covered his chest and reached up the column of his throat. She saw pearls, ships, tentacles, and sea beasts. Were tattoos some mark of manhood for pirates? Were they awarded and earned? Or did they simply look brilliant on the body?

Juliana peeked her head around his arm, her honey-warm coloring a direct contrast to the poisonous look on her face. The master gunner stepped from—from the hole. Anna had originally believed it was a door framing the two of them, but as her gaze traveled upward, she realized it was a hole in the side of a ship. She blinked a few times, gaze following the structure skyward. The aft of the ship went straight up past the canopy and the trees.

Good God, it had been a massive vessel.

How did it get here?

She stepped forward, eyes wide and hands on her hips. A board creaked, pulling her attention back to the Pirate King. He had stepped forward as well, no longer leaning on the ship. He looked fine, albeit unamused by whatever had happened. Every beautiful inch of him appeared unharmed, and she couldn't find it in herself to stop staring or stop the gratitude from flowering in her veins. His eyebrows pulled together as he inclined his head, a frown pulling at his lips.

Are ye okay, luv, his eyes seemed to ask. His dark gaze left hers and flickered to either side of her, searching for a threat she knew he wouldn't find.

Anna nodded, unsure of what else to do. She couldn't explain what had happened, not without sounding like she'd gone insane. She knew well how fast that could spiral out of control, how quick society would be to throw her somewhere nice and warm while they waited for her to die or be forgotten, whichever came first.

They'd call it humane, of course, a nice place to rest and get well.

"Wait, ye are Drake, aye?" Tate asked, drawing both her and Trevor's attention. "Or are ye the other one?"

Oh, bugger.

Anna stepped back, gaze traveling upward.

She thought Trevor and Markus were behemoths, mountains of men, but the two pirates standing before Tate dwarfed even the Pirate King. If not for the sheer expanse of the men and the damage she knew one swing of their fists would do, their size might have been comical.

The two living mountains stood between the Lovelace brothers, blotting out the sun like the wall that bisected the Xing countryside. Anna glanced between the two as they crossed their arms, motions completely in sync with the other. Hardly a hair was out of place between the two, their sashes wrapped in mirror images, swords on their outside hip.

Identical twins, then.

The man on the left sneered down at the Tate, but the quartermaster had already tipped his chin up, a vicious grin on his face. Tate's fingers twitched near his hips, clearly anticipating some form of resistance or scuffle. It was too bad they had all carelessly left their weapons aboard the *Pale Queen*. The cutlasses made of ink that hid beneath his shirt might look wicked, but she doubted they would be much help in a fight.

"Ye sure ye want to pick a bloody fight wi' me, bucko?" Tate growled through his grin, eyebrows waggling.

The twins exchanged a glance before the one on the right kicked a massive crate forward. Laden with as many weapons as it was, it groaned against the ground. The sun reflected off a particularly nasty-looking saber with serrated edges. Tate stared at the crate before turning back to the twins. He pulled his boots from his feet and tossed them over his shoulder.

"Fine, but if ye think I'm putting my pants back on, you're fucking mistaken," he said, fingers making quick work of his belt before he pulled his shirt over his head.

Stepping from his trousers, he stood in nothing but dark underthings. True to form, they were tight on his thighs and left indentations against his hips. A flush rose hot against her cheeks and Anna crossed her arms against the reminder that she'd seen his bare rump earlier.

Just over his shoulder, she saw the Pirate King, his gaze as dark and endless as the night sky. Shoulder pressed against the door frame, he was strung tight, arms crossed tightly against his chest. If Anna hadn't spent weeks constantly in his presence, she wouldn't have noticed the tension at the corners of his mouth or the uncomfortable glint in his eyes.

"Well?" Tate asked, spreading his arms wide and turning in a circle. The twin on the right frowned disapprovingly at the tattooed blades on the quartermaster's skin. He glanced at one such blade on his forearm and planted his hands on his hips. "Ye bloody well know there's naught I can do about these."

The twin on the left (Drake, perhaps) made a face and waved the quartermaster forward. He turned his almost almond-shaped eyes on Anna, the coloring of them a strange brownish green. The shape reminded her of Bryce Cunningham and his sister Hadley. He stepped forward, blocking the hole in the ship and those standing within its confines almost completely.

Anna stepped back. Good God, she didn't want anyone with hands like that near her. The damn things could easily twist her head from her shoulders if given the chance. She met the Pirate King's gaze over the twin's shoulder. His brows raised sharply as something vicious made itself home in the abyss of his eyes.

The twin took another slow step forward.

Steeling her spine, she held her ground, fingers slowly closing into fists.

Trevor Lovelace cleared his throat, drawing both of their gazes like a moth to flame. They turned, casting their attention over their shoulders in one fluid movement. Anna frowned; she had never liked the synchronicity identical twins had, as if they truly believed they were mirrors of each other.

Markus had never mimicked her movements, not unless he had been trying to provoke her ire.

"Do ye really think I'd give the female a fucking weapon, Drake?" the Pirate King asked, scowl deepening.

A grin twitched at Anna's lips as both monstrous pirates stiffened beneath Trevor Lovelace's scrutiny. The one on the right, likely Drake, shook his head. "No, king, but you know the rules."

The hair along her arms prickled. One of the twins looked skyward. The sky above them was a bright robin's egg blue, framed in lovely white cumulus clouds. Anna rubbed at the bridge of her nose and frowned at the unexpected pressure encompassing her.

The Pirate King smiled then, something dark and deadly.

The twins shifted their weight, boots dragging against the ground as they stepped away from him.

"Ye keep yourself respectful, aye?" Trevor said quietly as goosebumps formed along her skin. "I don't have all bloody day."

Back straightening, she turned an annoyed look on the Pirate King.

Bugger, he was doing it again—that damn thing where he thought she needed his protection like some dark knight in gilded armor.

Running her tongue over her teeth, she ignored the twin that lumbered before her. Anna spread her arms wide and turned in a small circle. Hopefully, a similar display as the quartermaster would be enough.

It wasn't.

He frowned, stepping forward and crouching. Even on his knees, the man was nearly taller than her. Anna looked past his shoulder as his hands slid up her arms. Tate glanced between his brother and the twins nervously, a grin pulling stiffly at his lips. How splendid, the quartermaster found at least a pound of amusement in this farce.

The pirate's hands slid down her ribcage, thumbs brushing her breasts despite their small size. She hardly believed the touch was intentional, but the twin still glanced imperceptivity to the side.

Did he expect Trevor Lovelace to gut him at the infraction?

Anna glared at some innocuous patch of earth, grinding her teeth as she refused to make eye contact with anyone—that didn't mean she couldn't see the Pirate King lurking against the door frame in her periphery, though. Lovelace leaned forward as if pulled by some invisible thread as the twin's hand slid over the curve of her rump.

Eventually, he stood and waved her forward, but not before his hands slid down the backs of her thighs and into her boots, checking for stray blades. The Pirate King's jaw ticked as she approached, and she saw the words simmering in his gaze. But before any sound whispered from between his lips, he turned away and stepped into the shadows.

It was probably for the best. Anna had a plethora of words pressed against the roof of her mouth; if he had uttered a single sound, she would have said ten. Withheld words were cousins with the raging water behind a dam; they exerted a pressure and wanted the freedom to run their course.

Anna approached the hole in the side of the ship apprehensively, the patchwork of shadows had completely shrouded the quartermaster and her captain. Stepping within, she breathed deeply—the scent was surprisingly pleasant, smelling faintly of lavender and leather oil.

The floors sloped terribly, only furthering her suspicion that the Pirate King planned on descending from the bowels of this sleeping giant and into some circle of hell. Candelabras in sets of two and three were spaced intermittently down the long winding hall. Thick stacks of white wax sat upon them, dripping and casting a ghoulish grey light that hardly did anything to improve visibility.

A soft memory curled at the edges of her mind, one filled with trumpets and smooth piano numbers. Smoke filtered upward in swirling stacks only to be lost to the devouring dark just like this in one of Markus's favorite haunts in Bellcaster.

Anna, you'll love it, Markus had said, cheeks pink from the cold, *I promise you'll love it.*

How many holes in the wall are we going to grace with our presence tonight?

He had grinned then. *This one has a piano and a woman who sings brilliantly enough that even I cry—and with how low they keep the lights, we'll hardly be recognized.*

A feeling of homesickness nearly overwhelmed her. It was a tightness in her chest and a longing in her veins. Her mother had always said home wasn't a place one could go, a location to be pinned down and pined after. When their mother had still possessed mastery over her mental faculties, it had never come as a surprise to her that Markus and Anna rarely frequented Bellcaster.

She had never wanted to lord over Bellcaster nobility at social functions, and surprisingly enough, neither had Markus.

Something rough and fleeting bumped her fingers as a shiver of heat crawled up her arm.

Lifting her chin, she tried to catch the Pirate King's eye, but he kept his stiff appraisal on the encroaching darkness in front of them. Walking with a lazy, confident gait, he stuffed his hands into the pockets of his captain's coat as if to hide the evidence of his infraction. The dark, inky cloth trailed him like ill will and lost promises.

She squinted at him, a soft smile flickering against her lips before she could smother it.

Did he think she wouldn't know him by touch alone, that hiding his hands would somehow negate the specter of him lingering on her skin?

A heavy, purple curtain adorned with delicate gold flowers stood guard at the end of the corridor, separating them from whatever lay beyond. The Pirate King didn't break stride, and dust wafted off the curtain as he threw it open and stepped from her sight. Bodhi and his smelly bag trailed behind Anna as she stepped beneath the curtain and into what she hoped was the secret sanctum of the Coalition of Pirates and not some fresh hell.

There were few who weren't scoundrels (or worse) that made it to Tiburon and back, but none had made it to this secret hidden away from the world.

Not a soul with their faculties intact would ever attempt such an endeavor—luckily, few had accused her of such sanity.

Anna stopped, boots dragging against the ground as she gaped; the innards of the ship had been gutted until only a cavern remained. The planks looked more akin to something chiseled from stone than anything she had ever seen crafted from lumber. Her attention dragged upward along the hull until she spied broken boards set against the sky.

Good God, they were splendidly reminiscent of broken teeth.

Every tomb and ruin Anna had ever explored crafted a story all its own, one that usually began before she even stepped foot within them. Gaze flickering from left to right, she searched the immediate area. Grey-blue moss hung from the hull like long, curly tufts of an old man's hair, and the mist that trailed along the floor made the cavern feel wet and musty, as old as age itself.

Which fine gentleman had crafted this space, and why did he want to imbue it with whatever wretched wrongness lived out in that jungle?

"What fresh hell is this?" she murmured, mostly to herself.

"Are you scared, Miss Savage?" Bodhi asked.

"Absolutely not; this is positively brilliant."

And it was, despite the visceral reaction that frothed inside her.

They passed a distorted mirror, and for the first time, Anna saw herself and Trevor standing next to each other. The mirror was coated in grime and grease, but it took her breath away. She'd seen them in splendor at her father's gala, but even then, it had felt like a farce, like she stared at two people pretending at something they weren't.

The Pirate King had looked stunning in his dinner jacket and dress pants, a dark backdrop next to her glittering gown—the night sky to her stars. As breathtaking as he had been then, he was something unearthly now in his pirate's attire and kohl-rimmed eyes. It fit him the same way her dirty breeches and unbuttoned shirts did. It made them look like a pair and she was angrier for it.

Slowing, he caught her gaze in the misshapen mirror. Something softened in his features, lasting all of a second before he paced away from that wicked glass that revealed entirely too much. Anna swallowed hard against the rising emotion flooding her chest. Why had she felt the need to lean into this disastrous sense of belonging?

As if she could ever belong in the tapestry of his life. If anything, Anna was a single weave, a pass of fingers that would only be lost in the fray.

"We call it Corazon," Trevor Lovelace said over his shoulder.

Anna cocked a brow.

Corazon?

What a fitting name. It certainly felt like the dark, despicable heart of the island.

Her boots padded softly against the hardened dirt path. Treasure of every size and make blocked her view of the destination. The path wound this way and that around large, gold statues embossed with diamonds and pearls and through what had likely once been mounds of gold. In the soft light, she caught the glimmer of gems and precious metals. Trunks, probably housing more treasure, were tossed haphazardly among the priceless trinkets.

It was the trunks and boxes covered in chains and locked tight that drew her eye.

With all the wealth around her, what could possibly be locked in a box?

Anna's gaze centered on one such trunk. It wasn't the box's small size or the interlocking chains encompassing it that drew her eye. It was not even the locking mechanism flanked in fleurs and pearls, whispering of a good challenge. A grin twitched at her lips as she devoured every detail of the image engraved above the lock.

A swan crowned in stars stared back at her.

She had seen Aepith carvings of stars, and she had seen swans, but never the two together. Spinning her mother's ring around her finger, Anna's gaze narrowed on the swan—something about it prickled at the edges of her mind.

There was a book in her mother's collection, one full of Aepith stories and rhymes. As a child, she had curled up with the dusty tome in her lap, lost in tales of the Kraken gobbling ships whole and of Eero's Chalice, which granted immortal life to those willing to brave the weight of time. If the swan appeared anywhere in Aepith legend with significance, she would find it in that book.

Hello, new friend, she cooed quietly to the small box, hand already rising to procure a lock pick from her hair. Her arm dropped. She had left the *Pale Queen* without the security of the small slips of metal.

"Keep moving," Juliana growled as she stepped around Anna, her eyes glowing in the dim lighting like gold-green lanterns.

Anna glanced back over her shoulder at the swan box. She might not be able to stuff it in her pockets now, but she'd be back for it later when the Pirate King's crew was good and drowsy during the little hours of the morning.

The path they walked narrowed and curved sharply around a copper statue that had oxidized into a lovely green and blue. Anna stared up at the statue as she passed under the woman's hand; strands of pearls and silver hung from her finger. Hushed voices filled the space in front of her, and the fog thinned to reveal the heart of this monstrous space.

Anna wasn't entirely sure what she had expected. Bodies lying in rot on a gilded marble floor?

Good God, that might have been better than the monstrous, ornate table that seemed to grow from the ground. It grabbed her attention and drew her in closer.

A map completely composed of gems and precious metals had been laid into its surface, giving it depth and vibrancy. A ship carved from ivory glowed softly, anchored off the coast of what looked like an island. Anna nodded her head; that was the *Pale Queen* sitting atop a sea of sapphires, which meant the mass of land was likely Tiburon.

She cocked her head at the delicate details on the tabletop. Her brows furrowed as she strode closer. Anna had anticipated maps; she didn't know a sailor worth his salt that didn't have a weathered paper shrine dedicated to their voyages. Markus even penned her adventures spelunking through tombs and ruins as a pastime, using her letters to recreate every twist and turn. But what scallywag of the sea commissioned a map that reflected only a piece of the known world and not its entirety?

Was it a reflection of their hubris?

The hushed voices quieted completely, and it was then Anna noticed the six chairs and their occupants.

Stilling, her gaze traveled from one seat to the next. There were five seats in total, one for each of the pirate chiefs, one for each of the Eternal Seas. The chairs were large and beautiful, filled to the brim with time in the same way the rest of the cavern was. Just behind the pirate chiefs loomed two or three of their most trusted.

Despite the prickling along her neck and the thundering in her heart, Anna realized she wasn't the one they trailed with their gazes.

"How kind of you to grace us with your presence," a female voice drawled kindly. It was easy to imagine the languid way she likely grinned.

"Viper," the Pirate King growled by way of greeting, stalking toward the only empty seat in Corazon.

It was a simple slab of bone-colored wood, sanded to a fine sheen. Something shifted above, moving the light within the cavern. Anna's jaw clenched, gaze narrowing at how the light distorted the pale throne's surface and made it look like a skull.

Had the ghoulish seat been crafted for Trevor Lovelace specifically?

Anna tracked him with her gaze, ignoring the heat along her skin as the pirate chiefs turned to her one by one. The Pirate King might walk with the authority of one with an armada of pirates at his beck and call, but he couldn't hide his fraying nerves from her. Glancing left and then right, she found Bodhi with a narrowed gaze and Juliana Gray with a look that bordered animosity.

Did anyone else see the tight line between his powerful shoulders or how perfectly timed his breaths had become since stepping in front of the Coalition?

And if Anna was the only one who had, what did that say about her?

What might that mean?

Lifting her chin, she focused on Lovelace's slow, confident steps along the calcified jungle floor, on the way he slumped into his skull throne. Every movement he made exuded flippancy, from the way he crossed his feet at the ankle to the way he planted his chin on his fist and stared at the Coalition expectantly.

The Man-Eater bumped Anna once more; she must have stilled at Lovelace's theatrics.

Anna glared down at her. The woman's elbows could be utilized as rib spreaders. Juliana Gray did not look amused, but Anna could hardly find it in herself to care.

Trevor patted the arm rest, grin curling at his lips deliciously.

He didn't—

Squinting, she glanced from the armrest and back to the delightfully wicked look in the Pirate King's eyes—bugger, the prick did.

Her cheeks heated and something stirred lower in her gut. Unsure of what game the Pirate King played, she stepped forward confidently, letting her hips sway more than she usually would. He followed the motion, gaze dipping to the ample curve of her thighs. Anna's heart thundered in her ears and her chest tightened.

Juliana and Bodhi split, striding to either side of his skull throne until Anna saw nothing but the golden glow of Juliana Gray's eyes from the shadows. She stood in front of the Pirate King, his kohl-rimmed gaze darkening as he cocked his head and winked.

Something the matter, luv? the cool breeze in Corazon seemed to whisper, mimicking his deep voice near perfectly.

Anna cocked a brow back at him. *Only that I can't wrap my hands around your damn neck.*

Her boots scuffed against the step up to his skull throne. Breathing deep, she sucked on her teeth before sitting down on the bone-white armrest. It had been smoothed with time and use—Anna doubted she was the first woman to sit at the Pirate King's side like this.

Settling his arm behind her, heat wafted off it in dense waves that were difficult to ignore. Anna crossed her legs, trying to create space between them where none existed. Bugger, if this was the price of sitting at this meeting and fettering out delicious secrets, so be it— she would sit here, look positively splendid, and play his dangerous game.

And it would be dangerous; she had acknowledged enough of the tension between them to admit that much.

"This your latest toy, boyo?" a man asked, though she hadn't been paying enough attention to identify who.

Raising her gaze, she looked from one chief to the next.

Chardae Badawi.

Marshal MacGrath.

Carsyn Kidd.

John Black.

Lir the Unchanging.

Something deep down, some instinct that had likely kept her ancestors alive murmured to keep her attention anchored on her boots or the brilliantly crafted table. Or maybe it was her father's voice, echoing back up from a plethora of childhood memories.

Glancing down, she ran her tongue over her teeth. With Trevor Lovelace slouched at her elbow, arm around her, the pirate chiefs were the least of her concerns. Anna knew without a doubt what to expect from the Coalition if given a chance—death, dismemberment, hanging. The rub lied in that she did not know where she stood with the Pirate King.

He had said he would keep her safe, that he wanted her alive and whole.

His actions claimed as much, but—

"No' exactly my type, but she's a sight if I've ever seen one," the pirate chief continued, gaze skimming her.

He was a large man, clothed in a dark shirt and trousers. A cape of white and grey fur hung from the corner of his seat. Anna stilled, attention landing on the shiny scar tissue decorating the alabaster skin of his throat; it was far fresher than the two marks that bisected his left brow and dragged down his cheek.

She met his gaze then, a strange ruby red glittering with an unidentifiable madness. Her mother's gaze had dulled with a fever of the mind before she had passed, the ravings of the sick leaving in hushed breaths. The madness in this man's eyes was something else entirely, this was a madness chosen, a madness embraced.

Marshal MacGrath, she named.

Only men and women from the Blood Isles had red eyes like that.

Winking, he ran a hand through his hair, brushing the strands from his gaze. The rest of his dirty blond mop hung haphazardly to his chin, his part falling far to the right. Anna stared at him, committing every visible mark to memory. Knowledge was power, and sometimes information was the teensiest manifestation of that.

Marshal MacGrath cocked his head, grin growing. "Are ye fucking her?"

She blinked, listening as his words echoed around the cavern.

Did he really just—

Good God, if given the chance, she'd shove those precarious words right back down his damn throat. Anna's face grew hot with the reminder of what they had done all those years ago—she might not remember tumbling the Pirate King, but that hardly meant his memory of the night was compromised as well. They hadn't broached the subject, nor did she intend to, but not talking about something and not thinking about it were two entirely different tasks.

Success had been easily found with the former; it was the latter that was proving increasingly difficult.

"Could ye blame me?" Lovelace said roughly.

His thumb brushed the outside of her thigh once, twice, a third time. Anna pressed her tongue against her teeth, breathing deep as the sensation of his thumb against her thigh became a constant pressure of strong, slow strokes.

Bugger—*did* he remember?

"Must not be satisfying her," MacGrath said. "She hasn't taken those gorgeous eyes off me yet."

"Would no' recommend it, mate." Lovelace's voice slid over her like a second skin. "My wee beastie has a poisonous bite."

"'Tis just so then, I fucking love teeth."

Lovelace grinned, canines making an appearance. Shifting slightly away, she caught the look in his gaze—oh, that was not a grin, it was a baring of teeth. A warning, one in a primal language, one that any of these alpha males would easily understand. Anna spun her mother's ring around her finger as the mist dampening the air formed beads of condensation at the ends of his thick wine-red strands.

"I couldn't care less that you're fucking her, Lovelace, but why's the girl here?" another chief asked, this one robed in evergreen silks.

He slouched in a dark chair just to her right; it wasn't a position born of confidence like the Pirate King's or from boredom like MacGrath's. Illness was a weight on this man's soul, pulling him down into a crumbled pile of flesh. His cheeks maintained a bright, feverish flush, the only spots of color against his waxy skin and thinning, light brown hair.

"You should care, Black." The Viper snorted. "That...*that* is a Savage."

Anna swallowed past her confusion. How could the Viper possibly know who she was? She had never met the woman personally and doubted her resemblance to Markus led Chardae Badawi to her accurate conclusion. Despite her brother's notoriety at sea, even he hadn't crossed paths often enough with the Coalition chiefs to warrant recognition on sight, and Anna had had far fewer dealings than he.

Another leaned forward, his skin darker than even Bodhi's, a rich umber that contrasted splendidly with the coppery color of his eyes. Exhaling his disappointment, the man's unamused gaze bored into the Pirate King. She recognized the breath well, the way it left through his nose in annoyance—her father had claimed a very similar sigh as his own.

Archaeology? he had asked, gaze on the stack of papers on his desk. *Just like mother.*

Her father had sighed, gaze narrowing. *Just like your mother.*

"Is it your intention to claim every last ounce of ire from the Briland Senate?" he growled. "Peace is precarious, Trevor."

"Bloody hell, Lir. Haven't ye heard?" the Pirate King asked, a cheerful note raising his voice. "I'm always pissing those bastards off— and usually for shite I've naught to do wi'."

John Black, the sickly man, stiffened at Lovelace's words, brows drawing together before his watery, blue gaze landed on Anna. This felt nothing like the heat on her skin when she found herself under the Pirate King's scrutiny. If Lovelace's attention was like smoldering coals, John Black's was swamp water—musty and warm, leaving an oily film in its wake.

"Where is it, Lovelace?" the Viper asked again, accent flourishing her words.

Anna looked away from John Black as he failed to contain a coughing fit and turned to the only woman who had ever become a pirate chief.

If she respected the Viper for anything, Anna respected her for that.

Chardae Badawi wore a veil of spun gold; only her eyes and the curve of cheekbones were visible—and both looked sharp enough to cut steel. Familiarity hid in the way she lined her eyes in kohl and the summer brown glow of her skin. Nostalgia warmed Anna's chest; something about the fearsome woman felt like coming home after a very long time away.

Anna clenched her jaw.

Of all the places her mother had loved, she had loved Abu Shazar best, with its sprawling markets and sticky desserts. Anna saw every day, every hour, every *minute*, she had spent toiling in the dust and desert with her mother and brother in Chardae Badawi, and it hurt.

Her hair tumbled well past her breasts in thick, straight strands, a ribbon of white highlighting the right side of her face. A vague sense of surprise settled in Anna's gut—she hadn't realized the Viper was likely her mother's age.

"Where the *fuck* is what?" Lovelace echoed, shifting forward as his gaze narrowed.

Lovelace removed his arm from behind her and placed it over her thigh. Her cheeks heated as she stared down at him, the warmth of his body soaking into her. Beads of condensation dripped from the ends of his hair and down the back of his neck, trailing beneath his shirt.

She imagined the path that droplet might take between his shoulders and down his spine.

Anna breathed deep, rather disappointed in herself. She had acknowledged his dashing good looks as soon as she had stumbled upon him, ignoring any red flag they should have raised. In the wild, the most dangerous beasts were often the most beautiful, and Trevor Lovelace was hardly an exception to the rule.

"The map," she said, one manicured brow raising. "The one you were instructed not to return without. *The chalice's map.*"

Trevor shrugged and leaned more of his weight onto her. "On its bloody way to Calaveras on a Briland ship."

From this distance, Anna couldn't discern the exact color of the Viper's eyes, only that they were a positively brilliant shade. She lounged in her throne atop a feather cushion, one leg cast over the side with the other tucked beneath her. It wasn't the chief's relaxed stature that held Anna's attention in a vice, it was the woman leaning against her throne. Her eyes were closed as Chardae Badawi played with her hair, twirling the chestnut strands and dragging her nails against the woman's scalp.

Anna stiffened as a bitter shade of jealousy knotted behind her ribs and twisted her stomach.

When was the last time someone had showered her in sweet caresses and soft, leisurely touches?

Lovelace leaned back. His dark, spiced scent filled her lungs as his palm dragged up her leg. His callouses caught on the smooth fabric, and his fingers left a trail of fire in their wake until the only point of contact between them was where the Pirate King had wrapped his hand around her thigh.

Anna blinked, inhaling stiffly at the familiarity of it. She remembered few things about their time together that disastrous night. Convincing herself it was better that way had been an easy affair—one could not fantasize about or fixate on things they could not remember.

But the remnants of his touch plagued Anna at the strangest, most irrelevant times.

A man stood, and something heavy clattered against the packed dirt floor. He shoved his hands through short, blue-black hair. She recognized him from an old wanted poster. He had been a teenager at the time it had been drawn, but his timeless aristocratic features and the scar cutting across his forehead hadn't changed.

Carsyn Kidd, she thought, focusing on his brilliant blue-green eyes.

Squinting at him, Anna ignored the way Lovelace's hand tensed against her thigh and the butterflies that flapped annoyingly in her gut. Carsyn Kidd hardly looked the age he should, from the dimple in his chin to the sharp line of his jaw.

"Do you realize what've you've gone and done?" Carsyn growled, fingers splaying against the sapphires on the tabletop. Anna cocked a brow at the leather trousers hugging his thighs before forcing her gaze away. "You know what sleeps on that blasted island."

Were all pirates gorgeous?

No, John Black certainly proved that wrong.

"Captain," one of the pirates behind Carysn Kidd whispered hesitantly.

Carsyn held up a hand, silencing any other protests that might follow. "You're an idjit, Trevor." His burning gaze shifted to her. "All this for *one* woman?"

He didn't say it, but Anna heard the implications between the spaces of his words all the same—not worth the time, not worth the effort, not enough to show for it.

Not enough.

"Once upon a time, ye'd have agreed one fem was worth everything, mate."

"Well." Kidd snorted. "We know how that turned out, don't we?"

"Plus, she's no' just any female. Ye heard the Viper—she's a *Savage*." Anna nearly snorted; Lovelace's tone suggested she was some mythical unicorn. "She is worth more than her gods-damned weight in gold."

Something cracked in the distance, casting an eerie echo through Corazon. Stone scraped against stone dramatically. The pirates in the cavern strained left and right, squinting out into the dense fog blanketing the trove of treasure. The sound grew louder, pulling her forward until her boots touched the ground, her right hand pressing into the armrest. Trevor's hand slipped to her hip as he too scanned the area for the sound.

Tate's rump broke through the fog first. Anna blinked several times, eyebrows furrowing as he struggled to drag something along. What was he up to? If the general read of the room had not been so serious, the sight would have been comical. Tate stopped only when a stone chest sat between the table and Anna, his long-sleeved shirt tied around his shoulders like a cape.

Bugger, she'd completely forgotten about the quartermaster.

Where the hell had he been this entire time?

"Apologies," he said sheepishly, stretching his arms high above his head before sitting with a huff. "I could no' find the bloody stool."

Anna couldn't see around his lean, muscular body—had that been intentional?

Was he blocking her from the Coalition's view, or was he hiding something from her?

Tate glanced over his shoulder, gaze twinkling with mischief as he noted where she sat.

The armrest of the Pirate King's throne was not comfortable, but what it lacked in cushion, it made up for in dignity. Or at least that's what Anna had told herself until Tate waggled his eyebrows suggestively and turned back around.

If he kept those shenanigans up, she'd see to it that he didn't have any eyebrows left.

"Tate," Trevor said, tipping his head back and exposing the tattoos at the base of his throat.

"Aye, Captain?"

"Did ye find anything in your wandering?"

"No' much more than a lovely place to situate my ass, Captain." The quartermaster paused for a moment as if considering his words before adding, "Looks to me like the lass found a fine seat as well."

"Mm."

"Aye."

Anna's cheeks heated even as her lips twitched into a near grin.

"Fucking hell," John Black snapped, fingers digging into the armrests of his seat. "What are we doing waiting around? I don't care if she is John Savage's whore daughter, I say *kill her.*"

A few pirates sounded their agreement.

A shiver crept up her spine as the air around them grew dense with something she could not quite describe. The temperature in the cavern plummeted until her breath nearly fanned from her face. The Pirate King was a well-fed furnace she found herself leaning toward as she searched for a reprieve from the cold.

Whatever this strange pressure was, it was cousins with what she had felt in the jungle.

"Are ye fucking done?" Trevor asked quietly.

John Black opened his mouth, cheeks flushed.

"I would no' recommend that, boyo." Tate *tsk*ed from his seat.

Something sharp glimmered darkly in his hands, catching the soft lighting of the candelabras. Anna leaned forward, gaze narrowing on the small object—a *knife?* He'd stripped nearly naked before entering the threshold of Corazon, how had he smuggled a weapon past those mountain-sized men?

As if feeling the weight of her stare, the quartermaster turned toward Anna with a lopsided grin on his face. There were secrets hidden in the corners of his smile, like small breaks of sunlight through the clouds. She shook her head at him as he dragged the small, black blade against his fingernails, making a show of cleaning the dirt and grime from beneath them.

How the hell had he smuggled that damn blade in here?

The Viper motioned vaguely in Anna's direction with her free hand. "We cannot trade damaged goods, Trevor Lovelace—and before you speak, yes, fucking *you* is considered damaged. Corrupted. Contaminated. I doubt even the Senate is stupid enough to trade a silly, ruined, little girl for that map, especially one who stole from the Pirate King."

Words of retaliation bubbled up her throat like acid. Chardae Badawi was not wrong about the Senate. Her father wouldn't pay for her return—at best, she'd be labeled a criminal and carted off to Chesterhale, and at worst she'd find herself stuck within the walls of the same ward her mother had wasted away in.

Just like her mother, John Savage would concede, a veneer of woe on his face.

An unfortunate circumstance of the blood, the physician would agree.

"The one who..." John Black paused, hands clenching his armrests. "*This* is the little whore who burned Cash's ship! I hope you're not too attached to your fucking head, girl!"

The room erupted.

John Black stood and stepped in her direction.

Anna wasn't entirely sure if she was more surprised by the chief's display of arrogance or that his sickly body sustained his weight without support. What did John Black possibly believe he could accomplish, especially without a weapon of any sort?

The Pirate King was wicked in a fight, a brutal force of nature when he wished to be.

Already, that feral grin twitched at Lovelace's lips as he slid forward. Movement from the corner of her eye drew her attention to the right as a pirate lunged from behind John Black's throne. Rushing backward, she slammed into Trevor's chest on impulse. Anna dug into his belt, searching for a blade—for *anything*—to defend herself with.

Her hand closed around something else entirely, bringing a hot flush to her cheeks.

Good God.

Trevor wrapped an arm around her waist and pulled her into his lap in one fluid motion. His hand splayed against her stomach as his little finger slipped beneath the hem of her breeches. Opening her mouth, she looked up at him. Any words she might have said froze on her tongue at the hellish look in eyes.

She was fairly certain a word did not yet exist to paint an accurate enough picture of the ire simmering in his gaze.

For a moment, the depth of his irises almost bubbled outward, flooding the whites like ink.

But then a vicious gust whipped through Corazon, nearly ripping her hair from its bun. Closing her eyes, she buried her face in the Pirate King's neck and turned into his chest to escape the wind. It howled and roared in the background, untucking her shirt and whipping her hair.

It ended abruptly, and the silence that followed pressed tightly against her skin.

Swallowing hard, Anna peered over her shoulder.

The wretch that had lunged at her stood as still as a statue, body trembling and arm raised. She tracked a tear as it rolled from wide, terrified eyes and down his cheek. The air in the room drifted forward and backward with each of Lovelace's breaths—but nothing seemed to have been touched, not a hair or item of clothing stood out of place on any of the chiefs.

Looking down, she saw a deep gouge along the floor that had not been there before.

How had that happened?

Lovelace leaned back, taking Anna with him. One of his warm hands settled behind her, elbow on the armrest while his other hand sat like a weight over her knee. Anna glanced from her arm draped over his shoulder to the hand resting against his chest. Where else was she supposed to put the damn things? Unsure of what else to do, she leaned into him and froze at the hard length pressing against her.

Bugger.

Chuckling uncomfortably beneath her breath, Anna turned away from the Pirate King. She couldn't look at him without thinking of the impression he'd left in her hand.

To think she had grabbed his—

The skin along her arms prickled, a sense of unease plucking chords in her spine like a pianist might keys. Anna's gaze slowly drifted away from where her hand rested on Lovelace's chest. She met the gaze of every Coalition chief. Most had a cruel curiosity sparkling from their depths, but John Black's pale blue eyes had grown poisonous.

Their keen observance and interest likely didn't bode well, but Anna would burn that bridge to the ground when it was required of her. Teasing through their assumptions and opinions required the careful examination of the unnamed thing lurking between her and Trevor Lovelace. The Coalition wouldn't hesitate to name what they believed it to be, thinking they could use it to rot and manipulate, but worry over their perceived findings was rather low on her list of concerns.

Lovelace tipped his head to the side, some of his hair tickling the shell of her ear. His hand tightened on her knees before his thumb started drumming to a tune—the shanty he'd whistled, the one she had hummed on the *Contessa*.

A question, she realized, as she glanced at him.

I'm not afraid of them, she thought as she met his dark gaze.

He turned away, either unconcerned or uninterested in the thoughts lingering in her gaze. "Let's be fucking clear, if ye lay one gods-damned—"

"She has the black spot," John Black growled, pale eyes glowing the same blue of a mottled corpse. "Death is her due."

Trevor waved his hand.

A moment later, that disgusting, smelly bag that had been tied to Bodhi's waist sailed over their heads and thumped with a squelch against the tabletop. Several pirates jumped, reaching for weapons they had been forced to leave behind at the door. The sack scattered the brilliant itty boats, gems, and coins that littered the surface.

That smell—she recognized it now.

Old blood.

Carsyn Kidd leaned forward cautiously, his blue-green eyes focused entirely on the bloodied bag. Looking over his shoulder, he nodded to one of the pirates at his side. A shorter, stockier man with pine-green hair stepped from the shroud of shadows. The quartermaster of Carsyn Kidd's flag ship did not have a formal name that she knew of; he simply went by the Fox.

Tentatively, he strode forward, eyeing the bag with a gaze nearly as dark as the Lovelace brothers'. In the murky darkness of Corazon, Anna couldn't be sure what color they were, but they were offset by the pale color of his skin and framed by shoulder-length, wavy hair.

The Fox lifted the bag by one end, spilling its contents over the beautiful table.

Bile rose in her throat, stomach contracting as she gagged. Good God, she had smelled some truly fearsome things in her life, but none compared to the rotting head on the table. Forcing herself to breathe through her mouth, she swallowed the bile back down and squinted at the fleshy, oozing stump.

He looked...familiar.

"Who the fuck is he?" Carsyn Kidd asked as he inspected the head. His face twisted, gaze rising to meet Lovelace's. "And what the hell did he do?"

"Say 'ello to the last male that tried killing our lovely wee lassie."

Our.

The word and its implications were not lost on Anna.

Anna turned to the Coalition chiefs. She might have been more concerned with their increased interest if not for the imagined feeling of dark, heavy waters pressing in on her. A phantom hand reached out, squeezing her heart as she stared down at the man who had taken her overboard with him.

Was she a fallen star?

Were the stars hiding beneath his skin, or hers?

Anna leaned away, pressing back into Lovelace in an effort to create distance between herself and the head. It was splendid, really; she'd have yet another rubbery face to add to the plethora already haunting her dreams. The Pirate King cleared his throat uncomfortably, shifting his legs beneath her. Anna swallowed hard, recognizing the solid length pressing against her rump for what it was.

Honestly, he should have thought this plan of his through more.

What did he think would happen after pulling her into his lap?

She turned to face him, expecting to find the same light-hearted expression on the Pirate King's face that she'd heard in Tate's voice. That was not at all what she found lurking in the handsome planes of his face. He held no such amusement, no sliver of mischief nor glimmer of playfulness. This was not a man who found joy in decapitated heads, and this was not her rake of a pirate.

This creature was the Pirate King, and not an ounce of him feared reminding the Coalition of that.

"And why is he here, Trevor?" Lir the Unchanging asked, leaning forward with his hands wrapped around a cane that had been carved from what appeared to be driftwood.

"That's the quartermaster of the *Independence*, sir," one of the wretches behind Lir murmured. "Male was tough as shit."

Trevor laughed, fury finally breaching the surface. "That cunt tried offering her up as a tithe—as safe fucking passage across my seas. There are ships sailing under my gods-damned banner, under *my* protection, that are tracking slaves." He paused, gaze landing on John Black. "Your wee shite-stain of a nephew is aiding that bloody trade. He brought the lass to Tiburon on his fucking ship. If no' for him, that cursed map never would have left."

The animosity present in John Black's gaze dissipated until only fear remained.

The Pirate King breathed deep. "Ye know what the fuck comes next, Black."

Marshal MacGrath cackled, his ruby-red gaze smoldering.

The sound proved to be the only warning for what happened next.

The pirates behind John Black lunged forward as Trevor stood, shucking her into the seat of his throne. Anna blinked, confusion rippling through her as several pistols clicked and fired. Smoke filtered around John Black's seat, burning her nose, and the wretches in his retinue were now on the ground, unmoving.

A blade whistled through the air, quickly followed by a dense, wet thump.

The Coalition chief's screams bounced off the walls of Corazon until it was the only sound registering in her ears. Shifting her attention, she stared first at Lovelace's rump as he held the screaming chief by the back of his neck against the tabletop.

How did he get all the way over there? she wondered, raising her gaze.

Trevor Lovelace stared down at her, a drop of blood slipping from his nose. His wicked gaze darkened as it dropped—she followed it, stilling at the deep gauge set into the armrest next to her. Just over the edge laid a pair of worn boots, a puddle of blood blooming around them.

That had been brilliantly close; she hadn't even realized one of the scoundrels had snuck up on her.

Swallowing hard, she found Lovelace's eyes once more. Blood continued dripping from his nose and had sprayed across his face at a diagonal. He'd split his upper lip, and for a moment, her heart stuttered and her lungs tightened.

He could have been killed, same as her.

Trevor offered her a small grin—it was more of a reassuring twitch of his lips than anything—before facing the Coalition chiefs.

Ye have naught to worry about, he had said.

She thought back to the sound of his voice breaking over the wind, pleading and screaming.

That might have been true once, she thought just before the sword ran through the Pirate King, *but not anymore.*

CHAPTER TWENTY-FOUR

The red crept from his gaze, if only a wee bit.

Enough that he would no' outright kill the fucker in front of him.

But, shite, he wanted nothing more than to wrap his hands around Black's throat and watch the gods-damned life leave his eyes. If no' for the fact that Cashton would inherit his uncle's ship and seat as a chief, he might have.

But that wee cunt would be worse on the seas. The lad already thought he was bigger than his britches, like being John Black's nephew protected him from the monsters swimming through deeper, darker waters.

Trevor was no' a forgiving male, and it seemed the Coalition needed reminding of that.

As John Black's fist passed in front of his nose, he saw Anna huddled against his bone throne from the corner of his eye. Bloody hell, he wished she didn't have to see this, but there were some things that couldn't be helped, some truths he could no' hide.

John Black's head cracked against the table; Trevor's fingers wrapped around the back of his neck. The bastard's fists thumped against his body as he struggled and wheezed. He hadn't expected there to be this much of a fight left in a body that was riddled wi' disease. Trevor leaned down hard, cutting off the prick's air.

Either he'd calm the fuck down or he'd pass the fuck out.

Black's tattoo crept from beneath Trevor's fingers, a gods-damned spider wi' needle-thin legs and a swollen body. He'd always hated the sight of the bug, even when Black's grandda' had worn it before him. John Black looked up at him, spit dripping from his maw, a filthy look in his watery blue eyes. The prick didn't understand just how lucky he was; if he'd been any other gods-damned male in the room, if he'd had any other gods-damned relative...

The next thump sunk into him, and it wasn't until Trevor felt the warmth running down his stomach that he paused. A scream ripped from Anna, one that chilled him to his core and left him wi' the itch to move—to do something, *anything*, to keep that grief out of her voice.

Looking down, he found the reason for her scream.

Trevor nearly broke the chief's neck right then and there as he stared at the grip of a sword, blood running down his stomach and into his trousers

Fucking shite.

This was his favorite gods-damned coat.

CHAPTER TWENTY-FIVE

Anna hadn't realized the sound had torn from her until everyone in Corazon stared at her—everyone except for John Black, his heavy gaze remained on the Pirate King. She heaved a breath inward, staring wide-eyed at the blood-slicked end of a saber. The blood was not an issue, the rub lied in the sword protruding from Trevor's back. Strands of his captain's coat hung from the blade.

For a moment, it was Markus standing before her, blade planted in his gut, but then she blinked and it was the Pirate King once more. Her hands shook at her sides as she stepped forward on legs she wasn't entirely sure would hold her weight. It didn't matter if they gave out, she'd crawl to him if she had to.

But what in God's name could she possibly do?

She wasn't a surgeon; she didn't have extensive medical training.

The saber would have ripped through some rather integral organs; simply stitching them wouldn't do. Anna ran her lip through her teeth—blood loss was already becoming an issue, but it wouldn't be long before sepsis was one too.

Bugger.

Tate latched onto her wrist, halting her forward momentum. Her gaze whipped to the quartermaster, eyes burning.

She needed to staunch the bleeding.

It was a quick affair, a look that lasted less than a blink because she couldn't take her eyes off the Pirate King for long. Anna noticed Trevor staring at her then; his dark eyes were completely void of pain or concern for his encroaching end. If anything, he looked annoyed, though his features softened when he met her gaze.

A soft hiss curled against his lips as he slowly pulled the saber from his gut. Anna winced, closing her eyes against the sickening sound of steel sliding through innards. A small part of her was morbidly curious at the affair, but it wasn't an image she wanted lingering in the littlest hours of the night.

The saber clattered dully against the dirt floor, drawing a flinch from her.

Good God, she had questions—but Anna didn't think she could bear the thought of asking them.

"This is a fucking warning to the rest of ye," Trevor growled through his teeth. "This happens again and I'll burn your ships. I'll slaughter your crews. I'll take more than your gods-damned hand. Ye would do well to remember my seas do no' traffic slaves."

Anna looked then, staring as he made eye contact with every other pirate in the room.

It wasn't until he threw a severed hand onto the table that she realized what the wet thump had been earlier—why John Black had screamed with such fervor.

Trevor leaned forward, whispering something into the chief's ear. As soon as the Pirate King released him, John Black flew backward, his stump clenched to his chest. Blood ran between his fingers and down the front of his silk robes.

"Bodhi," Trevor murmured, gaze trailing the man as he nearly ran from Corazon.

The surgeon nodded, tucking a pistol into his belt.

Where had that bugger come from?

"Told ye they'd require Bodhi's services," Tate murmured, throwing his brother a cloth.

"*Them?*" Anna stumbled over her words, eyes burning as she

stared at the blood soaking Trevor's shirt and the sash around his waist. "He's been—"

"We'll talk later."

She stared at Trevor.

Her worry for his life knew no bounds, and they would *talk* later? He'd been run through with a saber, it had punched its way out of his back not even two minutes ago, and they would be talking *later*? A word had not been invented yet for what she felt. Anna clamped down on her lips, the trembling in her fingers shifting to shaking fists.

Talk.

Anna cleared her throat. "But you're—"

"*Fine*," he said with a finality she had never heard before. "I am always *fine*."

The Pirate King wiped his hands off, making sure to clean every finger and knuckle. He tossed the bloodied cloth to the ground as he turned to face her. Anna's attention immediately dropped to his abdomen, where blood seeped slowly through the fingers he pressed to his stomach.

This was fine?

A saber skewering his internal organs like a shish kabob was *fine*— it wasn't something that mattered? Anna's head slowly shook side to side, a small huff of laughter pressed against her chest. Did that mean all the times a bone-crumbling fear had risen up with concern over him had not mattered?

And when she had believed he'd died—that some of her had died right along with him—that hadn't mattered either?

It had been fine?

Fury roared through her like a forest succumbing to flame.

As splendid as a discovery like this might be if it were true, it meant nothing to her right now.

"It is a good thing, Trevor Lovelace, that you are hard to harm," the Viper started slowly, her gaze seeking out Anna's, "and even harder to kill."

Was Chardae Badawi weighing her again?

Had something happened that increased her value in the woman's eyes?

The lines of Lovelace's body tensed at the pirate chief's interest. Ignoring her comment, his gaze slowly slid toward Lir. The dark-skinned chief straightened in his throne, fingers gripping the head of his driftwood cane tightly. Anna squinted down at the man's finger-nails, noticing they were painted black.

"Now that that's settled." Trevor exhaled. "*Stand.*"

Lir stood.

Anna tracked upward, jaw slackening.

They should have given him the moniker Lir the Unending—he just kept going, standing a head even above Trevor Lovelace.

Lir rolled his shoulders back once, achieving his unfathomable full height, and let his cane support some of his weight. He was by far the most well-dressed of all the pirate chiefs, standing before her in an ebony waistcoat and a maroon shirt. The gold buttons on the waist-coat had been shined until they gleamed, and the intricate, thin lines on the fabric reminded Anna of a topographical map. His dress pants were dark as well, and she was only mildly surprised to find him barefoot.

"Ye think I canno' tell when the Mer are fucking wi' me?" Trevor Lovelace said quietly, chin tipped up.

"I have never presumed such."

"Are ye telling me this wasn't your bloody doing?"

"One would think the Pirate King would be appreciative of the efforts taken by the Coalition to claim what was stolen."

"One would think if a male wanted to keep his fucking head, he wouldn't do things that gods-damned beg me to take it," Trevor growled, gaze burning. "I'm leaving in seven days for that map, but I'll no' be leaving wi'out the lass. Fix the fucking spot."

"Can't blame him," MacGrath murmured from his seat, chin resting on his fist. "If I'd planned on sailing for Calaveras, I'd want a lovely tart like that in naught but silk in my bed too."

Anna's jaw clenched.

Tart.

Crumpet.

Whore.

There were so many words to describe the sexual promiscuity of a woman—none of which ever seemed to be problematic until that woman was some man's wife. Anna was no man's wife, but she was a senator's daughter—*the* senator's daughter, some would argue. She could only imagine the headache this would cause her as soon as the rumor made it back to the mainland.

She had told her father she was pregnant with the pirate's baby; it wasn't much of a stretch to say she was his whore as well.

Lir leaned his head to the side, gaze narrowing into coppery slits as he stared at her.

Anna knew a man with questions when she saw one.

Trevor Lovelace leaned his free hand against the brilliant tabletop, the other was still fisted against his abdomen. "I will no' say it twice."

Lir stepped toward her, hand outstretched, palm up. Anna curled the fingers of her left hand inward, hesitant to let the splendidly tall wretch touch her.

What could the pirate chief possibly do to make this damnable spot disappear?

The Pirate King might ascribe to this mythic mumbo-jumbo, but Anna had yet to be irrevocably convinced the otherworldly presence on Tiburon was anything more than manufactured aesthetics by whomever had first settled here.

Lovelace's fingers brushed the back of her arm gently—a soft reassurance, perhaps?

I can keep ye safe.

Anna stepped toward Lir and away from the heat radiating from the Pirate King, not because his reassurance had given her enough courage to close the gap between herself and the chief, but because she was not afraid of Lir the Unchanging and wanted him to know that.

Sticking her hand out stubbornly, Anna raised her brow. She hoped the chief saw the challenge in the action. A soft smile that did not reveal teeth smoothed his features and softened his gaze.

Lir brushed his long, dark locks back and leaned down. "You remind me of my granddaughter."

"You hardly look old enough to father a child, let alone have a granddaughter," she said, shivering at the cool feeling of his fingers as they wrapped around her wrist.

One large hand grasped hers, holding it palm up for inspection. Her hand looked so incredibly pale in his. Lir stared down at the ugly thing occupying her flesh, turning her hand this way and that.

"I have many grandchildren." He sighed, brows pulling together as his gaze trailed the darkening veins of her arm. "We do not all age as you do, Miss Savage."

Juliana snorted from somewhere behind her.

He tapped her forearm near her elbow, humming softly as he did so. Anna frowned, feeling a soft thump in her chest. He tapped again. A matching thump again resounded from behind her ribs. Well, that was certainly unexpected. Clearing her throat, she ignored the strange sensation and all the questions burrowing into her bones.

It was an easy enough task until Lir pressed his index and middle finger against the inside of her elbow. His coppery eyes met hers as he dragged his fingers downward with an intention that spoke to secrets she did not know and a logic she did not understand.

Anna gasped, eyes widening as the pressure in her chest pulled outward and away from her as well, as if following the guidance of the pirate chief's fingers.

"The discomfort is to be expected," Lir said, though he was not looking at her.

Discomfort?

She nearly laughed, tears burning at the corners of her eyes. Bugger, if only this was mere *discomfort*. This was something else entirely. This was bottled nightmares and glimmering lighting. Her arm shook as Lir's hand tightened around her wrist, pulling her to him. Had she leaned away? She must have. Anna's breaths shallowed as the tight dragging sensation in her chest crawled up her throat and stole her breath.

What is this? she thought, eyes stinging.

Anna tried to steel her resolve, to bludgeon her panic, but that damnable *pulling* made it nearly impossible. The trembling started in her fingers, small and almost unnoticeable. Her gaze dropped to her palm, and all the color drained from her face. The blackened skin along her left hand shifted, charcoal-colored fumes wafting off it. Nearly gagging at the briny, putrid smell, she turned away as her skin began to bubble.

Her breaths came in short stops and starts, arm trembling. Lir's fingers pressed against the center of her forearm. She hadn't wanted the Pirate King to bother removing the damnable spot before—now? Good God, she would have rather taken the mark to the grave. If not for Markus's current state of damsel, Anna would have considered an extended vacation on Tiburon.

The black spot at the center of her arm pulsed and then began to drain. Bile crept up Anna's throat and soured her mouth as dark, oily sludge leaked from her palm and between her fingers, dripping to the floor with soft hisses. She blinked, gaze widening at the blasted mess of her hand.

How was one supposed to wrap their head around something like this? Her chest ached and her breath hardly filled her lungs, unable to shake the inescapable pull of Lir's fingers. The pirate chief's attention remained on her hand, brows drawn together in focus.

Good God...

She hissed, teeth sinking into her lip as the pressure of his fingers reached her wrist.

A squeak of discomfort forced its way between her lips as he held his fingers to her wrist, watching the ooze pulse from the wound. Anna grew lightheaded and savored the brush of the cool breeze against her cheeks and neck. It wound its way around her forearm and up her bicep. The slight gust of wind was proof enough that miracles could happen in hell.

"Are you done?" she growled, eyes pinching shut at the fiery ache in her palm.

"Almost," Lir murmured, fingers tightening around her wrist.

Her knees trembled, knocking together before collapsing beneath her and cracking against the ground. Lir kept a steady hold on her wrist, forcing it high above her head. Anna wasn't sure how much she had left in her; exhaustion curled in the crooks of her body, and shadows darkened the corners of her sight.

"I can't breathe," she whispered, throat tightening.

She hadn't thought anything could be worse than the pressure of icy water pressing against her and squeezing the air from her lungs, but this was.

"Lir," Lovelace growled from behind her, his voice a mere echo in her ears.

"Almost there, king."

Almost.

There was that word again. She hated it, the darker, distant cousin of *yet*. If "yet" saw the world as full of possibility and wonder, goals attainable and within reach, "almost" was the opposite. There was no worse word in existence than almost. It spun a tale of nearly there but not, a fine web of lost and crumbled potential—it had always implied failure in her life.

"There," Lir said, releasing her hand and stepping back as if she had burned him.

Anna's arm dropped, knuckles cracking against the rock-solid ground. Her chest loosened, breaths coming in deep and gasping pulls. For several erratic beats of her heart, all she could hear was the blood pumping through her ears, so similar to the roar of the tides of the sea.

Tentatively, she turned her hand over. What had become of her palm? Had that black ooze eaten through it until only bone remained? She stared down, brows pulling together. It looked as it should, as it always had, except for a coin-sized sore at the center of her palm.

"Time will heal that," Lir said, "as it does most things."

Coughing, she dragged her gaze upward and found every scoundrel in the damn cavern staring at her, gazes filled with a cruel sort of curiosity and wonder. Carsyn Kidd stared down at her, rage simmering beneath the surface of his eyes. It was an anger Anna matched, her body heating with it, trembling with the effort to keep it locked beneath her skin.

Lovelace placed a hand against her back, his touch tentative and gentle.

She frowned, muscles stiffening beneath his fingers. Swallowing past the bile and ire caught in her throat, Anna pushed herself to her feet and shot him a glare over her shoulder. She didn't care if it was childish; she didn't care if her anger felt misplaced. Eyes burning, she held the Pirate King's gaze until he turned from her.

"This does no' happen again, am I bloody clear?" Trevor Lovelace growled, fingers fisting his ruined shirt as he faced Lir the Unchanging. "Make sure ye tell all your fishy friends."

A shiver ran its course along her spine at the dark amusement hidden between his words.

Not all promises need to be spoken to be heard.

"I am not their keeper," Lir said quietly. "But if it does happen, it will not have been because of me."

Anna glared at her boots, at the ground—at anything that wasn't the Pirate King.

Good God, her insides burned hot enough to smelt bone. Perhaps she'd smash his stupid head in and see if that killed him. Anna had all the time in the world before they were back at sea to wring answers from him.

"Are we done here?" she asked, staring down at the blackened puddle sinking into the hardened ground. Bile burned the base of her throat as the distress tightened in her chest.

"Aye," Trevor whispered as he held out his hand, fingers coated in dark blood.

Turning away, she dismissed his hand and whatever offer he had intended it to be. Carsyn Kidd watched her carefully, and Lir's copper-colored eyes remained on her hand and the red, irate sore that now occupied it. Unconcerned with decorum and proper protocols, she stalked off.

"So angry," the Viper mused as Anna walked past. "You look just like your mother."

Surely, she was mistaken; Anna looked nothing like her mother. They shared the same high cheekbones and pear shape, but other than that, she was her father's daughter, her brother's sister, all springy blonde hair and glacial eyes. Her mother's eyes had been dark blue and her hair had often fallen to her shoulders in a straight, soft, brown sheet.

Even if Anna looked like her mother had when she was in her prime, how would the Viper know that?

Chardae Badawi shook her head, gaze narrowing in what could have been disappointment or annoyance. "Not your face, you stupid girl. Your *spirit*—it has the same shape."

Bugger, what did that even mean?

Lovelace's hand brushed the small of her back, warm and brief, a quick reminder that they were leaving Corazon and its cutthroat Coalition. Leaving the treasure trove she so wished to explore too. The desire was a pinprick in her soul, a small sensation beneath the ire that pushed and pulled beneath her skin like a tide.

She hardly noticed anything as she followed the winding path. She crossed her arms against her chest tightly, anchoring her gaze along the ground. She heard the light taps of Juliana's boots and saw the brief dust the quartermaster kicked up, but for as much as she tried to keep her attention on the pirates in front of her, she felt Trevor's gaze on her back like twin stars casting heat.

Talk.

Oh, they'd have plenty of time to talk over the next week.

Seven days, Trevor had said.

Markus was resourceful; he'd find a way to survive Bryce Cunningham. He was just as stubborn as she was, and, though she didn't want to give Bryce any credit, he could weave a blade between a man's ribs like a master seamstress might thread a needle. He wouldn't have hit anything vital if for no other reason than the embarrassment it would bring his father for murdering John Savage's son.

A sense of urgency had buried itself in her gut since watching that ship sail away with her brother on it, but Anna hadn't experienced the numbing grief.

Was her confidence in Cunningham's swordsmanship the reason for it?

Or was it because the Pirate King should not have survived being thrown overboard with a cannonball trapped to his boots?

Anna sucked on her teeth, shoulders raising.

The splash echoed even above the thunder.

When they spilled out into the warmth of the jungle, it wasn't to blinding sunlight. Somewhere off in the distance, the sun set at a leisurely pace. The last rays cast every surface in buttery yellows and simmering reds. Anna stormed past the twins, past the chest of cast-away weapons, past the treeline that raised the hair along her arms as soon as she stepped beneath its canopy.

"Savage," Juliana Gray called.

Anna ignored her; she knew the way. She had memorized the twists and turns, but her feet would not go any further into the living dark. She glared at the wide-leaved flora. The breeze sifted through the small petals and threaded its way through the moss that hung like fetid hair.

"Anna," Trevor murmured before he cleared his throat, his knuckle brushing her shoulder. "Can I—can we talk?"

Talk.

There was that word again.

Like she could even entertain the idea of a conversation between them when all she wanted was to do her best interpretation of a maelstrom, ripping everything asunder and drowning it. Question after question surged forth, each one pulling at her like a hellish riptide.

Trevor *hadn't* drowned in the storm.

He *hadn't* been mortally wounded by the saber.

Had she not gotten him the antidote, he wouldn't have been killed by the poison either.

How? The word rang through her mind like a death knell. *God-damnit, how?*

"I don't want to talk," she snapped, rushing forward and away from his soft touch.

"Anna..." He coughed, breaths coming labored—*fine*, he'd said. "Anna, wait!"

"Take a fucking nap, Trev!" Tate called over the soft buzz of insects.

She remembered the way he had slouched against the crates before Cunningham kicked the door in, how groggy his voice had been.

Had he planned on napping the injury away then as well?

Splendid, positively splendid—another question for when her anger no longer drowned out the mere inklings of curiosity.

"Bloody fucking hell, if ye would just slow down, lass."

"Piss off, Lovelace," she cracked, glaring over her shoulder.

His cheeks had flushed, and the rest of his skin looked washed out, the color having drained away. She supposed that's what happened when one had been stabbed, but this was apparently *fine*. His hand fisted the fabric at his gut, putting pressure on a wound that seeped profusely even now.

Though it wasn't a mortal wound for the infamous, nigh-unkillable Pirate King, it certainly wasn't agreeing with him.

Anna turned away, nausea churning her stomach at seeing him hurt, seeing him bleed. Anna could only shoulder so much before fissures formed in her self-assurance. When she closed her eyes, Markus was bleeding out on Cunningham's deck, and that damn splash echoed on repeat in her ears.

Too much, there was too much. The cracks had formed in her walls, and now she had to shore them up.

"You're angry."

"Splendidly so."

She had been so afraid for him. Her fear had rotted her from the inside out, made her reckless with her body and decisions that impacted her brother.

What had been the point of it?

What had been the point of worrying about a man who did not require the sentiment? She swallowed stiffly, nose burning. She had wasted energy and time burning her concern. What choices might she have made if she'd known he couldn't die?

"If ye would just let me explain—"

Good God, she didn't want an explanation.

What she wanted was to scream at him, to take apart the dam holding her anger in check brick by brick and flood him with every last drop of it.

What she wanted was to scream at him, but she felt the desire to fall into his arms and cry her eyes out more. She couldn't think straight when he was near; she had always had a difficult time mastering herself when he was in such close proximity.

Anna didn't *want* to be alone.

But sometimes, one needed to be.

CHAPTER TWENTY-SIX

Fucking hell.

Trevor scrubbed his hand against the stubble of his jaw, smearing gods-damned blood against his skin. Was it no' enough that he felt like a monster? Did he have to look like one too? He'd been following the wee lass through the jungle and toward the beach. It surprised him naught that she'd found her way just fine, stomping the entire way like a wee giant.

She'd likely memorized which side the moss faced along wi' the twists and turns.

Anna was crafty like that.

Soon as the dirt trail opened to sandy beaches, the lass made a beeline for his tent in the distance. It was no' an overly large thing, but something wee and homey. Shite, he wouldn't be seeing the inside of it—no' that he'd planned on it. Anna had taken over his quarters on the ship in a matter of hours, he'd expected no less here.

On their left, the *Pale Queen* lay on her side, glowing softly in the growing moonlight. The stars were just peppering the sky in wee bright spots. Full moon was bloody good luck; the crew would need it if they were to get the careening done in a week.

"Captain," one of them called, "ye look like Bodhi needs a good look at ye!"

"Aye, aye." Trevor waved him off, clenching the fabric of his shirt tighter.

Prick had stabbed him.

If a male'd told him John Black had the balls to swing at the Pirate King, Trevor'd have laughed himself to an early grave.

The steel in his gut bothered him less than the hole in his favorite coat. Even that was naught compared to the wee condition that'd plagued him for years now. No' being able to die sounded a fancy thing until a male truly couldn't.

The lass stumbled, arms pinwheeling before she found her balance again. He glared at his hands; both of the fuckers had shot out in front of him, ready to keep her upright. Sighing, he opened his mouth and closed it, trying to find the right words to say to her.

He didn't think they existed.

But he'd try looking for them anyway.

Halfway to the tent, Anna stopped and whipped around as quick as a bloody whip. Her lovely mouth opened, a wee finger pointed at him. Good. If she wanted to yell at him, he'd let her. Anna could scream and argue and call him a shite head all she wanted so long as she talked to him. He didn't think he could take another voyage of the lass locked away in his gods-damned room, hellbent on keeping to herself.

It had been a strange form of torture, knowing she was in there and no' being able to see or speak wi' her.

Trevor's eyelids were heavy, growing more so wi' each passing second. Shite, he needed to talk wi' her before the abyss pulled him under. He needed a nap about as much as he needed a bloody hole in his head at current. He could only imagine how falling asleep in front of the lass would piss her off.

Trevor yawned, and the lass's jaw snapped closed before she spun on a heel, eyes wet and glassy.

Bloody hell.

He followed her under the flap of his tent, surprised when her hands planted themselves against his chest and shoved him right the fuck back out. Trevor took one step forward before freezing, listening as the first shaky breath left her lovely mouth. He ran his hand through his hair; it was still damp from being in that gods-damned crypt.

"Luv?" he asked, voice hoarse.

The lass did no' reply, and the wee prickle on his spine told him everyone's eyes were on him—on how he'd react to the lass.

Shite.

This was such fucking shite.

"Anna," he tried again in a whisper. "Are ye all right, lovely?"

He leaned his forehead against the post spanning the center of the entrance and sighed. Gone and fucked this one up at every gods-damn turn today, and he'd spent the better half of the walk back through that cursed jungle trying to figure out exactly what had angered her so.

She'd been furious before stepping foot on Tiburon—oh, aye, she'd been livid.

But she'd cooled off for a wee while in Corazon. He didn't know what had calmed her, but there was no' a doubt in his mind that whatever had ignited her temper had something to do wi' him, and bloody hell, he just wanted to apologize for whatever it might be.

No' that she'd accept anything from Trevor after watching him take Black's hand like a gods-damned butcher. Suppose all that really mattered was offering up a wee bit of himself in hopes she'd understand. Even if she didn't, at least he could say he'd bloody well tried.

Trevor's head swam.

If he wasn't careful, he'd pass out right here and the lass would stumble over him in the morning. Sighing, he leaned away from the post. It felt wrong to leave her in there, stewing in grief and rage.

"No, I'm not okay," she said finally as he stepped back. "I'm not some common whore."

"No, you're no'," he said quietly, the words scraping against his throat.

Of course, the Coalition thought sleeping wi' him meant she was a whore—no' a single fem had ever crawled in his bed because they wanted *him*. For Trevor, it had always been an exchange of sorts. Even though it'd felt different wi' Anna that first time, he'd woken up to find the same.

The lass'd tumbled him to find that bloody map.

It hadn't been about *him*.

It had been about what he had.

"And—and I thought we were friends," she said softly, and if his heart had no' already been bleeding in his chest, it would have started then.

"*Friends?*" He closed his eyes and tipped his head back.

"I said as much on Bryce's ship, didn't I? That I couldn't leave you behind because it wasn't right, that I couldn't do it? I care too much and—" Anna paused. The gods-damned word *care* bounced around his skull like a loose bullet. "But Markus is still on that ship and they are on their way to some god-forsaken island in hopes of seeking out a mythical beast, and I cannot for the life of me understand why you kept everything from me. I could maybe understand before we were thrown in the brig together, but *after?*"

Trevor huffed, a fucking angry laugh creeping up his throat.

"Did you see what he looked like before they tossed you overboard?"

What *he* looked like?

No, he could no' remember what Markus Savage had looked like before that wicked deep swallowed him whole. Could have told the wee fem exactly what she'd looked like, though, straight down to the pins in her hair and the bruises on her skin.

"Cunningham *stabbed* him, Trevor. Markus was bleeding out from his stomach. If I had known *you* would be fine, if I had known that *you are hard to harm and even harder to kill,* I might have been more concerned with getting my brother off that ship instead of rescuing you. Things might have been different. I don't know if Markus is alive or dead, and now I am apparently your whore, and I'm stuck on this damn island while he's—"

"Lass, I—"

"As soon as I have my brother back, I am leaving. I had a life—I had a flat, a career! I threw it all away for what? It certainly wasn't so I could be considered your whore. It wasn't so I could have the constant worry that my brother is dead or dying. Every time I look at you I'm reminded of choosing—" Anna paused, breathing deep. "I can't—I *can't*, Trevor."

Something in him...stopped.

Might have been his gods-damned heart, he couldn't be sure.

It hadn't been beating for a while now, no' truly. Sure, it had skittered back to life at the mere suggestion of a smile from Anna, and it warmed uncomfortably when he caught her staring, but it had been a bloody long time since he'd really felt the fucker thump in his chest.

Trevor scrubbed at his neck, glaring down at the sand.

Was this one of those times ye didn't leave when a fem asked?

Shite, he didn't know.

But Anna was hurting, and despite every inch of him burning to rush in there and take her up in his arms, he didn't. Likely muck this up worse if he stayed; the least he could do was listen.

He stepped back, swallowing stiffly.

Another step.

And another.

"I..." he said quietly before turning around. "I had a sister, Anna. A baby sister. And because of me, she's..." He cleared his throat, feeling that all too familiar burn in his eyes. "That guilt eats away at me a wee more every day, makes it a wee harder to live wi' myself. I promise ye, lass, that brother of yours'll be right as rain even if it costs me my bloody life."

If Taylee had taught him anything, it was that he couldn't keep the people he loved safe.

His feet dragged against the sand as he made his way to the fire in the distance. He saw the shadows of his crew dancing and drinking—could even hear Silas singing. The bastard couldn't carry a tune to save his life.

Trevor stumbled, foot scraping against the sand before he hit the ground. The air left his lungs in one deep grunt and then he just laid there and stared up at the stars. The Tides of Fate stared down at him, and it felt a wee bit like being mocked by the gods.

As a lad, he'd been told the Tides of Fate were there to lead sailors forward to their destiny and future—to greatness and glory.

Trevor snorted.

To fucking hell wi' greatness and glory.

CHAPTER TWENTY-SEVEN

It had been four days since the Coalition meeting.

Four days since she'd last spoken to the Pirate King.

Anna had never run from a man in her life and yet she'd run from Trevor Lovelace repeatedly. It had been a different sort of fear that twisted her insides, placing her on a path that *should* have led her away from him—as far away from him as she could possibly get.

Except every road always brought her straight back to him.

She was adequately frustrated with the whole damn thing.

Anna stared at the pale planks in front of her face.

Sleep had been a cruel mistress of late; every time she closed her eyes, she saw her brother bleeding out on the deck. Sometimes it was worse—sometimes it was staring at Trevor's back and blood dripping from a blade. If it wasn't those two brilliantly inconvenient images, it was the rubbery, grey faces of all the men she had cut her way through to get to where she was now.

Anna did not regret what she had done, but that did little in deterring their ghosts from haunting her at all hours of the night.

"If you're in here, bloody well say so." Tate groaned, stomping through the captain's quarters of the *Pale Queen*.

Papers shuffled.

Various trunks and drawers were opened and then promptly closed.

He's been saying her name, you know, someone had said quietly just last night.

Her gaze shifted from the bone-white flooring to the matching boards along the walls. She did not want to go back to the beach where she could hear about the state of the Pirate King's health in every whispered breath. At the very least, putting distance between herself and their concerned murmurs *should* have improved her sleep.

Only it hadn't.

If Trevor Lovelace was whispering a woman's name, she wanted no knowledge of it.

The solitude on the *Pale Queen* was supposed to help, but retreating here had only spawned more horrendous questions. Never in her life had she dreaded her curiosity or the depth of her wonderings, but if she wanted to snare these answers, she would have to find the Pirate King.

Why was a consistent war drum in the back of her mind, buzzing forth like carrion flies at every moment of still silence.

When she had tiptoed into the captain's quarters, Anna had been surprised with the additions to his quarters. Several ashwood trunks now sat next to his, lined with navy velvet and overflowing with clothes that had been tailored to fit her. Ballerinas and carousel horses had been carved into the sides of the trunks by a meticulous hand.

Those gorgeous trunks hadn't been all, either.

There was a matching changing screen in a soft mint with gold trim.

Additional throw pillows on the bed and feather-soft blankets in jewel tones.

Several journals had been stacked on his desk, empty of wonderings and tied shut with ivory ribbons.

"I've no' had enough sleep to deal wi' your shenanigans," Tate said, chipper tone coating his annoyance like a fine veneer. "Did ye know my brother has been driving us like slaves the past four days?

Determined to set sail tonight, he is, and I've a whole list of tasks to accomplish before then."

Anna nearly rolled her eyes, unconcerned with the quartermaster's whining.

"And ye, lass, are going to be helping me wi' one of them."

Unless it was setting a course for her brother, she didn't want anything to do with the quartermaster's damn tasks. Or the Lovelace brothers. Or this hellish feeling in her chest. Bugger, was a weensy moment of silence or a single good night's sleep too much to ask for?

Tate's feet padded across the floorboards softly. She paid little attention to his rummaging and pressed her face into the crook of her elbow. Maybe if she ignored him, he would simply go away.

A bottle fell—broke.

Tate inhaled sharply. "Now I smell like a gods-damned garden. I hope you're happy, lassie."

Happy, she thought, turning the word over in her mind.

Oh, no.

She was not *happy.*

Fear, despair, and anger were not the only reasons she had started avoiding Trevor Lovelace at every opportunity. Lying to herself had been easier than she would have thought; it was simply saying one thing when she felt another. It was giving meaningless rhyme or reason to the ghost of a touch, the whisper of words against the shell of her ear.

Anna hadn't run from what Trevor Lovelace was.

She had run from what he could be.

Tate's weight sunk into the feather mattress. "Interesting, this. Trevor hasn't slept in silk since ye stole that bloody map." She heard his hands smooth over the sheet's surface. "The bed is still warm. I know you're in here, Anna."

Bugger.

The quartermaster snapped several times, and even though she couldn't see him, she felt the weight of his gaze as it roamed the captain's quarters from one side to the other as he stood. Then, his steps grew closer until she knew he lurked directly above.

Tate sighed softly, nudging her with his god-awful *toe* of all things.

"Touch me with your foot again..." she warned, glaring at the toes in front of her face.

Anna's gaze wandered up from his toes to his impeccably sculpted calves and rough-spun, brown trousers that ended above his knees. North of his trousers were many abdominal muscles, all of which were uninspiring. Crossing his arms over his chest, he stared down at her with a grin.

Honestly, how had all the ballads been written about *this* Lovelace?

Tate might be pretty, but he was no match for his older brother.

Anna's jaw clenched. "Piss off."

"'Tis time to rise and shine, my wee bonnie lass."

"And why in the name of all that is holy would I want to spend time wi' ye, my wee lad?" Anna mocked, lifting to an elbow.

"I have a task I thought ye might enjoy—and the gods know that'll help my bastard of a brother out of his foul mood," he said, nudging her ribs with his toe. Anna swatted at his foot angrily, drawing a booming laugh from his lips. "Bloody hell, ye need a bath. Ye look like a raccoon wi' those wee chubby cheekies."

Sniffing, Anna scowled.

The man was right.

Too bad she couldn't climb in the copper tub of her own accord.

Her bones creaked and popped as she stood, and Tate whistled an obnoxiously felicitous song as she walked to her vanity. Planting her hands onto its pale tabletop, she stared past her own reflection. Tate leaned against the wall behind her. Pirates were not supposed to possess devilish good looks, they were supposed to be grimy and dirty, and yet here the Lovelace brothers stood in clear contradiction of that.

Their sister must have been quite stunning as well.

Anna swallowed hard, gaze dropping as she shoved thoughts of their deceased sister from her mind. It lived too close to the fears she possessed. Moving several bottles around her vanity aimlessly, she raised her gaze, meeting her own icy blue eyes in the mirror.

She looked like a partially drowned raccoon.

"What are the chances of allowing me to wallow in self-pity if I say please?"

"None."

"You're an abhorrent disappointment." She sighed, wiping the dried makeup from beneath her eyes. Anna frowned, repressing the growl threatening to rise in her throat as the kohl merely smudged, adding to the bruised look her sleepless nights had left in their wake.

"A fem has never told me I'm a disappointment before." Tate chuckled, head shaking briefly as he met her gaze in the mirror. "Especially no' so close to a feather bed."

"Keep your silver tongue to yourself," she found herself saying, selecting several small bottles and a tin basin. "Magic only works when one doesn't understand the tricks—and I understand yours quite well."

"Careful, lassie, ye say shite like that where the wind'll whisper it to my brother and you'll get me skinned."

"Only skinned?" she mused. "What do you suppose the weather will be like today?"

Tiburon had been an absolute paradise for two of the four days she had been wasting away and twiddling her thumbs. The other two it had rained until her fingers pruned from the moisture in the air. Anna was prepared for every potential disaster, though—the new chests and trunks had seen to that. With a sigh, she left the vanity and went to one such trunk.

"We're in paradise, chances of it being beautiful are about the same as ye catching my brother working shirtless on deck—all...*sweaty*." Tate paused, distaste as clear on his face as it was in his voice. Her hands stilled on the deep purple shirt she'd pulled from the trunk. "It'll be fucking hell for me to endure, but at least you'll enjoy the show."

Anna blinked several times, mouth drying.

She hoped she wouldn't see him—and certainty not all lathered up and lifting heavy boxes. The Pirate King had not made it difficult to avoid him; he'd been sequestered away in an unknown destination for nearly three days. But just before nightfall yesterday, as the sun was setting and painting the world in warm yellows and reds, Anna had seen him—and felt things.

Her fingers continued sifting from one item of clothing to the next. "You do realize I'm furious with him, yes?" she reminded Tate, her voice coming quieter than intended.

"Aye, I know. We all know. Between refusing to talk wi' him and doing everything in your power to piss him off. The crew's taken note. 'Tis like ye know exactly what will cause him the most distress. Fuck, you've thought of things no' even I have, and I consider myself to be a gods-damned expert in pissing him off."

"Maybe I simply know him better—fresh pair of eyes and all that."

Her gaze centered on the off-white shirt between her fingers. The cut in the chest was steep, and three brass buttons adorned the front.

It was a splendid item, clearly well-made like everything else in the trunks.

Where had it all come from on such short notice?

Anna turned to another crate.

The shirt would do just fine. Now she needed a fresh pair of trousers and underthings.

"Ye know my brother better than me?" Tate laughed. "No, lassie. Ye spent, what, ten minutes between the sheets wi' him and a month rummaging around the continent? I've known Trevor longer than you've been alive," he said, voice proud. "But I do think you're reckless and don't have a single fucking ounce of fear for consequences, and that helps wi' your wiliness."

She flushed at the reminder of her night with Trevor. "The trunks are new."

"Aye, he can be a wee beast, but my brother understands shite like basic amenities and clothing. Ye should thank him." Tate brushed a stray hair behind his ear; the rest was as chaotic as a magpie's nest with glimmering bronze beads woven throughout. "Though, I'm a wee curious as to how he knows all your sizes."

"Use your imagination," she said, pulling out a pair of thin, dark shorts that would end mid-thigh.

"Fuck, no. I don't want those images knocking around in here," he said, motioning dramatically to his head. "'Tis bad enough knowing ye wanted to play peekaboo wi' my brother's vein cane."

His brother's—

A grin twitched at her lips.

"I mean, you're lovely enough, lassie, but *Trevor?*" Tate snorted. "I love him, but he's a wee dense when it pertains to the wants and fantasies of a female. I've always thought it's because he's the bloody king."

"Why's that?" she asked.

"He can't always do and say what he likes, canno' admit to what he wants because of who he thinks he is. He's the king, aye, but he's more than that. Always has been, no matter what he believes."

"If anyone could say or do what they like, one would think it would be the Pirate King. Sail wherever the winds take him, burn ships that hail him, pillage towns, transport women—bed them too," she added as an afterthought. "Debauchery and all manners of unsavory activity befitting one bestowed with the title of Pirate King."

"Aye, you'd think that. But you'd be wrong. Most just want something from him, and being the Pirate King just means he can't do any of those bloody things. Sometimes I wish he would—like when we were younger. The bastard thinks he's an old man now."

"Old?"

Positively ridiculous.

"Aye, ask him how old he is sometime." Tate grinned, a mischievous twinkle in his gaze.

Anna strode back to her vanity, filling the small basin with water from a pitcher. A washcloth sat next to it. She watched more and more of her scar become visible, each undone button revealing more of it. Once she reached the end of her scar, she glanced at the quartermaster behind her. At some point he'd laid down on his back with his arms pillowed beneath his head.

Something about his demeanor reminded her of Markus.

"Your supervision is no longer required," she said quietly.

"Spending time wi' ye is no' supervision; I'm enjoying myself."

She glanced at her reflection and then back down to the quarter-master on the floor. When Tate didn't move, Anna whipped her dirty shirt over her head and threw it at his face. If he truly thought his brother would have an issue with promiscuous words, this should send the quartermaster scrambling from the captain's quarters. Crossing her arms over her bare breasts, she turned and stared down at him with a raised brow.

Tate had scrambled to his feet, clutching her smelly shirt to his chest in alarm. A panicked noise croaked from the back of his throat as he looked from her shirt to her naked torso.

His throat bobbed.

And then the door slammed shut, leaving her in glorious solitude.

"The fem is trying to get me fucking killed!" Tate yelled in response to some question she hadn't heard.

"The fem is trying to take a bath!" she called, slipping her disgusting cotton trousers down her legs.

"Do ye need the tub?"

A cold sweat formed between her shoulders at the thought of the copper bathtub.

"Very brisk sponge bath," she corrected.

Turning from side to side, Anna frowned at her reflection in the mirror.

This was the thinnest she had ever been, but no one would accuse her of emaciation. Her hips still flared, accentuated by thick, toned legs and a muscular rump. Normally she held a little more weight through her waist, but all those missed meals had clearly had an impact. Her breasts were still their same tragically small masses, perfecting her pear form.

Suppose she should be thankful for that.

Anna traced the shiny white scar that cut from her neck and down between her breasts. Her clavicles bordered the ugly thing like little wings.

If she stared at it for too long, memories of that night filtered forth with the utmost clarity. Gentle fingers holding her as fire wove itself through her skin. Her brother's murmured prayers and the heat of his hand wrapped tightly around hers. The doctor's surprise that she had survived a pirate's blade separating facia and biting into bone.

The doctor aboard her brother's ship hadn't been the only one filled with surprise.

She'd been equally aghast at seeing the swollen wound, stitches barely keeping it together.

Anna knew now who those gentle fingers had belonged to. She likely owed him her life.

The sponge bath passed far too quickly, cool water sliding against her skin. Anna wiped the sweat and grime from her body one bowlful at a time before massaging a tonic into her hair that would detangle and tame her curls.

She flushed, only half surprised the underthings fit as well as they did. It was as if she'd picked the cotton bandeau bra and matching thong out herself. Threading a dark belt through the loops of her shorts, she tucked her shirt in and slipped on a pair of ankle boots.

Pulling her hair into a knot that resembled the quartermaster's, she stepped onto the deck of the *Pale Queen*. Anna looked left and right as she wrapped a bit of cloth around her left hand and tied it off with her teeth. The sore that had been left behind was still tender to the touch and sensitive to the warm air of Tiburon. The sound of the crew preparing to set sail echoed about, men calling down from the rigging as others rolled barrels across the deck or tied off ropes.

Business as usual, it seemed.

Bodhi was a dark splotch in the distance, one of many pulling a behemoth of a rope. Over on the port side, Zarya talked animatedly with the man Anna had seen scrubbing the decks on multiple occasions. His hair shone nearly blue in the light, like a raven's feathers.

The temperature rose drastically as she stepped from the shadows of the helm and into the direct sunlight, looking for the quartermaster.

Good God, it wouldn't be long before her toes stuck together within the confines of her boots.

Her attention slowly slid right—

Trevor stood not even ten feet away, carrying a large crate. With a heft, he set it down and wiped at his forehead with the back of his hand, grinning briefly at something someone must have said.

Anna couldn't breathe, gaze searching for evidence of his wound even as she stepped in his direction. She found nothing in her observation except for the sheen of sweat on his body and the flush of exertion on his cheeks. Leather strips had been wrapped around his wrists and, true to what Tate had claimed, the Pirate King wore no shirt—only a pair of shorts.

Bugger, why was he so tragically handsome?

"Captain!" Juliana's call cut through the general noise on the deck.

Trevor turned, feet carrying him across the planks.

His strides were perhaps a hair slower than they should have been. Swallowing hard, she stared at the tattoos spilling down the column of his throat and over his pecs before ending at his middle knuckles. They moved with his body, fitting like a second skin made of myth and ink.

He leaned over the taffrail, exposing the tattoos on his back, and ran a hand through his hair, causing the thick, wine-red strands to stand up.

"You're staring, lassie," Tate said, nudging her with his elbow.

Anna cleared her throat. "Where've you been?"

"Right here the entire bloody time."

"Tate!" Trevor yelled, turning with the action.

Bugger, he was going to see her.

They were going to have to talk.

Talk.

"Aye, Captain!"

What amusement that had been present in his eyes winked out near immediately as he met her gaze—her icy blue with his born of shadows. Trevor's body straightened and she held his gaze, hoping for anger to bubble up. That wasn't the emotion that tumbled through her gut and climbed its way up her throat. It wasn't the one heating her chest or causing her heart to flutter as if a hummingbird had taken up residence behind her ribs.

"You're staring," Tate whispered. "*Again.*"

"Piss off, little Lovelace."

Trevor cocked his head, looking away from her and back over the taffrail. "Come again, Jules?"

Bumping her with his elbow, Tate grinned down at her and walked off after his brother with quick, long-legged strides. She followed hesitantly. She had no real choice in the matter; Tate would likely throw her over his shoulder if she refused to aid him.

Then she'd have to embarrass him by putting him on his back, and she'd rather avoid that.

"Captain Kidd would like permission to come aboard!"

Trevor slumped, and even though she couldn't hear it, she knew he groaned as he rolled his whole head in exasperation. She had spent too much time with him to miss the little tells he showed, to miss the tense line of his shoulders.

"Send the lad up," he called, gaze shifting to Tate. "Careful out there"

"Aye," he replied quietly. "I'll let naught happen to your wee lassie."

Shaking his head, Trevor avoided her stare. "'Tis no' the fem I'm worried about."

If he wasn't worried about her, why did Tate have to be careful?

Anna strode past the Pirate King without a word, eyeing the ramp before turning her gaze upward to the blue skies and big cumulus clouds that reminded her of cotton candy.

They passed Captain Carsyn Kidd about halfway down the ramp.

When Juliana had said the chief wanted to come aboard, Anna hadn't realized the woman meant right now.

The chief slowed, turning to face her with a small frown.

Did any of the men on this damned island wear proper clothing?

It wasn't a *complaint* but...

Her eyes drifted downward of their own accord.

The chief was leaner than either Trevor or Tate, though he certainly wasn't lanky or spindly. Clearly defined muscles waited beneath his tanned skin like a predator waiting to strike. A line of hair trailed into his trousers and peppered the center of his chest, the same blue-black as the mop atop his head. Intricate leather vambraces were buckled over his forearms, and a green cloth had been tied about his waist, a cutlass waiting at his side like a loyal dog.

Anna ran her tongue over her teeth, staring at the tattoo wrapped around his bicep. It was a stunning raven standing atop a skull that was missing its mandible. Other images framed the bird on either side, but he passed by too quickly for her to make them out.

His gaze darted over her shoulder and narrowed at the quartermaster. Brow furrowing, she glanced at Tate. His grin didn't reach his eyes as he blew a kiss back to the pirate chief and continued his way down the ramp.

It was no rumor that Carsyn Kidd and Trevor Lovelace did not play nicely; their disagreements were rather infamous. One could not step foot in any drinking establishment, reputable or sordid, without hearing about the notorious accolades of the Pirate King and Carsyn Kidd.

That, of course, did not account for the look he'd given Tate.

Though after witnessing the Coalition meeting, she wouldn't put it past the quartermaster to get up to his own mischief where the chiefs are concerned.

If Carsyn Kidd had a sister, Tate had likely tumbled her.

Feeling goosebumps raise along her arms and warmth heating her back, Anna looked over her shoulder. Sucking on her teeth, she turned back toward the beach and ignored how the Pirate King blanketed her with a careful gaze as he leaned his forearms on the taffrail, fingers laced together.

Did he think keeping her within his sight would keep her safe?

Nonsense.

Trouble found no one quicker than it did Anna, and it would likely find her faster here.

Tiburon stretched in front of her, white beaches arching to either side of the ramp. Her gaze dropped to the crystal-clear waters below, skin prickling. The cerulean waters glimmered with the morning sun, revealing gemstone-colored fish darting back and forth through the tides. Between the splendid beaches and itty fish, the waters of Tiburon were a treasure trove all their own.

Untangling the web of secrets surrounding Corazon might have been her initial reason for exploring Tiburon, but Anna very well could have stayed an extra week if for no other reason than to wake up to this view.

Maybe she should have taken Trevor up on his offer.

"I'm pretty sure my brother was using ye to hide his cock, lass."

Anna stumbled as they stepped off the last plank and onto Tiburon's beach. "Excuse me?"

"Ye know exactly what I said. I'm quite certain ye accidentally grabbed the gods-damned thing in Corazon."

She couldn't help it—she laughed.

"Can't really blame him, lassie like ye sitting on his lap." Tate prattled on, staring up at the sky with his fingers threaded behind his neck. "Should probably thank ye. No' one of us wanted to see it while discussing such. Would have been rather distracting if his raging erection decided to sit at the bloody table too."

Anna laughed hard, turning to meet Tate's gaze. He was already smiling down at her, his charcoal-colored eyes so like those of his brother. "What is wrong with you?"

"Wrong?" he asked, mock offense layering in his voice. "Naught is wrong wi' me, I'm perfect. My mum told me so."

"I think she might have lied to you."

Tate shrugged, unconcerned. "Most do."

She opened her mouth before closing it softly. What a sorry existence to live if most everyone around him told small lies here and there —if it was true, that is. Sometimes the perception of one's words and intentions were actually quite different than the reality of them.

Like Trevor, she thought as they fell into companionable quiet.

She listened to the birds cooing quietly in the jungle's canopy and the slow roll of waves breaking against the shore. Relief flooded through her as Tate turned from the jungle; if Anna could avoid that cursed jungle and its screaming echoes, she would.

A few crew members plodded around the sands, breaking down

the camp. She assumed most of them had been delegated to ensuring the *Pale Queen* was tip-top before departure. The sun warmed her as they walked, and soon the muffled calls of the crew quieted until they were no more than mere suggestions of speech on the wind.

She wasn't entirely sure how much time had passed before the rough outline of brightly colored buildings broke through the dim darkness of the jungle. The walk, with its soft ocean breeze and rolling waves, had been pleasant. Silence was not what she'd expected from the quartermaster of the *Pale Queen*, but it seemed even he valued it on occasion.

Cutting inland, the beach shaped a splendid cove. The calm, clear waters were peppered with small boats, their triangular sails painted with all sorts of designs. A smile twitched at her lips. There was an anchor, a skull, and a sun held within the confines of a circle. Her gaze slid from the pretend pirate ships to the play swords crisscrossed in the sand and the mismatched pairs of shoes lying alongside them.

She smiled as she watched children sail their mock pirate ships. A dark-haired boy fell into the water with a splash. For a moment, she stiffened and held her breath. But then he broke the surface of the water, head shaking as he laughed and paddled back to his boat.

Anna glanced left and then right.

This was not the Tiburon she remembered.

This was not the island that had caged and kept her, even if it was for a short while.

Her gaze narrowed on the path ahead, where the trees thinned and revealed buildings made of brick. Someone had painted over them in pastel tones. She saw mints and cotton-candy pinks, lavender and canary yellow. Another building had even been painted a soft blue, pinstripes the color of cranberries stretching from its foundation to the rafters.

They were organized, spaced, and planned along the road. Signs painted with clear, crisp pictures hung from the fronts of all the buildings. The lavender one sported a needle and thread; the blue, pinstriped building had an outline of a cow. They were old—but how could that be? It would have made more sense if they had recently sprouted up from the wicked depths of Tiburon, but that wasn't the case.

These buildings had stood here for *years*.

And there were children—*happy* children.

What is going on here? she wondered, brows drawing together.

Tate veered down a smaller dirt path, taking her farther into the quaint market where men and women walked from one store front to the next. A few women wore skirts, but most wore trousers or shorts. There weren't many shoppers, but there were enough to make the hairs on her arms rise—enough to start scouring the landscape for an escape route.

The first rule of survival usually started with an escape route.

She nearly bumped into the quartermaster when he came to an abrupt halt in front of a mint-green building, its paint peeling and cracked. Her gaze rose to the symbol painted on the weathered sign.

A...cake?

Disbelief soured her tongue. Bakeries were little slices of heaven on earth, a true reprieve from the world. A jungle rumored to be cursed? Acceptable. Children laughing on its beaches? It was a stretch, but children were often a product of a pirate's favorite pastime and were known for felicitous giggles.

But a *bakery* on Tiburon?

Her head whipped toward Tate, but he was already grinning down at her.

"You jest," she said, glancing back toward the supposed bakery.

An arched window stared at her. On a lovely display sat a layered cake, the crumb coat thin. Freshly cut strawberries circled the top, making Anna's chest tighten. Her mother had always commissioned strawberry shortcake for Markus on their birthday.

Anna had gotten him one on their twentieth birthday, but it hadn't been the same.

"My sweet tooth knows no bounds, lass; I do no' jest about pastries."

Anna shook her head.

Could it be possible that Tiburon, the crown jewel of the Coalition of Pirates and seat of the infamous Pirate King, had a building dedicated to baked goods and frosted delights?

"It's not your sweet tooth that surprises me; even I've heard about your misadventures with tarts," she said smartly, ignoring the choked laughter that came from the quartermaster. "It's that Tiburon has a bakery."

And it was a damn good one if the smell was anything to go by.

"We're not proud of it," he sighed, a strange sadness chasing any amusement from his voice.

"Not proud of what?"

"Tiburon. Our legacy." Tate stepped toward the door. "It has taken a bloody long time to reclaim wee sections of the island. After all these years, this is all we've fucking managed."

Not enough.

Anna knew the feeling well.

"It wasn't always the capital of pirates, ye know." Tate shrugged a shoulder, hands in his trouser pockets. "I like thinking it might be more again one day. We might be more again. Now, ye wait here. I'll be back in a minute."

A bell chimed, and then he was gone.

Anna stood awkwardly outside the bakery, shifting her weight from one foot to the other. Quick glances left and right revealed only three individuals—two women and one man, on the other side of the street.

He'd left her alone.

Swallowing nervously, she dared a glance at the bakery door. She could run for it and commandeer a ship, sail it to her brother. Anna didn't have to worry about storms overtaking her now that the Pirate King had taken care of that damn spot on her palm. Bryce Cunningham rose to the surface of her mind, the way he had been saturated with wine, the way he held himself when he pushed Trevor overboard.

There would be no better ending for him than death. She only needed to figure out how to deliver it.

How did one kill a man like Bryce Cunningham?

A gust carried the smell of fresh bread back to her, quickly followed by the metal *ding* from moments ago. Whatever freedom she'd been gifted had come and gone. Tate held a brown paper sack in one hand, the top rolled shut. As the quartermaster neared on long, lazy strides, he rummaged in the bag until he held a pastry in front of her.

Anna stared down at the small shell-shaped pastry.

A madeleine.

Markus had always fancied strawberry shortcake, but these were Anna's favorite. The small sponge cake sat in the palm of her hand, roughly the size of an egg and shaped like a seashell. Powdered sugar lightly dusted the surface, and it smelled of delicate vanilla and delicious almond flavoring.

How had he...?

Trevor.

Spinning on a heel, Tate shoved one of the delicacies into his mouth and cut across the packed dirt street toward a weensy path that sliced through the jungle. Anna had to jog to catch up with his long strides.

Why were they in a hurry all of a sudden?

Tate started whistling, the tune different from the one Trevor knocked his knuckles to. Anna searched for the sun. Judging from its position, they were heading farther north.

What was north?

He held another madeleine out for her.

She shook her head, the murmured ocean breaks growing louder with every step.

"Thinking?" he asked around the pastry in his mouth.

"Always."

"All the gods-damned time? Sounds bloody exhausting."

"Why else would I require so much sleep?" she asked, swatting at the buzzing insects.

Tate snorted, drawing her gaze. "We both know ye don't sleep."

"Do we?"

"Aye, *we* do." He nodded. "Who the fuck do ye think followed ye

249

about every time ye snuck out of your tent or around the *Queen* at night? Was no' my brother. Prick's too bloody big to sneak."

Anna had suspected as much.

But she grinned at the thought of Trevor tiptoeing after her while she inspected the cannons and dug through the crew's trunks while they slept.

"Did you know the one named Silas has women's underthings in his trunk?" she offered, grinning wider as she remembered finding pale pink lace in the box sitting near his hammock. "Splendid pink, lacy things."

Tate's laugh erupted, and the sound was nothing short of contagious. The genuine chime of it pulled an amused chuckle from her as well, and before she knew it, they were laughing as they walked down the narrowing path. Shaking her head, she turned to look at him. The smile slipped from her face.

His mouth had the same shape as Trevor's when he laughed.

The path turned sharply and the loose dirt beneath her boots quickly gained a layer of sand. Tall, brownish-green strands of beachgrass grew from either side in thick clusters, creating a high arch above their heads. The few noises from the market grew further away, and soon the only audible sound was the hush of the breeze through the trees and the rumble of the ocean.

Where was he taking her?

"All right, lassie, what are ye thinking about?" he asked, bumping her with a bony elbow. "I see those wheels turning."

"Too much," she said without thought, though she wouldn't have been able to find truer words if she tried. "Why I agreed to take an afternoon stroll with the *Pale Queen's* quartermaster, naked of any weapons, for one. But mostly my brother."

"I don't know if ye know this or no', but your brother is a fucking prick. Out of all the Briland captains that have almost caught us, your brother has always come the closest. I'm sure he's fine."

"Last I saw Markus, he'd been gutted like a fish—and unlike your brother, mine is not as likely to survive an altercation of that caliber."

Tate nodded his head thoughtfully. "Aye, Trev is the biggest bastard I know. Even when he's good and fucked, he does no' let on. Are ye the oldest?"

"I am."

"Trevor is too, but Taylee was always pretending to be our mum. If no' for her, we wouldn't have ever bathed. She could sweet talk our way out of anything. She saved my brother's hide from more than a few lashes."

"Taylee," Anna echoed, remembering the way it had rolled off of Trevor's tongue, still full of grief and guilt.

"Aye."

A terrible sadness fell over his features then. The smile faded from his face with an uncertainty Anna had never seen before—not just from Tate, but from anyone. He turned his attention to the ground, looking out and away from her, shielding his face.

Bugger, what had happened to their sister?

Anna remained quiet, unsure of what else to do or say.

She more than recognized the grief that hung about Tate's shoulders like a mantle. After their mother had passed, Anna had seen the same signs of loss in her own features and mirrored in those of her brother. It was easy enough to spot loss once one had experienced it, to see the cracks one might attempt to shore up.

Like called to like, after all, and misery loved its company.

Grasping for something to lift the heavy blanket of unspoken emotion from their shoulders, Anna cleared her throat. "Markus is...*easy,*" she said on a sigh.

"Lass, even *I* have heard of your brother's—"

"That's not what I meant." She grinned. "But that too, I suppose. He's easy in a way I could never be, genuinely happy about everything. And it takes a great deal of effort to shake him. Smiles and sunshine, grit and grandeur...I think you'd like him."

Honesty came easy with Tate Lovelace. Maybe it was because there weren't any truths held between them like lightning bugs trapped in a bottle. Or maybe it was the lack of investment Anna had in how Tate saw her.

"Your brother has tried blowing one too many bloody holes in the

Queen for me to *like* him," Tate muttered as he stuffed another pastry into his mouth.

The path opened over a hill, stopping her in her tracks. Off to their right stood an outcropping of rocks, the formation resembling hands in prayer. The jungle they walked from jutted against the outcropping.

Squinting, she cocked her head. The position of the trees reminded her of a sleeve.

Sea stacks rose from the water in all sizes and shapes, their bases easily seen through the crystal-clear waters. The beach had a natural ambiance to it, one wrapped in intimacy with nothing but the lap of the ocean against the shore.

A seagull called overhead, the only witness to whatever the quartermaster had planned.

Splendid.

Absolutely splendid.

"Secluded beach, warm day, brilliant view...and would you look at that"—she nodded, attention roaming the sands in either direction—"not a soul in sight. I am flattered, but I am not interested."

"Would no' dream of it! You're absolutely gorgeous, lassie, big blue eyes and whatno', but Trevor would kill me—fucking *kill* me. And despite what everyone believes, I do have a wee sense of self-preservation. This way. Bigger steps, lass."

Anna stared at his back for a moment before following him down the sandy hill and toward the outcropping of rock stretching high into the air. It took a short amount of time to cross the beach. Sweat meandered down her back with the intensity of the sun.

The rockery rose before her, stones porous and dark. Small alcoves had whittled their way through the stone like ants boring tunnels through dirt. Some were large enough for Anna to kneel in, though others wouldn't have fit a mouse.

Trailing her fingers against a fine line of green algae that grew against the rocks, she glanced forward. This was where the water would sit at high tide. A light shiver crawled up her spine now that she stood within the shadows of the outcropping, the sun somewhere on the other side. Tate motioned her forward with a tip of his head and then stepped into the dense patchwork of shadows.

Were the tunnels naturally occurring, or had someone carved them?

Bugger all that, where the hell did they go?

As Anna's eyes adjusted to the dim lighting, intentional lines began to stand out along the walls. Leaning forward, she squinted at the scrawled carvings. They took shape, relaxing into a language that looked strangely familiar. She scratched a fingernail against one symbol before walking to the other wall and glaring at another.

She'd seen these before, but where?

Oh, this was going to piss her off.

Tate waded through puddles and deeper into the cave. She followed him, trusting he knew their heading. Every now and then, Anna stopped to inspect another symbol or sign, picking at the algae or grit that had accumulated with time. One vaguely resembled a crown with a single horizontal line and three arrow points above it.

The sun played hide and seek as they meandered through the tunnel's lazy curves. On a few occasions, an entire wall would open, allowing for a cutout of the ocean beyond. The sky looked painted through these porous frames, like the clouds had been designed by a deft hand.

Every step further into the outcropping fell heavier than the last, like time was trying to pull her backward until she could reconsider traipsing around this potential death trap.

The quartermaster stopped at a fork in the path and stared at a cluster of carved pictographs. She suspected he was looking for the grouping of rectangles and the almost-crown that had decorated each turn they'd made so far.

He turned to her then, a grin on his face.

"Well, are ye ready?"

"I was born ready," she told him, anticipation eating her insides like a cancer.

He followed the split to the left, Anna right on his heels. A gauzy, red coil of cloth blocked their path, the tassels along its bottom blowing faintly in a gust of air. The very same kiss of briny wind tousled the small corkscrews of hair framing her face and hanging near her ears.

A curtain was all that stood between Anna and whatever wild goose chase of a task Tate had dragged her on. She wanted to know what was behind the curtain, though, what could possibly be hidden away in a labyrinth of a rock outcropping. Honestly, with the pictographs and twisting tunnels, it was vaguely reminiscent of Heylik Toyer.

Anna strode forward, gaze anchored to the sheer fabric glimmering with small threads of gold. It was a little too coincidental, wasn't it? A labyrinth with symbols carved into the walls to denote the safe passages? She barely paused before tossing the fabric over her shoulder and—

She slid to a stop, eyes widening.

"I..." Anna swallowed hard, gaze trailing up, up, up to where the ocean misted, forming rainbows in the sunlight filtering in from cutouts in the ceiling.

"I've always been rather partial to this place," Tate commented from behind her.

"It's a library."

Her eyes burned as her gaze devoured the cavernous space in front of her. Shelving had been carved straight into the rockery, climbing tens of feet into the air. She followed it in disbelief. There was an innumerable number of books here.

Every wall, every niche, nearly every surface had been covered with old parchments and leather-bound tomes. To her left, the floor dipped down, giving way to a small cove, carpeted in powdery, white sand. Fish zigged and zagged through the water, breaking the surface in colorful arcs.

She had been wrong earlier.

Corazon was not the treasure trove on Tiburon; it was this place, this secret salt-water library.

"Your powers of deduction are truly uncanny, Miss Savage," Tate mocked in her Bellcaster accent. Throwing himself to the sandy ground, he reverted to his natural brogue. "Of course, 'tis a bloody library. What the fuck else would it be wi' all these books, fem?"

Anna drifted past a small nook covered in throw rugs, their bright colors and intricate pattern hardly grabbing her attention in the presence of all the books. Good God, there had to be thousands. What task could Tate possibly have that involved a library?

She'd stab him if they were meant to dismantle it in anyway.

"Why are we here?" she asked, turning to him.

Tate had closed his eyes, but he grinned at her question. "Fuck if I know, I'm just the messenger."

"What do you mean you don't know?"

"Bloody hell, Trev said to bring ye here. So I brought ye. He didn't say what to do when we arrived."

Her feet dragged forward of their own accord until she stood in front of a long line of books. Anna ran her fingers along the leather spines—there wasn't any dust, though sand and shells sprinkled the shelving in dense patches.

Closing her eyes, she breathed deep. It smelled like old leather and cool sand. Anna opened her eyes, gaze roving the shelves. From what she could tell, the salty air hadn't decimated the books. She honestly didn't care *why* they'd gone untouched by time and weather, only that they had.

Her attention drifted upward once more to where rainbows danced among the shafts of light.

Bugger, how did she reach the books all the way up there?

Was she supposed to climb?

Anna stepped back and squinted into the distance. There had to be a ladder around here somewhere. Instead, her gaze fell on the quartermaster lounging about on ornate rugs, his arms tucked under his head. Nodding to herself slowly, her attention dropped to the absurd length of his arms.

Finally, a productive use for his ridiculous height.

He wouldn't be able to reach all the shelves, but Anna had lurked in archives before, she knew the creativity required for reaching books along the topmost shelves.

"Why are ye looking at me like that?" he mumbled, mouth pressed against his arms.

"Oh, the plans I have for you quartermaster, sir."

"Bloody hell, if ye do no' curb that tongue, lassie, I'm the one who'll end up wi' a lashing."

Anna snorted.

"Ye think he wouldn't?"

She ran her tongue over her teeth, attention roaming from one book to the next. So many books and so little time. "I think you overestimate whatever it is that's..." She trailed off, squinting at a dark spine with an inky shine. "Not that there is...anything..."

Tate spoke, but his words were lost to her; only his general intonation made it to her ears as she stepped toward the ghoulish book.

Sometimes when she walked into a library, Anna went looking for a specific book. It was an adventure of sorts in the Board of Antiquity's archives; the entirety of it used an outdated sorting system that one only figured out by trial and error. There were other times, though, when she would walk down those three flights and into the dim, dusty lighting and a book would find her.

This was one of those times.

The book was strangely cool to the touch, its onyx surface almost dewy beneath her fingers. Anna traced the great sea beast painted in white on the cover, following the tentacles as they wrapped around the spine and trailed onto the back of the book.

Hello, beastie, she thought. *Pleased to make your acquaintance.*

Anna examined the book as she stalked back to where the quartermaster lay sprawled on the ground. There was no writing on the outside of the book, and the page edges glowed silver and bronze in the warm light. Plopping onto a dark blue cushion with a satisfying *umph,* she sank into it until it nearly engulfed her.

When had she last curled up like this with a good book?

She couldn't remember.

Good God, it had been too long.

Settling in, she breathed deep. The book smelled familiar, like sand, brine, and something darker, like spices on her tongue. The strange smell sent a jolt of electricity through her veins and warmed her belly. Closing her eyes, she swallowed hard past the recognition.

Bugger.

"Bloody curious, ain't it, lassie, that ye would pick that chair?"

"Don't get too comfortable down there."

"And why the hell no'? My brother's been working us damn near till death," he said, leaning up onto his elbows to stare at her. "I deserve a nap."

"Nap away, you poor abused child," Anna said. "Just know you'll be fetching and carrying as many books as you can carry. I'm taking as many back to the ship as I can."

And she would.

With decent enough reading material, this endeavor might not be quite as terrible as she had originally thought.

"Ye just want to see me flex," Tate said, lying his head back on his arms with a grin. "'Tis fine so long as it stays between us."

Were all Lovelaces this full of themselves?

Anna shook her head and cracked open the book.

There were no words on the first page, nor had anything been written on the second. But on the third page, a heavy, red-black script started at the top and continued down until the very bottom. Scowling down at the messy script, she sighed. There were no margins, no paragraph breaks; it was all just one block of text smooshed together. The handwriting was nearly illegible and required her to follow every line with her finger.

Bugger, what demon had penned this gibberish?

Leaning down, Anna squinted at the writing and groaned.

Why was it always *Aepith?*

CHAPTER TWENTY-EIGHT

Fucking hell.

Trevor wiped the back of his hand against his forehead, the bite of cool wind no' at all bothering him. Felt bloody great wi' the sweat he'd worked up carrying crates to and fro, up and down the gods-damned stairs. He lowered a hand to his stomach where that bloody prick'd run him through; what was left of the wound ached something fierce from his hard work prepping the *Queen*.

It'd been good for him, making his body work so his mind could rest.

Anna's laughter caught his attention, damn near ripping his head in the other direction. It was the kind of sound that rang like music, the kind that made him lean in and listen a wee longer, fucking chancer that he was.

He craned his neck over the taffrail as the sun sank into the horizon behind him, casting an orange glow over his shoulder. Bloody hell. The breath loosed from his lungs in a long sigh at seeing the bonnie sight of Anna striding up the ramp in the shadow of the *Pale Queen*. Then she was on the deck, head tipped up to Tate, revealing the lovely stretch of her throat in the warm evening light.

She smiled, full and bright like a weight had been lifted off her wee shoulders.

Good.

Trevor frowned at the stack of books in her hands. He'd have to have a chat wi' his brother about having the lass carry all that. Tate held a stack too, but that wasn't the fucking point. The lass still kept her hand wrapped, she should no' be carrying a stack of bloody books. He leaned his elbows against the taffrail and stared at her smile like a man who'd never seen the sunrise before.

At least she looked happier, settled in a way that was soul deep.

Shite.

He would no' be jealous of his brother.

Her pale pink lips moved, but reading lips had no' been one of his strengths. Tate shrugged, that easy grin reaching his eyes as he bumped the lass wi' his shoulder. Prick had to bend down to do so. He hated the way watching them pulled at his ribs. Fucking hated how hard it was for him to be easy going like his babe of a brother.

Anna grinned.

Again.

Tate nudged the door to Trevor's quarters open and followed her in. He'd counted to ninety-fucking-four before Tate walked back out, waving goodbye over his shoulder, face cast in lanternlight. He didn't have the books anymore.

But that did no' stop the ticking in his jaw.

Despite the way he glared at his brother, Tate walked right up to him.

"Don't ye give me that look." He laughed, punching Trevor on the arm. "It's no' my fault your fem likes me better than ye right now."

"I'm no'..." He scrubbed his hands through his hair and took a deep breath. Shite. "She's no' mine, Tate."

His brother cocked a brow, crossing his arms as he leaned against the taffrail. "Oh, aye, Trev. Ye just keep lying to yourself like that and let's see how it fucking works out."

Trevor laced his fingers behind his neck. "She just isn't. She doesn't—she can't be."

"Why the hell no'?" Tate's smile stiffened and then shrunk. "Lass seems to like ye against her better judgment. She's just angry right now; it'll pass. Everything does. Feelings aren't fucking final."

"I'm no'—"

"You're no' what, Trevor?" Tate asked seriously.

Bloody hell, he wasn't about to have this conversation wi' his brother.

Turning away, he leaned his forearms against the taffrail, arm brushing Tate's. Heat radiated off his brother, warming the chill that had worked its way up Trevor's spine. He stared at the water for a long while and matched his breathing to the easy push and pull of the tides against the *Queen's* hull.

Tate remained silent.

Too bad good things never fucking lasted.

"I think you're caught in a tide," he said quietly. "I think that tide is going to pull ye forward whether ye like it or no'."

Trevor nodded, opening his hands. He turned them over, palms staring up at him and ink shifting over them wi' a devilish tickle. Fuck. Biting his lip, he tilted them left and then right, watching as the ink swirled and changed. His stomach fluttered for a moment, excitement like lightning in his veins.

'Tis the same feeling he got when he saw Anna—awe and wonder mixed wi' a wee bit of fear.

Tate twitched. "What do ye see?"

"A storm." He sighed, looking toward the horizon.

"Are ye going to tear it down?"

Trevor shook his head. "Saving the bloody energy."

Tate hummed his response. What was that supposed to mean? Trevor glanced at his brother several times from the corner of his eye, expecting him to open his gods-damned mouth about one thing or another. Beneath the quiet lap of the waves against the hull, he heard the crew laughing below deck.

"Ye got a plan?"

"No' really. Save her bastard of a brother. Anchor off the eastern shore and head inland. Bloody hell, I haven't thought much about it.

There's too much I don't know and even more that'll change soon as we set foot on that hollow shore."

"That's no' what I was talking about and ye bloody well know it."

Trevor lifted his chin and faced his brother. "Do me another favor?"

"Always."

"Keep an eye on her if anything happens to me."

"Fuck ye. Naught is going to happen."

"You're right," he said, but he didn't believe it. "Just go get some sleep, Tate. We're leaving at first light."

"Aye, but I told the lass I'd fetch her some bread first." Tate grinned, pushing off the taffrail and stretching.

Fucking prick.

"Hey, ye keep giving me that look for no damn reason and I might just give ye one."

Gods damn it all to hell—he hadn't realized he was glaring.

He stared at his brother's back as he descended the stairs to the galley, noticing for the first time in a long time how grown up he looked. He never thought of Tate as his actual age; for whatever bloody reason, he always remembered him as a lad of ten, same wi' Taylee.

At least the wee female was in a better mood and had something to occupy her time wi'. He pushed off the rail and looked up at the stars twinkling high above his head. The *Mer Queen* stretched toward the *Tides of Fate,* hoping to change her own.

Farther west, the *Kraken* lurked, lying in wait.

Trevor swallowed past a knot in his throat, gaze focused entirely on those bloody tides leading sailors ever forward—toward greatness and glory. His mum had always said the *Tides of Fate* led the lost to where they were *supposed* to be, where they bloody well *wanted* to be when they did no' know where that was.

Trevor knew where he wanted to be, he didn't need the stars to tell him that.

The door to his quarters closed and he put his hands on his hips.

Exhaling hard, Trevor glared up at the newly born night and the stars sparkling like spun sugar.

Bloody fucking hell.

He was jealous of Tate.

CHAPTER TWENTY-NINE

Anna supported the weight of a splendidly heavy tome on her knees as she read, nestled in a cocoon of blankets and surrounded by a mountain of plush pillows. The Pirate King's bed sat tucked away in a nook, curtains drawn to block out the surrounding world.

If she closed her eyes and ignored the way Trevor's lingering scent warmed her belly, Anna could almost pretend she was in her flat in Bellcaster. Books were piled inside the nook with her, some still open to a particular page, hand-scribbled notes written on torn pieces of scrap paper and tucked into spines. She had tossed most of the throw pillows on the floor to accommodate her reading material.

Turning a page carefully, Anna listened for the beginning of a tear in the rough, tanned paper. It was thick between her fingers and the script had been horrendous to decipher at the start, but her Aepith had come along nicely in the week they'd been at sea.

A week.

Seven days.

Anna sighed, scratching at the scar between her breasts. She wore nothing but a plain cotton thong and a large, long-sleeved shirt that laced down the chest. Scandalous, yes, but due to a hellish twist of fate, Trevor's clothes were more comfortable. Besides, she held no fear of someone walking in unannounced. The crew generally left her alone—even Tate and Zarya had started knocking half a second before trying to throw the doors open.

And Trevor...she hadn't seen him since they had departed.

She wasn't sure if she was thrilled he had decided to leave her alone or if it was disappointment that pooled in her stomach. Her gaze wandered above the book to the sheer curtains billowing softly in the breeze. Each inhale and exhale of the wind revealed more of Trevor's quarters, though Anna might as well have called them her own.

Her clothes, dirty or not, littered every available space on the floor. Books stood guard in clusters based on topic or language, and Trevor's desk had been completely covered by her notes.

She winced at the haphazard toe and heel prints made of ink running along the pale floorboards.

Then her gaze landed on a scrap of lace draped over the arm of a chair.

She would have to clean later—but first, research. The book thumped heavily against her legs as she closed it, a solid weight that absolutely delighted her. She had never been one to turn away from the girth of a good book; if anything, the stout number of pages made the experience more enjoyable.

Intricate designs of mythical sea beasts riddled both covers, and nearly all the pages between. There were accounts of salacious sirens and memorable mermaids, of sharks the size of ships and sea dragons that could swallow a man-of-war whole. As interesting as it all was, Anna wasn't searching every damn page for information pertaining to sea squids or sharks that lurked on land like phantom menaces.

No, the mythical monster she chased was the Kraken. Trevor had said that was what slept on Calaveras. But good God, if she stayed up one more night until her eyes burned and bones creaked without finding additional information on the bugger, she might throw something.

Anna didn't truly believe some terrible monster of the deep would be there, but Trevor did. For whatever ludicrous reason, that meant something to her.

Most of the accounts of the Kraken were vague. Either it was entirely make-believe, as Anna suspected, or it hadn't left enough survivors to accrue enough stories for comparison and analysis. Much to her displeasure, every song or legend was more nefarious and bone-chilling than the one before. It all left a terrible taste in her mouth, a sour foreboding that twisted her stomach and curled her toes.

The most recent text she had read said the blood of Kings was needed to wake it from its slumber.

Was it supposed to be a capital k, though, presuming importance and emphasis, or—

The windowsill creaked, drawing her attention.

One of her notes blew off the desk, dancing about in the soft, darkly spiced breeze.

How peculiar. She hadn't left the windows open.

Setting the book down next to her, Anna crawled forward on her hands and knees, brushing the vibrant sapphire-colored curtain to the side. Nothing appeared out of the ordinary, except perhaps the chaos she left in her wake. The pale planks were warm beneath her feet from the sun bleeding through the bay windows.

Anna stretched her arms high above her head, muscles rigid and sore. Good God, she had spent too much time avoiding the Pirate King; so many words threatened to spill from her mouth as soon as he stepped within her line of sight. Worse yet were all the words and phrases she imagined layered within his exhales.

She had never wanted reassurances and explanations from a man before.

It was pathetic.

She leaned forward on her toes, stomach pressed against the windowsill to reach the open panes. Her hip dug into the wood uncomfortably, fingers brushing the frame. She pulled the bay windows closed just as a warm gust of wind brushed the underside of her jaw.

The ocean stared at her, a stark contrast to the robin's egg blue of the sky above. She studied the sun-burned expanse, looking for the signs of calamity that had followed like a miasma all the way to Tiburon. She didn't find any; it was another brilliant day at sea with a warm sun and calm waters. Rocking back on her heels, she spun her mother's ring with her thumb.

Bugger.

Perhaps she owed Trevor a teensy thank you—if nothing else, at least an acknowledgement that because of him, she no longer had to take the train for every expedition. It would certainly save her in time and resources.

The skin along the back of her neck prickled, drawing her spine taut.

Something wasn't right.

"...is that Lovelace's shirt?" a masculine voice said from behind her.

The floorboards creaked as he stepped closer.

Without thought, Anna turned and swung. Her fist caught him square on the face before she landed several shots to his body. Grunting, his palm cracked hard between her breasts, launching her against the windows. The panes rattled fiercely as she floundered for breath.

"Shit," he swore, disbelief coating his tone. "I'm so sorry. I didn't mean to—it just—"

Set the pace and fight your fight, Markus had always said. *You are not a lamb to be led to slaughter.*

Anna was a Savage.

Savages didn't lose.

"Anna?" a voice called from beyond the cabin doors. She hadn't heard him speak in over a week, but his voice plagued her day and night with its soft brogue. "Luv, are ye all right?"

She shoved his concerned tone from her mind, foot cracking against the man's knee as she ducked his hand. Grunting, he stepped back. Anna almost laughed as she chased him—bugger, it felt *good* to move and exert pressure and force on another.

"If you would just—"

His head snapped back, blood spraying from his nose. Saturated with his ire, the man's gaze appeared greener—meaner too. He spat a wad of blood to the ground, attention narrowing to pinpricks. He blocked three of her punches, but Anna's knuckles finally cracked against his jaw, his ribs, and the inside of his bicep. He caught her leg as she raised it and swung her into the bookshelves. The air whooshed from her lungs and she fell against the floor, jostled by her impact.

Something warm ran down her lip. She was bleeding. His throat bobbed and he stepped back, gaze flickering from her eyes to her lip. Then the coward turned and tried to run.

Oh, she thought not.

Anna stumbled forward, trying to avoid the books scattered around her. She snatched silverware off a porcelain plate and threw them at random. Leg buckling, he came to a sliding stop and glanced at her before his attention dropped to the knife protruding from his calf.

"You're daft," he breathed as Anna cranked her arm back.

The man rolled right, straight into a stack of books. In the background, the doors to the main deck rattled, fists thumping hard against them as voices called to them. Anna and her idjit of an intruder were too busy staring at the fork as it oscillated up and down in the wall exactly where his head had been.

Anna stilled as she turned toward him.

It was the dark-haired man from the deck, the one with stunning abdominals—she hadn't recognized him with his shirt on. What was he doing in here? As of yet, she had only caught glimpses of him from a distance.

With a dramatic wince, he pulled the knife from his skin.

Her gaze shot to the knife. Bugger, she hadn't intended to arm him. Before Anna could contemplate maiming him with the spoon, the cabin doors slammed against the walls. A picture fell and glass broke as feet stampeded through the captain's quarters.

She looked for the man in the sea of crew members and watched him get dragged away by the nape of his neck like a petulant child. Arms, legs, and torsos blocked most of her view. She breathed deep— she'd know the hand wrapped around the man's neck anywhere.

Pushing herself to her feet, Anna strode from beneath the door frame and out onto the main deck. A small crowd had gathered in a semi-circle. Her attention fluttered from face to face in rapid succession. They were all men she knew, men she had seen laughing and singing as they worked, and they all looked positively ferocious right now, frowns on their faces and furrows between their brows.

"Are ye out of your gods-damned mind?"

"I'm sorry, Captain! It—it was an accident!"

Trevor growled something beneath his breath, his voice like gravel and death.

Tate stood behind his brother, a quiet amusement on his face, stance loose and unconcerned. She pushed past the crew and then past the quartermaster as well, smacking his hand away when he reached for her. She caught Trevor's bicep as he raised his fist to beat the dark-haired man—likely within an inch of his life.

Time had not erased her memories of the Pirate King caving a man's face in with the blunt end of a revolver, nor the landscape of corpses he'd stood before on the train.

His bicep tightened beneath her hand as he met her gaze. Anna counted the eleven or so freckles scattered over the bridge of his nose and up his cheekbones like lost stars. Surprise brightened his eyes as his attention dragged upward; she felt the weight of it against her thighs and then her chest before it settled on her face, on the small split in her lip. Brows furrowing, his lips pressed into a thin, angry line.

It hardly hurts, she nearly said.

"Anna..." He cleared his throat quietly. "What—"

"I can take care of myself, Lovelace," she said instead of speaking reassurances that weighed nothing more than the wind.

Anna ignored her current state of immodesty—she looked damn good in her underthings and one of his shirts. If the crew stared, it was only because they thought so as well. As easy as it was to recycle her embarrassment and adorn herself in it like armor, it was not so with the sensation of Trevor's attention on her skin.

It was electric and warm, a buzzing along her thighs and in her stomach.

More than that, it was distracting.

She looked up to catch his gaze and found a similar blush dusted along his cheeks just below the dark circles of his eyes. Her attention shifted to the mussed wine-red mop atop his head, and her chest tightened. It wasn't like him to sleep so late. She might not have seen him for days, but that hardly meant she wasn't aware of his comings and goings on deck.

Anna knew the sound of his voice even in her sleep.

Her gaze dropped from the bruises beneath his eyes to the rest of him. His shoulders straightened under her careful appraisal. Staring at his clavicles, her attention lowered to the bronze skin breaks between the ink stretching over his pecs and down his sternum.

Good God, Trevor wasn't wearing a shirt.

That shouldn't have mattered; she'd seen more of his tanned skin in the hot springs than was on display now. His bicep tightened beneath her hand. The damnable heat in her cheeks drifted lower, prickling against her chest and settling in her belly. The first row of his abdominals flickered, and her attention snapped upward.

Licking his lips, Trevor's dark gaze met the bright blue of hers.

Bugger, she'd been caught staring again.

"What the hell were you doing?" she asked, turning to face the man.

"I was just curious," he murmured, dropping his gaze.

"About *what*, Silas?" Trevor growled low. "Bloody hell, did Carsyn talk wi' ye?"

Silas's silence was answer enough.

"Why would Carsyn Kidd want to talk with a member of your crew?"

"I'm not just a...I'm a carpenter. *The* carpenter on the *Pale Queen*," Silas said fiercely. "But Carsyn is—he's my...cousin of sorts."

"Your *cousin?*"

"Yes, Miss Savage."

Anna turned back to the so-called carpenter and squinted, examining the features of his face. He was younger than the Coalition chief by several years, but shared Kidd's thick, dark hair and blue-green eyes, though Silas's were deeper—darker. The two men even shared a similar nose and jaw.

How did a relative of Carsyn Kidd become the carpenter on the Pirate King's vessel?

In her experience, one ended up in the employ of their family or a close friend. As his *cousin*, Silas should have found himself on one of Kidd's vessels. She had heard his ship, the *Devil's Delight*, was second only to the *Pale Queen* in speed and glory.

"How did you find your way to the *Pale Queen?*" she asked, brows furrowing.

"Same way anyone does, Miss Savage—through loss and love." He paused, squinting at her. "If you're wondering why I'm inked with a crown instead of a crow, it's because my cousin is a miserable bastard. He was a member of Trevor's crew too, you know," he added almost as an afterthought, like it would be some saving grace.

She laughed. "Truly?"

Silas nodded immediately, a broad grin on his face.

The Pirate King was not so quick to respond. "Aye."

"*How?* All the reports claim you can't stand each other. When— before all of *this,* I remember hearing about you and Carsyn getting into a scuffle at a tavern. Then while I was at a dig last summer, I heard you *stabbed* him."

Laughter barked from Tate, drawing a mean look from his brother. The quartermaster quickly tried to smother his laughter. It softened from a riotous burst to a strangled chortle. When Anna glanced at him, Tate was hunched at the shoulders with his hands tucked into his armpits.

"Bloody hell, I forgot all about that," he said with a smile.

"Ye telling me you've never had a disagreement wi' one of the pricks ye dig wi'?" Trevor asked.

"My peers? Good God, no. I have never slammed one of their heads through a bar top, no. Or—or *stabbed* them."

"The prick is lucky all I did was stab him," he grumbled, scrubbing a hand against the back of his neck.

Silas stood with a smile on his face, seemingly remembering his cousin's time being stabbed quite fondly. Some of the crew shifted behind her, their bare feet dragging against the smooth planks of the *Pale Queen*. Juliana's voice cut through the murmur of voices, calling many of the men back to whatever it was they had been doing before Trevor had incited a stampede.

Sighing, the Pirate King glared up at the sun-burned sky. "What the hell did the bastard want?"

"He just...he had questions about the girl." Silas scuffed the ball of his foot against the deck. "About Miss Savage."

Anna, she almost corrected.

"Did he?"

"He did."

"Was this before or after his visit?"

"After, Captain."

"Why did he come aboard in the first place?" she asked, turning to face Trevor.

The Pirate King groaned, rocking back on his heels as he scrubbed at the back of his neck. "The Coalition wanted someone to come wi' to monitor things—sign of good faith an all that shite after...*losing* the map in the first place. Far as I know, the prick volunteered to come wi' but I told him to fuck off. To hell wi' the Coalition and their gods-damned snooping."

Anna leaned back, cocking a brow at the Pirate King. "Why would anyone volunteer to spend time with you?"

"I've been told I'm delightful to look at," he said, grinning.

It was lopsided and boyish, and the muscles of his arms flickered as he crossed them against his chest, the tattoos of his arms layering on top of those on his chest. They were so splendidly crafted, with fine lines and brilliant whorls. Mermaids and sunken ships with jewels and coins playing between them.

Not for the first time, Trevor flexed brazenly.

"A damn *peacock* is what you are."

His grin grew, drawing her attention to his mouth and all the pearly white teeth sitting in it. His beard was more than sandpaper on his face, but not by much. He must have been trimming it, though she couldn't imagine why. Anna rather liked him scruffy with windblown hair and that boyish grin.

Her spine drew tight in her back and her stomach fluttered as she railed against the sensation that this was nice—that everything that was right and good in the world had finally found its way back to her. Gut twisting, she stepped away from him yet again, a chasm of briny sea air opening between them.

Anna swallowed stiffly.

Bugger, she had missed him.

Silas shucked his shirt over his head. "What I don't understand is why you're hiding, Miss Savage."

"I'm not hiding," she answered for Trevor, crossing her arms stubbornly. "I'm in the midst of *research*."

"Mmm." He nodded slowly. "Of course, of course. *Research*."

Anna frowned.

What the hell was *that* supposed to mean?

"Yes, *research*," she reiterated. "I don't like going into a situation blind if I can help it. I've spent the past week reading until my damn eyes crossed."

"Find anything useful?"

Anna snorted. "If you believe in fairytales and falsities, yes, I'm sure we'll find plenty of use for what I've read. From a practical, logical standpoint, I don't see how differentiating between a siren and a mermaid will provide much aid in our endeavor."

"Your mother was Sarah Sommers, yeah?"

Anna nodded her head slowly, brows furrowing.

What would a carpenter aboard the *Pale Queen* know about her mother?

Dragging his gaze from her toes to the top of her head once more, he nodded his head in consideration. "She had a penchant for pirates too. Must be in the blood."

"*Pirates?* My mother was an archaeologist, she didn't have time for pirates."

"I've learned that parents are rarely the people we think they are," he said. "They were all men and women in their prime once, living in a time where they could do anything and be anything. Is it really such a stretch that your mother might have gallivanted with pirates?"

Maybe not for most people.

Maybe not for Silas's parents, whoever they might have been.

But Gran would have lost her ever-loving mind if—

"Leave the lass be, Silas," Trevor growled, stepping between them.

There he went again, providing aid where none was needed.

Anna tightened her arms around her chest and looked around the redhead. It was easier said than done; his shoulders were broad, and he took up far more space than any man had a right to.

"Work needs doing, all of ye get to it," Trevor said to the lingering men. "Except *ye,* Silas," he added as the carpenter turned to abscond as well.

The muscles flickered in his stomach as he leered at Silas.

Anna turned, not one to be caught staring *again.*

"If you excuse me, I have work to do," she muttered, spinning on her heel. "It was nice to finally meet your acquaintance, Silas Kidd."

"Payne," Silas called back. "It's Silas Payne."

Shaking her head, she continued toward the captain's quarters. There was plenty of work to be had without getting in the middle of whatever verbal lashing Silas was about to be subjected to.

Anna closed the door to the captain's quarters quickly, leaning against the cool wood. Pinching her eyes tight, she pressed her thighs together and breathed deep. She didn't have time to ponder the hard, handsome lines of the Pirate King. The mountain of books she had yet to read was unending, a task that would not be completed by itself nor by anyone else. She doubted there was a soul within ten leagues who spoke and read as many languages as she did.

It was a rather brilliant problem to have.

Opening her eyes, her gaze roamed from one side of Trevor's quarters to the other, cataloging each piece of the horrendous mess. If anyone asked, she would absolutely blame it on the carpenter, but most of it had spawned from her general disdain of cleaning.

Anna propped her hands on her hips with a frown.

Perhaps some cleaning was in order.

She stepped forward as one of the doors opened behind her and froze as it closed gently. Was it possible to know a man by his footsteps or the heat of his gaze? She wouldn't have been able to answer with certainty before.

But now?

Now she wished for ignorance, she wished she couldn't pick the hitch of his breath out of a crowd.

Crouching, she picked up several articles of clothing and threw them into a wicker basket. Next, she shuffled papers on the ground, thumbing through them until they were back in the correct order. Placing her notes on the desk, she organized what was in sight as his attention warmed the backs of her thighs and spine.

Trevor remained silent through it all, a statue of a man lying in wait.

"I'm still angry," she said, staring at one of the empty ink wells on the desk.

"I know," he whispered in reply, voice hoarse. "And I know ye have questions, Anna. Ask them. Ask them all. I might no' have any bloody answers, but...but ask them anyway."

Bugger, if there was one thing Anna possessed in spades, it was questions.

Some of which had answers she wanted no knowledge of.

Others were kept pressed against her teeth by acidic fear.

Turning, she found the Pirate King leaning against the door, his arms crossed against his chest, showing off the swells of his biceps and pecs. Anna's attention fell like a dying star until it landed on a new, thin scar, just to the right of his belly button.

Creeping forward, her steps were slow and methodical. "How..." She cleared her throat, her voice so incredibly small. "How are you alive?"

"Disappointed?" he asked.

Something vulnerable and expectant lived in his gaze, swirling beneath the shadows of his irises.

Did he truly believe she wanted to see him harmed or killed right in front of her?

Anna's breath caught in her throat, guilt swelling in her chest. She had thrown nothing but brimstone and ash at him since waking up half-drowned aboard the *Pale Queen*, rage and wrath following her closer than her own shadow. What else was he supposed to believe when she had done little and said less to show otherwise?

She slid another step forward. "The only disappointment I feel is that you let that wretched bastard leave with his life."

"Ye would have rathered I killed him?"

Another step, and her toes were near enough to brush his.

"For trying to gut you? Absolutely," she said, gaze dropping to the healing wound at his stomach. "If I'd had more sense myself, I would have."

His throat bobbed as he tracked her gaze. "I'll be fine yet, luv."

Anna's fingers rose of their own accord until her index finger trailed against the mark gently. The muscles of his stomach twitched, and goosebumps pebbled his skin. There was a thin line of red in the middle of the waxy mark where blood had crusted. Her gaze rose to his, brows furrowed—it wasn't as healed as he liked to pretend it was.

"You'll *be* fine," she murmured. "Are you...does it hurt now?"

"No, no' like ye would think."

"That scared me," Anna admitted, breathing the words out. "After seeing Markus—I was terrified that you would...that you might..."

His hand came up to rest over her fingers, pinning them to his soft, warm skin. "I'll always be fine, luv. Ye don't have to worry about me. No' now, no' ever."

Anna's throat bobbed as she stared into his dark eyes. The heat of her anger rapidly dissolved into an entirely different burn as she focused on the press of Trevor's warm skin beneath her palm, the calluses on his hand against hers. Shifting his hips, he drew her attention downward.

Angry, she reminded herself as she stared at his erection.

She was supposed to be so very, *very* angry.

"Trevor, I..." she started, dragging her gaze up to his.

How did Anna begin to explain to the man before her that she was furious with herself, not with him? That she likely didn't deserve whatever this was between them—this inexhaustible, insatiable heat.

"Ye what?"

She wanted this.

Good God, how selfish did that make her?

"I want..." She hesitated. "...whatever *this* is—if you do. Call it a distraction, call it release, call it pent up hormones on a ship filled with beautiful men. Call it whatever you like but...but I want it."

Her core throbbed between her legs as memories from her father's estate bubbled to the surface. Bugger, one thing was certain—Anna would find release tonight, it was simply up to the pirate on if he'd be here when she did.

"Ye want...*me*..." he started, almost in disbelief.

Anna met his gaze, heart fluttering in her chest.

She felt so bold when he looked down at her like that, with his lips parted and cheeks flushed. Knowing she elicited such a response in him was more than a shot of adrenaline—it was ambrosia. If ever there was a sensation created to please the gods, it was this one, this lightning in her veins, this hummingbird caged in her chest.

Trevor tipped his head down, gaze half-lidded at best. Lifting to her toes, Anna pressed her lips against his and gently pulled his lower lip through her teeth. It felt real—*he* felt real, beneath her fingers and against her mouth. The heat radiating off him was like a small sun about to collapse in on itself.

Everything was too hot and too sensitive—his tongue against hers, his rough palms sliding beneath her shirt and settling against her hips. Anna was a live wire beneath his fingers, a powder keg ready to ignite. Teeth scraping against her pulse, Trevor coaxed a moan from deep in her chest. Warmth flooded her, stealing her breath as one of her hands trailed down his chest and stomach.

Her fingers brushed his newest scar, stilling in their descent to his waistband.

"I'm fine, luv," he said into her neck. "Let me show ye."

Let me show ye.

Pressing her hips against the wall, Trevor sucked and nipped at the sensitive flesh below her ear. His teeth grazed lower, following Anna's waxy scar downward, showering it with kisses as he swept one of his thumbs over her breast repeatedly. She closed her eyes, nearly shaking from the pressure building between her legs. All it would take is a single touch, a thrust, and she would come apart. Already, her thighs were slick and her underthings uncomfortable.

Show me, she thought, *show me everything.*

Looking down, her chest tightened as a hot flush scalded her cheeks and chest. Trevor had dropped to his knees, gaze dark and intent as he searched her face—was he looking for regret already? She nearly laughed. Here was a man with claim to a throne, a man who was supposed to bow before none.

And yet he had gotten on his knees for her.

Regret was not an emotion he would find.

Anna ran her tongue over her teeth as his hands trailed her sides and raised her shirt. He pressed a gentle kiss to her stomach first, and then another against her hip bone. The feeling of his warm breath against her center dragged a soft whine from her lips.

There was only one reason a man might find himself between a woman's legs like this, and good God, Anna was nearly panting with anticipation, with the knowledge of what he was about to do.

Trevor ran his hand up her bare calf until it slipped behind her knee, raising it. With his other hand, he slid her underthings to the side and paused. Breathing deep, she threaded her fingers through his wine-red hair and tugged.

Slow—he was moving entirely too slow.

"Eager, are we?" He chuckled.

They made eye contact.

And then his tongue slid against her center.

Good *fucking* God.

The sound that sprung from her was deep and guttural, forcing Anna to pinch her lips shut as he licked her again, and again, and again.

"*More,*" she breathed.

Always more with him.

She watched as Trevor shifted in front of her, dragging his hand up the inside of her thigh. The heat in her cheeks increased with every inch his rough hands slid up her leg. She knew what he would find at the apex of her thighs—all the slick evidence of her eager anticipation and want. Embarrassment wasn't quite the word for the feelings knotting themselves in her stomach.

Anna wasn't *embarrassed* by her body's reaction to his every move and spoken word, but perhaps the magnitude of the response was what forced the feeling.

His fingers stilled against her, gaze locking with hers. Surprise and something that might have been pride or satisfaction flooded his features. If Trevor Lovelace hadn't realized the agony his touch produced before, he understood it well enough now.

"More, luv?" he teased, delight in his gaze.

Please, she thought, nodding her head.

Without breaking eye contact, Trevor slowly sunk two fingers into her. Swallowing hard, she stared into the dark depths of his eyes.

Her breath shallowed as his fingers moved in her—in and out, curling against her only to spark lightning in her veins. And then he lowered his mouth back to her throbbing center, drawing a high-pitched gasp from her lips as his tongue rolled against her. Anna pressed her lips into a thin line, body trembling beneath the pirate's touch.

More.

Closing her eyes tight, she lowered her hips, pressing herself against his mouth harder. Just—she just needed... Her head tipped back against the wall, body strung tighter than a bow string. Anna cried out as Trevor sucked against her center, hips jerking away from his mouth—but the Pirate King was nothing if not thorough. The hand on her hips tightened as he wrung every tremor from her.

Breathing hard, Anna's hand fell to her side, her entire body relaxing at once. Her gaze lowered until she watched him through her eyelashes, legs trembling like a newborn foal. Trevor pulled his hand away from her body, and her core clenched with the absence of him.

"I told ye so," he said breathlessly.

"What?" Anna asked, smiling at his mused hair.

Trevor repositioned her underthings, placing a kiss between her navel and center before leaning away.

"That I know exactly what to do wi' a lady, Anna," he said, licking his lips.

She wouldn't admit he was right, of course.

That would only inflate his already engorged ego.

Trevor rocked all the way back onto his rump, a tired grin on his face. Anna stared for a moment, counting his freckles before dropping her gaze all the way down to his groin, where he strained against his trousers. Realizing where her attention now rested, his legs unfolded from beneath him and he leaned back on his hands, stomach muscles rippling.

He made no attempt to suggest she return the favor, simply made it clear that if she wished to, she could. There was an offer in the way he presented himself, in his quiet, considering gaze. He wouldn't push her to do anything she didn't want to.

But she wanted it. She wanted to see what sounds and expressions she could draw from him.

It would only be fair.

Sliding down the wall, she found herself between his legs, hands running up his thighs as she closed the distance between them. Her lips brushed his softly once, twice, tasting herself on him before kissing the side of his jaw, his neck.

Trevor's head lolled to the side as one of her fingers slid beneath his waistband, drawing a hiss from his lips as she brushed the head of his cock. Anna found herself panting with sheer want as she dragged kisses down his neck, fingernails grazing his shaft lightly. His fingers had felt good, this would feel even better. He shivered, his entire body twitching at her gentle touch.

A fist pounded on the door, drawing them both upright.

"Captain!" Tate called from the other side. "What the fuck are ye doing in there? Ye said you'd be gone five bloody minutes!"

Anna sat back on her heels.

What incredibly poor timing.

She glanced back toward the door suspiciously. Was it poor timing, or was the quartermaster exacting revenge for how ragged Trevor had run his crew those last days on Tiburon?

The Pirate King's legs pulled away from her, drawing himself to his feet as he adjusted himself in his trousers. She stared with a teensy bit of amusement as he found only glorious failure in trying to hide his obvious bulge.

"Come on, Trev!"

"Fuck off, Tate!" Trevor snapped, glaring at his door as he crossed his quarters.

"I could...if you came back..." she said quickly, cheeks aflame as he started closing the door.

The door stopped abruptly, and he turned to stare at her, gaze curious. "What?"

Bugger—what had possessed her to say *that*?

There was no lie in her words; if Trevor found his way back to his quarters, he'd find himself in a much better mood when he left. It was like waiting for a play to start, the anticipation and excitement while one watched the curtains, impatient for them to reveal what lay behind.

"I feel bad about—well—" she stammered, cheeks hot.

"Don't, I'll be—"

"*Fine*," she finished for him. "I'm sure you will be, but it doesn't seem fair."

"Fair? I didn't do that to be fair or get any gods-damned favors from ye. I did it because I wanted to...because *ye* wanted to," he said with a soft smile. "Worry naught about me, luv. It'll work itself out."

The door closed behind him softly and then he called after his brother, steps quick across the deck. Sighing, she picked another piece of paper off the ground on her way to his desk and the work she had intended on starting. Angling the paper sideways, she read the rough script.

Topography of Calaveras.

Anna blinked, thinking of Trevor's lazy grin as he had stared at her. Fanning herself with the paper in her hands, she leaned back against the desk and glared at the door. Heat lingered on her cheeks and chest, and her core throbbed gently between her legs at the barest thought of the Pirate King.

She wasn't furious with him or herself anymore.

CHAPTER THIRTY

Bloody fucking hell.

Trevor could no' walk past his door wi'out his cock surging to the surface and attempting a gods-damned jailbreak. Three times now, Tate had caught him wi' a raging hard on. So he settled for sitting his ass in the crow's nest until his blood felt less like fireworks in his veins.

Why did the lass look better in his bloody clothing than he did?

He glanced down over the edge of the crow's nest and to the doors of his quarters. It felt like a thousand years since he'd seen Anna, but it'd only been one bloody day. Trevor frowned up at where the sun hung its lazy ass in the sky—bloody hell, it'd been *less* than a day.

How had it been less than a day since he'd finally gotten a taste of her?

Trevor rubbed his jaw and scratched at the scruff on his neck. Anna's skin had been so fucking smooth in his hands, and the sounds she'd made were perfection. Shite, everything about Anna was perfect. Which was no' to say she didn't have her flaws, because she did.

But they made up for and matched his own.

The rigging creaked. Trevor turned just in time to see his brother peek his nosy fucking face over the rails of the crow's nest. He wasn't wearing a bloody shirt, but what else was new? It looked like Tate was in need of a good shave; wasn't like him to let his whiskers grow too long. Tate's hair was knotted on top of his head, the bits of random shiny shite he kept in there caught what wee light broke through the clouds.

"Do ye know how hard ye are to—" Tate stopped, groaning as he looked just over Trevor's shoulder. "Would ye put that away before someone loses a gods-damn eye?"

Trevor looked down.

Fucking hell.

"What are ye doing up here?" Trevor growled, shoving his pillow over his lap. He'd stolen it from his quarters while the lass was eating breakfast.

"Looking for the captain, ye happen to know where the bastard is?" Tate draped his elbows over the rail. "Ye think he's hiding out somewhere wi' your bloody dignity?"

"Tate—"

"What? You'll throw me overboard?" his brother interrupted. Arrogant piece of shite. "Maybe I should toss *ye* in, Trev. Looks like ye could use a nice, cold swim."

It was an honest gods-damned surprise that Trevor hadn't strangled Tate in his sleep yet. He could wrap his hands around the bastard's neck and squeeze, but the wee shite wouldn't even stay dead.

Normally, it was a grand thing.

Trevor glared at his brother and the smug smile on his face.

'Twas no' such a grand thing at current.

"What needs doing?" he growled through his teeth.

"No' a whole lot, just been thinking."

Bloody hell.

Naught ever ended well when Tate got thinking.

"*And?*"

Tate tugged a stubborn strand behind his ear and climbed into the crow's nest wi' Trevor, tucking his long legs to his chest. Looking up at the sky, he tipped his head back and rested it on the rail. "Well, I did some looking around like ye asked on Tiburon. I didn't find any bloody snakes...but the twins at the door, they had some ink that might have been snake bites."

Trevor stiffened. "Why didn't ye say something sooner?"

Figured snake bite tattoos meant working wi' the bastard running the slave trade. The mainland might no' realize it, but ink meant something to a pirate; they did no' just get it because it was pretty. The Viper was an easy choice for blame.

Didn't sit right wi' him, though.

She always had her crew tattooed wi' the whole snake, wee slithery tongue and everything.

But Chardae Badawi was no' the only one wi' a snake tied to her name.

"Oh, I don't know. Maybe because ye were fucking sleeping and then ye were more concerned wi' what the lass was doing—" Tate stopped and breathed deep. "And now ye are hiding from her. Its bloody hard to talk when I can't find ye."

"Did ye talk to the twins about their ink? Or get a closer look?"

His brother laughed. "You've met Anna. Keeping an eye on the lassie is a full-time job. No, I did no' have time to speak wi' the bastards. I was too busy following her out into the jungle and supervising her sponge baths. Did ye know she never gets in the tub? I go through all that bloody trouble of filling the damn thing up every day and she never even puts a toe in."

"The twins are supposed to be neutral, 'tis why they guard the door," Trevor said more to himself than Tate, trying and bloody failing to ignore the fact that Tate had tried peeping—and that Anna was likely scared of her bath.

That fucking gutted him.

"Gut says it's Black," Tate offered. "His uncle liked to nab females at sea and sell them on Tiburon, remember?"

"Aye, I remember, but Black isn't smart enough for this."

"No, but I bet if we follow that thread, it'll lead us straight to the gods-damn sweater."

Trevor laughed, the sound rocking his core. He tipped his head back, grinning at the sky before side-eyeing his brother. "What would ye know about sweaters?"

"Fucking naught, that's what." Tate laughed wi' him. "Seemed like the right thing to say."

His heart clenched painfully in his chest. "Ye always know the right thing to say."

"'Tis a skill I had to learn since ye always say the wrong thing."

"Fuck off." He grinned, throwing his elbow into Tate's side gently.

"'Tis true, Trev. Is that why you're hiding from Anna? So ye don't have to talk wi' her?"

"That's no' why." Trevor sighed and motioned to his cock, which was still taking up more room than it had the gods-damned right to in his trousers. "*This* is why."

"I figured the two were related," Tate said, glancing away wi' a smile. "Thank the gods for retreating, Trev. Ye could really do some serious damage on deck wi' that thing swinging about."

"'Tis no' funny."

"No, you're right. 'Tis bloody hilarious. Now, what are ye going to do about it? Ye can't hide up here forever."

"I'm no—shite, I'm no' hiding from her. I just—I know what I want, I just don't know if she wants it too."

"Have ye asked her?" Tate paused, smile dropping. "Who the fuck do I think ye are, 'course ye haven't asked her. Talk wi' Anna about it. Her answer might surprise ye."

"There are a few things that are a wee more gods-damned important than what I want. The Kraken. Her brother. Finally figuring this whole slave trade shite out."

"You've never let anything stop ye before, so what's wrong?" Tate asked.

Trevor didn't have words for his babe of a brother; he knew this wasn't something he'd fucking understand. All of this had always been so easy for Tate; smile, and the female melted in his hands. She'd stick around too, if he asked, and a fem had never expected anything in exchange from him.

"If the lass likes ye, why the fuck no' figure it out? And don't tell me she doesn't like ye, I heard enough of what was going on in there."

Frustration bled into Tate's voice, his gaze the most serious Trevor had ever seen it. "*Look* at what's between ye two. Why don't ye want to be happy, Trevor? We live too long no' to grasp at any happiness we can find for as long as we're allowed to have it. Eternity is a bloody long time to be miserable, don't ye think?"

It was.

"What if she doesn't like me?"

Riding his tongue and fingers did no' mean the lass liked him. He wasn't fucking daft. Anna could hate him plenty and still find satisfaction and release in what they'd done. Lass was still furious wi' him; she'd said as much more than once.

Tate blinked several times, grin growing. "The wee lassie likes ye, all right, I think ye and she are the only ones who can't fucking tell."

Trevor laughed.

"No, you're right." Tate sighed, standing. He threw his leg back over the crow's nest. "She only likes ye for your body."

"Have ye seen me? Everyone likes looking at me."

Tate shook his head. "Are ye ever going to put a shirt back on? Or is this part of your bloody scheme to draw Anna to ye since she only wants to feel ye up?"

"Does it bother ye?"

Tate nodded. "Oh, aye."

"I don't reckon I will, then."

His brother's laughter was followed wi' some nonsense about climbing down for supper, but Trevor ignored it, choosing instead to slump all the way down and kick his legs up and over the rail. The clouds passed above in dark masses, hiding his precious sky and the stars that would twinkle soon.

"I want...I want to ask her to stay," he admitted in a whisper.

Anna had chosen him once, picked him instead of her fucking da'.

Maybe if he asked, she'd chose him again.

CHAPTER THIRTY-ONE

"Savage, wake the hell up!"

Popping up, she wiped the drool from her cheek.

Bugger, what had she been doing?

Had something been scheduled for today?

Anna squinted through the remaining cobwebs of sleep, gaze skipping her surroundings to the papers on the desk in front of her. She doubted she had a conference to attend. It took another moment of reading her notes before everything came back to her.

Markus, the Pirate King, the quest to Calaveras.

Honestly, it all seemed more like a dream than the one she had actually—

It'll work itself out.

Cheeks flushing, she busied herself with shuffling papers and sounding productive. Perhaps her dreams were not all that unrealistic after all. Good God, the Pirate King's quarters had grown warm. Anna stood, feet padding across the plush rug to the window, and threw it open. The breeze rose up to meet her, threading through her curls and brushing along the underside of her jaw.

"*Get up!*"

"I'm awake," she snapped over her shoulder, catching her reflection in her vanity mirror.

She nearly rolled her entire head at spying the imprint of her writing on her cheek. Wetting a cloth, she scrubbed at the discoloring on her cheek before braiding the monstrosity living atop her head back. Anna had to crane her arms behind her head to finish the plait and tied it off with a scrap of leather.

Once presentable, she threw the doors open and stared down at Juliana Gray.

What was the master gunner doing here?

"Tate sent me," she said, crossing her arms. "You'll find supper in the galley."

Frowning, she stepped out into the light. It had been almost two days since she'd last seen Trevor and she still felt—uncomfortable wasn't quite the right word, but it was close enough. She had been so certain he would find his way back to his quarters, but he never had, and that left insecurities tunneling through her like a termite.

Had he really chosen his hand over her?

Had she done something wrong to incite that decision, or was it another matter entirely?

Juliana walked next to her, hands in her pockets, hair waving gently in the breeze. She heard the crack on the deck then and turned toward the abrupt noise, eyes widening and heart fluttering quicker than a hummingbird's wings. She hadn't expected the sound and had expected to see two full-grown men grappling back and forth even less.

Push and pull.

Two steps forward—two steps backward.

Anna cocked her brow at the two. What disagreement or misunderstanding had the Lovelace brothers gotten into now? She supposed throwing each other on deck was better than other alternatives, but... The Pirate King slipped behind his brother and lobbed him. She winced at the sound of Tate hitting the deck and the string of colorful curses that followed.

Markus would have found several of them entertaining.

Juliana raised a hand in caution as she shuffled closer. Waving her off, she ignored the Man-Eater's warning. Anna had absolutely zero intention of stepping between them or standing within reach of their powerful bodies.

Trevor glanced at her nervously as he ducked beneath one of Tate's long arms. His eyes met hers, full of curious concern. Anna understood the question in his gaze as easily as if he had spoken it.

Are ye okay, luv? she imagined him asking.

She nodded, offering a small smile.

Trevor's features relaxed a fraction at her acknowledgement—shoulders lowering and stance gaining a fluidity it had lacked moments before. The quartermaster danced backward and grunted. A brief grin flashed across Trevor's face and then Tate landed hard on his back once more.

Breathing deep, the Pirate King turned to face her. If his wicked, dark gaze was any indication, he hadn't been avoiding her because of what they'd done or the misgivings he might have about her. Bugger, she hadn't thought it was possible for the butterflies in her stomach to worsen, but they did.

"Afternoon, lassie," Tate called, lifting his head from the deck.

"Afternoon?" Trevor huffed, helping his brother to his feet. "'Tis nearly supper time."

"Is eating all you think about?"

Trevor's attention wandered to Anna once more, cheeks flushing. "More or less."

Good God.

She turned away, warmth pooling just south of her stomach, the apex of her thighs throbbing. Tate glanced between them, a quiet grin on his face as he rolled to his feet and hopped onto the taffrail next to Bodhi. Wiping his forehead against his forearm, he spat into the ocean.

"Tate said ye were working on a map, luv?" Trevor asked, stepping closer.

"That's correct," she said before clearing her throat. "I'm nearly done, I just have to figure out where a few of the sites are—or at least where they're supposed to be based on accounts from several of the books."

He shuffled forward another step. "I could tell ye where they are."

"You could?" she asked, chest tightening.

Asking for his help would likely mean more forced proximity in his quarters.

Proximity that would likely go unchaperoned.

"Aye, Anna. You'd have more time to sunbathe if I lent a hand," he said quickly, pausing only long enough to face the quartermaster. "Again?"

"Shite, no—no' unless ye give me a blade. We'll see who fucking wins then."

Anna snorted.

She'd seen Trevor with a blade; the outcome would remain the same.

Tate turned to Bodhi. "Reckon all she would have to do is say *please*. The wee lassie is much cuter than I am—'tis no' fair, Bodhi."

Anna knew when she was being baited, but altogether did not mind the prospect this time. Though she wasn't entirely sure what the quartermaster would get out of watching her wipe the floor with his older brother.

"I wouldn't have to win?" she asked, folding her arms across her chest. "Just put him on his back?"

"*Aye*," Tate said, grin growing.

"Are ye sure, luv?" Trevor asked, a handsome smile growing on his face as delight shone from his eyes. "Ye know better than some what I can do."

Anna was not in the habit of suffering delusions.

Trevor Lovelace was wicked in a fight and brilliant with a blade.

Wiping that smug smile off his face was the goal here, not claiming victory.

He had been built differently than she had, solid in a way her genetics would never allow no matter how hard she worked for it. But Anna had never entertained the idea of losing. She had boxed and sparred with her brother for as long as she could remember; he had always pushed and prodded, encouraging her to learn. If she could best her brother in a fight at least once, she could put the Pirate King on his back.

Anna was not wholly unprepared for this eventuality.

You must be quicker, Anna, Markus had barked at her on more than one occasion. *Smarter, too.*

"That may be," she said, rolling her sleeves to her elbows. "But all I have to do is knock you on your rump. Do we have access to weapons? A pistol or blade?"

"Abso-fucking-lutely no'." He shook his head, still smiling. "I know better than to give ye a gods-damned weapon."

"Our fists, then," she said, rolling her shoulders. "Are you prepared to lie down?"

Trevor raised his fists. "Use your manners, lovely, and I just might."

Anna walked on the balls of her feet as she approached him, steps cautious and fists ready. The Pirate King dipped into a stance that was far more casual than hers. He blotted out the sun, shrouding her in shadows. Anna wasn't small for a woman, but she might as well have been when standing before an alpha male of the extra-large variety.

"Five silvers say the captain wins," Bodhi murmured, leaning toward the quartermaster.

"Fuck that, mate. Make it ten," Tate replied. "Trevor hasn't yet learned pretty smiles are usually hiding something."

Grinning, Trevor opened his mouth—

Anna's fist struck hard beneath his jaw in a powerful uppercut. His head snapped back, words tucking behind his teeth. Tate's riotous laughter sounded from behind her, Bodhi's soft chuckle echoing beneath it. The pirate stepped back, surprise barely contained beneath his amusement.

Being skewered with a blade had left hardly any lasting damage.

He could handle having his damn teeth rattled.

Stepping inward and ducking beneath his arm, she struck the inside of his bicep—he laughed in response. His lighthearted grin twisted her heart beneath her ribcage, nearly stilling her in surprise. It wasn't entirely astonishing that the Pirate King's response to being hit was joyous laughter.

"Ye could say *please,* luv."

"I bet you like it when a woman begs," she said, glaring at his stupid, handsome face. "Probably inflates your ego and makes you feel *big.*"

"I'm no' above begging myself." Trevor winked, circling to her right. "'Tis a time and a place for manners, and the bedroom is one of them. Ladies first and all that."

Heat burned between her legs at the mere suggestion of Trevor Lovelace begging for anything. Her throat bobbed and her breaths became shallow. Anna had never gotten the chance to discover which touch or act might elicit a response from him, but she wanted to. She wanted to find every last desire of his, the ones that would coax throaty groans and breathy sighs.

Oh, wretched pirate, prepare to meet your match.

Gritting her teeth, she moved.

Anna was a flurry of fists and feet, stepping into and around Trevor before darting away from his callused grasp. His head snapped back and forth, gaze tracking her movements, hand raising to grab her fist one way or to catch her elbow. He leaned off one leg completely, adjusting his center of gravity, moving the balance in his body.

Holding his gaze, she grinned.

If she could not be stronger than him, she would be *faster.*

If she could not be faster, she would be *smarter.*

Her arms and legs tangled with his. They were nothing more than two bodies colliding, an impact that rattled her bones, heating every piece of her that touched him. It was a gamble of sorts, trying to predict which way they would tumble. At first glance, one might believe there was potential for either outcome—Trevor landing on his back or completely flattening her on the deck.

Anna knew better, though.

Trevor had never put her in danger, not directly. If anything, the Pirate King had gone out of his way to keep her from harm's way. He had stepped in front of knives and bullets, had forced the Coalition to remove that damnable smudge.

Trevor had done all of that and more.

He wouldn't land on her, not even accidentally.

Toppling backward, Trevor hissed a splendidly colorful curse into her neck. Turning, she stared into his eyes, grinning at the look on his face. Time held for that moment, if for no other reason than to allow her the satisfaction of watching the truth pass across his face. He landed hard on his back, breath loosing from his lungs as her chest pressed against his.

Anna wrapped her hand around his throat as he flexed beneath her, sitting up until he was leaning back on both elbows. She slid with the motion, landing in the cradle of his lap.

"Dead." She breathed hard through her nose, fingers of her other hand pressing against his throat like a mock pistol. "I win."

Trevor sat up completely, folding his legs around her. Good God, the heat rolling off him could heat a ship in the North Sea. Sitting up straighter, Anna pressed her knees against the warm planks of the *Pale Queen* and tightened her grip around his throat. He leaned forward, arms coming to rest on either side of her legs, unconcerned with the pressure.

He smiled, mouth only a whisper away from hers. "'Tis a matter of perspective, lovely."

"I got you on your back. It might have only been for a second, but it counts, pirate."

Trevor's grin grew immediately, satisfaction finding its way to his gaze as he glanced between their bodies. What had him so fascinated? She was nearly afraid to look, knowing full well the least of what she would find was tanned skin and hard muscles.

She wouldn't look.

She didn't want that image playing in her mind later.

Pressure trailed against her calves and then increased on her thighs. Anna stilled, trying to breathe past the feeling of his fingers trailing up and over her rump before settling on her hips. Her hand relaxed against his neck while the other lowered to his chest. His heart thundered against her palm.

Why was it beating so quickly?

"Rogue," she breathed.

"Pirate," he murmured, leaning forward a fraction.

Anna's heart skipped a beat, gaze dropping to his lips. It wouldn't take much to touch them with her own, to kiss every single one of his freckles. Press her lips to the skin at his temple, the space between his brows, his cheekbone.

His lips parted.

He must have said something—her name, maybe?—because he smiled. Anna realized she was leaning into him and stood.

She stepped backward, away from him—running, why was she always running? It was all too much, his breath in her lungs, the sound of his voice in her ears. Anna glanced away from the burn of his gaze as he tried to catch her eye.

Why was everything about Trevor Lovelace so magnified?

Was it because of what they'd done—because of everything she still wanted to do to him?

Bugger, it had been an age since she'd had any kind of physical release, and it had been even longer since she had found pleasure with a partner. The general response to tumbling in an underground temple rife with booby traps and looters was a resounding *no*, and she was rather talented in keeping herself extraordinarily busy.

Her intention had never been to starve herself of a man's touch or the benefits that came with a good tumble...but she had. And then Trevor had come along and reminded her how splendid it was to have a partner. Now that she'd had a taste, her body wanted more regardless of how she felt about it.

That had to be it.

Where else would these blasted feelings and hormones have bubbled up from?

Anna sneaked a glance at Trevor as he stretched and sighed.

His tragic good looks weren't helping in any matter.

Honestly, could he be any more handsome?

"Is there any water aboard his vessel," she said suddenly, turning to the quartermaster. "I'm absolutely parched."

"Grog or water?" Tate leaned away from the taffrail.

"Good God, *water*." Anna huffed a laugh.

The breeze increased, flowing around her as it pressed against her skin. The air was warm and briny. The only sounds around her were the calls of the crew and the ocean. Markus might have yodeled on despairingly about the plights of living on a ship, but there was a peace at sea that couldn't be replicated anywhere else.

A life on the ocean would not be such a terrible thing.

There were certainly worse fates to endure.

Tate laughed, drawing an entire chorus of chuckles. As she grabbed the skin of water from the quartermaster, she caught sight of his brother. A smile relaxed his features, and he stood with his hands on his hips, chest expanding briefly before he tucked his hands into his pockets.

It was a boyish thing that made Anna grin.

"Aye, lass?" he asked, meeting her gaze.

She lifted the hem of her shirt to wipe the water from her lips and chin, well aware of how his gaze sunk to her midsection. "As much fun as this was, I have work to do. Tate, I think I'll take supper in the captain's quarters."

There was entirely too much work to be had to stand around out here.

That, and she hadn't found anything quite as dousing as deciphering ancient Aepith.

"Again?" He groaned, "Lassie, I grow bloody tired of ferrying your dishes back and forth. I'm no' a maid."

"Oh, but imagine if you were," Anna said, turning toward the captain's quarters. "I'm sure we could find an absolutely adorable uniform."

Tate laughed, already on his way to the galley. "How do ye know I don't already have one?"

"With lace?"

"And frills," he added, steps taking him deeper into the ship.

Anna waved her hand over her shoulder and strode back into the captain's quarters. The door closed with a soft click behind her, muffling the calls and laughter on the main deck. Slumping against the door, she closed her eyes.

Idjit, she thought.

She had been entirely too close to kissing him in front of the entire crew. The audience wasn't what truly bothered her; it was the unknown. How was she supposed to know what to do and how to proceed around him? Did he even want to be kissed? She knew better than most that the desires of the body did not always adhere to the demands of the mind.

Opening her eyes, Anna stared at the ceiling of Trevor's quarters. Little spots of pale yellow and blue showed above. The markings were barely visible with the color of the *Pale Queen,* but as she squinted up at them, their arrangements appeared vaguely familiar. She glanced from one configuration to the next, until she finally recognized the shapes.

The *Tides of Fate.*

The *Kraken.*

The *Fishmonger with his Great Net.*

She knew these constellations well. Anna examined them for a few more minutes before turning her attention to the various papers she had covered the windows with. Deep lines inked in black intersected and crossed, forming the rough outline of an island.

Calaveras.

She'd been working on the damn thing all day and had nearly reached completion when she'd fallen asleep. The map was likely as finished as it could ever be, given her limited resources and meager understanding of Aepith. If given another week of studying the language of the ancient seafarers and a month in the catacombs beneath the university, she might have something presentable.

Anna had gleaned the general topography from four of the books Tate had carried back to the *Pale Queen.* Calaveras was composed of mountainous hills and deep valleys connected by well-fed rivers. Two sacred spaces had been mentioned, but neither were described thoroughly.

A knock sounded against the door, the rhythmic thumps echoing in her chest. Cracking the door open, she found Tate standing on the other side, a silver tray with tea sandwiches, a kettle, and matching cups in his hands. Disappointment fizzled in her veins. She'd known it would be the quartermaster, but that didn't mean a part of her hadn't hoped otherwise.

"Shite." He laughed. "I've never been the wrong brother before."

Anna snatched the tray from his grasp, closing the door with her foot. Tate's delighted chuckles carried through the frame, raising a hot flush in her cheeks. Oh, the quartermaster was lucky he hadn't delivered any cutlery with the tray. She had half a mind to find out if he'd survive being stabbed as well.

Setting the tray on the desk, Anna's gaze traveled to the sunlight brightening the back of the paper. She poured herself a cup of tea as she examined her crude map, soul sinking into the soothing warmth. She had added flourish to the map, mythical sea beasts in the water and large-leafed trees like those she'd seen on Tiburon. Markus would love every bit of this, making the map and assigning detail.

Her mother had loved maps, so he loved them too. He had made them as a game at first, little things that would lead past trials to treasure. From there, he started penning maps of their dormitories at boarding school and the surrounding area. After that, Markus recorded everything—every sea he sailed, every bit of land he traipsed about on.

Anna stood in front of the rough map compiled of layered paper and watered-down ink and crossed her arms. The island wasn't terribly vast. Based on her rough calculations it would take less than a week to cross on foot, but that hardly accounted for the steep terrain or any other features that might hinder their expedition.

She traced a section of jungle gently, ink not entirely dry.

"'Tis called the Avani," Trevor said quietly from behind her.

Anna's heart kicked against her ribs as she turned.

He leaned against the door, bringing a smile to her lips—was it genetics or conditioning that caused the Lovelace brothers to lurk against everything? She'd caught Tate on more than one occasion using the wall or the edge of a table to hold his massive frame upright. Her gaze narrowed playfully at the pirate, head cocking to the side—perhaps the Lovelace brothers were lazy.

"Why?" she asked, leaning back against the window's frame.

The smile slipped from his face as he scrubbed at the back of his neck. "Because...well, shite, the Aavani live there. They're...wee wood sprites that cause all sorts of bloody trouble on Calaveras. Mostly wee things, like moving the paths and turning ye about in circles, but sometimes they do worse."

She'd read about such occurrences in books as a child.

"You can't possibly believe every legend you have ever heard," Anna said softly.

"Tell that to the males strangled in their sleep by roots," Trevor said absently, gaze rising to meet hers. "Ye best start believing in legends, luv; you're in the middle of one whether ye like it or no'."

She walked around Trevor's desk and leaned back against it. If he planned on insisting there would be more than logic and the natural order of the world on this voyage, she wanted a crash course. The black spot on her palm had done more than ignite a curiosity of the unexplainable.

"A jungle filled with magical earth sprites, a mythical sea monster said to swallow galleons whole, and blasted Cunningham..." She paused, sipping her tea and settling it behind her. "What else is on that island that I should know about?"

"Enough that you're going to be out on deck wi' me every day, luv."

Oh, no.

She couldn't do that every day, not without wanting to ravage him.

"Why?" she asked.

"'Tis too much on Calaveras that could kill ye," he said, matter of fact.

"I think I've proven I am perfectly capable of keeping myself alive and whole."

"Aye, ye have," he agreed. "But ye have also proven ye need more bloody practice."

"Matter of perspective," she mocked lightheartedly. "I still flattened you earlier."

Trevor laughed at that, rocking back on his heels and crossing his arms.

Anna's gaze fell to the line he cut against the horizon and sky beyond the doorframe. The feeling of being caught in a man's orbit was foreign to Anna; she had never been left quite so unbalanced. A warm flush burned her neck and chest, her gaze dropping from his eyes to the bow of his lips as he spoke.

"*One,* ye do no' weigh enough to do that. And *two,* ye fucking cheated and ye know it." He let his gaze wander over her. "Ye knew I would choose landing on my back over landing on ye. But I'd be lying if I said the thought of being on top of ye hadn't crossed my mind at least once."

Trevor's cheeks had pinkened and his ears burned, but he held her gaze.

Oh, bugger.

Anna shifted, pressing her thighs together uncomfortably.

"If this adventure is anything to go by, pirate, I'd have to do all the work," she said, smiling at the way his eyes lit up. "Not that it's a complaint. You were an absolute vision with your head between my legs; the view would be even more brilliant while riding you."

Trevor kicked the door closed.

He had been waiting for an invitation, then.

Anna's heart nearly beat through her chest, her core feeling like it was cousins with a caldera. Anticipation shallowed her breath as the Pirate King stepped toward her with slow, leisurely steps, as if he had all the time in the world.

That may be so, but Anna did not—she wanted him here and now, with nothing between them.

"I've a list of things I'd like to do wi' ye, I've no qualms wi' starting there."

She bit her lip, watching as his chest rose and fell in breaths that were just as small as her own. It did not take long for the Pirate King to stand directly in front of her, chin dipping down as his hands pressed against the desk on either side of her.

His grin widened, and her heart stuttered, breath caught in her chest.

Trevor Lovelace was devastating.

"We could start here," she whispered, spreading her knees so he could step between them.

Lowering his head, his nose brushed against hers once, then twice. Her eyes drifted shut, savoring the gentle press of his lips against her cheek and the corner of her mouth. Anna dragged her hands down the hardened muscles of his chest and stomach, following the downy hairs to his trousers. His entire body shivered as her fingers dipped beneath the hem, pulling him closer until her knees curled around his hips.

One of his hands rose, fingers threading through her hair as his thumb brushed her cheek. The press of his lips grew rougher, nearly frenzied. His mouth was hot against her neck, and his hand dragged up her thigh, calluses catching against her breeches. Anna tipped her head back, angling it away as his hand slipped beneath her shirt and up her ribcage until he held her breast in his palm.

His thumb brushed over her nipple, sending a jolt through her. Every one of Trevor's touches scalded her, drawing pleasure-filled gasps and low moans. Anna found his mouth once more, tongue brushing his between each shallow breath.

More. She wanted *more*.

More of *this*.

More of *him*.

Anna popped the buttons on his trousers, slowing as every muscle in the pirate tightened.

Everything about him was of the extra-large variety, this shouldn't have come as a surprise at all. Her hand wrapped around his shaft tentatively, sliding from base to tip. He was hard and hot in her hand, the tip already slick. Trevor's lips hovered against the sensitive flesh where her neck met her shoulder, breath leaving his lungs in one fell swoop.

"Fuck, Anna," he groaned hoarsely.

"Tell me what you like," she murmured, embarrassment heating her cheeks.

"Tighter," he said on a breath, teeth grazing her neck.

Anna's eyes drifted closed as she tightened her grip around the length of him. One hand slipped behind his neck as the other continued to stroke him in long, strong pulls. Breaths huffing against her throat, soft groans escaped his lips and pooled warmth in her center.

The desk groaned as he leaned onto it harder, hips thrusting hesitantly into her hand. "If ye keep that up, luv—"

"I want to see you undone," she whispered into his ear, running his earlobe between her teeth.

Anna kissed his neck and down his shoulder, following the wing of his collarbone as she pumped him faster. It wasn't long before Trevor's breaths turned ragged and stiff, his muscles tight as he moaned softly into her ear. Every sound and breath only served to increase the heat that scalded her core, the apex of her thighs throbbing in time with his pulse.

"Captain!" the Man-Eater called, fist rapping on the door.

Trevor glanced over his shoulder, resignation already on his face. He sighed and muttered something unintelligible beneath his breath before shaking his head and stepping away from her. Sucking on her teeth, Anna glanced from the tight lines bracketing his lips to the engorged length bobbing between them.

This would be the second time he'd walk away without finding release, and she felt rather guilty about it. Guilty and selfish, if she was honest. She wanted to know what he looked and sounded like when he went over the edge

"Are you close?" she asked on a breath.

Anna wasn't entirely sure he heard her until he nodded his head.

It would only be fair, her words from earlier echoed.

She kissed his pec above his heart, dropping another kiss to the bottom of his sternum and another over his newest scar on his stomach. Sliding to her knees, she pressed her lips against each of the four freckles dusted along the deep V of muscle on his right side.

And then she sat, eyelevel with his swollen cock.

It twitched, drawing her gaze upward.

"Anna, ye don't have to," he breathed, staring down at her.

His gaze was heavy with need, muscles wound tighter than a spring.

"I want to," she said, licking the underside from base to tip.

Anna braced one hand against his hip and steadied his cock with the other. Holding his gaze, she wet her lips and then took him as deep into her mouth as she could. Trevor groaned and buckled forward, one hand tightening on the edge of his desk while the other threaded its way into her hair.

Wanton, the women of Bellcaster had whispered behind their hands and fluttering fans.

Tart, the men had grinned on the street.

Pirate King's whore, her father had growled at finding out what she had done.

Their murmurings and hushed whispers had never truly bothered her. The prospect of rumors hadn't stopped her as a child, nor had they kept her from pushing the pirate against a wall and kissing him in her family estate. They wouldn't stop her here either.

Anna had always known what she wanted—she had never been afraid to reach out and grasp it.

Trevor's breath was ragged as she sucked him into her mouth, one hand on his hip while the other trailed her lips up and down his shaft. He had been warm in her hand, but he was even hotter in her mouth, a salacious heat that burned her throat.

The desk behind her creaked.

Glancing up, Anna watched his head fall forward, eyes pinched shut as he breathed heavily through his nose. Trevor exhaled on a shaky breath, a raspy moan leaving his lips as his hips stuttered, plunging his cock deeper into her throat.

He had said he was close, and it had taken no time at all.

Anna closed her eyes, moaning softly as she swallowed—once, twice, until he was finished. Leaning back on her heels, she let his length slip from her lips. Trevor stared down at her through half-lidded eyes and thick lashes, a hot flush on his cheeks. She counted the handsome freckles on his face as he brushed his thumb against her cheek, fingers still in her hair. Anna looked away as he stepped back and tucked himself back into his trousers.

"Was...that to your liking?" she asked softly, meeting his gaze.

The pirate grinned, mischief and delight sparkling within his eyes.

"Captain!" Juliana called once more, fists rapping on the door.

His attention darted from the door and then to Anna several times. Such frustration welled in his gaze, quickly covering any satisfaction and pleasure he had felt. Trevor laced his fingers behind his neck and growled.

Did he wish to stay?

Did he have some expectation of reciprocating before he had to return to his duties as captain?

"Sometimes I hate being the bloody captain," he confessed quietly.

"I wasn't expecting anything," she lied through her teeth. She certainly had anticipated something as he laid her back against the desk, but not after dropping to her knees.

"Ye lie, luv," Trevor said, gaze darkening. "Ye wanted me to take ye there on the bloody table."

"It's probably for the best—those Aepith books aren't going to read themselves."

Trevor winked, opening and then quickly closing his mouth.

The quiet, smooth way that he walked always surprised her. Even now, his feet barely made a sound as they padded across the planks and over the plush rugs. Anna leaned back on her hands, watching him walk away from her. In a way, it reminded her of the sensation in her chest as Lir ridded her of the smudge on her palm—like something integral was pulling away from her and every fiber of her being protested it.

"Pirate," Anna said suddenly.

Trevor stopped with his hand around the intricate brass knob, turning to face her with questions lingering in her eyes.

"If you're not too terribly busy...I wouldn't mind the company while I toil away in here."

The smile that broke against his lips stole her breath. "Ye finally asking for my help?"

Her mouth soured, lips pressing into a thin line. She didn't like it, but she had been backed into a corner. She had no other option than to ask for aid and hope he had reliable, accurate information. If given the chance, she'd trade more than her left leg for Mihk or the university's catacombs.

More than that, she enjoyed his company—had missed it.

"Not your *help*," she said, rolling the word around on her tongue. "Your company."

He cocked a brow, adorable flush pinkening his cheeks.

"Not like that," she clarified, laughing at the wicked look in his eyes. "If that were the case, I would never get any work done."

A line would have to be drawn, and since Trevor seemed content to let her drive their pace and what they did, she'd have to keep her hands to herself. Anna had a sneaking suspicion it would be easier said than done, but she was nothing if not stubborn.

Trevor turned toward the door, a shy grin on his face. "I'd like that, Anna."

CHAPTER THIRTY-TWO

Trevor turned the brass knob, finding it unlocked for the first time since the lass had stepped aboard. He walked gingerly into the room and closed the door, holding the knob so it wouldn't make a sound. None of the lanterns had been lit; the only source of light came through the papers she had fixed against the bay windows.

He paused a foot from the door, scanning his quarters. Awe and surprise crept over him; he was impressed at how Anna had completely overtaken his space. The sheets on his bed had been tangled, and half the bloody goose-feather comforter had pooled on the floor. Makeup and hair trinkets littered the vanity, and she'd left her clothes in puddles all over the floor.

Shite, he wasn't entirely sure what was clean and what was dirty.

He walked to the nearest lantern and lit it—apparently, the wee beastie either hadn't noticed the dimming light or she was no' concerned wi' it. But Taylee had always scolded Tate for reading late at night, said reading in the dark was no' good for his eyes.

His quarters smelled like her too.

Like citrus and silk, warm and sweet wi' a wee bite to it.

Bloody hell, he'd never smelled something so lovely.

Trevor nearly tripped over a shirt on his way to where Anna sat at his desk, stomping about wi' his damn foot tangled in the sleeve.

"Is that you, pirate?" she asked in that wee way he'd learned meant she was concentrating on reading something, only half here wi' him.

Smiling, he turned and stared at the pale planks of the *Queen*. It had been a bloody long time since Anna had called him that. Hearing her say it warmed his stomach right before the feeling turned to acid. He had taken his brother's advice of enjoying this now, but fucking hell, Trevor did no' know how long it would last. It couldn't truly last, and that killed him inside, burned him straight to ash.

"Who else would it be?" he asked back, brow cocked.

The fem spared him a wee glance, reading his face faster than anyone he'd ever met. He could be dressed for the north sea and he'd still feel fucking naked beneath her gaze. For as much as he tried to cover everything up, she saw every bloody thing he felt.

Didn't matter how far he buried it, Anna was a gods-damned archaeologist in every sense of the word.

Lighting another match, he dipped it into the wick of a lantern. Wasn't surprised by her lack of response. He'd learned the past few days that when Anna was elbow-deep in one of those old books, it could be difficult to reach her. It bothered Tate something fierce, the fucker did no' like being ignored, but 'twas no' so wi' Trevor.

His female's work ethic was a thing of beauty.

Anna twirled and twisted a white-blonde curl around one of her fingers as she read. Fuck, the things he would do to be that strand of hair or one of the words on her book. He'd happily take another boon from the gods if it meant having her lovely eyes on him like that.

What was another curse when he had a female like Anna staring at him?

The light warmed her face, glancing off her high cheekbones and straight nose. Her hair looked like a wee halo about her head, the blonde strands glowing pinkish in the dying light. Trevor's stomach fluttered, and his chest tightened like a bloody lad wi' his first fancy.

Smile flickering, he kicked one of her wee boots from his path.

"Trevor?" Anna said suddenly, clearing her throat as she met his gaze.

His cheeks warmed, a wee embarrassed at being caught staring. "I—"

Anna stood and his mouth dried, jaw slackening. She was wearing another one of his gods-damned shirts. No' just any shirt, his favorite one, wi' the sleeves rolled to her elbows. It was an old thing, made of rough-spun cotton dyed a soft blue. She hadn't tightened the ties at the chest, showing off the beautiful swell of her breasts and that gods-damned scar that still haunted his dreams.

"I'm sorry," she said quickly, catching his attention again. "I was... angry and shouldn't have taken it out on you."

An apology?

Bloody hell, what the fuck for?

"When?"

"On Tiburon," Anna whispered.

He shook his head, smile slowly slipping from his face. "Worry naught about it, luv."

"No, it wasn't right. I'm not too big to admit when I'm wrong— though it rarely happens—and I am *trying* to apologize."

"Ye are no' very big at all, if ye ask me."

Anna's blue gaze narrowed into annoyed slits, lip stiffening.

"Accepted," he said as she leaned back against the desk. "But I can bear it, luv. All your hurt and pain, any anger ye have; I can carry it, gladly, if it means ye do no' have to." Trevor exhaled softly. "I know my breaking point better than most, and I haven't reached it yet."

She crossed her arms, snorting softly.

He still saw the sadness and worry in her beautiful blue eyes.

"*That* is precisely what I'm worried about."

"Ye...you're worried about *me?*"

Anna chewed on her bottom lip. They were already bright red— the lass must have been worrying at them all bloody day. Instead of answering his question, she looked down at the heavy book on the desk. She tipped her head back and stared at the pale planks above, at the stars he'd painted.

Taylee had painted constellations on the *Gods Beau;* this wasn't the same, but it was better than naught. It was another piece of her, even if he'd had to do it himself.

"Would you..." Anna trailed off, breathing deep before all her words tumbled from her mouth in an adorable rush, "Would you mind listening for a bit? There is a passage that doesn't make any damn sense to me, but there's another that looks vaguely familiar if I squint, and I just can't—"

The lass stopped.

They stared at each other, naught but the sound of the sea and ship to interrupt.

Trevor's heart hammered against his chest. He opened his mouth and then closed it. Fuck, what was he supposed to say to that? "Ye want me to listen to ye read?"

Anna nodded, blonde wisps floating around her head as she sat back down in the chair and looked at her hands. "It's stupid, I know—"

"It's no'," he interrupted, voice quieting, deepening. "I'd...I'd really like that."

"Okay," she murmured, turning to the book on his desk.

Trevor sat across from her, forearms crossed wi' his head lying atop them on the desk. The wee fem stared at his bare arms, following the curves of his tattoos wi' her eyes. Her gaze narrowed, probably noticing one of the bastards had moved. It was only a matter of time before she started asking questions he did no' have the gods-damned answers to.

He watched her fingers trail a line of gibberish, her mouth moving wi' the words as she read. The only ones that stood out to him were the common ones—the, a, and. Trevor'd never learned to read, and that had been all well and good; it had never seemed important until right now.

Anna tapped a section, squinting down at it as she leaned forward. From where he was, he couldn't quite see what she stared at, no' that it would have mattered. But he found himself sitting up and propping his head on his hand anyway.

Shite, she was gorgeous.

It was no' until the lass started reading out loud that Trevor realized he could get used to this—no' just the wee beastie reading to him, but all of it. Her clothes all over the bloody floor, the way his quarters did no' only smell like him anymore.

Anna looked up and winked.

She had never shied away from him, had never flinched at what he was doing or what he had to be—no' even when she was furious—and fuck, if he didn't love her more for it. Something cold ripped through him, holding his beating heart hostage. If he'd been standing, Trevor would have fallen the fuck over, as it was, his head slipped right off his hand.

Bloody hell.

CHAPTER THIRTY-THREE

They worked in companionable, comfortable quiet that first night, right up until the sun rose from beyond the horizon and Tate barged in, stumbling over her dirty clothes with breakfast, drinking all her tea, and badgering the good nature straight out of his brother. As soon as the ragamuffin left, Anna had spent the day reading to the pirate, watching his eyebrows draw together in thought at one phrase or another.

But those hours turned into days, and Anna wasn't sure about anything anymore—not their destination, not the state of her brother, not even how they would navigate the apparently very cursed island of Calaveras.

Worst of all, she didn't know how she felt about Trevor Lovelace.

Which was to say, she knew exactly how she felt and had been completely unwilling to name any of it. She had always believed language held more power than it likely should—speak of something, and you very well might speak it into existence. Speak of something, and suddenly it had a weight and substance all its own.

If she spoke of it, she would have to confront it, and she simply did not have the time for that.

Licking her fingers, she turned the page.

They were salty from the suspicious brine coating the books. She wasn't actively reading to Trevor right now, simply re-reading a text about hypothetical secret pirate locations, what treasure may or may not be found there, and the maps one might use to find them. Some splendid lore about the blood of Aepith kings had been tucked in one of the passages, and there was a symbol that stood out, one that was suspiciously familiar.

Anna tucked a hair behind her ears, twitching at the increased whistling from the pirate. He sat across from her, feet up on the desk, his fingers laced behind his head. The chair leaned back on two legs, groaning at the precarious angle he insisted upon. Anna smiled softly to herself; she had been tempted more than once to shove his feet if for no other reason to watch the surprise flash across his face.

But alas, there was work to be done.

"So you're an archaeologist," he said almost clumsily in his soft brogue.

Anna glanced at him, brows furrowing suspiciously. "...yes."

Trevor knew she was an archaeologist.

Just what was he getting at?

Her attention shifted until she could see over the tops of his bare feet. He had gone shirtless yet again. Normally, Trevor had responsibilities to see to and drifted in and out of his quarters, but he'd done nothing but laze about in a pair of dark grey shorts all morning.

Was it distracting?

Unfathomably so.

Trevor made a rough noise in the back of his throat, gaze narrowing to a squint on the constellations painted on the ceiling. He said nothing, so Anna returned her attention to the book in front of her. The tome was so very old, the pages thick and almost leathery between her fingers. The looping script was legible, which was more than she could say about some of the other books.

"So," he started once Anna had read a few sentences, voice dark, "how long does a male have to be dead for it to be archaeology and no' bloody grave robbing?"

She'd never thought of it that way. Looking down, she stared at her hands as she contemplated her answer, pen twiddling back and forth with an increased fervor. Was there a distinction between grave robbing and archaeology? It certainly wasn't black and white —this or that. Very few things in life were ever that splendidly simple.

"Answer the question, beastie," he said, drawing her gaze to his growing smile. Good God, the Pirate King was handsome. "Else I've to think ye are a wee grave robber too."

Anna laughed, putting her pen down. "Excuse me?"

"Ye heard me."

She counted the freckles she could see on his face before letting her gaze slip to the shadows of ink that climbed his neck and stretched over his shoulders. Her attention settled on the nautical imagery dripping down his chest.

"Having a teensy appreciation for beautiful things," she said, ignoring the way Trevor waggled his eyebrows at her. "Does not mean I'm a grave robber. Most of the oddities I procure are just that—oddities. It is quite rare that the tombs I investigate are filled with more than rocks and bones. They're hardly filled with jewels and gold. Looters have always pilfered them long before I arrive."

"Ye are obsessed wi' treasure, luv."

"I'm not going to dignify that with an answer."

"I saw ye looking at the trove. 'Tis no' a bad thing."

Trevor's deep, throaty chuckle rang like music in her ears. Licking her lips, she turned away from him and back to her book. This one was particularly dense with jargon Anna didn't completely grasp. Hopefully, the methodical task of deciphering the text would dredge her focus back to where it was needed in her skull.

Anna had managed to keep her hands to herself in all but two instances thus far and was trying her best to keep the tally at that.

She skimmed the passage, finger trailing beneath the elongated script quickly. This passage wasn't incredibly meaningful to their endeavor—Aepith traditions around map making and whatnot. Unlike her brother and most of the known world, the ancient seafarers hadn't made complete maps of the world. Rather, they had penned maps that would lead to something. Their maps were categorized by symbols in the corner, letting one know where they led and what they would find.

Her gaze stumbled from one beautiful illustration to the next as she tucked the Aepith treasures away for a rainy day. It took time to pull the phrases apart, sifting from one dialect to the next. The lovely pictures with their thin, elegant lines and swooping flourishes provided a surprising amount of aid.

There was a map for Helmi's Casket, a crown of stars and feathers at its side.

One for Alavassa, the City of Souls, a pillar of bones.

And another yet for—

Eero.

Anna squinted at the writing, at the picture showing a long-stemmed chalice flanked by a jaguar's skull. That couldn't be right. If the marking for Eero's Chalice had been on the map she had stolen, that would mean—

"Pirate?"

"Aye?"

"The map I stole from you—was it the King's map or something else?"

His chest expanded, something uncertain entering his gaze at her examination. "...something else."

Bugger.

"You never told me that!" she hissed. The throb of frustration in her veins quickly molded into a headache behind her eyes.

"Ye never asked. Between your gods-damned refusal to ask for help and your bloody habit of jumping to conclusions, 'tis no' my fault ye thought that cursed map was something it wasn't."

"What was I supposed to think? It was the only blasted map in your quarters!" Anna stopped, breathing deep as she splayed her fingers against her thigh. "It should have been the Pirate King's map. If there is only one map in the Pirate King's quarters, it should be that one."

"A map is no' always a map."

Anna growled in frustration.

What did that even *mean?*

Trevor crossed his arms against his chest, rolling his eyes. Good God, she wanted to throttle him with the stone cup she used as a paperweight. Shoving herself to her feet, she slid the book across the desk, spinning it so he could easily see the symbol. Anna jammed her finger at it, staring down at him expectantly. The Pirate King held her gaze, defiance layered beneath something that turned her stomach.

"What does *this* symbol mean?"

"I can't read," he said quietly, body stiffening.

Anna's brow furrowed. "On the train, you told me you'd learned when you were fourteen."

His face hardened, and she nearly regretted asking the question. Trevor lowered his chair and removed his feet from the table. "Ye were reading that book and I thought it would make me..."

The frustration eased from her frame. "I wouldn't have—I *don't* care if you can read or not. Knowing that doesn't make me think any less of you; if anything, it just gives me an excuse to read out loud to you." She exhaled slowly, nudging the book farther forward. "The Aepith serialized their maps; they used symbols to denote where one might lead, not words."

His throat bobbed, but he didn't look terribly convinced.

"Please?"

Trevor looked from her face to the book in front of him and sighed. Scanning the page, recognition flickered across his face when the symbol beneath her fingers fell into his gaze. "Eero's Chalice."

Nodding, she dropped her head into her hands as a harsh laugh bubbled up. To think she had believed she could steal the Pirate King's map. She had done years of research, formulated a plan that would shake the stars from the heavens and unseat those curmudgeons on the Board of Antiquity; and instead of an infamous map rumored to lead anywhere one wished to go, Anna had nixed a cursed map inked in what had appeared to be blood. It led to a cup rumored to grant immortal life.

Splendid.

Absolutely splendid.

"The whole allure of that damn map is that no one knows what it actually does or where it will lead you. My mother loved the mystery and intrigue that surrounded it. I thought what I had stolen was the Pirate King's map—your map—so now Cunningham does too." Drumming her fingers, she glanced away from the handsome planes of his face. "Do you think this will get Markus killed?"

Hubris, she thought angrily.

If Anna had to choose a fatal flaw for herself, it would be that.

Trevor rested his chin on his forearm. "No, lovely. He'll be fine. That damsel in distress ye call a brother is bloody lucky the Kraken has been sleeping on the same island the Chalice used to be."

"What do you mean used to be?" she asked, heart thundering.

"The Chalice hasn't been on that island for years," Trevor said, gaze rolling lazily to the old stone cup on the desk.

Anna blinked, swallowing past a knot in her throat.

She...had been using Eero's Chalice as a paper weight?

The infamous cup sat innocently enough on a bed of papers. The chalice wasn't adorned in jewels, nor did it have any inscriptions on it. There wasn't anything noteworthy, not a single detail to suggest that it was a cup of legend.

"You jest," she said quietly.

"No' this time."

Perhaps its name had been inscribed on the bottom and that's how she had missed it. Trevor leaned toward her; forearms pressed against the tabletop. From the corner of her eye, Anna noted the way his mussed hair fell to one side across his forehead. A thicker bit of scruff lined his jaw today, more than just stubble or sandpaper.

"Does it make you immortal?" she asked, hands hovering over the stolen cup.

Trevor leaned back, pressing his foot against the desk until his chair stood on only two legs once more. "No? I've killed my share of males who've drunk from that bloody cup. But short of chopping their fucking heads off, no' much else does lasting damage." He motioned vaguely to his stomach. "We hurt and we scar but we do no' die."

"You're not the only one?"

The Pirate King shook his head.

Anna nodded, questions and wonderings unfurling inside of her like a flower. Curiosity pulled her forward like a magnet as she examined him. Bugger, his scars were infinitely more interesting than they had been five minutes ago.

"Ask me," he murmured.

"Do your limbs grow back?"

"Are ye thinking of cutting a piece of me off?"

Anna waved him off. "No, it's purely an academic question."

"I'm no' sure; I've never completely lost a piece of me," he said, a nervous undertone in his voice.

"Oh, quit worrying, pirate. I promise I won't try and cut your finger off in your sleep."

"'Tis no' my finger I fret about, luv."

"This all makes much more sense now," she said, ignoring his comment.

"What does?"

"Why you never seemed hurt for long or concerned with any sort of injury you might have sustained." Anna traced the lip of the chalice with her finger. "Why you didn't bleed out."

"I would have told ye, but as I recall, ye didn't want anything to do wi' me," he said, scratching his newest scar.

Scanning the Pirate King from head to toe once more, she exhaled slowly. "You truly can't die?"

"As a fem of science, 'tis only one way to find out, aye?"

Anna stared down at the knife in his hand, unsure of where he had procured it from. Maybe he kept them sheathed beneath the chairs or the desk. The small bit of steel gleamed in the late afternoon light. Looking from the knife, she shook her head. The thought of marking his skin in such a way made her sick.

"I'm in no hurry to discover all your secrets," she said. "I have plenty of time to procure an answer. After all, while I'm on my deathbed, you'll still be—"

"A gods-damned specimen among men?" he asked playfully. It did little to hide the well of sadness within his eyes.

"I was going to say devastating," she whispered.

Because that's exactly what he was—devastatingly dangerous and handsome, wicked and brilliant. Trevor didn't speak, but she felt his attention on her like she might the calm before a summer storm, full of pressure and warm heat.

Had she said too much?

Or not enough?

Clearing her throat, she asked, "How old are you?"

"Old enough, why?" he said, sitting up straighter.

Anna stared at him.

Was he dodging her question?

"I just haven't figured that out yet," she told him honestly.

"Tate put ye up to this, didn't he?" The Pirate King tapped his thumbs against the desk furiously. "'Tis a rather difficult question, lass. There are two answers, depending on if ye want to know the age of my bones or that of my mind."

"Quit stalling," she told him, attention dropping to shuffle her notes. A purple tome embossed with gold filigree caught her eye from beneath a weighty stack.

"I drank from the cup the year I was supposed to turn twenty-eight. My body feels the same as it did then, looks roughly the same too, though I've added a few scars. I..."

Anna chanced a fleeting glance at Trevor as he stopped talking.

His lips had pressed into a thin line, gaze anchored on his hands. There was a hesitation she didn't understand in his eyes. She slowly opened the purple book, attention fixed on the pirate in front of her. His cheeks flushed and his jaw ticked, throat bobbing as he met her gaze.

Was he embarrassed?

"I am much older than ye are."

"How much older?"

"I'm...fucking shite, I'm forty-eight."

Anna blinked, eyes wide as the grin grew on her face. "Oh."

"Aye, *oh*," he snapped, flush creeping up his neck and onto his cheeks.

"Are you *blushing?*"

Oh yes, the Pirate King was embarrassed about his age.

"At least you don't look like you're half a century old."

"Would ye fancy living forever?" he asked tentatively, voice coming in soft stops and starts.

"No," she answered without thought. "Forever is an incredibly long time to exist. I can't imagine watching the people I love most grow old and die. I...I would like to leave something behind that might endure through the ages, but I would be terrified of doing so myself."

The prospect of living in a world without her brother in it was daunting and cold. She wouldn't be able to live with herself knowing she had chosen to live forever without him.

Immortality was a fool's gold, gilded in the promise of ages and entirely void of worth.

"No' even for a strikingly handsome male who may or may no' have drunk from the cup?" the pirate hedged. "I happen to know just the one, Anna. Bloody handsome and unspoken for at current...might know his way 'round a fem too."

"Brilliant effort."

A sliver of a smile broke across his face, and it might have been the most beautiful thing she had ever seen. It was lopsided, reminding her of how young Trevor likely wasn't—of the years he shouldered despite his appearance. It wasn't until he canted his head to the side and his smile grew that Anna realized she had started leaning forward, straight over the top of the book.

"See something to your liking, luv?"

"No." Anna grinned despite her lie.

Using the desk to stand, Trevor turned toward the door. "Shame, that."

"Is it?" she asked, genuinely curious.

"Aye. A female like ye doesn't come around every decade," he said softly, stumbling briefly as he walked backwards. "Though I suspect one like ye might never come back around."

Anna flushed, chest tightening. "I'm charmed."

"What if"—he paused, looking behind her and out the bay windows—"what if ye didn't have a choice?"

Her smile flattened into a thin line, gaze narrowing. "If you think about forcing me to drink from that damn cup for a second, I'll bludgeon you with it."

"I wasn't—I just—bloody hell. Never mind. I'll be back later, lass."

"Where are you going?"

"Chores." He shrugged, yawning. "Check the bloody course, see if Tate's been gutted by Jules yet. Maybe stop by the galley and see if Zarya's made any bread."

A frown pulled on her face as she examined the man in front of her. Exhaustion had lived in every line of his body for weeks now. "Are you all right?"

"Just a wee tired, beastie."

"If you're tired, you should sleep," she said.

"Aye, I will."

"You...could sleep here."

"I know I could."

Sucking on her teeth, Anna watched him walk away from her—and consequently, away from the completely unoccupied bed with feather pillows and deliciously silky sheets.

The Pirate King clearly didn't mind being in her presence, and it wasn't as if she was asking to share the bed with him. There was a line between finding pleasure in each other's arms and lingering comfort in the dead of night, curled together like pieces of a puzzle. It was a line she wasn't willing to cross, but...

Why would he choose to sleep anywhere but his quarters?

Before she had the chance to ask him, the door clicked shut, and she was left to her thoughts and the silence.

Anna laughed, shaking her head.

Forty-eight.

Good God, he was nearly as old as her father.

CHAPTER THIRTY-FOUR

Markus vomited into a cluster of ferns on his right.

And then he vomited again.

Bollocks, how did he have anything left in his damn stomach?

"Get moving," one of Cunningham's sailors barked, shoving him forward.

He struggled to get his feet back under himself and fell to his knees, fingers digging into the springy soil of this dreadful island. He'd been suspicious of it ever since it broke the horizon, this ghoulish grey rock with the ghosts of trees sprouting from every possible surface.

Mark his words, there was something incredibly unnatural about this stretch of land.

Something more unnatural than his sister's fascination with the pirate's abdominal muscles.

Breath fanning in front of his face, he spat what was left of the bile into the bushes, stomach wound feeling like it was aflame. It had started itching fiercely, a strange, sweet smell wafting from it every now and then.

The scent hardly concerned him; he wouldn't die from something as anticlimactic as an infection—at least not before this island killed him. He was far more annoyed with the ferocity of the itch. If he wasn't careful, he'd reopen the wound; so he gently massaged the area around it instead of the frantic scratching he wanted to do.

Pushing to his knees, Markus winced and his brows drew together. He had likely just torn the stitches again. He'd already done so twice, and the wet burn that dripped down his stomach was enough to support his conclusion.

"Do you think *this* island is cursed?" he asked Cunningham, though considering the man stood fifteen feet away, Markus had to scream it. "I've read *all* the Aepith islands are cursed."

He had read no such thing in any of the old, dusty books or his mother's journals. But one could easily make that assumption based on the accounts in his mother's theories. His lies had the desired effect.

The marshals in their black uniforms gazed out at the surrounding area, looking for some monster that may or may not be lurking there. While their faces remained mostly unconcerned, no tells except for the creasing of brows and lines bracketing their lips, the sailors trembled in their dark jackets and pale trousers. They had not signed up for some wild adventure past the Black Line.

They had not signed up for hurricanes.

They had not signed up for the Kraken.

They had not signed up for *cursed*.

These sailors wanted to go home.

Markus grinned, placing a hand on his knee as he stood. A breeze rolled through the forest, creating whispers in the black pine needles and waving pale branches above their heads. Moss like wet clumps of hair bobbed up and down. A stick cracked in the distance, and several men jumped, heads swiveling from right to left.

He couldn't have planned it better himself.

"It doesn't matter if it is," Cunningham replied coolly. None of the panic or wildness had returned to his eyes since that first night they had crossed the Black Line. "The Briland Senate doesn't tolerate failure."

"The Briland Senate or our fathers?" Markus shot back, stepping forward.

"Unlike your father, mine doesn't tolerate failure." Cunningham stopped and looked over his shoulder, offering Markus his profile. He'd combed his hair to perfection, brown eyes unfazed by the forest around them or eerie pressure hanging in the air.

Markus's hands curled into fists at his side, but the smile remained on his face. "You honestly believe failure is an option in the Savage household?"

"He tolerates you, doesn't he?" Cunningham walked deeper into the forest.

Staring at Bryce's back, his gaze narrowed as anger flooded his veins, dragging everything else down like a riptide until all he felt was that itchy heat crawling around beneath his skin.

Is that what everyone thought, that John Savage simply tolerated his son? That this was all a splendid misunderstanding and that Markus would eventually inherit his father's titles and holdings? He shook his head and ran his tongue over his teeth.

Good God, he had absolutely zero intention of ever doing that.

Markus had stopped thinking of himself as the one who would sit atop his father's self-made throne when he was very little. Just the thought of being in his father's office with its curtains the same shade as greed put the taste of ash in his mouth.

Everyone had believed Markus had joined the Briland Navy because it's what his father had done, and what his father's father had done. There had been a Savage in the Briland Navy for as long as Bell-caster could remember; Markus was simply one son in a very long line of them to enlist.

It was true that he had never known what he wanted, which is why he had wanted and tried everything at first. It was how he had found himself on a ship to begin with.

What could possibly be better than being leagues away from his father?

Nothing.

"Get moving," a sailor hissed at him, unwilling to come near. "Get moving, or they'll make you."

Waving him off, Markus trudged forward, one hand on his

abdomen as he walked. Joining the navy might have been an escape from John Savage and all his expectations, but it had led him home.

I should have let you drown, she had whispered against his lips once.

Juliana Gray had been naked and covered in sand, her hair gritty with brine. Even with seaweed tangling her legs with his, she had been the loveliest woman he had ever seen, and she hadn't let him drown even when she probably should have.

Markus glanced up at the trees, letting his gaze move from one shadow to the next before landing on Bryce Cunningham ahead. The captain crested a small rise in the forest, and tendrils of fog snaked their way toward him through the trees and fronds.

A shiver crept up his spine—something didn't feel right.

He devoured their surroundings, breath pluming thicker and darker in front of his face. Bollocks, the dip in temperature couldn't be a good sign. The marshals in his periphery all reached for a pistol or their rapiers, even Markus's hand did the same—

That's right.

Cunningham wouldn't let him carry a weapon.

He breathed in, listening to the rustle as the shadows around them deepened and darkened as if the sun had begun to set. His brows drew together, and he looked up. The sun shouldn't be setting quite yet; they should still have a few hours left in the day.

Cursed, the word whispered through the trees above them.

Maybe the island *was* cursed. Nothing would surprise him at this point.

He wanted to go home—he wanted Juliana in his arms again, wanted to feel her against him and the solid weight of her head on his chest. He never should have left her on that beach, never should have left her side at all.

If he could go back, he would.

I should have let you down, Juliana had said, golden-green gaze narrowed nearly into slits as she pressed her hand against his chest.

His throat bobbed. He might not be able to change the past, but he could change the future.

First things first, he had to survive this blasted island and find a way to stop Cunningham before Anna arrived and buggered the entire operation up. The man in front of him stopped, drawing him up short as well.

Markus shifted his pack on his shoulders, sweat dripping down his spine and from his temples. A low murmur picked up among the men as they too searched the surrounding area for whatever it was that caused the hair-prickling sensation, but he had turned away from the shadows and to the captain.

Bryce's shoulders had risen, one foot sliding back through the carpet of needles and loamy soil. Markus swallowed hard against the pounding in his chest and the approaching feeling of dread. One of the men standing next to Cunningham stepped back, hands shaking at his sides.

"Wh—what is—what is that?"

And then a man screamed, terror fracturing his voice before it abruptly cut off.

Brilliant.

CHAPTER THIRTY-FIVE

"Anna," he whispered. "Anna, wake up."

She shot up, blinking into the darkness, adrenaline rushing through her veins. Anna would know that voice and its incapability to whisper anywhere. There was a melody hidden beneath his tone, though, one she had never heard him use, but she cared little for the difference.

Markus was here—against all odds, he was here.

Adjusting the shirt on her shoulder, she breathed deep and squinted into the darkness.

Why did it seem strange that her brother was here?

"Markus?" she asked sleepily, crawling forward on the bed until she sat on its edge.

"Anna, where are you, Anna?"

"I'm right here, you buffoon," she said quietly, gaze searching for his massive form.

Markus chuckled beneath his breath, heavy steps rousing high-pitched whines from the planks of the captain's quarters. One of the double doors opened and closed, bathing the floor in a bright swatch of moonlight for less than a second.

Bugger, where did he think he was running off to?

The soft material of her night dress caressed her bare thighs on a rogue breeze. It was a beautiful nightgown with thin straps, trimmed and tailored from crushed velvet in a deep fuchsia. Anna had never been one for nightgowns, they were impractical and flimsy, but this one was lush against her skin and the floral pattern on the bodice was positively charming.

Anna opened the door and squinted into the late night; she looked left, then right, up, and across the deck. She didn't see her brother anywhere. Something tightened in her chest, dread hollowing her bones.

Why did it feel like he had fumbled his way into yet another egregious circumstance?

Had he slept with the wrong man's wife or daughter again?

She wouldn't put it past him to be involved in some form of debauchery that warranted a pound of flesh as payment. Trouble trailed Anna closer than her own shadow, but her brother was more than adept at hanging himself with self-created misfortune.

The sails above rustled, snapping in a vicious gust.

Markus's footsteps trailed onward across the main deck, pulling her attention toward their echo. She looked from the smooth planks beneath her toes, still warm from their time in the sun, to the large pale main mast. Panic wove its way between her ribs, pulling her spine tight.

Why was she on the *Pale Queen* in this ostentatious nightgown?

"This way, Anna," Markus breathed, voice slippery and soft.

"This isn't funny," she said, swallowing past fear and dread.

"You're not scared, are *you?*"

You.

You.

"You'll have to move faster than that to catch me." Markus's voice twanged, pitching upward like when they were children playing chase.

Anna didn't have time to play hide and seek, especially not on the infamous flag ship of the Pirate King. She crept forward, past barrels illuminated by moonlight and rolls of rope lying in wait. She winced every time her steps caused a creak or a groan. Every flap and snap of the sails sent her heart racing. She had narrowly escaped expiration on her last visit to the *Pale Queen,* she'd rather not test her luck again.

"Markus, *stop,*" she snapped in a whisper, breaths coming tight, shallow gasps.

The wind tugged at her nightgown, drawing her attention to the smooth material brushing against her skin. One blink showed the soft velvet with beautiful floral stitching, and the next revealed a man's shirt, laced loosely at the chest.

Anna stumbled, catching herself against a crate before she could truly fall. Staring down, she saw the velvet once more, her pulse ratcheting and head swimming. She sucked in a tight breath of air, staring at the fabric clinging to her body. The shadows painted it in beautiful velvet, but in the soft shafts of moonlight, she saw threadbare cotton.

What is going on? she thought, gaze roaming the deck wildly.

The *Pale Queen* rocked to the side, creaking in protest.

"Anna, haste!" Markus's voice cracked like a whip from directly behind her, venom twined between his words.

She turned, certain he would be there.

He wasn't.

...one below deck, Jules...doing out here, luv, a soft brogue whispered in her ears. The question faded as soon as he ceased speaking, there and then gone like a message erased in the sand.

"Quick, Anna," Markus hissed, ripping her attention back toward him.

A tall, hulking shadow darted off into the shadows; it could belong to no one else than her brother. The Pirate King's crew wouldn't be sneaking about like thieves in the night on their own ship. Ducking behind crates and crouching behind barrels, Anna hurried after her brother, slipping from one cluster of shadow to the next.

Markus slid to a halt, turning with the motion until he faced her. There was a smile on his face, one that encouraged retreat. Something was off about it—it was a little too wide and full of too many teeth. His eyes darkened from their sunburnt blue, deepening to the color of the ocean as the night sky reflected off it.

"Markus—"

The sound of water sloshing across the deck twisted her stomach, drawing her gaze to the mess in front of her brother. At seeing his entrails upon the deck, Anna screamed. Blood bathed the front of him—good God, there was more blood outside his body than likely left in. She had never seen a man lose so much and live. Her throat tightened as she stepped forward, hands shaking at her sides.

Markus stumbled back a step, blood dribbling down his chin as his mouth opened and closed like a gasping fish. His rump bumped against the taffrail, bloodied hand reaching out to steady himself.

It hurt.

Good God, it hurt.

His hand slipped, and he fell backward over the rail.

Anna dove forward, reaching for his blood-soaked shirt, his arm, *anything* she could but his body folded away from her like an accordion unfurling. She was in motion one moment and slamming to an abrupt halt the next. The complete stoppage of motion shocked her body and left her gasping for air as iron bands clasped around her waist and chest.

The splash echoed even above the thunder.

Flinching, she pulled her lip through her teeth. Markus was a strong swimmer, she just had to get him out of the water. Beneath the roaring in her ears, she heard that soft brogue again. Thrashing and screaming, she fought against what held her. A slice of cold steel dragged over her forearm, leaving a wet warmth in its wake.

She blinked.

And blinked again.

And *again*, until the fog clouding her sensibilities dissipated.

"Shh, Anna—I'm here. I'm here, luv."

Glancing from left to right, Anna realized she was halfway over the taffrail. The only thing keeping her grounded to the *Pale Queen* were the tattooed arms banded around her waist and chest.

Trevor.

Of course, it was Trevor.

If he hadn't stopped her, she would have gone straight over the rail after her—

That wasn't Markus. Those hadn't been his innards splattered over the deck. But it had felt so real. A sobbed gasp ripped itself from her soul, tears streaking down her cheeks as she fought for each breath. There wasn't a piece of the pirate she couldn't feel, from the corded bands of his arms to the hard lines of his stomach, the curve of his shoulders on either side of hers.

"I'm here," she heard him say again, breath warm against her ear. "I have ye, Anna, and I'll have ye even after the last star in the sky turns to dust."

Trevor held her until her tears dried, until her breath no longer came in shallow gasps and her heart didn't hurt quite as much. Swallowing, she leaned back against him, and her hands came up to hold the forearm wrapped around her chest.

"What the hell was that?" She exhaled, ire curling in her stomach. Head tipping back, she breathed deep, surrounding herself in his scent, in his warmth.

Markus might not have been real, but Trevor Lovelace was.

"A siren," he said against her cheek.

Anna laughed—*sirens?*

She had barely wrapped her head around the Kraken, but sea beasts with an unearthly ability to snare a man's soul?

"You jest," she said, turning to look up at him.

Trevor stared into the water, gaze narrowing.

Following his line of sight, she leaned forward. Moonlight glanced off the sea's calm surface, darkness nearly hiding the sea monster that lurked beneath. Bile burned her throat as she scanned the waters. As if on cue, a large silhouette breached the surface. If not for the full moon above, she wouldn't have been able to see anything. But the murky visibility did nothing to calm the visceral panic pooling in her gut.

Anna's blood ran cold, and Trevor's grip tightened around her waist. The siren almost looked human with its leathery, grey skin and large luminescent eyes. She was tempted to call it a she, if only for the ample breasts on its chest and the alluring, feminine way in which its lips curved. Regardless of whether or not the siren was male or female, it was beautiful and elegant in the way all creatures of the night or unknown should be.

Eerie and mysterious, a nearly grotesque oddity.

The siren's eel-like tail slapped against the water. A faint glow radiated from the sides of its tail and down its chest in soft circles and semi-circles. Grinning up at her, it showed a mouth that was a little too wide and full of too many teeth. Its eyes were completely black, but it tilted its head until it seemed to stare at Trevor. It waggled its webbed, narrow fingers and dove back down beneath the waves.

Trevor dropped his head to her shoulder and inhaled deeply, arms tightening around her. She turned until her arms were wrapped around his waist and her forehead pressed against his shoulder. Anna leaned into him. His heart thundered beneath her ear, belying his outward calm, giving her a shallow sense of how he truly felt.

Panic.

Worry.

"Are ye okay?" he finally asked.

"If I am, it's because of you," Anna whispered against his skin. "Are you all right?"

Hands sliding down the smooth planes of his chest, she searched his face. The scruff on his neck and cheeks had thickened, and the dark circles beneath his eyes looked like fading bruises. Good; he must have found rest somewhere along the line. But all the sleep in the world couldn't hide the wild, raw look in her eyes or how his jaw ticked.

Trevor Lovelace was hardly okay.

"Naught is wrong wi' me, except maybe ye scaring me half to bloody death," he told her sincerely. "I don't know what I would have done if ye had gone over."

"Something incredibly foolish like dive in after me," she said, remembering what he had said on the train. "There was some catch, though—something about a reward for rescuing me from the clutches of the sea."

"Aye." A small smile lit up his face. "A kiss in a place of my choosing, lass."

Heat flooded from her chest to the pit of her belly as a slow, insistent throb started at the apex of Anna's thighs. Her heart fluttered softly as she spoke, lightning zinging through her veins. "I owe you several, then."

A distraction sounded brilliant.

If anyone could chase away the frost in her veins, it was the man before her.

Lifting to her toes, Anna leaned into him, fingers scraping upward against his chest before tangling in his hair. The tight leash the pirate kept about himself dissolved in one fluid motion. Pressing into her, he walked her backward until her rump bumped into a crate or a barrel —bugger she didn't care what it was—and lifted her atop it before settling himself between her thighs.

More.

Swallowing hard, she fumbled with the ties of his teensy trousers. Anna didn't want his fingers or his mouth, not this time. Her core clenched uncomfortably, slick with need as she shoved the waistband of his trousers down and gripped his cock. There wasn't anything quite as heady or intoxicating as knowing she could coax brilliant moans from the Pirate King if she wished.

Anna kissed him on the cheek, the side of his jaw. She peppered the strong column of his throat with soft bites, sucking the sensitive flesh as she stroked up and down at a languid pace. Tightening her grip, she pumped him from base to tip—again—and again—and again. His gentle moans turned into a deep throaty chuckle, one she felt against her neck.

"Anna, ye keep this up and I won't—"

"I don't care," she said, kissing his jaw and spreading her legs. "I just want you—this. Something to chase whatever that was away—if that's what you want too," she added as an afterthought.

There was not a part of her, not a molecule or atom, that did not want all of him desperately.

Trevor Lovelace was a lifeline in a sea of uncertainty, he always had been.

Gripping her beneath her knees, Trevor slid her forward roughly. Bugger, it was about time his damnable self-control slipped from his fingers. He could have been a saint in another life, honestly. His attention dropped, and Anna followed it—

Oh.

His thighs pressed against the cradle of her leg, his cock gripped tightly in her hand. Trevor's gaze didn't move from her center as he stepped forward, the hot tip pressing against her. At hearing her hiss in delight, his eyes shot to hers, full of concern and hesitation.

More, she thought, nudging him forward with her heel. *Everything.*

Trevor held her gaze, hands sliding up her thighs as his cock pressed into her, stretching her with a delicious burn. A low, guttural moan left her lips on an exhale. Swallowing past the knot of arousal in her throat, Anna tried ignoring just how impossibly brilliant it felt. She nearly cried as he pulled away before sheathing himself wholly inside her with a clap.

"*Fuck,*" he growled, voice a tight rasp.

One of his hands pressed against her lower back, holding her to him while the other gripped the edge of whatever she was sitting on hard enough for it to creak. Anna wrapped her legs around his hips, urging him forward, deeper. His hips rolled in time with her pulse, quick and hard. Unable to do anything more than breathe and moan into his ear, she laced her arms around his neck as he pumped in and out of her.

Letting her head fall back, Anna opened her eyes to the night sky. The stars glimmered above them, jewels threaded into a dark, velvet tapestry. They were so incredibly small in the face of the great expanse above them, but when she closed her eyes, the world narrowed to no more than her and the Pirate King.

Had it been like this that first time, the time she couldn't remember?

Had Trevor taken her beneath a bed of stars or in silk in the captain's quarters?

Anna's core wound tighter than a spring, throbbing almost painfully with each thrust. It didn't take long for the pirate's pace to turn frantic. Everything inside of her coiled, toes curling as she bit down on his shoulder and tried to muffle every sound that might escape her lips.

So close—she was so close—

Her thighs pressed against his hips, and between one thrust and the next, she gasped and pinched her eyes shut. Molten heat poured from her, loosening the muscles of her stomach and legs, leaving her feeling ragged. Another choked moan broke through the cage of her teeth as he moved in and out of her.

"You feel so good," she said against his skin, breathing hard.

"Anna, I—" he said, pressing his forehead against her temple, hips stuttering.

The nails of her right hand bit deep into his back, and she widened her legs, trying to take as much of him as she could. Trevor's breath caught, teeth scraping against her neck.

Good God, she couldn't wait to see the look of satisfaction in his gaze after he—

Something thumped hard against the deck, like a sack of potatoes had been lobbed in their direction.

Trevor's hips stilled as they made eye contact, the thick, hot length of him still buried deep inside her. He stumbled backward, frantically trying to tuck himself back into his trousers. It wasn't until he turned completely that Anna glimpsed the quartermaster's hand wrapped tight around Trevor's arm.

Oh, bugger, she thought, scrambling to right her underthings. A deep flush heated her cheeks and chest, arousal and want hollowing into deep-seated embarrassment.

They'd been *caught*.

By his god-damned *brother*.

Tate laughed wildly, shaking his head and waggling his finger.

"Oh, shite no, Trev! If I'm no' allowed to fuck fems on the main deck, then neither are ye!"

Confusion tumbled through her veins like a child rolling haphazardly down a hill. Anna was torn, unsure of whether she should feel all-encompassing mortification at Tate catching them or profound amusement at watching Trevor receive a lecture from his younger brother. She leaned forward until her toes touched the soft planks of the *Pale Queen*.

This was an occasion that called for a necessary retreat.

Trevor glanced over his shoulder once at Anna, boyish humiliation painted across his features. His hand rose in the limpest finger wave she had ever seen. Despite the circumstances, she smiled at the sincerity and genuine discomfort in that single gesture.

Forty-eight years old?

Not with that expression on his face, freckles peeking through the red-hot flush on his cheeks like constellations in the night sky.

"Don't ye look at the lass, ye keep your eyes over here," the quartermaster snapped. Trevor's attention whipped toward Tate. "What in the bloody fuck do ye think you're doing? Shite, Trev, when I said enjoy yourself, I did no' mean on the gods-damn deck! If ye fuck this up for me, I will kill ye and dump your gods-damned body where naught will find it."

"Fuck this up for *ye?*" Trevor echoed, shoving his brother away from him.

Anna blinked, gaze flickering from one brother to the next as she took one small step in the direction of the captain's quarters.

Good God, this was almost comical.

"Oh, aye. I like her. You're no' as much of an ass wi' her around," Tate said, pausing long enough to cross his arms and lean forward petulantly. "Did Mum never tell ye how babes are made? Fucking hell, Trev, me walking in on ye in the *middle of the gods-damned deck* is the least of your worries."

Trevor growled something beneath his breath and shoved his hands into his trousers.

Anna slid her foot back further.

"Now, I might no' have been old enough for Mum to talk to me about this," Tate announced despite the look on his brother's face. "But Taylee made sure to beat the finer points of knocking boots into my bloody skull. I'll recite them for ye, since ye seem to have forgotten."

A hasty retreat, then.

She backpedaled toward the captain's quarters, content to let the Lovelace brothers hash this one out on their own. Anna possessed a rather ample knowledge of reproduction; she had asked her mother's physicians plenty of questions on the matter. They hadn't exactly been forthcoming, but Anna had been able to weasel little bits of information out of them—even if that information had been silence.

Their voices faded into the distance as she crept across the deck, thankful to be forgotten. The door to Trevor's quarters opened silently. Moonlight illuminated the bay windows in a soft silver glow. The shadows appeared even darker against the pale planks. Anna padded quietly to the bed and slumped onto it, pressing the heels of her hands into her eyes. She had well and truly buggered that up—what had she been thinking?

Tumbling the Pirate King *on the main deck?*

If Markus were here—

Anna laughed, head shaking softly.

If Markus were here, that never would have happened. As much as she loved him, he found some strange, morbid enjoyment in ensuring they always had a chaperone. Anna could only imagine what he'd be like with a daughter in tow—he'd likely stand between the poor girl and the object of her affections like a veritable, sulking wall.

The presence of his memory added weight to her shoulders, and despite the heat lingering on her cheeks and pressing against her core, Anna shivered and fell back against the bed. Her toes barely brushed the planks, and she stared up at the ceiling of the bed's nook.

If sirens existed, what was stopping the Kraken from taking up space on this plane of life instead of the imaginings of men?

There had been little to no information on the Kraken and even less on what to expect once she arrived on the island. Trevor had filled in some of the holes, like how the trees on the island grew tall and narrow, specters of the pines she had grown up with. But she had stifled her questions, letting what information he wanted to share pour from his mouth like honeyed wine.

Should she have spoken every wondering aloud, even the fleeting ones?

Likely, she thought with a groan, running her hands up her face.

Anna shook her head as she crawled further into the bed and settled deep beneath the covers. She would figure it out; there wasn't anything on that island she couldn't handle, not when it stood between her and Markus. Most learned rather quickly that placing oneself between them was not a location they wanted to stake a claim.

If she breathed deeply enough, the blankets still smelled like Trevor. It sent her heart tumbling, shallowing her breath even as the scent pulled the strain and stress from her muscles. A grin worked its way onto her cheeks. Once, she might have tried to name what this feeling was, but naming something gave it power. It felt soft and it came in little starts and stops. She feared it might make decisions for her instead of the other way around.

If she ignored it, maybe it would go away.

The door creaked. Anna couldn't see it from where she lay swaddled in Trevor's bed, but she knew the sound for what it was. Only two pirates on the *Pale Queen* were brave enough to enter these quarters in the middle of the night, though she doubted Tate would be the one to abscond into her quarters after what he witnessed.

That left the Pirate King. Had he come looking for completion?

His feet hardly made a sound as he crossed the room. The deep, satisfied ache from earlier made its home between her legs. But then his steps stopped, and the room descended into silence. She opened her eyes, brows furrowing.

Why was he just standing at the edge of the bed?

Anna ran her tongue over her teeth and breathed deep as she tried to squash every little insecurity threatening to scream to the surface. Trevor had been more than interested in her earlier, what kept him from crawling into the bed now? What kept his feet tethered to the damn floor in front of her?

Was his hesitancy because of what Tate had said about babies?

That seemed a likely suspect.

Perhaps she should tell the Pirate King he shouldn't be worried about conceiving a child—not with her, at least. Anna wasn't entirely sure she could.

She pinched her eyes shut for several beats, trying to form the words in her mouth. Admitting something as small as this shouldn't be difficult. The words should have sprung forth like a well-fed spring, gurgling and warm. Just as Anna told herself it wouldn't matter if she told him, that there was nothing between them aside from convenience and mutual attraction, he stepped back.

Anna sat up, feather blanket pooling around her waist. "Where are you going?"

Trevor turned quickly, nothing but another dark shadow in the room. The soft moonlight glowed against the angle of his jaw but revealed nothing of importance—not the expression on his face nor the glint in his gaze.

"I—well—fucking hell..." He raised his hand to the back of his neck. When he spoke, his voice dropped lower, nearly to a murmur. "I wanted to see that ye got back all right since ye wandered off wi'out saying goodnight."

Anna clenched her jaw, playing with a loose thread on the comforter. "Just that?"

He nodded.

"...did I do something wrong? Is it because of what Tate said?"

Not enough, hummed through her mind.

His gaze snapped to hers and then he stepped close enough that she could see the surprise on his face. "No. Of course no'. Did it feel like ye were doing something wrong?"

"No. In case you couldn't tell, pirate, I rather enjoyed myself."

"I..." He paused, lowering his hand with a sigh. "It's no' a...*good* idea."

337

"Oh," she said, voice thick. Anna nodded her head slowly. "It seemed like a perfectly good idea at the time. What changed?"

"I'm no'...it's no' safe, luv. I'm the Pirate King; getting involved wi' me is a dangerous business. Most don't live through it."

"That's it?" She gaped, "You're worried about...*me?*"

Did Trevor honestly believe she wouldn't want whatever that had been because he was the Pirate King? Her brows pulled together, surprised that this had nothing to do with what his brother had said and everything to do with a title she no longer feared.

"*That's it?*" he echoed, striding forward. "No, that's no' it, lovely. I—I didn't even realize Tate was fucking standing there. There's enough on that bloody island that could bloody well kill ye wi'out me being distracted by this."

"*This,*" she said quietly.

"'Tis no' that I don't *want*—I—I thought I could, but I can't," he said quietly, hoarsely. "I know what the fuck *this* is, lass. Can ye say the same?"

Anna couldn't—she wouldn't.

Names granted power, they granted ownership. They made something real and offered expectations and definitions to feelings that may be fleeting. Names forced people to admit and confront and Anna wasn't willing to do any of that.

Maybe she would tell him what she thought this was when it was all said and done.

But that didn't mean she wanted Trevor wallowing and believing himself to be too dangerous for her. Hadn't he realized she did not mind a dangerous endeavor? Anna would pick potential peril over safety so long as it was authentic any day.

"Fine." She looked away, a wall built purely of stubborn spite rising up within her. A bit of humor crept into her voice when she spoke next. "But I am hardly to blame. This ship is full of remarkably gorgeous men."

"*What?*"

Anna shrugged, forcing the grin from her face and smoothing her voice into an even, casual tone. "Please. As if you hadn't noticed

338

everyone aboard is positively beautiful? Is that a requirement when joining the Pirate King's crew? It couldn't possibly be an accident that your brother—"

"*My brother?*"

"—Silas—"

"*Silas?*" he asked, a strained breath leaving his mouth.

"Don't worry, pirate, I hardly intend on breaking up your crew." Anna's sigh descended into a small, breathy laugh. "But I doubt any harm has ever befallen anyone from looking."

Trevor grunted something beneath his breath, but she caught the gist of it: "*maybe no' to ye*," and "*flog the fuckers.*"

Anna grinned as she wrapped her arms around her legs.

Clearing his throat, Trevor stepped forward tentatively. "There are fems aboard as well...and other ways of releasing a wee pressure, lovely."

Zarya.

Juliana Gray.

There were splendid women aboard, but she cared little for the wiles of a feminine body.

"I did notice them—the women, I mean. If you recall, Markus and I don't share the penchant for scandalizing the masses indiscriminately. I'm a fair bit pickier than him. And if you think I haven't already done all in my power to temper myself, then you are mistaken."

Breathing deep, his frame tightened handsomely in the soft glow of moonlight.

Good.

Let him be goaded; let him forget about thinking himself dangerous.

A splash echoed in the distance, drawing their attention to the bay windows. The moon hung heavy in the sky, brightening the nearly black waters. In a way, the slow, sifting amble of the tides reminded her of the shadows on Tiburon. Both had a seemingly innocuous surface that hid something far more sinister beneath.

"I thought sirens were supposed to be beautiful," she said, thinking back to all the descriptions she had read.

Trevor was quiet for a long time. Just when she believed he would ignore her question completely, he cleared his throat. "They believe they are, and, in a way, 'tis true. Some wear the skins of the fems they drown, others simply feast on their flesh, thinking that'll grant them the beauty they desire. Lovely nightmares, those beasties."

"Aren't they supposed to sing?"

Anna couldn't remember hearing a tune.

"Aye," he confirmed as another splash filled the room, this one farther away. "That's how they lure ye. 'Tis a beautiful, lonesome song. It does something to the mind and makes ye see things ye want deep in your soul, things that ye would follow to your death. That's how they get ye to jump into the water where they eat ye alive...and if they deem ye pretty enough, borrow your skin."

Anna turned her attention away from the dark sea, centering it on the Pirate King. "That can't be...that's not..." she said, frowning. "I don't want Markus dead. This entire voyage is in the name of keeping him irrevocably the opposite."

Her stomach twisted itself into knots as she remembered the sound of his innards hitting the deck and seeing his intestines on the outside of his body like long, bloody ropes. It hadn't been real, but that didn't make it feel any less so. The knowledge itself didn't erase the fear that had been, nor the panic that continued to build behind her eyes and tighten her chest.

"Aye," he mused. "But ye were ready to follow him over the gods-damned taffrail."

"Why weren't you affected?"

Why wasn't the crew, for that matter?

"The siren's lies and tricks are in no' knowing, and I know more than my fair share about this stretch of sea," he said.

Her brows pulled together, curiosity sparking. In her mind, she traced latitudes and longitudes, calculating how quickly they had traversed. They had covered far more distance than she would have thought possible. "We're...we've passed the Black Line, haven't we?"

"'Tis why the water looks black now. I fell asleep—if I hadn't fallen asleep the siren wouldn't have swum as close as she did." He nodded his head, voice tightening. "She must have wanted you desperately, Anna. She would no' have come so bloody close otherwise."

He blamed himself for sleeping?

"What makes you say that?" Anna asked quietly.

"You're the loveliest female I've ever seen," he murmured. "Ye could lure a great many males to their death, and they'd all go willingly."

"Oh," she breathed.

The quiet stretched between them.

Anna frowned as he scrubbed at his scalp. A fist closed around her heart, digging its nails in and twisting. Perhaps the pirate needed a friend more than he needed a bedmate right now—someone he could talk to and share his thoughts with. Perhaps she did too; she had always had Markus or Mihk as a sounding board and as of late, she had neither.

"Well, I'll leave ye to it, lass." He waved gently, gaze downcast as he walked toward the door, off to inhabit whichever mysterious hole he had crawled out of before rescuing her.

Panic flared up from deep within her, uncertain yet arresting.

She didn't want to be alone and...she didn't want Trevor to be alone either.

"*Please*, wait," she said. Trevor stopped, hand around the knob. She saw the curve of his cheekbone over his shoulder. "Tell me more about the Black Line."

"Lovely, I shouldn't stay..."

"Why not? You could stay. We could talk," she said, feeling bold. At his silence, she gnawed on her lip. "Honestly, I had no idea the Pirate King, Scourge of the Seas, would be terrified of sharing a bed and conversing."

"I'm no' afraid," he said stubbornly, turning around. "And I never said I'd get in the bloody bed."

"Prove it." Anna grinned. "I am at least confident in my ability to resist your roguish charm."

"Ye think I'm charming?"

Was that delight she detected in his voice?

"I admit it, even I could see the appeal in this dull lighting."

Dull lightning, she nearly laughed at herself.

She'd be able to see the appeal even if she were blind.

Anna listened as he walked from the door and lit one lantern after the next. Trevor had chased the shadows away and now he intended to stay, in whatever capacity that might be. The vice around her heart loosened as she watched him move gracefully throughout the room until he stood awkwardly between the desk and bed once more. Looking from Anna to one of the chairs in front of his desk, he grasped one and dragged it toward her.

By the time she had climbed back beneath the comforter, the pirate had slumped in the old chair with his feet kicked up on the feather mattress. She snuggled down into the blankets and pressed her head into the pillow, making sure she could still see him from where she laid.

"I'm only staying until ye fall asleep."

"Whatever helps you sleep at night, pirate." She yawned. "Now, tell me about this Black Line and all the nasty buggers in it."

Her heart clenched painfully. It hurt to look at him, the feeling of falling altogether consuming and not entirely unwelcome. Trevor's face softened, a small smile tugging at the corners of his lips. Clearing his throat, something odd gleamed in his eyes.

"All right, luv," he said quietly.

Anna's eyes fluttered closed as he wove a tapestry with his words. Each tale was a thread in the overall work, each one more glorious than the last. He was well-spoken, his voice like a metronome to her exhausted, addled brain.

And to think Trevor had said he was no good with words.

CHAPTER THIRTY-SIX

Anna thought he was charming.

He did no' think any single thought could fuck him up as thoroughly as that one had. The female could have thought anything about him, but he hadn't thought that charming would be one of them—especially no' after fucking her like a gods-damned animal on the deck.

But she did.

Bloody hell, would Calaveras require his sanity as its price this time around? Because the lass was fucking testing it. All that talk about the crew twisted him up inside. His jaw ached, muscles still coiled tight. Soon as he left his gods-demand quarters, Trevor planned on throwing Tate the fuck overboard.

And Silas?

Bastard was getting stabbed.

Trevor shifted for the eighth time in half as many minutes. He was a chancer for turning her down, for refusing what she'd been ready to offer, but it was better this way. Still couldn't believe he hadn't noticed Tate and he hadn't realized Jules was at the helm and had likely seen everything. When the lass was around, he couldn't focus, couldn't keep track of what was around him to keep her safe, and he'd need to be at his best on Calaveras.

Trevor wasn't even sure he'd be getting off that island. It wasn't fair to start something wi' the lass he couldn't bloody finish. He shifted again, putting his feet on the floor and stretching his hands high above his head.

For as fucked as this was, leaving her like that would be worse.

"Trevor?" Anna asked, sleep riding her voice.

He glanced back to the bed where she lay on her side, wee fists clenched in front of her face. Couldn't be sure if she was awake, no' wi' her eyelids fluttering as gently as a hummingbird's wings against her cheek.

"Aye, luv?"

"I want to make," she said, speaking past the yawn interrupting the middle of her sentence—gods-damned adorable. "...to make something abundantly clear to you, pirate."

He chuckled. "I have no intention of doing anything naughty in your sleep."

"I'd remove your favorite hand before you got that far." She grinned softly, and his heart leapt.

"But, lovely, I need my right hand to handle my steel," he said quietly.

Anna opened her eyes, something critical in her tired gaze. It caused him to straighten, muscles of his abdomen twitching—it wasn't a reaction he could stop if he fucking tried.

"You are a brutal and wicked thing," she started.

Shame set in.

Shame and something close to self-loathing.

Of course, the lass had come to her senses.

"But—"

"But?"

Shite, there was more?

Anna glared at him, a clear sign to quiet himself—he might've said that last part out loud.

"Aye," she mocked. "You are a brutal and wicked thing, but I'm not scared of you. I have never been scared of you," she whispered quickly as if she did no' get the words out now, she might hold them

344

in forever. "I've never feared you, only your title that you wear like a mask—like it's a curse. I care quite little for the Pirate King, but I have found I care quite a lot about Trevor Lovelace."

He swallowed hard.

Fucking speechless.

Her gaze flickered from where it had settled over his right shoulder back to his face. Despite her beautiful blue eyes being heavy wi' sleep, a clear purpose shone from them. Must have been satisfied wi' what she'd said and wi' his silence because she settled back into the feather pillows and closed her eyes.

Maybe she cared naught if he said anything.

Maybe a response from him hadn't been the bloody point.

Anna fell back asleep, and Trevor focused on the rise and fall of her chest, the way a rogue curl fluttered wi' each breath. He imagined they were different, that this life they found themselves in was different. A thousand lives played out in his head in a million different ways and in each one, he was hers.

Shite, in every single one of the damn things, Trevor was hopelessly Anna's.

CHAPTER THIRTY-SEVEN

Calaveras crawled into their sight a week later.

Seven days of falling into blissful, undisturbed slumber with Trevor no closer than that pale chair.

Four hundred and twenty minutes of working side by side, near enough that she could hardly smell anything else but him, dark and spiced.

Twenty-five thousand, two hundred seconds of pretending she did not know what this was.

The main deck was a rush of men preparing to dock. The motion was dizzying, swathes of clothing snapping in the breeze, boots and bare feet pounding against the deck. Despite it all, the crew remained eerily quiet, as if they worked with their breath held. Swallowing hard, she pinned Calaveras beneath her gaze. Startlingly steep mountains rose from the ocean, completely covered in trees that appeared black from this distance, just a smear of shadows, indistinct and chilling.

"Welcome to Calaveras, the island of blood and despair," Trevor said from next to her. "No' as pretty as Tiburon, but...well, I don't have anything nice to say."

Anna glanced toward him, eyeing the way he watched the approaching island.

Did he think it would come over here and bite him?

His cream shirt snapped and billowed on a vicious, ice-cold gust. It had been laced loosely down the front, calling attention to the swell of muscle and the tanned skin swirling with ink beneath. Trevor's shirt billowed again, tightening against his torso before filling with air. The movement pulled her gaze to the space at his throat and then lower to where he had failed to tie his shirt.

Good God, she wished it was a complaint.

Swallowing hard, she faced the island once more. "Do you even know how to lace a shirt?"

Trevor straightened. "Are ye offering to help?"

"Absolutely not. That would mean covering up your tattoos, and I am rather fond of them."

His chuckle brought a smile to her face for no other reason than she was the one to cause it.

The wind blew again, drawing Anna toward him if only by a miniscule increment. Heat rolled off the Pirate King in waves, enveloping her in a tight embrace while she scanned Calaveras. A large channel bisected the island from east to west from its coast nearly to its center. Trevor had already planned on anchoring in the shallows after its second bend, where the ship would be safe from prying eyes.

Something felt off about the island, there was no denying that. Anna had walked through a plethora of cemeteries and sacred spaces before, and none had felt quite like this.

Not even the khan's necropolises deep beneath the earth had hollowed her out like Calaveras did, and they were true cities of the dead.

Anna squinted at the trees as they sailed up the river, noticing they were covered in inky needles, the white bark a stark contrast. Even the sand was a gruesome shade of grey, like moonlight cast off a tombstone.

"Do you have a plan?" she asked, clearing her throat.

"Of course."

Anna frowned up at him, concern bubbling its way up her throat. Exhaustion clung to Trevor closer than his own skin; it was clear in the strain of his frame and the circles beneath his eyes. Anna had caught murmurings from the crew that it should not have been possible to cover the distance between Tiburon and Calaveras as quickly as they had—not without his help. She wasn't sure how the Pirate King had rushed their journey along; none of the ideas she had conjured made any sense.

Not that any of this made any sense.

"Then why do you look so stressed, pirate?"

Shrugging, his attention strayed away from her eyes and back to the dark line of trees. "Ye sure I can't convince ye to stay aboard while I find that brother of yours?" Trevor wouldn't meet her gaze, but from the corner of her eye, she saw Silas and Bodhi turn an ear toward them. "If I had to choose between stepping one gods-damn foot on that bloody island and spending the day in bed wi' ye, I know what I'd pick, Anna."

She rolled her eyes, leaning her forearms against the taffrail. "Careful now, you'll give the crew *ideas*."

He snorted. "Wi' what happened on the bloody deck and sleeping in my quarters all week, oh, aye, the crew has some fucking *ideas*, all right."

Trevor turned then, glaring over his shoulder at their eavesdroppers. Silas and Bodhi turned away, suddenly very interested in the knot Bodhi had tied, their heads tipped together. Anna saw Bodhi's bright smile against his dark skin as he turned away completely.

"All of them brilliantly scandalous, I'm sure."

"Have ye met ye?" he said, cocking a brow at her.

Anna smiled at that, leaning into the icy breeze and away from the Pirate King's cocoon of heat. Ever since crossing the Black Line, the temperature had plummeted and ice floes had ambled by as slowly as molasses. It reminded her of sailing off the coast of Bellcaster to the north, where sheets of ice floated in their own armada. She had decided to wear thick breeches and knee-high boots with a hooded coat and gloves, but the rest of the Pirate King's crew didn't seem to notice the cold.

The wisps near her ears tickled her cheeks in the breeze. Looking down, she tucked one side back once more, focusing on the water below. It was black as pitch, darker than even the night sky. Not even the shallows had lightened as the *Queen* approached them, like most did. Anna wished they had; she did not like possessing the knowledge that something she couldn't see likely swam beneath the ship.

"All jesting aside, are you sure we weren't spotted?" Anna asked, leaning her back and forearms against the rail as she turned her face up to the Pirate King.

She knew Bryce Cunningham better than most. The task before them would be made easier if he didn't know they approached. Good God, the man could hold a grudge almost as well as her father could.

"No' unless ye think the prick can see through this fog better than I can," Trevor bit out. "Following that gods-damned map would have put him on the western side of Calaveras."

"Here I come, Markus," she said quietly, tipping her head back to stare at the thick, grey clouds above.

"We, lass, here *we* come."

Her heart thumped wildly in her chest as she glanced back at Trevor. The wind tousled his hair, and the pallor created by his exhaustion only highlighted the bruises beneath his eyes and the freckles on this side of his face. Tate appeared at his brother's back, a rifle slung over his shoulder. Her gaze trailed from his boots to the haphazard way he wore his hair in a knot on his head.

"You're not bringing the entire armory today?" she asked.

"Afraid no', lassie." Tate winked before smothering the smile on his lips and coughing as he turned to his brother, the air tense between them.

Anna glanced between the two, suspicion curling at the corners of her mind. "What's this about?"

The quartermaster's attention wandered up to the sky and focused on some point she couldn't discern. Following his gaze anyway, she only found clouds and rigging. Squinting at the Lovelace brothers, a frown pulled against her lips.

With the way Trevor stared at Calaveras, she'd think it had slandered his mother.

"Well?" she pressed before kicking Tate's shin and raising a brow.

"Hell if I know. The prick's been acting like this for a bloody week." Tate rolled his eyes. "Shite, if anyone should be upset, 'tis me. I'm the one who saw more than they bloody well wanted to."

Anna's cheeks heated and a small grin twitched against her lips.

She was exceptionally aware of what he had interrupted, but she also remembered what she had said to Trevor as well—that his brother was one of the beautiful men aboard the ship. Her grin widened as she faced the Pirate King. "Is this about what I said?"

Tate groaned dramatically, tossing his head back in exasperation. "What the hell did ye say to him?"

Trevor grunted, lips pressing into a thin line as he stared at the nearing bend where they would drop anchor. Elbowing him gently, she laughed and turned to the quartermaster. "I might have mentioned how pleasing to the eye you were, that's all."

"Why the hell would ye do that?" Tate said, staring at her like she'd grown another head. Shaking his head, he stepped back. "Well... well, when ye two are ready, the bloody boat is as well."

Trevor shot his brother a look that had him spinning on a heel and walking in the other direction. She didn't miss the smile on the quartermaster's face as he left, nor the wink in her direction. Once Tate was out of earshot, she turned to the pirate with a raised brow. A blush tinted his cheeks, bringing color to them even when the icy caress of the breeze couldn't.

His throat bobbed, and he glanced away from her. Anna knew which words were caught in his throat. Trevor wanted her to stay on the ship but knew better than to ask.

"No sense in waiting," she said gently, stepping forward. After a moment, she added, "I promise I'll be fine."

He nodded, resignation hiding in his gaze.

The trip from the *Pale Queen* to the shore was hardly worth climbing in the boat, especially with Tate and Trevor both rowing. The water of the inlet was as smooth as a mirror, hardly a ripple marring the surface as it flowed out to sea. Anna kept her attention trained on the shore, on the shadows between the trees and the fog that weaved between them in dense pockets.

She sat elbow to elbow with Juliana Gray; Bodhi trailed in a smaller boat with their supplies. Trevor, as captain, had decided a small expedition on Calaveras would serve them better, and she was inclined to agree with him. The only detail that had her rolling their options like coins between her knuckles was the knowledge that Bryce could have made it to the island with formidable numbers.

The Lovelace brothers jumped over the sides and dragged the small boat the rest of the way to shore. Their boots sloshed, and the bottom scraped angrily against the beach. Shivering from the damp sea spray, Anna followed them over as soon as it was completely beached. Her feet hit something solid, and a quick glance revealed slick stone.

Bugger, she already hated everything about this island.

Tate slipped several times as he and Trevor hauled the small boat farther up the rocky beach, Bodhi just now spilling over the edge of his taffrail. The surgeon glared down at the water as if it burned. Juliana Gray stepped close to Anna, gaze downcast as she watched the tide lap at the rocky shore.

Good God, she was far closer to the Man-Eater than she had any interest in being.

Anna looked left, then to the horizon where the crew moved about the *Pale Queen* like little figurines. Finally, her gaze crept toward Juliana Gray. It felt dangerous to do so, like creeping up on a big cat as it napped.

The master gunner of the *Pale Queen* stood with a wide stance, lean arms crossed against her chest. Her golden-green gaze narrowed, completely focused on the men as they struggled to push the small boats up the beach. As Anna turned to her, the sun broke through the clouds, painting Juliana in warm, buttery tones and complimenting her light brown skin and the honey color of her hair.

Markus had been captivated by her, and in this light, it was easy to see why.

Juliana wore a burgundy and cream striped shirt void of sleeves with tight, black leather pants that laced along the front. They dipped into tall, worn boots. Two rapiers hung from a thick belt, and knives were strapped to her thighs and glimmered from the leather wraps she wore along her forearms.

The Man-Eater tapped her heel against the ground, and a small blade shot forth from the toe of her boot before sinking back in on her next impatient step.

How did Markus live through their encounter? she wondered.

"Thank you," Anna said suddenly, thinking of her brother. "I didn't realize you would be coming with us, but words will never describe the gratitude I feel. I'm in your debt, Man-Eater."

Juliana turned slowly to face Anna, a finely manicured brow raised in the subtlest surprise. She stilled in the way only a well-practiced predator could. Throat bobbing, she was unsure of how to proceed—she hadn't meant to say anything to the woman, let alone that.

Anna drew herself up taller as the Man-Eater's gaze narrowed to burning green slits. She had at least six inches on the master gunner and was excellent in a scrap, but Anna wasn't entirely sure that would be any help with the feral look lurking in Juliana's gaze. Even the cutlass's pressure against her thigh was hardly a reassurance.

"I'm not doing this for you."

"Oh," she replied. "Trevor is incredibly lucky to have a crew that—"

"I'm not doing it for him either. I have my reasons."

Anna straightened, brows pulling together as the wind ruffled the Man-Eaters lovely locks. Her honey-colored hair barely brushed her shoulders in soft waves brought on by years spent out in the salty spray of the sea. She wore her waves parted down the middle and tucked behind her ear, showing off the sharp lines of her jaw.

There truly was nothing soft about Juliana Gray.

A distant part of Anna suggested pressing and prying as to why the master gunner would volunteer to come on a certainly dangerous expedition. An even smaller, quieter part of her whispered that Juliana could be trusted, that she didn't possess a malicious intent toward Markus. But it was difficult to listen to that small voice when it refused to speak louder than a murmur.

"Well," Anna started, watching the men stalk up the slick rocks with packs on their backs and smaller ones in their hands—it would appear she and Juliana would be carrying those. "I owe you regardless. Name your price and it's yours."

"You may not like what I ask for."

"Markus is worth any price."

A small smile curled at the corner of her lips before they pressed into a thin line, shaped by arrogance and something else—a knowing, maybe, or a secret. "Your brother very well may be my price."

What was *that* supposed to mean?

Surely, Anna had heard her wrong. The master gunner raised a shoulder dismissively and turned her attention to the horizon. Her eyes were large and round. Anna closed her mouth, caging any questions before they could escape as Tate and Bodhi approached.

Bodhi bumped the quartermaster with his elbow a pleased grin on his face. He held his hand open and waggled his eyebrows. "Not a drop of blood between the two."

Tate swore beneath his breath and dropped five silver coins into the surgeon's waiting palm.

"Fucking pricks," Juliana said flatly as she shouldered the pack from Bodhi and stalked off toward the forest.

Trevor came to a standstill next to her, offering a small smile as he held her pack out. Anna grabbed it from him, shouldering it with ease. His fingers followed the sack of canvas to the straps, attempting to help her settle it along her shoulders and back. Grinning to herself, she waved him off—this wasn't her first rodeo. Anna likely had more experience traipsing through unknown locations shrouded in myth than any of these four combined.

"Which one of you has the machetes?" Anna asked, looking at the dense path.

"Lassie," Tate said, pulling a bit of brush away with a grin, "this is no' a jungle ye cut into."

She cocked a brow, glancing toward Trevor, but the Pirate King had already stepped onto the path.

"Watch your step, Anna," he said over his shoulder.

Juliana forged ahead, straight into the brush. The layers of debris on the forest floor and the eons of decomposing needles swallowed any sound their steps might have made. Fern fronds tall enough to brush her elbows and ribs had sprouted up between the trees, and dry, greying moss hung like matted hair from broken branches.

Trevor walked between Juliana and Anna with Bodhi and Tate following behind. Somehow, he always managed to position her in the safest place possible. Anna looked around at their surroundings and snorted beneath her breath. There likely wasn't anywhere on this island that could be misconstrued as safe.

Finally, her gaze fell on Trevor as he walked in front of her, steps sure and head tilting from left to right as he searched their surroundings for potential conflict.

"All well, luv?" he asked softly, glancing over his shoulder.

Anna nodded, gripping the straps of her pack tightly. If not for the urgency in rescuing her brother from certain doom, this was not an island she would have ventured to willingly. If they had found Calaveras as she had planned, with just the pirate and her brother, Anna likely would have opted to sail away.

"It's just this place," she whispered, sure the spaces between the white-barked trees were listening.

"Aye. This island has a taste for blood, one no' even Tiburon can match."

An island with a taste for...blood?

Splendid.

The island could fancy whatever it liked, but it was the stiff silence that bothered Anna most. There were no insects and no animals, and the breeze did not rustle the branches of clumps of moss. One step never sounded louder than the last nor the next; not even the pirate's breathing reached her ears after several hours of hiking uphill. Anna knew she breathed hard, she felt the burn in her lungs and the heave of her inhales, but it hardly sounded like she breathed at all.

Glancing up for the hundredth time, she saw nothing but darkness. Her attention wandered to the tall, straight trees—all of their branches had been broken until thirty or so feet. The buggers were wide at the base, and their bark was chipped and white, a thick skin to what hid beneath.

Was the wood just as pale?

Would the rings be black like the tree's needles, or grey like the rest of this damnable island?

"This is surely the most horrid forest I've had the displeasure of gallivanting about in," she said between breaths.

Anna stepped over the last of the incline and shook her head, glad to see a terrain that would not be so demanding to traverse. The pirate's head shot up to the canopy far above and arced over his shoulder, clearly tracking something Anna hadn't seen or heard. Squinting up, she searched the air above before closing her eyes and listening. Faintly in the distance, she heard the beat of leathery wings.

"'Tis no' a spot I would choose for myself," he muttered wearily, attention returning to the path ahead of them.

"Well, if this fresh hell isn't your vacation spot, then pray tell, what is?"

Trevor was quiet for several minutes; the soft murmurs from the other pirates sounded muffled despite their proximity. The path broke into two, and Juliana curved to the right ahead of Trevor. Hardly any light filtered down, and it had only grown darker since they had entered the forest.

Was it because the sun had lowered or because the forest had grown denser as they neared its center?

"Anywhere my female would like to be," he said with finality.

Anna stared hard at his pack before dropping her gaze to the blackened needles along the forest floor. "Truly? No intentions of living out your life on Tiburon once this is done and over with?"

"No' unless that's where she wanted to be. Home is where your heart is, luv, and I'd rather tether myself to the female I love than a place I could live wi'out."

Throat tightening, she looked away. "Growing up, Markus and I attended every boarding school imaginable. Believe it or not, we were rather difficult to manage."

"Ye? Difficult? I never would have thought so."

"When we weren't at school, we were with my mother at her excavation sites. The only time we spent in Bellcaster was for holidays, or upon my father's insipid request—it should have been home, but it never felt like it." She swallowed, unsure of the words leaving her mouth. The cursed things did so of their own accord. Anna could do nothing but listen and see what blasphemy came into existence next. "Nothing has felt like home since she died."

"Loss never gets easier, luv. It doesn't hurt any less, but after a while ye find it easier to bear." He paused. "Taylee, ye see, she loved to read. I—I can't look at books wi'out thinking of her now, but I bought the damn things for her wi' whatever coin I could scrape together in every port I docked in. Still do."

"...those books, the ones Tate showed me...?"

He nodded, the motion short and curt. "Still can't breathe when I go in there; 'tis fucking pathetic, I know, but I like knowing I'm surrounded by what she loved."

"It's not pathetic," Anna told him

Trevor shrugged, and they didn't speak much after that.

CHAPTER THIRTY-EIGHT

"It's been almost a week," Cunningham said by way of greeting.

The flap to the tent snapped shut behind him, obscuring Markus's view of the outside world. Not that there was much to see, just pale trees, dark bracken, and the stacks of sailors they had lost the previous night, piled up and waiting to be burned.

The blasted flap could remain closed—it was doing God's work, with obscuring the view and deterring the stench from entering the small tent he and Cunningham shared.

"Yes, another fresh day in hell," Markus deadpanned, gaze falling back to his work. "It must be before breakfast; they haven't started burning the bodies yet."

Cunningham's stare prickled the hairs along the back of Markus's neck, but he was well past the point of caring. Let the rat bastard stew in whatever meager feelings of frustration and guilt he might have. He could have turned the blasted ship around at any point and sailed back to Briland.

But instead of choosing what was right, Bryce had chosen obedience—the consequence of which was watching his men fall one by one in front of him.

"What's the count now?" he asked, throwing salt in Bryce's proverbial wound. "Fifty-four?"

No response.

"Honestly, leaving a skeleton crew on the *Oceana's Ire* was one of the smarter choices you've made thus far. I'd hate to be marooned *here* of all places when this plan of yours falls through."

"I need answers!" Cunningham finally cracked, voice low and deep.

"I don't have them," Markus said, pushing his chair back as he turned to face the brunette. "If you wanted answers and wanted them posthaste, you shouldn't have driven my sister away!"

Anna.

His heart tightened in his chest painfully.

Admittedly, Markus hadn't thought all that much about his sister past what she would do if she were here. Guilt occasionally plagued him when he realized he thought more about Juliana and how to apologize to her if he ever had the chance than he did about his sister.

Anna was alive, though.

Markus would have known if something terrible had befallen his twin. He would have felt it like a phantom pain, sensed it like an animal might an incoming storm. They had come into the world together, taken their first breaths one right after the other. If Anna had taken her last and passed into whatever came after, he would have known.

Why would he pour energy into thinking about where she was and what she was doing beyond the acknowledgement that wherever she was, she was alive and well?

Especially knowing wherever Anna resided, it was with the Pirate King—blast it all to hell, he dodged *those* thoughts like a gambler evading loan sharks.

"I didn't drive her away," Bryce said, stepping forward.

Markus leaned straight into the furious pressure radiating off him. "Do you honestly believe that? You threw her pirate overboard."

"*Her* pirate?" Cunningham scowled, inching another step closer.

Ire sparked in Markus's veins, heating his chest and tightening his skin.

He wasn't scared of Bryce.

He would never fear another man again, not after what he had witnessed on this island.

"Yes, *her* pirate. I certainly didn't claim the damn wretch." Markus stood; he was taller, had more mass. In a fight, he could wipe the floor with Bryce Cunningham, but with those rapiers hanging at his waist...well, he wasn't looking to be impaled again. "What did you think would happen when you tossed the man into the sea?"

"She had *you*," Cunningham bit out, furious. "She was supposed to listen!"

"When has Anna ever done what she's told?" Markus laughed, pain spiking through his abdomen with the force of it. He raised a hand to the healing wound; it was warm beneath his touch. "I'll answer that for you, prick. *Never.* You let your petty jealousy get in the way, and Anna responded tenfold."

"We are running out of time, Savage."

"No, what you're running out of is *men*," Markus cracked back, scowl deepening.

Bryce crossed the small space in three large steps, fist thumping hard against the back of Markus's hand—the one gently caressing his slowly healing wound. The hit dropped him to his knees with a wheeze. He hardly had time to laugh before the brunette's backhand cracked against his cheek, splitting his lip.

Markus swallowed hard, one hand on his stomach, the other planted in front of him to keep him upright. Slowly, he sat back on his heels and breathed through his nose. Blood welled in his mouth and beaded down his lip, dripping from his chin. A drop hit the ground in front of him, and he watched as it soaked into the forest floor, hissing softly as it went.

Brilliant.

Apparently, every blasted thing on this island had a taste for blood.

"Is that all?" Markus asked, voice quiet. "Or are you quite finished with your tantrum?"

Cunningham's hands fisted at his sides before relaxing, drawing Markus's gaze from the brunette's feet to his face. His chest expanded on a deep breath, something cruel and painfully familiar settling in his gaze. "I didn't come here to argue with you. I came here for answers."

"And I told you, I don't have them."

It was a bold-faced lie, but Cunningham didn't need to know that.

Oh, Markus had answers.

The rub lay in that he didn't understand any of them.

His stomach muscles twitched beneath his hand, rebelling against the movement Markus coaxed forth. Rolling his shoulders back, he sat up straighter, forcing the wince from his face as he stood. He couldn't remain on the floor.

"You never said how you came by all these journals," Markus started, sucking his lip into his mouth.

John Savage was a master of manipulation, but Markus had picked up on some of his father's sleight of hand and tricks steeped in misdirection. He breathed slowly, watching as Bryce eyed him carefully. The captain's gaze dropped from his eyes to his lips, likely tracking the blood still on his chin. Dragging the back of his forearm against his face, Markus smeared the blood and further stained his shirt.

Cunningham's shoulders stiffened, and he looked away. "Your father gave them to me. Apparently, your mother had quite an unhealthy obsession with pirates."

"Those were his words?"

"They were," Cunningham said, stepping back. The toe of his boot dragged against the forest floor. "You have until nightfall. I know you have acclimated to the feeling of someone's disappointment in you, but trust me when I say this is not a feeling you will want to evoke when I return."

Acclimated?

Acclimation implied that he cared.

He did not.

"You asked before, man or woman?" Markus grinned at Cunningham's back as he approached the flap. "She's a *pirate*."

Bryce immediately stopped, shoulders rising.

"Do you think that'll finally get my father to disown me? Do you think being in love with a pirate will be the thing to finally tip the scales of his constant disappointment in my favor?" Markus pulled himself to his feet and slumped into his chair. He spoke quietly next, mostly to himself. "Maybe it'll finally convince him I don't want his estates. I never have. You might want to reign as the perfect prince in Bellcaster, Bryce, but you are alone in that endeavor."

Cunningham stormed silently from the tent, letting the flap snap over his shoulder.

Markus looked left, then right. Blast it all to hell, he'd been left alone with his deceased mother's journals once again. Honestly, he might have preferred Cunningham's company. But no, the bastard had left him alone in the deafening silence with the smell of burning bodies wafting under the tent walls.

At least he had a task to keep him occupied now, a task with a time limit.

Nothing quite like the pressure of potential dismemberment and torture to motivate oneself. Markus relaxed, slouching in the small, creaky chair and threw his feet up onto a pitiful crate. The carefully organized stack of his mother's journals and leather-bound books stared at him from the corner of his eye.

They wanted to be opened, to be read.

Stacks of books always seemed to have a strange sentience around him. It was why he hated the library, every book a collective conscious put to paper and sat in a row.

His mother's signature caught his eye at the bottom of one of the pages. If what Cunningham had said was true, his father had proclaimed Sara Sommers had a fascination with pirates. Markus's gaze narrowed slightly at that.

His mother had never been obsessed with the unlawful scoundrels out at sea. She had been obsessed with the khan and finding the Pirate King's map because of its potential in locating the man. Markus frowned down at her handwriting, tracing her large, looping script with his pinky.

There had always been stories, though—the ones she had hushed as rumor and hear-say.

Those pertaining to her misadventures and faceoffs involving the Viper.

Nothing boiled Markus's blood like mention of Chardae Badawi. Not even Bryce Cunningham could ignite such an instantaneous reaction from him. Markus wiped his sweaty palms against his trousers, ignoring the press of his skin against his bones.

Poisoned, his mother had said, and he had believed her.

It had done him little good, of course; his father had confided that it was retaliation against his fleet of merchant ships and then simply sent her to Xiang where the weather was pleasant and the convents more accommodating of the ravings of a dying woman. Guilt bubbled up, burning his throat. He'd thought it was the right move for his mother at the time—she had always spoken so fondly of Xing.

Now, though?

Poisoned, she had whispered, glancing uneasily over Markus's shoulder, *by a snake.*

"Focus," he told himself, forcing the creeping feeling that he was wrong about something back into its damn box.

Markus didn't have time for self-doubt.

He had a puzzle to crack before Cunningham returned and did something unspeakable like smile. Glaring at the ceiling, he sighed heavily through his nose. His mother would never have written a lie, but nothing in these journals made—

Markus sat up straight, legs falling from the crate in his haste.

Sara Sommers never would have *lied.*

But she would have written in code.

He was already exhausted at the prospect of translating her notes from this dead, decrepit language and then trying to decode it. Honestly, writing in a dead language and then having him decode it was something Anna would have done to drive him past the point of madness. She had gotten her difficult nature from somewhere, and it hadn't been their father. John Savage had always been difficult by necessity.

If one made business easy for him, the senator would repay the gesture.

If one made it a hardship, however, his father would return the favor tenfold, reigning ruination and bankruptcy down upon their head.

Markus drummed his fingers against the table before scooting in tight. With the stacks of dusty tomes as his witness, he would figure this out. Squinting down at his mother's writing, he frowned.

Bollocks, where would Anna start? Markus wondered with a sigh. His attention jumped from one book to the next before settling on the smallest journal. *Likely from the beginning.*

Markus opened the oldest journal amongst the stacks and began.

CHAPTER THIRTY-NINE

The forest came alive hours later.

"Which way, Captain?"

The Pirate King looked down at something in front of him before motioning to a rather large tree that split their narrow path. One trail peeled off narrowly to the left and the other opened wide on their right. As they strode closer, Anna realized it wasn't one massive pine but five intertwined and braided together.

"Left." He sighed. "At this rate, we'll reach the bloody ruins around dusk."

"Going to be shite if it's after that. I *hate* the guardians," Tate said loud enough that his voice carried to her.

Trevor had never mentioned guardians.

"Don't forget about the staircase," Juliana deadpanned, sounding hardly winded.

"Fuck," Tate groaned as they all stepped onto the needle-thin path.

"Stairs?" she wondered out loud.

Anna had climbed a plethora of stone steps in ancient ruins and hidden temples.

"Aye," the quartermaster said with a sigh. "Lots of bloody stairs."

Fern fronds curled beneath her elbows and brushed her triceps, feeling like fingers. The path opened into a small clearing with a brook bisecting it. Anna's mouth dried as she stared at its slow-moving water, clear enough to see the round, flat rocks along the bottom. She imagined it was quite cool, a balm to her parched throat—though if Anna's luck decided to rear its ugly head, the water would also be poisonous.

Inching a foot forward, her gaze dropped to the ring of rocks outlining the clearing and the wall of white-barked trunks behind them. Anna's attention followed them upward—at least the sky was visible from here.

Several packs hit the ground as she stared at the furious clouds above. Her own pack *whuffed* softly against the black pine needles, and Anna looked from one member of their small expedition to the next. They stretched quietly from within the circle of rocks—though it was not lost on her that they kept their attention on the trees and their backs to the center of the clearing.

Well, all except for Trevor—she wasn't entirely surprised to find the pirate staring ahead with his back to the forest. His penchant for disregarding or encouraging dangerous encounters nearly matched her own. Tracking his gaze, she froze, breath emptying from her lungs. Surprise stilled her breathing for a mere moment before curiosity burned at the corners of her mind.

Bugger, how had that happened?

A skeleton peeked over the brush, weathered and browning. The remains of its clothes were in barely discernible tatters around it. Roots had woven between its ribs, and its skull was half-covered in dirt, a violet cluster of flowers sprouting from its left eye. Anna swallowed hard, fingers brushing against the pirate's knuckles gently.

"Was it the Avani?" she asked slowly, recalling the earth sprites he had described on the *Pale Queen*.

A chill crept up her spine as an eerie breeze wove through the trees, sounding like murmurs.

"Shh," Bodhi whispered, staring at the skeletal remains. "We do not speak their names here—name something and you might call it forth."

One by one, their gazes dropped to the skeleton—Juliana's tiger eyes and then Tate's inky eyes, the same pitch as the night sky in winter. Varying shades of grief colored their expressions, Tate and Trevor most of all.

Were those the remains of their sister?

Anna prayed to every god and goddess she could think of, hoping and pleading she was wrong.

Trevor stepped forward, jaw clenched tight.

Good God, please don't be their dead sister, she thought, stepping with him.

"'Ello Johnny," Tate whispered. Anna looked in his direction in time to see his throat bob before he met her gaze. "Trevor told the wee bastard no' to wander off but...reckon he was seventeen. Thought he knew it all."

Oh, the poor boy.

Any relief that loosened her lungs quickly curdled to guilt. Those browned bones and tattered cotton clothes might not belong to their sister, but they belonged to someone—someone's son, a friend.

Anna swallowed past the lump in her throat, brushing the outside of the Pirate King's hand once more. He stiffened, lacing his fingers with hers and squeezing. His hand was hot and calloused, trembling like a leaf on the wind. She didn't think the others could see his nerves, but she felt them like the pulse in her veins.

"Fifteen," he finally said, squeezing tighter. "Tall, lanky lad. He tried convincing everyone he was older. He really was a bloody prick. Talked shite. Broke shite. He was a shite shot. Bloody idiot even took a go at Jules once...but he did no' deserve this."

Anna listened quietly, brows drawing together.

Johnny's remains had to be at least twenty years old, but Juliana Gray hardly looked any older than Anna. Had she drunk from the chalice as well, or was she something else entirely? Her gaze slowly roamed to Tate and Bodhi. Were they all immortal in the same way the Pirate King was, completely safe as long as their heads remained attached to their bodies?

"No one deserves this," she told him, pulling him toward the brook to fill their canteens. Trevor squatted with her, dipping his hands into the stream and scrubbing them. Anna frowned at the action—it was more akin to washing the sins from his hands than sweat or dirt. "And you can't hate yourself for this. Blame is not yours to monopolize, Trevor."

Holding the canteen out, Anna was unable to form even the smallest of smiles. Trevor sighed and took the outstretched canteen. Despite the general wrongness of the island, he drank from its stream.

"Thank ye," he said, wiping his mouth with the back of his sleeve. "But knowing that does no' help me sleep at night, and it doesn't help wi' the guilt."

"Perhaps you require an incentive," she said with a smile, a bright flush warming her chest and face. "I could think of an activity or two that might wear you out."

Tate choked on his water in the background, raising a light laugh from her lips.

"Captain," Juliana whispered, unease blooming like a rare flower in her voice. "It's starting."

Trevor hissed through his nose, immediately scanning the trees and brush as he stood. Anna tracked his gaze—the trees, the sky, the ground near Tate's feet. A group of ferns shivered several feet from where they stood, drawing her attention as a snake slithered forth.

Anna blinked.

Bugger, it wasn't a snake—it was a blackened root.

It moved enough like the scaled reptile, bobbing and wavering back and forth like the serpents the Kurder coaxed from wicker baskets in their markets. Her stomach churned as she watched the thin tip of the root turn one way and then the other.

Was it searching for something?

"What," Anna said quietly, eyes wide, "is that?"

One of his arms circled her waist, pulling Anna tight against his body. She wasn't entirely sure which was more preposterous—that Trevor growled at a root and it responded by pulling back into the ferns, or that he did so in a language she hardly recognized.

Closing her eyes, she repeated the rough, fast phrase.

Some of it sounded familiar, but he had spoken too quickly, too hoarse for her to grasp where one syllable ended and the next began.

Looking up at him, a flush rose in her cheeks.

Good God.

Just when she thought the Pirate King could not possibly be any more handsome, he had to go and spout off in another language.

"Are you okay?" she asked.

His heart thundered beneath her palm, and sweat dripped from his temples, but he nodded anyway. He held her for a ten count, waiting until the ferns no longer trembled beneath his gaze before pulling away from her. Anna looked from his fingers where he'd chewed his nails raw to Tate, Juliana and Bodhi. They had already hefted their packs onto their backs and stood on the opposite side of the brook, where the needle-thin trail continued.

"Best that we get on our way, Captain," Juliana's voice interrupted the silence. "Everything will be waking soon."

"Aye." Trevor sighed, lifting Anna's pack for her. "The bloody sun will be setting too."

No one spoke as they walked, their gazes darting back and forth, scanning every wretched meter of the jungle. The flapping of leathery wings increased above their heads, pooling dread in her stomach. Now that she had seen evidence of the Avani, she noticed their presence more—the curving of trunks as they walked past, the shaking of ferns and movement of roots beneath her feet. The brush and scrape of plant life no longer felt incidental.

Anna glared up at the darkening canopy of the forest, bumping Trevor's shoulder with her elbow. The path here was wide enough for them to walk two abreast, but the pace the Pirate King had set was brutal.

"I have a working theory," she huffed, "that we do not want to be caught out in this damn forest after dark."

"Oh?"

"Yes, *oh*. Between the conversations I've overheard and the fact that every single structure I mapped on Calaveras is within a day's walk of each other, it was a rather easy conclusion to stumble toward. I would like to know why."

"My wee beastie does use that head for something." He grinned, though it didn't reach his eyes. "'Tis because of the guardians roaming the forest after dark."

"Guardians?" she murmured before Bodhi shot her a look over his shoulder. "That doesn't sound too terrible."

The first level of a brilliantly ancient step pyramid loomed in the distance, peeking between breaks in the trees. It was the same ghastly grey as the rest of Calaveras, but that did little to quell the nostalgia fluttering in her stomach.

Anna's gaze narrowed at the splendid structure.

Could it be one of the khan's?

Shivering, she turned away from the towering pyramid and rubbed her hands against her arms. The chill was likely from trudging through small rivers when she couldn't step over them—Anna was far too dignified to take Trevor's offer to carry her. The hair on the back of her neck prickled, coaxing her to turn her head. Juliana had stopped several feet back, hands at her sides as she stared at the ground.

Anna stepped toward her, hands around her pack's straps. "Juliana...?"

Her head snapped up, eyes frantic and wide. "Walk faster."

The feeling of being watched intensified until the moment crystalized into two: the time that came *before* and that which came *after*.

A lush frond reached out, brushing Anna's hand as her breath plumed in front of her face from a sudden drop of temperature. Something deep and primal hummed in her veins at seeing the eerie spot of green weave through the trees.

Good God.

Predator, predator, predator, her senses hissed.

"Trevor," she whispered.

He stopped immediately at hearing his name. "What is it?"

Several hundred feet behind them were the shapes of six sharks, each one a ghastly green and casting a soft light against the black of the forest. Anna had no illusions of being a marine biologist, but the beasts looked like great whites.

Anna blinked several times, mouth dropping open.

The buggers moved through air like their marine counterparts did water, tails swishing back and forth.

It shouldn't have been possible.

None of it should have been possible—not the damn wood sprites, not the sirens, and certainly not the god-damned immortal men.

Trevor's hand slid into hers, jerking her into motion and down the path. Anna was still looking over her shoulder as Tate cut into the forest to their right, heedless of the brush. Bodhi and Juliana split from each other, disappearing into the fog as the pirate pulled her to the left and down an embankment.

They ran as fast as they could down the slope, their hands clasped together. Trevor glanced over his shoulder as they hit the bottom and took off at a dead sprint, dragging her along. Her breaths came in harsh stops and starts, reducing her to the *thumpthumpthump* of their boots against the pines. Her thighs burned and lungs ached pitifully, already spent from the full day of hiking and rough terrain.

Flying sharks?

Anna almost laughed, the cold stinging her eyes as a colorful string of expletives growled from Trevor's mouth.

"Don't look back, Anna, *don't look back*," he panted, coughing hard as he dragged her up the embankment.

Anna looked.

She should have listened to Trevor.

One of the beasts had closed in on them impossibly fast, simply swimming over the embankment, its tail ripping back and forth as its maw gnashed. All it took was a single glance at all the layers of pearly white teeth for the trembling to start. Cloth, likely that of a pant leg, trailed from one side of its mouth.

Instead of slowing down, its jaws snapped through a sizable branch like it was mere tinder.

Anna stumbled, choosing to look forward instead of at her potential doom. Trevor bore her weight while she fished for better footing in the loosely packed pine needles. One moment he held her weight and the next he stopped, and her arm went painfully taut between them.

Anna was weightless, vaguely aware that the trunk next to her had exploded, sharp chunks flying in every direction with a deafening crack. She saw the black of the shark's eyes and then Trevor let go—simply released her into the air. Rolling down the embankment, she tumbled head over heels as time was captured in snapshots with each blink.

Trevor leaping backward, midair, the shark slamming into the ground where he had been.

Debris raining down on her.

A tree exploding into splinters and tinder.

She landed at the bottom of the embankment, breath knocking from her lungs in one fell swoop. Coughing and gasping, she turned to her stomach and dragged her legs beneath her. As she shrugged her pack from her shoulders, an agonized yelp echoed down to her before it was completely smothered by an echoing boom of thunder.

Good God, Anna thought she had known every face of fear.

She hadn't.

Dropping her pack with a frustrated growl, she started the hike back up the embankment. His inability to die hardly quieted the terror chewing holes in her stomach. It was a vicious maestro, painting a picture of Trevor suffering a thousand different ways in a hundred different lifetimes.

Where is he? she thought as she broke the crest and scanned the area.

A felled pine smoked, lying on its side. A flash of blinding light forced her gaze away, deafening thunder on its heels. The air prickled and popped as she sprinted through the surrounding forest. Roots, ferns, and God only knew what else reached for her, scratching and tearing at her hair. Another bout of lightning had her stumbling, tucking, and then rolling back to her feet.

The pirate growled, a short scream tearing from his mouth in the distance.

"*Trevor!*" she screamed, vaulting over a fallen tree.

Her gaze swam left to right, breath stuck in her lungs. The shark laid on its side on her right, bubbling and hissing as it dissolved before her eyes. The front half of its face was blackened and cracked like a fish that had been over a fire for too long. Liquid seeped from a wound on its side, and its jaw hung limp at an angry angle. Everywhere the damn thing dripped, the ground smoked and burned.

Anna looked away, frantically trying to make sense of a scene that hardly seemed possible. Everything about it made her headache and tightened her chest. The great white shark was melting, but it had been glowing and flying. The area had been trashed, and there wasn't a sign of—

"Trevor," she whispered, lunging forward.

The Pirate King lay propped against several broken trunks as if he had gone through them. His head laid against them, arms resting along them like they were the back of a chaise. She watched the shaky rise and fall of his chest, heart pounding painfully against her ribs.

He couldn't die.

He was supposed to be immortal.

Anna shook her head. As much as she wanted to believe him, hearing it when he was whole and flirting in his quarters was far easier than seeing him caked in blood with his shirt slicked to his torso, showing off every hard-earned line.

Good God, there was so much blood.

Anna slid to his side in seconds, dropping to her knees. What the hell was she supposed to do first? Swallowing past the panic, she pressed her hand to his cheek gently. Trevor's brow furrowed, and his jaw ticked. Only one of his eyes opened as he turned his head toward hers.

He might have grinned, but it looked more like a grimace.

"Told ye no' to look, lass," he wheezed.

"The guardians are flying great whites that glow in the dark?" she asked, gaze roaming his torso.

There were holes in his shirt, blood pouring from them in steady pumps. They arced from his shoulder, his chest, and down to his hip in a nearly perfect crescent.

Bugger, had the shark tried taking a bite of him?

If that had been the case, the beastie had paid the price.

"Remind me not to bite you," she commented quietly.

"I'd never turn ye down; I almost fucking came when ye bit me last," he said, his eyes far off and glassy as he tried sitting up. Slumping, he growled in frustration. "Gone and fucked this one up good and true, I did. Ye need to find a spot to hide until morning, luv."

Anna winced, attention dropping back to the blood, some of which now coated her hands. Slipping a knife from her boot, she sawed at his shirt and peeled it away from his skin. Trevor groaned, teeth sinking into his lip as his body shook.

Oh, bugger.

Her mouth opened and closed several times in shock as she scanned every puncture the shark had left behind. There had to be at least thirty or forty wounds and a stream of red flooded from each one.

"If ye wanted me naked"—he gasped, eyes pinched shut—"all ye had to do was ask."

Anna glared down at him. "Quit jesting and take this seriously."

Helpless, she looked at the fauna around them. She recognized some as having medicinal purposes. Her father had been right, all that time spent with him in the greenhouse at their estate would amount to something.

"Sun is setting," Trevor said on a sigh.

All the half-conceived notions of scattered thoughts fell away until a course sat firmly in Anna's mind, like pieces of a puzzle falling into place. First thing first, they needed somewhere safe to sleep. Then she had to find a way to keep him alive—or from dying further, she wasn't entirely sure of the semantics on that one.

"Ye can leave me here," he whispered, eyes fluttering open. "Find a place to hide, and I'll find my way to ye in the morning, I promise."

Anna laughed outright.

Leave him?

Didn't he understand she would never be able to do that?

"I'm fuck—" He coughed suddenly, blood spraying. Wiping at the back of his mouth, Trevor drew a shaky breath. "I am bloody serious. Do no' make me beg."

She stared down at him for five seconds, then ten. It was thirty before she finally inhaled slowly, gaze narrowing viciously. The possibility of losing him nearly caved her insides. "I would never leave you in the middle of a god-forsaken forest to die alone—even if you won't stay dead."

"As much as I'd love to see your bedside manner, reckon I've had worse. I'll be fine yet." He grinned, eyeing the bite marks with a careful glance. "Aye, they'll scar, but I'll be fine. I've been told females love—"

Trevor's eyes rolled back, and his head thumped hard against the trunk.

"Trevor," her whisper broke as she poked his chest.

Bringing her fingers to his neck, she felt for a pulse. He had one, but good God, it was fretfully weak, and the rise and fall of his chest stuttered to a near standstill. The knowledge that he couldn't die didn't matter. It was a fanciful thought, but it didn't cease the what-ifs whispering in the back of her mind.

Did it matter if he fell asleep?

What if he never woke up?

Were there rules she did not know?

Bugger it all to hell, she should have asked more questions—should have pried the answers from his lips.

"You have to wake up," she said through gritted teeth, starting on chest compressions. "You have to wake up because I—"

The truth of what Anna felt nearly killed her.

She had not said it, had not even admitted it to herself, let alone the pirate. She had denied it, cornered it, and beaten it nearly to death with a stick until it had become so incredibly small and unrecognizable. Anna ripped her coat over her head and pressed it to his abdomen to staunch some of the bleeding, hot tears running down her face. Every compression was an admission of the truth, every thump against his chest mirrored in her heartbeat.

She loved him.

She loved him.

She loved him.

The knowledge pounded through her ears, stronger and louder than any pulse. Clenching her eyes shut, she tried to count to ten, to take a deep breath, but nothing else was important in the face of her acknowledgement, not even breathing.

Anna was in love with the Pirate King, and there wasn't a single damn thing that would come between them.

CHAPTER FORTY

·

Trevor stared down into the endless abyss, watching it ripple and wi'draw.

He'd been here a hundred times, maybe even a thousand, and each time it was the same, naught but darkness and this gods-damned pool. He'd tried walking into it once, thinking that was what the hell he was supposed to do, but the fucker had nearly eaten him alive and he'd woken up wi' the burns later to prove it.

It would never take him into its sweet embrace no matter how much he might want it to, no matter how much he'd prayed for gods-damned release after all these years of fighting, guilt, and pain.

But drinking from that bloody cup had guaranteed him thousands more.

Trevor heard the choked sound of crying and rage held at bay distantly above his head. He'd told the wee lass to go, to find somewhere safe, but he should have known she wouldn't bloody well listen. Her frustration grew, he heard it in her voice and in the wee sounds she made before pressure gathered over his chest.

It was like holding a hurricane back wi' just her hands, though. It did no' take long for something warm and wet to slide down his cheek. He knew he wouldn't find the tears here, but he touched his cheek anyway. Shite, his heart wrenched at the sound as thunder cracked over his head—the first stutter of a beat in his bloody chest.

You said you couldn't die, pirate. Wake up, I said wake up, Trevor.

A minute passed before another clap of thunder echoed and nearly knocked Trevor to his knees. The abyss in front of him hardly registered the bloody sound other than to scream its own high-pitched wailing.

Trevor clutched at his chest, knees cracking against the ground as a ragged breath filled his lungs His back warmed, leaving him tingling as he tried to breathe past the feeling of acid in his throat. Grinning, he stared down at the abyss—aye, sometimes he wanted to burn, to be done. Other times, he remembered why that was a fucking terrible idea. Tate and his crew needed him; but more than that, it seemed dying would upset his wee beastie, and her disappointment was no' something Trevor thought he could stomach.

Trevor, she said, steel in her voice, speech broken by ragged breaths, *wake up.*

What the fuck was his daft female up to now?

Raising hell, most like.

I don't know if you were telling the truth. But I do know I won't let you go willingly. Lady Death will have to pry you from my hands, and even then, I will find you. This is not your end. It is not our end. I need you to wake up, if not because we have unfinished business, you and I, then because you are incredibly heavy, and I misjudged how much you weigh.

Trevor smiled and pushed himself to his feet. Turning on a heel, he walked into the warmth as the black pool hissed and sputtered behind him.

Bloody hell, he loved her.

For her, he'd come back from anything.

CHAPTER FORTY-ONE

Anna had never known exhaustion could quite feel like this—like holding a live wire and drowning all at the same time. Muscles aching, she shifted and licked her lips with a wince before dragging the back of her hand against her mouth. The rusty taste of old blood invaded her senses, serving only to remind her of how many times the Pirate King had required mouth-to-mouth resuscitation.

The low dirt ceiling forced her into a crouch, her face entirely too close to his.

Anna breathed deep. Held it.

Nerve-wracking was not quite the word for what she had just experienced but it was the only one that did not slip from her addled wit's grasp. All forty-eight of his wounds stared up at her, a crescent of neat white dashes that curved from shoulder to hip. They were about an inch in length, and deep enough that Anna had glimpsed flecks of bone while working on him. There was a matching wound on his back with thirty-three punctures—not that she had been counting.

"Come on, pirate," she whispered, gaze dragging from the pallor of his face all the way down to his boots. "We're on a tight schedule. The sun is up, and I need you."

Trevor had assured her anything short of a beheading wouldn't put him within death's cold grasp. She had never heard of anything more preposterous, yet she refused to believe any different. He would be fine. He would wake up. This was nothing, the infamous Trevor Lovelace had lived through worse.

If Anna believed him invincible, it was only so he would be.

Dabbing at his forehead, she caught a stray bead of sweat as it rolled down his cheek. His pulse had fallen to a soft murmur that alarmed her, and his chest had stilled for minutes at a time, but Trevor hadn't irrevocably expired.

His eyes moved behind his eyelids, causing his lashes to flutter lightly against his cheek. Holding her breath, she brushed the back of her knuckles against his cheek and traced his eleven or so freckles for the hundredth time that night.

Sleeping, she told herself, *he is merely sleeping.*

Anna remembered Tate suggesting he take a nap after being run through with John Black's cutlass. She nearly snorted, gaze dropping to his wounds. She hadn't slept since dragging his sorry carcass into this hole. Having his life in her hands and his blood in her mouth had made the task rather difficult, and any bit of sleep she had greedily clawed at had been filled with nightmares.

Markus, gutted like a fish.

Trevor dangling from a hangman's noose.

Her mother in the last hours of sickness, her waxy skin paper thin.

Cold steel running through her stomach before the hot rush of blood.

Shaking the images from her head, she ducked awkwardly to the side and tried stretching her back. Every muscle in her body was stiff and sore from sitting in a hunch for too long. She shot an annoyed look up at the dirt ceiling, fingers digging into the sore muscles of her neck when she heard it—a soft scraping.

The sound changed from scraping to something sliding through the dirt. Her gaze shot to the ground as she searched for any sign of the Avani and their tricks.

God help whatever beast might try to kill her pirate next; she'd flay the bugger and cook it over a spit. There wasn't a monster or myth that would make a liar of her.

Anna scanned the ground, looking for the beginnings of her next nightmare. But roots hadn't sprung from the ground, and none had sunken into Trevor or threaded between his ribs. Anna breathed deep, watching as the pirate's fingers slid against the ground and clenched into a fist in the light candlelight.

He was waking up.

Trevor raised his knees until they were bent, feet flat on the ground. Hot tears rolled down her cheeks as he lurched to his side, stomach emptying with a vengeance. Anna didn't care. She reached forward, hand pressing against his back, feeling the warmth of his skin move beneath her fingertips.

He looked over his shoulder at the touch. Anna's body moved of its own accord, hand pressing against his neck as her lips touched his, gentle and soft. He had lived when he shouldn't have, but she didn't care. She didn't need to know how. The curiosity that so often sparked at the unexplainable remained quiet, content with the outcome.

Anna's nose brushed his as she pulled away, opening her eyes. Trevor stared at her, confusion on his face, lips parted. But his uncertainty was hardly the cause for the concern sinking into her stomach. The veins in his eyes had darkened to a near black, their edges greyed and blurred. Taking a deep breath, she leaned forward curiously, squinting into the murky light cast from the candles she'd found in his pack.

"Trevor, your eyes..."

He blinked, attention dragging from her waist to her face.

Recognition didn't spark in his velvet gaze.

Anna held her breath, feeling like the world had dropped out from under her.

Trevor didn't remember her.

Why didn't he remember?

Scooching forward, her knees dragged against the ground until they rested against his hip. Anna's heart hammered in her chest as his brows drew together, all the pain and years he'd lived through gathering in that small space between his wine-red brows. Trevor touched one of the forty-eight angry, red marks marring his body, nearly marveling at the raised skin.

Most were concealed by his tattoos, but the ones arcing across his stomach stood out.

He looked up suddenly, gaze fixated on her face.

"Anna," he breathed, reaching forward. His palm was cool against her skin, and he wiped away a tear with his thumb. Something in his eyes changed. "Fuck, what happened? Why are ye crying, luv?"

Why was she...

Clenching the fabric of her pants in her hand, she dropped her attention to the ground, unable to sustain the quiet wrath simmering in his. "I—I didn't know if you would wake up," she sniffed, a tear rolling off her nose and onto her leg. "Bugger, Trevor, I didn't know if I was doing anything right or if it helped at all. The thought of losing you terrified me."

He fidgeted as he examined his wounds and how she had treated them, attention sliding from one puncture to the next. Trevor winced as he prodded the mark nearest his groin. After several minutes of self-examination, he looked up at her from his spot propped on his elbow, one arm draped across his midsection and his legs crossed at the ankle.

"Are you...okay?" she asked.

"Ye kissed me."

Bugger.

Is that why he was so quiet?

"What of it?" Anna shrugged, chest tightening. "We've done far more than kiss, pirate."

"This was different," he said, words weighted. "Why?"

Just like that, everything she had felt and acknowledged hours ago came roaring back to the surface. The adoration, love, and crippling fear ripped through her faster than lightning. Anna could hardly think straight with her pulse thumping to the tune of *because I love you,* let alone when he stared at her, with such sincerity and distress.

The words were right there, caught in her throat, just waiting for her to open her mouth so they could color the air with their truth. But the fear, the prickle of potential pain, knotted them into a lump she could hardly breathe past.

He deserved the truth.

"Because I—" She stopped herself, dread squeezing her throat. "I —I told you, I didn't know if you would wake or if I was doing anything right and I was terrified you wouldn't open your eyes."

Coward, she hissed at herself, breath hitching.

"I told ye I would find my way back, lass."

"Well, knowing in advance and truly trusting it while you are bleeding out all over me are two completely different things."

Trevor stared at her then. He must have seen the blood on her hands, trousers, and shirt; he probably noticed the exhausted bruises beneath her eyes. His head canted to the side. Sloughing off the vulnerable curiosity like a pair of dirty lace, Trevor Lovelace stepped right back into his role of the rake.

"Ye sure there wasn't another reason?" he fished, a small smile growing on his face.

Anna's lip twitched, thankful for the distraction and familiarity "What other reason could there possibly be?"

"I'm a rather stunning male. Wouldn't blame ye for kissing me," he mused, looking just below her face but not quite at her breasts. "I've heard a good tumble will put a fem right to sleep, and the gods know I'd love to help ye catch up on yours, Anna. Bloody hell, ye look tired."

Her toes curled and warmth pooled in her center as she thought of the delicious feeling of being stretched and filled by him. It had been fast and frenzied, hands and lips touching and tasting while fingers and teeth scraped sensitive flesh.

If not for his injuries and Markus's life hanging in the balance, she would have climbed on top of him then and there, covered in blood, dirt, and God only knew what else.

Meeting his gaze, a small mischievous smile pulled across her face. "As much as I would love to climb atop you and ride you until your hands tighten on my thighs and you're gasping for breath…" She paused, watching his throat bob. "We don't have the time."

Anna didn't have the time to waste, didn't have spare seconds for what-ifs. Too many unknowns circled them like sharks in the water. Unease had long since settled into her bones, but there wasn't anything she could do to dissolve it. So she did what she could and started packing.

She had to reach over the Pirate King several times to gather their belongings. His gaze warmed her face and shoulders, dipping down to burn her thighs. Leaning all the way across his body, her hair tickled his face as she clasped a pile of clean bandages she had made from his shirt. Trevor blew at the rogue strand, his breath caressing her cheek gently.

Such a child.

Turning to him with a raised brow, she stuffed the bandages into her bag.

He licked his lips, holding her gaze. "Ye are a bloody tease, is what ye are."

"We live through this and perhaps I'll make it up to you."

"We live through this, lass, and ye said you're leaving."

Her soul sagged at the disappointment in his voice. "I don't think that's a road I wish to walk anymore."

"What changed?"

"I'm rather fond of living, and the way I see it, pirate, it will be rather difficult to maintain my freedom with my father disowning me. In all likelihood, he'll send a splendid number of marshals to apprehend me and escort me to a lovely convent where the weather—"

"Ye are welcome to the *Queen* as long as ye like, but that's no' what I'm talking about and ye know it."

"I don't know what you're—"

"This." He motioned between them with his finger. "It doesn't feel like a joke anymore, like I'm the only one rowing. It feels…real."

Anna swallowed hard, glancing to her hands as she rolled the bandages. "It's always been real, from the moment I met you. We've been through a lot together, you and I. It hasn't always been easy or fair, but it's never been fake—not to me," she whispered, mentally side-stepping all the other words that gathered in her mouth. Clearing her throat, she gave the pirate a quick once over. "Are you ready?"

"Aye, aye." He sighed, running a hand through his hair.

She blew out the candle and set herself to the task of pushing her pack down the tunnel. It was a small thing, only fifteen feet from the hollowed-out hole where they had taken shelter to the entrance. She had quite literally stumbled into it while searching from somewhere safe. Trevor struggled behind her, his motions stilted and stiff.

"Are you sure you're okay?" she asked, glancing over her shoulder, hoping for a glimpse of him.

She found nothing but shadows.

"I'll always be fine, luv."

"The inability to die doesn't equate to fine," she said stubbornly, thinking of the purple discoloration beneath his eyes and the way the shark's bites raised his skin. "Well?"

"I don't—shite, I don't go *that* far very often, Anna." Another few beats passed before he sighed softly. "I ache. Everything fucking hurts when I come back, no matter how I...*go*." His voice dropped lower. "But this time, it was no' so bad."

Anna frowned, stomach churning.

He might have been trying to comfort her by regaling that this time wasn't as horrendous as it could be, but that only illuminated the fact that there had been other times that had been worse. Good God, what could have possibly been worse than being mauled by a glowing, green shark?

Poking her head through the hole at the end of the tunnel, she was thankful for the light. Nightmares were too easily conjured in the dark, and hers were filled with Markus and Trevor's potential horrific ends.

Her head had only been in the cool grey light a moment before the pirate's hand wrapped around her ankle and dragged her back. Body pressing hard against hers, his groin dragged over her rump as he climbed over her. Anna leaned back into him, reveling in the friction and the sound of his hoarse chuckle.

"Remember, luv, I go first." He smiled over his shoulder, barely illuminated by the light filtering into the hole.

Trevor was already standing with his face tipped to the canopy by the time she pushed her pack out the hole. The black pines were clustered too densely to see the clouds, but a wet fog loomed about their pale branches. The light mist dampened her skin, a chill forcing her breath to fan in front of her face.

Bugger, this was likely as close to a bath as she would get.

Anna's teeth ground against each other as she dusted her hands off on her knees. The forest around them devoured any noise caused by her steps as she walked in a small circle and stretched.

Which way? she wondered, squinting into the distance.

In one direction lay the destruction Trevor and the guardian had left in their wake, and in the other, she saw the small path they had started on. Anna propped her hands on her hips, the icy air burning her lungs. They couldn't be that far from where they had separated from Tate, Bodhi, and Juliana. Turning to the pirate, she was about to say just as much, but his gaze was anchored to his open palms, her pack shouldered on his back.

He glanced up. "This way, luv."

Pushing a giant fern frond to the side, he paused with his arm in the air and turned to look at Anna over his shoulder. Trevor stood before her bare-chested, tattoos on display, in trousers that hugged his thighs. She let her gaze sink, trailing his legs, noting how his left pantleg had ripped away below the knee.

Even stitched to high heaven and covered in blood and detritus, the man remained a vision.

Anna walked forward until they were shoulder to shoulder and glanced down at his hand. She knew what the ink along his palms looked like. She had traced the shifting lines after Cunningham had had Trevor beaten nearly to death. They had been covered in blood and bruises then, and they didn't look much different now.

The Pirate King stepped away from her and into the forest, grinning down at her softly.

It took twenty minutes for Anna to work up the nerve and ask him a question—any question—about himself, about what he could do, to explain the unexplainable to her. "Why were you looking down at your hands?"

He swallowed, lifting his palms. "I—ye wanted to see the Pirate King's map, aye?"

The—

The Pirate King's map?

Anna gaped up at him before her attention plummeted to the intersecting lines of his palms. Good God. Cupping both his hands in hers, she ran a finger over the lines of his palms and nodded her head—latitude and longitude, even lines showing topography and elevation. Her gaze narrowed down at his hands, tongue running over her teeth.

These were not the marks she had traced on Cunningham's ship, though.

"How does this work?" she murmured, raising her eyes to meet his.

Trevor wore a bashful expression, his attention fixed on her small hands cradling his. Finally, he looked from her hands to her face and pressed his lips into a thin line before sighing. "Ye act like I know how any of this fucking works."

Amazing. He was absolutely amazing—no matter the fact Anna couldn't make heads or tails of it. Was that the point of this, though, of a life well lived? To understand and quantify, to break it down into manageable pieces she could explain away?

Or was the point to enjoy it?

"How did you get them?" she said, stepping closer. "Is there some magical artist, or is it the ink that makes them something straight from the legends of old? Was a ritual involved?"

He shook his head. "These? I don't bloody know. They just...sunk into my skin as a lad."

"And the others?"

"I don't understand it. I don't understand any of it. I've never tried too, either," he said, gaze skimming the ink along his forearms. "They all appeared after one gods-damned adventure or another."

He might have never tried to understand the tattoos moving against his skin, but she wanted to. Good God, Anna wanted to stare at them for as long as she wished, to trace them with more than just her fingers. She wanted to know the stories behind each one. "You are incredible, Trevor. This is incredible, and I don't understand it, but I'd like to one day."

"It doesn't scare ye?"

"Why would I be scared?"

"It scares me," he said quietly.

The Pirate King, scared of some silly shadows living on his skin? "Why?"

She looked back at his hands, tracing one of the lines denoting elevation. Was it the loss of control that scared him? In Bellcaster, she had grown up with every man weighing in on what they believed was acceptable for her to do with her body. That had been hard until she decided she didn't give a rat's ass about their opinion.

Anna didn't know how she would have reacted to the sudden appearance of tattoos on her skin, especially without knowing how or why.

"It's no'..." Trevor's throat bobbed and he pulled his hand from hers, clenching it at his side. "I'm no' normal—"

"Stop right there, Trevor Lovelace," she said, stepping back and crossing her arms against her chest.

His head snapped up at hearing his full name, gaze anchoring on hers.

"First, I would like to inform you that normal is dreadfully boring. Second, the sudden onset of tattoos is hardly the strangest thing I've heard lately. In fact, I would rank"—one of her hands popped free as she ticked off her comments on her finger— "sharks that swim through the air, sirens that steal your skin, and trees with a mind of their own as far more outlandish. But let's not forget about the Kraken and the absolutely devastating, deathless man who I have grown rather fond of despite his old age."

Trevor's lips twitched at that. "Hush, ye."

Anna laced one hand with his, walking backward down the narrow path. "Come on, old man; we have people to be and places to see."

Trevor looked at the palm of his other hand and veered to the right. On the other side of a thick grouping of bracken, a narrow trail appeared—honestly, it looked closer in kin to a game trail. It wound ahead of them between two willowy pines, moss waving in a breeze high above. Droplets of condensation dripped from their tangles in icy orbs.

"Me—"

"*First*," she interrupted, allowing him to step in front of her.

Anna's breath fanned in front of her face. She dragged the back of her hand against her forehead, keeping her attention anchored on Trevor's back and the way his pack hung off one shoulder—the right strap had been torn and rendered useless.

It had likely been severed when the shark tried taking a bite out of him.

"How many others have drunk from Eero's Chalice?" she asked, looking up at him.

"I don't know, luv." Trevor shrugged. "Reckon too many. Most of my crew. Fucking Carsyn Kidd too."

"Only Carsyn Kidd, not the rest of the Coalition?" Anna hedged. Trevor nodded stiffly, velvet gaze glaring at something in the distance. "How is that?"

"Fucker was there wi' me when I found the bloody thing—we... we were best mates, once."

She laughed. "Best friends? Truly?"

The Pirate King was not so quick to respond, gaze shifting from the pale pines in the distance to the shifting brush at their bases. "Aye."

"*How?* All the reports claim you can't stand each other."

"No' *now*, before," he said quietly, a small chuckle warming his words. "I met the whelp on the Old Crow's crew when I was fifteen. He was one of the cabin boys at the time; later I learned he was the son of one of the Coalition chiefs too. He was only ten and reminded me a wee bit of Tate, so I tried looking out for him."

"Oh." Anna's brows furrowed as she looked up at the canopy. "For being five years younger than you, he looks older."

"Aye, he is." Trevor nodded slowly. "Prick did no' drink from that gods-damned cup until...maybe thirty-five? I think that's when he finally made up his bloody mind."

Peculiar.

Being caught in limbo as a child or teenager, let alone at all, sounded like an absolute nightmare...but if forced to choose, she would have wanted to remain in time's grasp at an age where the body wasn't naturally falling apart.

The poor man likely suffered from knee pain and would continue to do so until expiration.

"Why wait?"

"Carsyn wasn't sure if he wanted it after all we lost—I wouldn't have, but it was too fucking late for me," he said, craning his head to look up at the mist and shadows above. "When I got the *God's Beau*, he came wi'. She was my ship before the *Queen*, ye see. Smaller, near as swift, but bloody hell, Anna, she was a gods-damned sight. Blackened hull and blood-red sails. I started running down the slavers on the *Beau*; she was swift enough to take them but no' strong enough to sink them. After Taylee died—"

Anna ran straight into Trevor's back, entirely focused on the sound of his voice while she examined their surroundings.

Loss never gets easier.

It doesn't hurt any less.

Wincing, she opened her mouth to tell Trevor he didn't have to talk about his sister, but his head swiveled back and forth. Had he heard something? He looked over his shoulder, eyes closed as he cocked his head this way and that.

"What is it?" she whispered, her mind conjuring images of mythical beasts.

"I hear something...almost like groaning?"

"Do you think—"

"No," he said, sounding completely sure. "'Tis no' my crew. We'd hear Tate cursing loud enough to curdle milk in gods-damned Bellcaster if it was him."

"What about the others?"

Trevor shook his head, pushing past fronds and other foliage. "You'd never hear either of them—Bodhi on principle and Jules out of bloody spite."

As they strode forward, the groaning became loud enough that Anna heard it too—something deep and pitiful like a wounded animal. The pirate paused, brows drawing together, arm automatically stretched to keep her behind him. She nearly smiled at the gesture. If it had come from anyone else, Anna would have been offended, but coming from her pirate, it caused a flutter in her stomach.

One of his tattoos moved; a mermaid along his forearm swished her tail, and her expression changed to match his, one of surprise and caution. Which adventure had she appeared after? One of these days, if they were allowed the time, she would ask him when and where each and every mark on his body originated from—scars, tattoos, all of it.

"Should we..." She trailed off, a chill trailing up her spine.

Trevor shook his head. "Let the fucking gods take the poor bastard. He's no' me or mine. I'm no' risking it."

Risking ye, she heard echoed in his words.

Anna snorted, stepping around the over-protective Pirate King. "My intentions aren't entirely philanthropic, pirate. If they're not one of yours, they're one of Cunningham's and that means they might have answers."

Careful of every step, Anna walked around Trevor like a satellite around the sun. A small clearing laid ten or so feet away, though it didn't open to the sky. Large rocks covered in strange, burgundy algae stood sentinel on her left. The fog slunk through the gaps in the trees, caressing the plant life like a lover's fingers, but still, she didn't see any of Cunningham's—

Good God.

If not for the twitching of the man's foot, she never would have seen him. Anna's breath caught in her throat, chest tightening as her gaze stilled on the man. The pirate stepped around her, the stiff lines of his body the only indication he had noticed as well.

The man sat propped up against a behemoth of a tree, no shoes and no shirt. Blood leaked from everywhere—his nose, ears, and mouth. The man's eyes were milk white and yet he made eye contact with her, gaze steady and strong. Anna swallowed uncomfortably, a buzzing starting up in the back of her skull like a hornet's nest.

Trevor and Anna's footsteps didn't make a sound, their attention wholly focused on the man before them. She couldn't take her eyes off him. It wasn't his milky, sightless gaze following her eerily, and it wasn't the dark blood gurgling forth; her attention was on the roots woven around his torso. Her gaze shifted to the ones that were still moving. They twisted their way into his ears and beneath his nails, coiling in and out of his ribs like stitching.

"I see ye...met the locals," Trevor said casually.

The man attempted a laugh, foot twitching as he wheezed.

"I've some questions for ye."

"Thought you might—dead anyway," the man grumbled, glaring at the Pirate King with surprising accuracy. "So what's the fucking point?"

"Aye, you're dead either bloody way, but a lot can happen between now and then, bucko," he said, shoving his hands into his pockets and puffing out his chest. "If you'd like, I can cut your wee bits off first."

The sailor grinned, attention dropping to his groin. "Reckon it's literal wood right about now, king. Imagine that."

Anna focused on the man's face instead of all the wrongness the island had woven through his body. The sailor canted his head in her direction, sending her stomach tumbling. It was an unnatural movement, like an invisible hand had come up and broken his neck. His neck cracked, twitching his head from left to right in a harsh snap before those sightless eyes of his bored into her.

There's no way, she thought eerily.

He blinked once, then twice, licking a split in his lip as a root escaped his torso.

Could he see her?

The intensity of his stare suggested he could, but the white color of his eyes meant he shouldn't be able to. Anna froze at the curious light in his gaze, teeth gritting at how his features changed from someone who had been caught to a man staring at prey snared in his trap.

"Ah, would you look at that? If it isn't the little cunt that dragged us to this bleeding island to begin with." He paused, exhaling a hard, shaky breath. "And hand in hand with the Pirate King, no less, imagine *that.*"

Trevor's knuckles popped in what she could only describe as a warning. Looking down, Anna saw his hands had rounded into fists, and the veins along the top of his hands and forearms stood out against the ink on his skin.

Bugger, had every muscle in his body gone taut at the sailor's words?

His gaze narrowed to dark pinpricks. As he stepped forward, Anna lifted her hand.

"I did not bring you here," she said, staring down at the dying man.

His laugh sounded closer to breaking glass, a wet wheeze following in its wake. "Of course, you wouldn't think so—no one is ever the villain in their story. But we wouldn't be here if not for you and that bit of warmth between your legs."

"What is between my legs has nothing to do with this."

"Oh, it does." Black ichor leaked from the corners of his mouth and nose, running like tears from his eyes. "We love the captain. I've watched him come up in the ranks since he was a lad. But he's not much for imaginative plans, you see. You think he would have come up with the idea to chase the fucking Pirate King if you hadn't gotten it in your head first?"

Bryce had always wanted to strut one step ahead of her, to claim her every achievement as his own.

Why would this have been different.

"I see you're warming to how I see things. No, Captain wouldn't have wanted that blasted map if not for your having it first—if not for your father wanting it too." The sailor shook his head slowly, gaze wavering toward Trevor. "Captain saw the way you look at Lovelace that night too, we all did. What's a captain in the Briland Navy when you can have a king?"

The warmth of Trevor's attention worsened the burn of embarrassment and disappointment on her cheeks. "That's *not*—" She stopped and breathed deep. "His thoughts and emotions are his own; if he is too small to rein them in, that is on him. I will not be blamed or held accountable for his actions."

The sailor scoffed. "Would it have been so difficult for you to marry him and pop out a brood of babies? To live an easy life, well-fed with naught to worry about except for where and when to lie down?"

She thought about it then, all the years that stood between her complacently marrying Bryce and death.

It would have been torture.

"Did you know your father made a proposal to the captain before we set sail? Whatever is on this blasted island for your hand? Deal's done, all he has to do is bring you back to Bellcaster and it'll be white lace and linens for you." He paused as Trevor's attention settled on her with an even heavier weight. "Shouldn't be a hard decision, really, save your brother's life, sail home, live a life of luxury—and all you have to do is marry the captain. What more could you possibly want?"

Anna wanted a love and a life to rattle the stars.

Life with Bryce would have hardly shaken the cupboards.

"That's nice," Trevor said, stepping forward. "Now, back to my bloody questions. I have a lot of the fuckers and no' much time, ye see."

"Changing the subject, are we?" The sailor's smile twitched, the movement closer to a shiver. "I see you, Trevor fucking Lovelace, and you can't tell me it doesn't bother you."

"Oh, aye, I'm no' hiding anything. You'd be fucking bothered too if ye were standing on an island ye swore you'd never sail close enough to see again," he said dramatically, crossing his arms. "Or are we talking about their tumbling?"

Anna flushed, turning to stare at the pirate. His jaw ticked, and lines bracketed his eyes and mouth. The scruff on his cheeks and jaw had traveled down his neck, and his wine-red hair tickled his ears. It had grown long enough that a cowlick kept some of it off his forehead.

Where was he going with this?

Trevor angled his head, meeting her gaze—waiting, always waiting. He'd let her interject, make it clear she wasn't a thing to be spoken about like a doll in the room. One look at the patience and simmering annoyance on his face confirmed that.

But did that knowledge bother Trevor?

Damn it all to hell, she wanted to know.

"Aye, it bothers me," he said, grinning.

Anna's heart nearly stopped in her chest.

Bugger, why wouldn't it bother him? Bryce had tied cannonballs to his boots and thrown him over the taffrail.

"But only because the lass could do better. Her business is her own, and if she wants the wee bastard, so fucking be it. But she'll no' be forced into any gods-damned arrangements—no' while I breathe." Trevor held her gaze while he spoke, voice softening. "We've been through a lot, she and me."

Anna breathed past all the words wishing to spring forth from her soul. An impossible amount of love was trapped in the four chambers of her heart, all of it waiting to escape and pour from her lips. The words were trapped in her chest, though, and now was not the place to voice them.

But when was the time?

In a few days?

A month?

Was there a time that would be too late? If Anna waited even a day, would she miss her chance?

Trevor looked away from her, his focus back on the sailor. Or perhaps it wasn't the sailor, maybe it was the unnatural movement beneath his skin. A flower bloomed from within the sailor's ear, a small burst of periwinkle in the cold grey of Calaveras, before it wilted and fell, landing on his shoulder.

"Tell ye what, ye answer my questions and I might put ye out of your bloody misery."

The sailor straightened as best he could at that, head slumping to the side.

When Trevor spoke next, he was the image of cool confidence—a king by might and right with no one to contest his reign. "Now, where the fuck is the wee shite?"

"Probably raising the sea king. Big plans, that one."

"I'm the only king these bloody seas know. How many survived?"

"Less than a quarter—blasted storm was brutal. Three hurricanes and swells bigger than I've ever seen. I'm not sure how many are still alive; we were attacked two nights ago by damn sharks, if you can believe it. He knows about you, Lovelace, and he'll use everything you love against you—use it right up until its naught but ash. Including her."

The pirate remained quiet. Just when Anna thought he wouldn't speak, he shifted, powerful body turning toward her. "Come on, lovely, we've a wee more walking to do."

Anna turned with him, craning her neck to look over her shoulder. Something cold chewed on her emotions, guilt or surprise, maybe. Leaving the man to suffer unnecessarily felt wrong. As far as she knew, he hadn't committed a crime other than following Bryce Cunningham in whatever scheme they found themselves entangled in.

"Wait!" he called weakly. "You said you'd kill me!"

Trevor didn't turn at the man's words, his attention anchored on the dark spaces between the trees in front of them. The commotion of

395

convulsions, of boots kicking and scraping against dirt as a body flailed, followed in their wake.

Good God, she had never heard anything louder, anything more tragic or chilling.

"I said might," Trevor muttered, fingers sliding between hers and tightening. "But your body is already dead, mate, it just doesn't know it yet."

The sailor's laugh echoed around them, the sound choked and full of fear.

CHAPTER FORTY-TWO

Trevor's fingers tightened around Anna's as the sounds of the sailor died wi' him. It never got any bloody easier, and there was never a way to prepare someone for seeing that shite. He watched his beastie from the corner of his eye, how her wee chin tipped this way and that, gaze devouring every inch of their bloody surroundings.

Fuck, what he'd give to be devoured by her.

He thought of his sister then. Might have been strange if no' for how Calaveras pulled his memories of her from where he'd locked them inside his fucking chest.

First time Trevor'd taken his sister out to sea, she met a lad.

He had no' understood it at the time, and frankly, wi' the pain in his ass that the lad'd been, he still did no' bloody well get it. How she'd picked *him* out of all the males on the planet was beyond Trevor.

He'd asked her about it once, what it was she felt, and she told him: love. Wi' her deep eyes shining and her hell's fire hair caught in the salty gusts ripping off the swells, she'd said it was *love*—as if that was all the bloody explanation he'd need.

Took a long time to get over her loving another as much as she loved him or Tate, that she'd had more room in her heart to spare. Fucking hell, he hadn't had more room in his heart at the time. All the space in that lonesome thing in his chest had been taken up by Tate, Taylee, and his crew.

But she'd found room for a pirate like Trevor.

A ruthless killer wi' blood on his hands.

Despite that, she'd wanted every gods-damned minute wi' him and his blue-green eyes.

Once, she'd said that they were the kind ye could dedicate poetry to. Trevor'd immediately thrown up everything in his stomach over the taffrails of the *Beau*. Couldn't imagine writing poetry to anyone. He'd hated words; the wee fuckers had a nasty habit of getting caught in his throat. Taylee had loved them, though, and Tate had learned how to spin them into a tale to catch some tail.

Back then, Trevor could no' imagine loving someone as much as he did Tate and Taylee, no' after raising them. How could he have any more room or energy to devote to a fem like that? He'd hated the no' knowing—no' knowing if it could ever happen for him, no' knowing when it would if it did.

No' knowing if he'd love Taylee and Tate less because of it.

"It's almost like suffocating," Taylee'd said quietly.

He remembered it like it'd been yesterday—leaning against the taffrail, eyes on the blanket of stars above. The air had been a constant chill wi' the sail north, and they'd both been dressed in warm clothes. Even then, Trevor had draped his coat around her shoulders.

He'd wondered what in the ever-loving fuck went through her mind as he stared at her. Taylee had more freckles than Tate and Trevor combined; they cascaded over the wee bridge of her nose and up her cheeks, and speckles of them colored her forehead and chin.

"Suffocating? Why the fuck would anyone willingly do that?" Trevor'd asked after a while.

"Pirate, are you listening?" Anna asked, tone full of lovely amusement. "I think the jungle is thinning."

He grinned at the sound of the wee fem's voice before glancing at one of his hands. "Aye, beastie, no' long now."

Looking at her like he was now, every breath came easier, filling his lungs to a fullness he'd rarely experienced in his gods-damned life.

Sure, his chest ached, but doesn't everyone's after holding their bloody breath? Shite, he was dizzy wi' the sensation of her fingers threaded through his. Bloody fucking hell, Trevor hoped she didn't mind how sweaty they were. His heart pounded against his ribs, but this was no' suffocating.

He'd done that enough times to know the bloody difference.

No, this was finally breathing.

They stepped from the shade of the forest and out into the open air, the grey light of the sun beating coolly against his back. Shite, he was cold, but Bodhi likely had a fire going in the temple. The male was good like that.

Rolling his shoulders, his gaze moved casually over the forest. The stitching the lass had done pulled against his skin wi' every movement. It pained him naught at this point, more hassle than anything.

Anna stopped, eyes widening and mouth opening in surprise. Then the awe slipped from her lips in a soft sigh, quickly replaced by excitement. Her throat bobbed, and she shuffled forward one step, turning to look up at him excitedly, and fuck, if that didn't floor him.

Is it to your liking? he thought softly.

I love anything old, he imagined her replying.

Bouncing on her heels, her fingers pulled from his as she stepped forward. Shite, he did no' know what the lass was looking for or if the layout meant anything to her, but he wanted to. He wanted to know every wee thought in her mind, wanted to know why she stared at the ruins in front of them wi' questions on her tongue and wonder in her eyes.

But if it made Anna happy, he'd watch her take this forsaken temple apart brick by bloody brick.

She crossed the clearing carefully, steps light against the crushed shells. Scrubbing the back of his neck, he followed her. Bloody hell, she'd make someone happy one day. She'd already made him happy by just being, and—and he knew how this would end. He'd had a sinking feeling since first stepping foot on Calaveras.

Did you know your father made a proposal to the captain before we set sail?

Trevor's fingers folded into fists before he stuffed them into his pockets, mood souring in a second. The fury came cold like wind nipping at his calves and shoulders, muscles bunching and itching for a fight. Knowing John fucking Savage had offered up his daughter pissed him off.

"Do you know how old," she paused and waved her hands as she stared at the temple, "*this* is?"

"Nah, lass," he sighed, dragging his attention from the foundation to the tippy-most top. "Then again, I've never given a shite how old the rocks are."

Anna snorted. "Some help you are, pirate."

"You're the wee grave robber, ye tell me."

She turned and smiled. His chest ached and the grin he'd had on his face slipped from his lips as she turned around and set off down the path. Something had bloody-well changed when he'd woken up; he knew it the second her gaze had met his. He wasn't sure what had changed, but it was poor timing.

Trevor was in love wi' her wi' everything he had.

It wasn't something ye could lay at a fem's feet, especially no' one like Anna and no' at a time like this.

She walked faster now, tossing another smile over her shoulder. It was brief, full of excitement and the blue of her eyes looked more akin to lightning. Poor lass couldn't get any words out. Trevor nodded at her—he understood. He'd been in awe the first time too. Anna bounded forward through chunks of stone, navigating the debris wi' ease.

She looked so bloody happy.

Breathing deep, Trevor slowed. She wasn't coming wi' him. Either he'd get her killed, or she'd be dragged back to marry that fucking cunt. Could he live wi' himself if something happened to her?

Shite, no.

A wee plant wi' wide, crackling leaves caught Trevor's attention, and he almost smiled.

Bloody fitting, he thought.

CHAPTER FORTY-THREE

Anna didn't have any words to describe the temple and its surroundings other than heaven—and even then, the word seemed inadequate in the face of the structure before her. Spinning, she turned in circles as she walked, taking everything in. The step-pyramid rose high above the treetops, the sun a ghastly grey ball hanging like a crown just above the topmost step.

Intention lived in the landscape surrounding the step-pyramid. It wasn't the first piece of ancient architecture she had seen that had crafted the surrounding area to match the builder's vision. Leveling the forest allowed for the pyramid to dwarf them, to make those who approached it feel small, almost like a peasant kneeling in prayer. And the bright white shells leading to the temple felt like a welcome mat, pulling her closer to the steps.

Anna looked down curiously at the blanket of crushed shells and white pebbles, something tugging at the back of her mind. She'd think on the familiarity of it all later; right now, she was simply too giddy.

The curious recognition disintegrated as she stared up at the statues standing sentry. Each was grey in color, the same grey as the step-pyramid, veined in tan and gold and standing at least thirty feet in height. Anna stopped in front of one, gaze working from the base it stood on to its toes which were eye level with her. Long, lean calves dragged her attention up until her neck ached. A short sash had been carved to ensure the statue's modesty, which was rather splendid.

Bugger, she'd seen enough stone carvings of the male anatomy to last her a lifetime.

Abdominals and the impression of a navel curved beyond the statue's hips, but everything crumbled away above the bottom-most rib in the ribcage. Weather had not been kind to the statues; it had smoothed over the intricate details until they were barely discernible. The pattern of the sash was now as fine as a fingerprint, and the tattoos trailing down their legs looked no more important or powerful than tracery, the equivalent of faded watercolor on a canvas.

Despite the calamity erosion had set upon them, they were still extraordinary.

"They're positively splendid," she told Trevor, gaze skipping to the next statue.

The next statue had an arm and a shoulder, its body cleaved diagonally from clavicle to hip. Her attention dropped to the ground around the sentinel, searching for whatever had been grasped and later dropped. A scattering of broken stone had settled haphazardly around the base.

Had it been a sword?

A staff?

Bugger, she didn't know, only time did. It was the only thing that remained constant when everything else changed at the drop of a hat.

The pirate shrugged, fingers trailing something along one of the statue's bases. "Aye, if ye like that sort of thing. No' much of a bloody fan of a male's legs, myself."

Ignoring the arc of stitching on his back, she stared at the curve of his shoulders and the way his trousers tightened around his thighs as he kneeled. One of his pant legs still hung about the top of his boots, the skin of his knee and calf out for her to see.

"I do," Anna admitted, staring at the Pirate King. "I *really* do."

Trevor looked over his shoulder, the rakish smile on his face warming her belly. It didn't quite reach his eyes, though she supposed there could be any number of reasons for why he felt the way he did—Tate lost, the crew scattered, Cunningham up to no good.

Turning away, she squinted in the distance and counted the remaining statues—thirty-two total, sixteen on one side and sixteen on the other. The last statue had fallen long ago, its legs smashed asunder and its base tipped on its side.

What had caused it to fall?

Anna stared down at long, black singe marks along the base. An incendiary would have caused those, but...she shook her head, glancing toward Trevor. The long look he gave the sentinel suggested he might know what had caused the fall. She followed his obsidian gaze until her own landed on the statue's head resting on the ground in the distance.

Good God, what were the chances?

Her steps felt distant as she stepped closer to the masculine stone face. Trevor said something in the background, but it was lost to the din of ringing in her ears and the pounding of her heart in her chest.

Bugger, she had seen that handsome, freshly shaven face before.

She knew the story of how he had acquired the scar running through his eyebrow and over his eye.

And if none of that stood out to her, the jaguar headdress would have been sufficient to identify whose image had been cast into stone.

Granbaatar Khan.

What are you doing here?

Anna didn't know how or why the damn khan had been on Calaveras, but now that she looked around with this knowledge as a lens, she saw him everywhere. Leaning forward, she pressed her hand against his cheek and studied his face. The stone was cool to the touch and moist with condensation, just like the jaguar she had found at GBSP-21.

So my weensy kitty was carved from stone originating from here, she figured, bright blue gaze narrowing on the khan's features.

There was an echo of familiarity in the square angle of his jaw and how his eyes had been set into the stone. Reaching forward, she trailed a finger down the scar through his brow and stepped back. He had always been depicted younger than Anna thought he should be. She had fancied him as a teenager, but as she stared into his eyes now, they belonged wholly to a boy just shy of his twenties.

Her lips pressed into a thin line as she leaned forward and scratched grime away with her nail.

Why would any king desire immortalization as barely more than a boy?

Perhaps the answers she sought were inside; the khan had the nasty habit of writing all over his walls.

The step-pyramid had five layers that rose into the sky, blotting out everything around them from this angle. A seemingly endless staircase led up, up, up, with a thick partition dividing them into two sides. Masses of sculptures sat at regular intervals the entire way up.

"...I need my bag."

"What bloody bag?"

Anna's hands twitched at her sides, the skin along her arms prickling. She had stumbled upon something greater than any expedition she had gone on. Was this where the khan had been hiding all this time? No wonder she had never been able to find him, he might never had been on the continent to begin with.

Oh, nay, the khan might have buried himself on a cursed island in the Black Line.

It was entirely too fitting.

Anna was here now, though, standing in front of an entirely intact step-pyramid just waiting to be explored, waiting for her to speak its secrets back into existence, to unearth what had been lost and restore knowledge to the world. The top—she should climb to the top, that's where he should be resting.

"My dig bag. This place...I have no doubt it belongs to the khan. If there ever had been a landscape so thoroughly molded by a singular person, it is this one."

"I do no' know who that is, lass." He trailed off, scrubbing the back of his neck with his hand. "But..."

"But what?"

"This place belonged to the Aepith king, no' your khan."

"The Aepith had five kings, everyone knows that," she muttered, studying the profile of the statue. Something more than recognition unraveled in her gut.

"Aye, and one who oversaw them all."

Oh.

The pirate referred to *that* Aepith king.

"How do you know that?"

"This is his bloody island, lovely, everything on it is his—I wonder sometimes if that's why so much is fucking wrong wi' it."

Anna stepped away from the head and turned to the stairs stretching toward the sun, innumerable and unknowable.

Was the khan the Aepith king, the one who had been exiled and cast out for unleashing a terrible plight upon the seas? It made sense now why he had filled his sacred spaces with nautical imagery, the constellations, and his obsession with the sea.

Bugger.

Granbaatar Khan might be the exiled Aepith king of legend—he might be in the temple in front of her—but she couldn't go looking for him because her brother required rescuing.

If Markus wasn't already dead, he would be when Anna found him.

She couldn't remember when she had closed the distance nor when she had faced the pirate, but she must have because he stared down at her now. His brow arched and he crossed his arms against his chest, curiosity sparkling from his dark eyes like stars in the night sky.

He cleared his throat, a small grin tickling his lips as it fluttered her stomach. "Why are we killing your brother?"

Had she said that out loud?

"Because I doubt we'll be in the mood to partake in a brief vacation here after rescuing him and foiling Cunningham's plot."

"Really are daft, aren't ye?" he asked, taking a step toward the pyramid and its staircase that seemed to reach toward the sun.

Anna's thighs ached at the prospect of following him.

"Am I daft for wanting to spend more time on this fresh hell in order to prove a theory and claim that damn seat among the Board of Antiquity? *Absolutely.*"

"'Tis a good thing, then, that your brother is in trouble."

Anna snorted. "Markus is always in trouble."

"Granbat—whatever, that's the male who tunneled beneath Abu Shazar, aye?"

"The one and only." Anna sighed, slowly slogging up the steps after him.

Glaring down at the stone steps, she sucked on her teeth. She wouldn't be able to explore the step-pyramid after scaling all these steps—oh no, Markus required saving.

"Do ye think there will be any bloody traps?"

Anna chuckled, cheeks heating. "Oh, traps are the least of our worries. We might find something far worse inside."

"What could be worse?"

"The wings dedicated to his harems and concubine, for a start. If I had to pick, I would choose the torture chambers. They might be dangerous, but they are far easier to forget."

"Ye sound like ye speak from experience."

Oh, such unfortunate experience.

Anna nodded her head, forcing memories of those chambers away. The only fate worse than walking through one such room would be doing so with Trevor in tow.

And it had been such a splendid day already.

The pirate swore beneath his breath, and the rough sound of it pulled a grin to her face. She trudged up another few steps, watching the way the muscles in his lower back moved. Running her tongue over her teeth, she dropped her attention to his rump.

Climbing ten thousand steps might not be such a terrible fate after all.

They climbed for what felt like hours. The cool light of the sun warmed her face from behind the clouds. From this height, they could easily see over the tops of pines and to the other side of the island. The gusts of wind had grown in strength and cooled considerably, causing shivers to run up and down her spine as beads of sweat dripped down her back.

"Bloody fucking hell, I do no' remember there being this many steps," Trevor groaned as they approached a landing of sorts.

"When," she said, legs trembling as she stopped and wiped the back of her hand against her forehead, "was that?"

Trevor looked up at the clouds in thought. "Twenty years, maybe?"

Grinning, she leaned her hands on her thighs. "Well, that might be why. Twenty years is a long time, pirate. Or...perhaps you've forgotten that bit of information in your old age."

The pirate scowled at her half-heartedly, spinning and sitting on the steps in one swift movement. He kicked his legs out in front of him and stretched his arms high above his head. Anna followed his lead, massaging her thighs and knees after sitting. Her feet ached fiercely, but she didn't dare remove her boots. If she took them off, she might not get the buggers back on.

Anna's gaze wandered from where her fingers massaged her knees to the pirate. He sat with his hands in his lap, staring into the distant tree-line. Something about the tense line of his shoulders and the frown pulling at his lips felt off. One of his thumbs tapped against his thigh, and she immediately recognized the rhythm. It was that damnable sea shanty.

Something was clearly bothering Trevor, and she wanted to know what, if only to smooth the furrow between his brows.

"Is something wrong?"

Stupid question, she told herself, *everything is wrong.*

"Aye," Trevor said after several beats, velvet gaze anchored on where the horizon might be in the distance.

"Do you...want to talk about it?"

"I..." He sighed, lacing his fingers behind his head as he leaned back into his pack. "I don't know that it's worth the bloody conversation."

"If it's bothering you, it is," she said, pulling her knees to her chest. "It is if you want to talk about it."

It could be anything and yet she believed she knew exactly what weighed on his mind like rocks stacked on his chest. The sailor had said Cunningham would use everything against Trevor, and she didn't doubt that. Bryce had learned to apply pressure, to find what it was one cared about and manipulate it to his advantage.

"Is it about what that sailor said?" she asked quietly.

"Oh, aye. I'm fucking furious that your da would marry ye off like that."

Anna nearly choked, head whipping to face him.

The ghoulish haze hanging in the air only highlighted his features, the sharper planes of his face and the bruises beneath his eyes. Is that truly what had upset him? Out of all the ridiculous notions that had left the sailor's mouth, the pirate had fixated on the one where her father had tried dictating her future?

Her sire had tried matching her with eligible men of Bellcaster for years; he had an entire drawer of unsuccessful correspondences in his office to show for it. Each attempt had either been foiled by Markus's penchant for overprotective, alpha-male behavior or her own reputation and desire for notoriety and adventure.

Just behind Trevor's head, the sun glowed above the top of the temple like a torch through thick fog. He looked away from her, digging into the pack he had carried for a skin of water. Throat bobbing, he drank deep, all the while Anna's attention remained firmly on him.

Her heart flipped in her chest, and something warm and fluttery made itself home in her stomach—maybe to some capacity, his feelings mirrored hers.

"Really?" she asked, refusing to acknowledge the hope climbing from her chest. "Is that so hard to believe? Senator John Savage, concerned with his legacy and growing merchant empire?"

"Would ye do it?" he asked, droplets of water caught in the short length of his beard.

"Marry a man without a say in the matter?" she murmured, trying to keep the grin off her face. "No. There isn't a force on this earth that could make me bend to the will of another. I wasn't exaggerating when I said I wanted a life and a love loud enough to rattle the stars, pirate."

Trevor's attention dropped to his hands, elbows now on his knees as he leaned toward her. He turned his palms this way and that, following the lines there with a finger. His brow creased and he looked very young then—a boy with something worth holding in his hands, something he wasn't sure of.

"What about a male of your choosing?" he asked.

Anna's heart skipped a beat. "Not many believe me when I say this, but yes. I have always wanted someone who loves me unconditionally, who sees me for who I am and not all the things I could be if only I was less." Her lips pressed into a thin line as she dropped her gaze to his boots, fearful he would look up and see the truth hiding in her eyes. "I want my home in someone's heartbeat and theirs in mine. Like you, I've just been waiting."

But I found you, she wanted to say, *I found you against all odds.*

"Ye remembered what I said, lass?"

Anna smiled. "Of course. I remember everything you say, pirate."

Trevor's smile finally reached his eyes and she counted his freckles —even the ones that became lost near his hairline—waiting for his shoulders to loosen. He didn't relax, though; if anything, he looked like a man who had come to a decision he did not like.

She didn't like the idea that something troubled him so, but Good God, some sick sense of satisfaction flooded her system.

Trevor Lovelace liked the idea of her father's plan even less than she did.

Scratching at her scalp, she stood and offered him her hand to stand. He stared at it, smile falling as he clasped her fingers and they continued to trudge up the temple. They quickly neared the top; the entrance hung shrouded in shadow between large columns.

The last ten steps mocked them both, her legs trembling, and Trevor's breath coming in uneven, choppy inhales. Anna frowned, watching how the pack swayed at his back and how he gripped the strap at the shoulder. Every step forward brought them closer to relief, to solid, flat ground, and hopefully his crew, but with every step, he seemed farther away.

Anna squinted at the spaces between the pillars, trailing a figure as they peeled away from the shadows and stepped into the grey light. She guessed it was the quartermaster based on the way he carried himself—that and how he'd been using the damn pillar to hold himself up.

The pillars themselves were made of the same grey stone as the rest of the step-pyramid and the jaguar she had found in GBSP-21 and stood at least twenty feet in height. The landing was slick, the spaces between the stone filled with old debris and a suspicious mauve growth.

Stepping beneath the entrance of the tomb, she caught sight of a second figure too tall to be Juliana Gray. Anna squinted in the murky light, searching Bodhi and Tate from head to toe for injuries like the ones the Pirate King had sustained. Relief warmed her belly and dropped a sigh from her lips as Trevor inhaled stiffly.

Tate wasn't any worse for wear, though it seemed he'd forgone his shirt. The sight of his bare chest wasn't entirely surprising. Her gaze dropped to the tattoos on either side of his hips and the ones adorning his arms.

Were they no more than ink and shadows, or did they haunt him like Trevor's did?

The Pirate King's steps lengthened, and his pack dropped to the ground as he swallowed his brother into a hug. A smile stretched Tate's cheeks, pulling at the three thin scars and stealing Anna's breath away.

Markus always crushed her to his chest in a similar fashion.

Trevor pulled away, his hand lingering on his brother's shoulder as he glanced to Bodhi. "Where is Jules?"

"Waiting on ye, where the fuck else would she be?" Tate's laughter filled the space, the carefree sound easing some of the worry that had stiffened her spine. "Ye know that one has a way wi' beasties."

Trevor went to shoulder the pack, but the remaining strap snapped as soon as it touched his shoulder. Stifling her laugher, Anna pressed her lips into a thin line as she watched the pirate's look of disbelief turn into exhausted annoyance. His nostrils flared, and he picked it up by a loop on the back before stalking off into the dark corridor, shoulders nearly touching his ears with how tightly he was strung.

Tate's wide grin fell into a small twitch of his lips as he stared after his brother, gaze narrowed. He shook his head and jogged after him, leaving Bodhi and Anna standing in the dusky light of Calaveras.

Anna glanced at the surgeon from the corner of her eye. Why was he staring at her like that? The completeness of his attention caused uncomfortable flutters in her stomach, like he was slowly stripping away every layer until he saw straight down to her soul. His head turned and he stared after where Trevor had stormed off, nodding to himself slowly. Anna stared at him, meeting his gaze as he turned.

Oh, bugger.

Bodhi smiled softly, offering her his arm. "Come, Miss Savage, you shouldn't be out here by yourself. I was just pulling dinner together."

"Food sounds brilliant," she said, stomach grumbling.

Bodhi raised his arm, a splendid grin on his face. Threading her arm with his, she turned with him into the shadows. Down the corridor, Trevor and Tate whispered back and forth, though she couldn't hear exactly what they said. But from their tones and the fervent pace of their whispers, it was easy enough to conclude they were arguing—and even easier to ignore when she noticed the glyphs on the walls, blanketed in dust and grime.

"Have you been here before?" Anna asked, trying to make polite conversation.

"Yes. I was on the *Beau* when Trevor sailed for Eero's Chalice the first time," he said with a sigh, meeting her gaze.

"You know Carsyn Kidd, then."

"I do."

Anna swallowed past the knot in her throat. "Do you know why he waited so long to drink from the cup?"

"I do." Bodhi smiled sadly, hand closing over hers on his forearm, much like Trevor's had at her father's gala. "When we see him again, you will have to ask him."

The surgeon led her down another curve, and the shadows opened into a spacious room covered in debris and dust. She scanned the ground, gaze meandering from the large chunks of stone to the cracks and divots in the ground.

Did Trevor have an inkling of what had happened here, or had time been responsible?

Following the dreary light upward, Anna spied the culprit of the destruction—some of the supports for the ceiling had collapsed in large chunks, leaving rubble in their wake. Skylights opened along the ceiling like holes in a tapestry, the space between them carved with imagery of the ocean—rushing waves, garlands of pearls, and not-so-mythical monsters.

Anna squinted.

Bugger, the clouds beyond the skylights were nearly black.

As she turned to Bodhi to inquire about the weather on Calaveras, she saw the dais.

It was front and center in the middle of the room, and the stairs leading up stretched several levels. Pillars at the top reached toward the heavens before crumbling away into empty air. It was nearly a miniature of the temple they were in now. Anna narrowed her gaze at the structure, filling in the negative space where the barrel-vaulted arches must have connected with the pillars once—like a bridge between heaven and earth.

Her fingers twitched on Bodhi's arm.

What was at the top?

The surgeon gave the Lovelace brothers a wide berth, eyeing them carefully as he walked toward where Juliana lounged on the stairs of the dais, a knife in one hand and a half-peeled apple in the other. Bodhi sat slowly in front of a large smoldering fire, roasting something on a spit. The grease dripped into the flames with hisses and pops, coaxing another greedy growl from her stomach.

The Lovelace brothers hardly noticed Bodhi and they didn't turn to acknowledge her, entirely distracted by the words hanging between them heavier than silence. Motes of dust sparkled in the tense air between them; the murky light only served to illuminate the sharp planes of their faces and the shadows hiding in the hollows of their bodies. Trevor knelt with his back to Anna, back bowed over what must have been Tate's pack.

The entire situation was nearly as tense as holiday dinner at Gran's.

"Bloody hell, Tate, will ye just fucking drop it—"

"Then why did ye even bring her? If ye were this worried about the lass, ye should have left her on the damn ship," Tate hissed back.

"What was I going to do?" Trevor bit out, frustration evident in his voice and every hard line of his body. "Tie her to the bloody bed? Anna...the lass can take care of herself. I fucking know that. It's like the bloody island knows, Tate. It knows, and I didn't realize how bloody hard it would be for me—fuck."

"What are ye supposed to do? Talk wi' her, maybe? Explain how ye feel? Ye got feelings, Trev, ye can fucking talk about them," Tate snapped, frustration laying in his voice. "Ye really think leaving her alone in this gods-damned temple is any fucking better?"

Anna's heart raced in her chest, thumping wildly out of rhythm. An angry flush heated the skin of her chest and worked its way up her cheeks. He...he thought he could leave her here? Is that why he had been so quiet on the way up, why every step toward the top of the pyramid had felt like a step further away from her? Her anger became a physical thing, crawling beneath her skin and buzzing in her ears like flies around carrion.

"She would no' be alone," the pirate said with finality.

The only sound in the void around them was that of Bodhi's crackling fire. The angry smile that had been on Tate's face fell flat.

"What the fuck did ye say?"

"Ye heard me. Anna wouldn't be alone."

Tate crossed his arms against his chest. "Well, I'm no' babysitting her," he said quietly. "Fuck that shite."

Trevor turned enough to send his brother a vicious look, but it was not enough to see Anna standing in the shadows of the corridor's opening.

The quartermaster met his brother's gaze, unfazed. "Ye know she's no' going to stay here of her own damn accord, no' because ye tell her to. Ye going to tie her up? Reckon she'll slip any knot ye bind her wi'. Chains won't work, wouldn't put it past the lassie to keep picks in her bloody boots. And that's all if ye can catch her. Did ye parse out this plan of yours? Because I don't know if you've fucking noticed, but your fem does what she wants, to hell wi' anything anyone says—especially ye."

Trevor stiffened, mouth opening to argue with his brother, but something in her untethered and she stormed forward, fury in every step. "You are out of your god-damned mind if you think I'm going to stay here and twiddle my thumbs while you go gallivanting off into the sunset like some mythical hero of old! That is my brother out there, and I'm going with you!"

Head dropping forward, the pirate swore beneath his breath as every muscle along his back tightened. What had he expected, that she would stay silent and go along with whatever half-baked plan he had concocted? A growl of a laugh ripped through her—oh no, she would not stay silent.

"Do you know what happens to heroes?" she asked, every word steeped in venom. "Every single one of their stories ends in tragedy. Beheaded. Drawn and quartered. Hung. Flayed—and worse."

"What could possibly be worse?" Tate asked on a breath.

"According to you alpha males?" she asked, stalking closer to the Pirate King. "Losing the rather useless bit swinging between your legs."

"I'm a Lovelace, lassie, the cock swinging between—"

"Not one word, Tate," she snapped, pinning Trevor beneath her gaze.

His knee popped as he stood, scrubbing his hand through his hair. Trevor turned to her, letting out an angry breath, arms flexing against his chest as he crossed them. Even in this piss-poor lighting, she saw how tightly his fists were clenched, the whites of his knuckles nearly glowing against the black of his tattoos.

Gaze meeting hers, a frown pulled tightly against his lips.

That's right, Lovelace, Anna thought with a huff. *I heard everything.*

"I understand ye want to find Markus, Anna. I do." Trevor glared at the ground, throat bobbing "I'll rescue the gods-damned damsel and we'll all be back aboard the *Queen* laughing about the whole fucking thing before ye now it. I'll even bring ye Cunningham's head as a gift."

"Alone?"

Trevor met her halfway, glowering down his nose at her. Craning her neck upward, Anna puffed out her chest and tried ignoring the warmth of his proximity—without the barrier of his shirt, the heat radiated off him in waves like a furnace. Anna narrowed her gaze at him, keeping it focused on the inky dark pools of his eyes.

Good God, he was beautiful even when he was furious and acting like an ass.

"Aye," he finally said, "*alone.*"

Anna nodded her head. "Because that worked out so well for you last time."

"The bloody island'll leave me alone if it knows what's good for it."

"What the bloody island did is try to take a bite out of ye," she mocked in his accent.

Trevor stood before her one moment and in the next, his countenance shifted until something else entirely stared down at her. The change into this new and cold creature was subtle. She'd seen the transformation before, knew his newfound relaxed position for what it was. Trevor's hands left his chest, shoulders rounding as he leaned closer to her, thumbs snagging in the waistline of his trousers.

Hello, king, she thought with a savage grin of her own.

Did he think she was an absolute idjit?

His throat bobbed, and he nodded slowly, eyes darkening until they looked more akin to some ungodly pit of hell instead of the lovely dark between the stars. The air chilled then, a rogue breeze caressing the line of her jaw and threading through her hair.

Anna had always been able to tell when someone picked a fight with her intentionally; the Board of Antiquity did it often enough in an outlandish attempt to discredit her work. But why would he want to instigate a reaction from her *now* of all times?

She snorted. If that was his goal, she wished him luck. Anna loved him, and if there was a vein of truth she would always hold to, it was that she could never fear someone she lo—

"You're afraid," she whispered, clarity sinking into her chest.

It had never occurred to her before that Trevor Lovelace, Scourge of the Seas, might feel something as small and vicious as fear. She had thought it was anger staring back at her from the void in his gaze, but it wasn't. If Markus and Anna were two sides of the same coin, then fear and anger were as well.

He laughed. "I'm no' fucking scared."

"It sure looks like it," she challenged.

"I'm the Pirate King. I'm no' scared of whatever shite Cunningham has planned, and I don't need the help of some gods-damned lass. Ye are staying here."

Anna felt wild and bold as she stared into his eyes. "I'm not letting you go off on some ridiculous plan that's only success will be getting you tortured since you are apparently so splendidly difficult to kill. I care about you too much to let you do that. I thought—"

"Ye thought what?"

She forced the flourishing acknowledgements of love back down her throat.

If there ever was a time, now was not it.

"Ye thought *what*, fem? That Calaveras would be a fucking tropical get away? That ye might no' die saving your gods-damned brother? Fuck that. Ye are staying here, Anna."

"You can't make me—"

"I'm the fucking Pirate King, what I say goes."

"You honestly believe that?" she said, crossing her arms beneath her breasts. "That I'll fall in line because you're truly some scourge of the seas, the biggest bastard to ever sail the Black Line? Well, I know different, Trevor. I see you, and I will not be swayed by some ridiculous act—"

"*It's no' a fucking act!*" Trevor roared, chest heaving. A look of horror flashed across his face, and he spun away from Anna, hands scrubbing against his scalp as he tried to catch his breath.

Staring at his back, she took one tentative step forward and then another, until she could brush her fingers against the warm skin of his back. Anna's heart tightened painfully in her chest as he flinched away from her touch. Inhaling slowly, she pulled her fingers into a fist and dropped them to her side.

Bugger, she thought, sadness welling in her stomach.

"The truth is, *I* am afraid. I'm afraid Markus isn't even alive, and I'm afraid that all the legends I have ever learned about are real. And" —she breathed out—"I am afraid I can't do this on my own, that I'll have to ask for help. I'm afraid that when it comes down to it, I won't be enough."

Tensing, a ragged breath left the pirate's mouth. He turned enough to meet her gaze over his shoulder and nothing more. Anna's chest hollowed as she held his gaze and the misery that lay within it. His eyes deepened to a shameful and embarrassed shade of obsidian, devastation and defeat in his gaze.

"I don't deserve you," Trevor started quiet enough that Anna surely was the only one who heard him. "How is it you think you know me so well?"

"I honestly can't quite remember what life was like before you stumbled into it, and the thought of what it might look like after you brings me pain. We have been through a lot, you and me, Trevor. Despite everything, our beginnings and middles and any end we might find, we are *friends*. Friends don't let each other think the worst of themselves or follow through with some silly plan—at least not by themselves."

"Friends," he whispered, jaw ticking.

Anna opened her mouth to say more, but he turned his back on her and made haste toward the darkest corner in the chambers. His steps were sluggish, as if all the air had been knocked out of him. Sliding down the wall, he thumped to the ground.

Maybe his fear and anger had been the only things keeping him on his feet.

Should she go comfort him?

Tate shook his head at her as Trevor laid down and faced the wall. Her heart hammered painfully in her chest, but she understood what it was like to want to be alone. Anna had locked herself away in his chambers enough times in the past few months to recognize the need for solitude.

CHAPTER FORTY-FOUR

It had taken six hours, but good God, he had done it.

He had cracked the code and translated the whole damn thing.

Markus pushed the small leather-bound journal away and pinched the bridge of his nose. His mother had never lied to him before. She had always believed words had power and meaning—she never would have scribed an untruth.

According to his dead mother's decade-old journals, Bryce needed a copious amount of blood to wake the Kraken and the blood of a very specific Aepith lineage to subdue it, to bind it to a purpose. Markus had grinned then, realizing he would have to break the horrid news to Cunningham—they wouldn't be able to find the blood of the last Aepith King, he had been dead for thousands of years.

This had been a splendid problem at first.

No infamous Aepith bloodline to bind the Kraken?

Brilliant, they could all sail home and laugh about it over tea and biscuits.

But then his mother's writing had continued.

Markus had learned the ancient seafarers were not as dead as everyone believed them to be. The poor bastards had supposedly been cursed, their islands corrupted, their homes swallowed whole by the sea. Their royal lines had survived through the ages, though, their

419

mantles passed from father to son—or in the Viper's case, from mother to daughter.

Markus had more than a suspicion about who claimed the title of Aepith King of Kings, and the poor bastard was likely on his way here right now, with Anna in tow.

"Why do my problems always involve pirates now?" he wondered out loud, rather frustrated with this entire business.

Bollocks, who gave the bastards the right?

"Because that is their nature," Bryce said, tone clipped as the tent flap snapped in a feral gust.

Markus pinched the bridge of his nose and tipped his head back.

His headache had returned with a vengeance.

It's like blasted clockwork, he thought, frustrated.

"I assume you have the information I require?"

Markus clenched his jaw, focusing his attention on his work.

"Well?" Cunningham prodded, the soft pop of knuckles echoing from behind.

Blast it all to hell.

Breathing deep, he slouched in his chair. "I do. But it's not a plan you could possibly go through with."

"Your father was quite clear in his instructions," he said. "Now, if you would care to share how to raise the Kraken and bind it to the Senate's will, we could get started and be on our way back home by sundown tomorrow."

"But we *can't*. You would need to sacrifice good men—men who trust you!"

"It's a small price to pay for Briland and for safer seas. Imagine what we could do with that kind of power. Pirates would think twice before plaguing our waters—what happened at Tremble's Bay would not happen again."

"You are mad," Markus barked, coming to a stand. "Even if you were willing to slit twenty-five of your men's throats, that does not solve the problem of the Pirate King's absence. He is not here, Bryce. He is probably sitting on a beach somewhere drinking bubbly pink drinks out of coconut shells with my blasted sister! We might as well pack our bags and sail home."

"You're wrong," he said.

"They're here?" Markus whispered, stomach dropping to his boots.

"Are you truly surprised?" he asked, cocking his head. "If anyone knows Miss Savage's tenacity, it's you. An advance party spotted them earlier today, hiking toward the step-pyramid in the distance. I may have doubted your ability to parse information from these books, but I have not doubted for a second that she would find her way here to rescue you."

"That still doesn't solve your problem. You would have to catch them first. I don't know if you recall, but Anna is quite good at dodging traps. Try to think back to your time courting her, Cunningham. How often was she in Bellcaster?" Markus paused, cocking a brow. "Let me remind you, most of your time with her was spent on a boat traveling to and from her expeditions in tombs and temples *just like this*."

"I remember. I remember all too well our time together—enough of it was spent with her nose folded between the pages of a blasted book that I picked up on some of the ancient script," Cunningham growled. "But I read through the damn things four times and couldn't make heads or tails of any of it." He paced along the forest floor, stroking his thumb across his lower lip. Pulling up short, his gaze slowly shifted back to Markus. "You're right. if I'm going to catch Miss Savage, I have to think like her."

"I never said—"

Bryce spun on a heel, striding toward the tent's exit.

"What are you going to do?"

"Burn his books. Burn his notes," he said as the tent snapped open. "Everything I need, I have up here."

"No," Markus hissed, stretching his arms out to protect his mother's journals. "Bryce, *no!*"

A sea of sailors in their damnable evergreen uniforms flooded into the tent.

If he lived through this, Markus would never don his again—in fact, he had brilliant plans to burn them in a bonfire during his next birthday, perhaps smoke something delicious over them.

The first sailor stepped forward, jaw set and eyes red—it could have been from his state of distress or the constant plume of smoke wafting off of the pyres of burning bodies.

"You're not burning my mother's journals," he growled, raising his fists.

But in the end, they did.

And Markus fell asleep that night with his arms curled around his torso, eyes burning as he forced his breathing to be even.

CHAPTER FORTY-FIVE

Anna stood awkwardly in the center of the room, arms curled around herself in a tight embrace. The cavernous space darkened as clouds bloomed over another skylight, drawing her attention upward. She could take a look around, poke about in the temple's bowels if she found a door or a way down that wasn't the stairs outside.

With her brother's state of distress, this was likely the only time she'd have to do so.

"Welcome to our humble abode, lassie," Tate said, making a grand gesture with his hands. "Bodhi's got dinner roasting on the spit, no' sure what it is, but it smells bloody delicious. Trust me when I say it looks much prettier skinned and roasted."

"It does smell rather splendid," she said with a smile, forcing her gaze away from where Trevor laid on the ground.

Sleeping sounded brilliant.

Anna's attention returned to the dais.

Sleeping was for the weak.

Markus be damned, she had every intention of cataloging that dais before the night's end. Anna reached to her side where her satchel normally hung; she'd need charcoal and paper to take impressions of the engravings she was sure would be there. Her hand brushed her thigh, the air empty of what she required.

"Should have brought the damn bag," she muttered to herself.

Anna forced her feet in the direction of the dais, to the pillar Juliana Gray's bag leaned against. Muted blues and greens had wormed their way into the cracks of the inscriptions cutting into the stone. Leaning into it, she mouthed the words, the Aepith fumbling off her tongue sluggishly. Bugger, it was the verbal equivalent of trudging through sludge; the sounds formed words, but lacked overall meaning.

Another cool breeze rustled her hair, pulling her attention to the opposite pillar. Fabric as thin as mist billowed gently. A quick glance revealed it must have hung from the ceiling at one point, but with its collapse, the curtain had rained down too. The delicate fabric might have been purple once, but Calaveras had stolen its vibrancy, like it stole nearly everything else.

How had the curtain survived the years at all?

"So," Tate started, voice loud in her ear, "what do ye think it is?"

Anna started, turning to face the quartermaster. She jumped back at his proximity. His head hovered just above her shoulder as he stared up at the broken pillars and the twenty or so steps up to the landing. Her gaze skipped from the torches and mounted vases alternating along the walls—most empty and smashed—to the drapery and the skylights.

What, indeed?

"Well..." She cleared her throat. "The step-pyramid was likely built by Granbaatar Khan, and this room could be one of many things. I'm hoping it's a sacrificial altar up there."

Good God, please be a sacrificial altar.

The only fate worse than walking arm in arm with the Pirate King down a hall of salacious wonders was doing so with his younger brother.

"Who the fuck was that?"

"The khan, bless his heart, was a prolific builder. At least seventy percent of all major monoliths, necropolises, tombs, and pyramids can be attributed to his reign. Trevor told me this island belonged to the

Aepith King in exile, and I think he and the khan might be one in the same."

Tate ran his hand against the sandpaper of stubble along his jaw—it made him look strangely older, more roguish, but Anna preferred the quartermaster clean-shaven. "How do ye figure this khan might be involved? No' like the male's name is on the bloody temple."

"There are clues everywhere—the shell path, the nautical imagery along the ceiling. But it was the feline headdresses and what remained of his face on the statue that truly gave it away. I've seen depictions of Granbaatar Khan enough times to recognize him."

"That bloody handsome, aye?" Tate asked, an air of amusement in his voice that Anna didn't quite understand.

Her gaze had already returned to the Aepith scribbled across the pillar. Squinting at the rough letters and vague symbols, she answered quietly. "I suppose. I fancied him as a girl, but he's a little young for me now."

Tate laughed, the sound near music to her ears. It was more playful and carefree than Trevor's, but it lightened her soul all the same. Anna walked from one step to the next, gnawing on her lip as she traced the words and followed the sentences with her finger. At first, most of the symbols remained distant, close enough to be cousins to any language or dialect she knew but not friendly enough to be on speaking terms.

"Well?" Tate asked impatiently.

Head cocking to the side, she picked at one jaguar-esque symbol. "It's not as easy as it looks."

"Reckon 'tis just reading."

"Reckon ye would be wrong," Anna muttered under her breath. "At university, they teach a very standard version of a dialect that looks a little like this if one squints. But *this* one"—she tapped another symbol, going up another step and leaning around the pillar to see the next one—"is very odd. It reads like the Aepith on the map, but that one had been washed with—"

And then she saw it.

The name Eero next to a crude depiction of a jaguar.

Hello, there, she cooed.

A story unfolded before her, one she had read a thousand times in a thousand places. She had seen it in GBSP-21 months ago, had trailed her fingers along its length in a necropolis just north of the Xing border. Anna had even found it in Heylik Toyer when she was a child. The story she followed with her gaze had generally become known as the khan's coming of age story—how he had been tossed into the sea at the ripe age of sixteen and it had spat him back out.

Anna gently scrubbed at the dirt and grime that had accumulated. Every now and then, she looked to the rest of the room to see exactly how everything lined up from a certain view. Granbaatar Khan hadn't just leveled forests and built a step-pyramid for the grand notion of it; he had filled his spaces and used every inch of them to convey who he was and to tell his story.

Lips pursing, she stumbled upon a word.

Anna recognized it, but depending on the time of its inscription, it could mean a number of things. Most commonly it had been used as a euphemism for death, defecation, and—

"How old are you?" she asked, squinting at it.

"Older than I bloody look," Tate replied easily, and Anna realized she had turned to look at him as she spoke. "But I guarantee no' a fem has complained—all the experience wi' none of the age."

Anna shook her head, scowling at the stairs separating her from the landing at the top of the dais. There were too many damn steps in this temple. "Not that. I have determined this is either a crypt, a restroom, or...a room dedicated to one of the khan's harems."

She turned in place again, walking up the stairs backward. Tate followed her up one step at a time, his tangled wine-red hair hanging loose around his shoulders for once. Bits of bronze glimmered from the thick strands, and his tattoos stood out against the skin of his forearms and biceps.

Squinting into the distance, Anna traced the adornments with her eyes, from the jaguars lurking like crown molding to the pattern of constellations carved into the floor She never would have noticed them had she not ascended to where she was on the dais. The detritus scattered haphazardly around the temple floor made distinguishing one constellation from the next difficult, but...

She glanced toward the landing.

What secrets would be revealed when she looked out from up there?

"What are ye waiting for, lassie? I can tell ye want to look around some." He smiled, glancing over her shoulder to the top. "We won't be leaving till bloody morning anyways, ye have time."

Anna frowned.

Did she want to investigate the contents atop the dais?

Absolutely.

Did she want to do so with Tate Lovelace?

Good God, no—no, she did not.

The dais' use as a royal restroom could only be described as the best-case scenario, and it said quite a lot that Anna hoped they would find fecal matter if they ventured to the top. Turning back to the pillars, she skimmed over the symbols, mouthing the words. Her back warmed, bringing a smile to her face—there was only one reason her body would elicit such a response.

The Pirate King must be staring at her.

Anna shifted her gaze downward but couldn't see him—only Juliana with her hair tied tight in a knot and Bodhi walking toward a hall at the back.

"What does it say?" Tate asked, motioning to the inscription on the pillar. "It's no' like anything I've ever read."

"You can read?" she asked quietly.

"Aye, why?"

"I..." She paused, turning to face him. "I assumed because Trevor couldn't—"

"—that I could no' either?" Tate finished, smug. "No, fem. Taylee read to me near every gods-damned night until I was fourteen. It helped keep the nightmares away."

"Oh," Anna breathed out.

The images continued to wind and bend around the pillar. It was such a shame that time had worn them into shallow imitations of what they had once been. Scrubbing at the suspicious mauve growth that had taken root in parts of the inscription, she squinted.

Anna laughed, shaking her head.

Bugger, sometimes she hated it when she was right.

"Something interesting?" Tate asked, stepping into what little light was left with the darkening clouds.

"That depends, do you find the idea of sacrificing virgins interesting?" she muttered, scrubbing another bit of grime away with her sleeve.

"He sacrificed..." Tate started incredulously. "Why the hell would —what a bloody waste."

Anna smiled at the quartermaster's distress. Oh, bugger, she had missed the small moments of panic that came with deciphering ancient script while trying to make heads or tails of it.

"I think"—she pursed her lips, gaze narrowing—"he sacrificed their virginity here, not their lives."

"This is where...fucking shite. Did the bastard really build an entire gods-damned temple in the middle of a forsaken forest just for knocking boots? A bed was no' good enough for him?"

"The khan was rather dramatic. I'm honestly surprised we haven't tripped any booby traps yet," she said, following the length of the pillar up until she reached its broken peak.

There were so many truly wondrous things just waiting to be uncovered or committed to living memory in this temple, if she only had the time and opportunity to do so. Once she had discovered a penchant for locating obscure knowledge and artifacts, she had felt rather obligated to do so.

Stepping down a step, Anna sighed as her stomach growled at them. The quartermaster glanced down at her abdomen and laughed, shaking his head.

"Come on, lassie, dinner should be about done," he said with a grin.

"Hush, you." She grinned back, ruffling his hair—though she had to stand on her toes to do so.

Swatting at her hand, he chanced a glance at his brother as his grin turned a little embarrassed.

"If Trevor catches ye, it's my throat he'll slit, Anna—*shite!*" Tate swore, raising his voice. "Ye are a gods-damned terrible cook, Trev, get away from that bloody pot!"

That certainly explained the over-boiled, leafy concoctions that had appeared in Trevor's quarters sporadically. Anna grinned as she descended the steps to the main level. Even if the tea itself had been positively horrid, it had been rather sweet of him.

For a man with as many monstrous rumors circulating about him, the Pirate King had never been anything but sincere and respectful of her—even with his alpha-male tendencies. Despite the lick of anger he had shown earlier, she knew that that wasn't who Trevor was, but the fear speaking through him.

Everyone was allowed a bad day. Anna knew she'd had her fair share since stepping onto that train all those months ago.

Her brows pulled together as she thought of all the little things he had said or done over their course of time together. Each of his actions pressed together like pieces of a puzzle, the accumulation of them forging an image she wasn't entirely certain of.

I know what the fuck this is, lass. Can ye say the same?

Good God.

Hope unfurled in her chest, and like a moth chasing after a flame, Anna followed him with her gaze. He stood in front of the cook pot as Bodhi ladled something that smelled delicious into his bowl. She flushed as he caught her staring at him but refused to break eye contact. If the eyes truly were windows to the soul, maybe he would see everything that had been left unspoken between them.

Maybe he would see everything he needed to.

Maybe he already had, and she was just a fearful creature, unable to speak her feelings lest they be forgotten or ridiculed.

Trevor grumbled something beneath his breath, a wooden bowl and spoon in hand as he stalked back to his spot against the far wall. Sliding down it, the Pirate King put the bowl on the ground and tipped his head back, eyes closed and long wine-red lashes brushing his cheek.

Anna turned back to Bodhi, chest tight. The surgeon held a small bowl and spoon out for her. Offering him a smile, his fingers brushed hers as she took the bowl. The contents were hot enough that steam curled upward, and the soft wood warmed her hands.

Mystery soup, she thought fondly as she sat on the first step.

Tate sat down across from her, blowing on his spoon with a devilish grin. Turning her attention to the gaping hole in the ceiling, she closed her eyes and breathed deep. The conversation droned out until it was nothing more than a dull hum in the background, and if she closed her eyes, she could have been anywhere in any number of archaeological sites.

In GBSP-21 with Batu.

In the Emerald Isles with Director Tamm.

Or even in one of the memories she had of her mother, back bent over some inscription or broken shard of pottery, touch feather-light as she brushed away dust and films of dirt. Anna opened her eyes and inhaled deep. It was easy to convince herself she could smell her mother's perfume in old, decrepit tombs like this, but the truth of it was that her mother had smelled like this.

Sara Sommers had kept her hair short, a vicious mop sheared to her shoulders and often parted far to one side. Anna had inherited her high cheekbones and round face, but she remembered her mother's relief that she hadn't inherited her nose—it had been a rather prominent thing, but it had always looked just right on her.

She sang to them and raised meticulously thin eyebrows in question or wondering, and life had been positively splendid until it wasn't. Heart tightening in her chest, she set her bowl down on the step as exhaustion pulled her back into a hunch. Anna pressed her elbows into her knees and wiped her hands over her warming face.

It had been years since her mother passed, and still the remembrance of loss cracked her chest open, revealing all the raw and wounded pieces of her that had yet to heal.

Maybe if it had been different—

The sound of steel on stone echoed in Anna's ears, drawing her attention to the master gunner in a rapid turn of her head. The whole world tilted on its axis and sloshed the contents of her stomach as bile rose in her throat. She saw a double image of Juliana Gray.

Anna squinted, blinking until the images of Juliana layered back into one as she collapsed backward, head cracking against a stone step.

"Juliana?" Bodhi asked, a slur to his tone.

In his haste to stand, Tate knocked the cook pot over before collapsing to the ground with a growl like a wounded animal. The cacophony around her was muffled despite the proximity, forcing her heart to beat wildly in her chest.

Have to do something, she thought sluggishly, staring at the ceiling as something cold pressed against her spine.

When had she laid down?

Anna's head flopped to the side, debris on the ground scratching against her cheek. Squinting, she watched a shadow peel itself from the wall. It grew closer, steps deceptively slow as black encroached on her vision in murky patches. What was left of the world finally blurred to indistinct colors and shapes, none of which made sense.

Trevor, she thought as his dark, spiced scent rolled through her senses like a miasma.

Alarm bells ran in her head, and icicles threaded their way through her veins.

She couldn't breathe—she truly couldn't breathe.

Gasping for breath, Anna listened to the shadow as it walked away, its steps the only sound in this strange void.

How splendid that she could hear that.

CHAPTER FORTY-SIX

The temple Trevor said he'd never return to stared at him from beyond the treeline. It had been built along the shores overlooking a cove; the waves echoing up were near deafening. He could picture the meat grinder the currents created perfectly. Anything that was lobbed into them would be broken against the fucking rocks or sucked under to drown, never to be found again.

Trevor'd never wondered what happened to the Old Crow's body.

Breathing deep, he let all his bloody nerves sink into his boots as grey stone sharpened into monsters and myth. Most everything on this circle of hell had big cats carved into it or painted atop it—signs of the khan, or at least that's what the lass called the bastard.

But no' this one.

This temple had gods-damned sea beasties.

He brushed some leafy shite from his view and glared at the structure. It broke from the forest, standing above the ocean like how the Old Crow used to wi' a lash—in need of assurance that he was the biggest and meanest male to sail the ocean blue. Despite the terrible oily feeling sliding down his spine as he looked at the monstrous temple, there was a loveliness in the way the creatures laid against every curve.

Reminded Trevor a wee bit of how his tattoos slept on his skin.

Too bad he had plans to topple the fucker. Anna would have loved it.

Icy ribbons of dense mist clung to the outside of the temple and threaded through the trees, stretching out like a witch's knobby fingers. Lightning struck the sea with a hiss, brightening the area for a single bloody second. The clouds above had only grown darker wi' every step he took, and the spaces between the trees smelled of broken bones and old blood.

Whatever was required to wake the Kraken had begun; he felt it in the way his bones ached and wi' how the air popped and crackled around his ears.

Fucking shite, every bone in Trevor's body howled warnings at him

But he wouldn't turn around, no' now.

"On to twisted tides and salted fair ladies," he sang under his breath. Mum had hummed it when he was wee; he remembered the tune better than he did her. "On to hollow shores where hell waits for me."

Another flash lit the door to the temple like an entrance to one of the pits of hell his mum had always warned him about.

Five seas for five gates.

Five keys for five kings.

Slowing, he pressed his lips into a thin line. Last he'd walked through those bloody maws, he'd come out a changed male and the price had been steep. Tate'd always argued that the two weren't connected—finding that bloody cup and Taylee dying. Her death had always been easier for his brother. Tate had no' caused the gods-damned thing, after all?

Knowing he'd played a hand in his sister's death had always been hard to swallow, but the thought of Anna dying—or worse—because of him?

Bloody fucking hell, it choked him.

She was going to hate him when this was done. Whatever she felt for him now would burn away into an ash he did no' think would ever rekindle. Shite, just thinking about it left his gut twisting. Naught else mattered except his wee beastie walking away from Calaveras, even if it meant walking away from him.

Something soft clicked beneath his foot, snatching all his bloody attention.

His gaze dropped to the forest floor.

"Fu—"

Trevor didn't finish the word.

Metal jaws snapped closed wi' enough force to nearly split his lower leg in two. Bones snapped, dropping him to the ground. He cut the scream off, clenching his lips tightly between his teeth. Pain—such gods-damned pain—ripped nearly all the senses from his head.

He saw naught.

And then Trevor blinked, staring at the tree tops wi' their blackened needles and ghostly branches, body trembling. Inhaling deep, he closed his eyes and forced himself to his bloody elbows. Sweat dripped from his temples and ran down his chest from the effort.

His vision blurred at seeing the mess Cunningham had made of his leg. Bits of white bone poked through, pinkened by blood and torn strips of muscle. Turning, he threw up until everything that had been in his stomach painted the forest floor.

Shite.

Trevor leaned on his hands and tipped his head back, scowling at the sky. How the hell was he supposed to weasel his gods-damned way out of a bloody bear trap?

Fuck this island.

Fuck Cunningham.

Fuck his fucking leg—he did no' need it to get this shite done.

Ten minutes, that was all he could bloody do. His fingers were raw, and he'd sweat through his trousers. Or maybe the blood had soaked them. Likely a wee of both. There were other fluids he'd rather have all over him, but that was neither here nor there.

Bloody hell.

If Anna were here, what would she do? Lass likely would have found her way out of this bloody mess faster than Tate could eat a bag of biscuits. Trevor swiped at the sweat dripping into his eyes with the back of his hand, but it was the light casting shadows on his leg that made him stiffen.

"You know," a voice said, his tone mocking. "I honestly didn't think this would work."

"If ye think I'm going anywhere wi' ye," Trevor growled, breaths coming in sharp pants, "ye best think again."

The prick scoffed, settling a hand on the rapier at his side. "Oh, no, I don't intend on taking you anywhere. Not when I can use you to draw the others out."

Fucking hell.

CHAPTER FORTY-SEVEN

Anna ducked a low-hanging branch, amazed at how Tate contorted his unseemly height under it. A single cutlass cracked against her leg with every step, but Tate had forgone all steel—he'd said something about *improvising later* and *no' wanting the bloody weight*. He was a man on fire, a machine that couldn't be stopped. Her legs had long since lost their ability to feel anything but exhaustion, feet numb and traumatized by all those steps, and yet the quartermaster seemed to feel nothing but the urgency to find his brother.

It was a sentiment she understood quite well, made only worse by the intensity of her feelings for the Pirate King. Trevor could take care of himself, he had proved that point beyond a shadow of a doubt on multiple occasions, but something was *wrong*. The clouds she glimpsed through the canopy swirled, nearly pitch black in color.

Lightning flashed, thunder quickly following in its wake.

Oh, bugger.

Nothing quite like a thunderstorm to set the ominous mood for their encounter with Cunningham and his crew. The next bolt lit the temple in front of them, brightening it as if it were daytime. A second passed, and the forest descended back into the murky dark that dogged their heels. Water churned in the distance, a mad gurgle that sounded more akin to the furious chortle of a daft god.

Slowing, Tate exchanged a look with her over his shoulder as he came to a near stop. They both scoured the temple with their gazes, looking for any sign of a disturbance as they heaved air in as quietly as possible. Anna leaned her hands on her knees, and Tate laced his fingers behind his head, expanding his chest as he inhaled deeply.

Bodhi and Juliana hadn't reached the temple yet; she imagined it would be a bit louder once they did.

Light not far in the distance brightened the spaces between the trees. Ducking behind a pair of ghostly pines, they crept closer. Anna squinted into the shadows, watching as Tate brought a finger to his lips. She nodded her head and she peeked around the massive trunk, ignoring the way the pale bark scratched at her cheek. Four silhouettes crossed in front of them; the sound of fronds grasping their clothes was the only sound they made.

"They're looking for something," Anna murmured a hair above the wind.

"Trevor must be near," he said, a determined smile slowly gracing his handsome face.

That couldn't be good.

Anna stepped toward the quartermaster, intent on grabbing him before he could do something incredibly stupid, but Tate was faster.

Lunging forward, he bungled through the brush like a boar.

All four of Cunningham's men whipped their heads in his direction as he turned in a circle. Squinting, she followed the arc of his hands, how his left hand slid against his opposite forearm. One of the sailors jerked backward, a black, ornate blade sticking from his throat before his back hit the ground.

"Stay out of fucking sight," he hissed between his teeth.

"It's the quartermaster of the *Pale Queen!*" one man screamed.

Anna shivered as the *shing* of various blades drawing whispered across her skin.

"It's fucking Tate Lovelace!"

Tate, the idjit, ran toward the men, drawing a black-bladed cutlass at his hip. He swung it with precision; the sound of blades dueling rang through the night between the sounds of men calling for help.

Spinning, he disarmed one man as he took the other's head on his backswing. Another dropped dead, intestines curtaining his torso in her next blink.

Good God, she hadn't realized what a swordsman the quartermaster was.

Anna watched in quiet anticipation as Tate took steps away from her, pulling the sailors with him. Grinding her teeth, she glared at him. He planned to lead them away from her, did he?

She stepped forward and a stick cracked beneath her foot, drawing the quartermaster's dark gaze. He mouthed something as he bent under a rapier and opened a man at the femoral artery, another black blade in his hand.

Where had he gotten those?

She didn't remember seeing him strap any to his body or hide any in his boots. Her brows drew together, gaze narrowing on the cutlass in his hands. He hadn't brought a sword with him, where the hell had that come from?

A funnel of sailors rounded the brush from the left, stopping in unison in front of the *Pale Queen's* quartermaster as if he'd drawn a line in the sand. Half of Tate's hair was pulled back into a loose knot; a few strands had come loose in the mayhem and framed his face. He smiled at them, rotating his black-bladed cutlass with one hand. The other reached to his side where the tattoo laid against his skin and—

Anna's breath caught in her throat as Tate Lovelace, quartermaster of the *Pale Queen,* pulled a blade from his skin.

So his tattoos were like Trevor's, then, more than just ink and shadows.

Chaos ensued as Cunningham's sailors tried to flank him, but he danced back and forth, swinging with a daft grin on his face and an electric kind of madness in his eyes. In six moves, Tate had drawn the contingent of sailors farther away until their backs faced her, far more concerned with meeting the pointy end of either of his cutlasses than whatever task they had been deployed to complete.

Find Trevor.

Of course, Tate delegated the difficult task to her. Fighting off a band of sailors seemed rather easy compared to the daunting challenge of locating the Pirate King. Staying low, she crept away from the fighting men, confident that Tate could take care of himself; at the very least, he could play opossum. Tate and Trevor's inability for expiration seemed rather splendid right about now.

What had possessed her to turn the Pirate King down in his offer of immortality?

Life would not be meaningful or worth the trouble without her brother to inconvenience her at every turn, but she couldn't deny the safety net drinking from the chalice would have provided.

Bugger, it went beyond that—she wouldn't be any use to anyone dead.

The shouts and clangs of steel grew farther away, the carpet of pine needles softly *whuff*ing beneath the balls of her feet as she padded away from Tate. Another torch hovered in the distance, bringing Anna to a standstill, her breath coming in slow, deep pulls. She squinted into the sphere of light cast from the torch, looking for the outline of a sailor's shoulders or the glimmer of the lion's pin at a marshal's throat. Curiously enough, she found none.

Her mother had always said if something looked too good to be true, it likely was.

The soft breeze rustled the foliage around her, ruffling her hair and flora that was tall enough to brush her elbows. She leaned down, fingers grazing the top of a knife in her boot. Anna paused and looked through the fronds of massive ferns to the brightly burning torch. It hadn't moved, its flames dancing and waving in the growing gusts.

One of the shadows on her right moved at the same time a stick snapped. Her hand tightened around the handle of her knife. Ducking, she raised the blade just enough to catch the low swing of a rapier. A great gust pressed against her elbow, holding her arm in check as light sparked where the blades ground against each other.

Stepping in, Anna's free fist pounded against the man's jaw before she disarmed him. His head whipped to the side, but the momentum did little to keep him from slamming her to the ground. Bollocks, the ground on Calaveras was closer to granite than dirt. Anna wheezed, back likely already purpling from the hard landing. The cold seeped into her skin as she thrashed below the marshal straddling her hips.

She buried her knife between his ribs even as his hands tightened around her neck. His fingers dug in, thumbs pressing into her throat. Coughing, she pulled the knife from his side and buried it in his armpit and then his spleen before tearing it down through his triceps. The marshal only grunted in response, clearly determined to suffocate her.

Well, Anna had other plans.

Gritting her teeth, she brought the knife to his wrist. The marshal would be releasing her throat one way or another, either of his own accord or after she sawed through his ligaments and tendons. He glared down at her, gaze narrowing to dark pinpricks filled with despair and hate. Anna leaned up, ignoring how easily her blade cut through the skin atop his wrist, showing bone near immediately.

This would not end the way he hoped.

Anna would not succumb to death because a man had wrapped his hands a little too tightly around her throat. Humans could survive more than they thought they could, they could persevere and find strength in the smallest of spaces and darkest of nights. The man said something, but her ears rang loud enough to block it out, and black spots flanked her vision.

And just like that, the marshal was gone, taking his weight off her hips and throat. Anna choked, eyes watering and lungs burning. Turning over onto her side, her hands slid through deadened pine needles. Her eyes widened, eyebrows rising at the sight of the marshal on his back, legs flailing and arms clawing at something she couldn't quite see.

Anna squinted; something dark had wrapped around the marshal's throat, cutting off his air. Between the movement of the man's arms, she saw the tail of a mermaid and coins dripping into the sea. She would know that forearm anywhere.

A grin split her face as relief cooled the anger at his actions.

She'd found him—she'd found Trevor before Cunningham could take him and hurt him.

"Trevor, is that you?" she asked, eyes stinging.

"Aye, lass," he grunted between ragged breaths. "'Tis...me."

A snap punctuated his sentence, not like that of a stick but of a neck.

Then the only sounds permeating the air belonged to their breathing.

Anna shucked her knife back in her boot, one hand rising to feel the tender skin at her throat. Trevor shuffled in the dirt, a pained noise caught in his chest. Gaze darting to him, she watched him roll the marshal off his body before he leaned back on his forearms and hung his head all the way back, exposing the column of his throat.

He had already been bruised and bloodied from his encounter with the guardian, but Anna had tried to remove as much of the blood from his skin as possible. His hands hadn't been painted red when they had crawled from that hole, and they certainly hadn't been so when he left the temple.

Where had all the damn blood come from, then?

Covered in dirt and blackened pine needles, Trevor's head tipped up as if he felt the weight of her gaze. She ignored the curious look on his face, starting at his neck before letting her gaze follow the drip of sweat between his pecs and then lower still. She eyed the ropes of muscle at his abdomen, internally flinching at the scar John Black had inflicted. There weren't any new injuries beyond the shallow, seeping scratches the marshal had inflicted.

But then her attention settled on his legs, and she gasped. His left leg had nearly been severed from his body at the calf, muscle and skin holding it together between the jaws of a rather wicked-looking bear trap. Some of the fear clawing her throat dissipated as a new truth settled like an anvil on her chest: he wouldn't die, not from blood loss or infection. She had time to fix this, but—

"Aye, might need a bloody peg after this," he sighed, jaw ticking. Trevor didn't look directly at her, only slightly to her left.

Was he embarrassed?

"Don't jest about that," she hissed, wiping at her traitorous eyes as she crawled toward him.

She wouldn't think any different of him without the leg, she hadn't fallen in love with him because of his splendidly muscular calves. His limbs were just an extension of who he was, of where his soul lived. They had a job to do, though, one she thought might be rather hindered by the loss of a leg.

Could she build a makeshift lower leg if they severed and cauterized it?

Stupid question—she could do anything given the proper timing.

But did she have time to construct a prosthetic or for Trevor to sleep the injury off?

Likely not.

"No' jesting, I'm no' sure if it'll fucking heal. I've"—he swallowed, throat bobbing stiffly—"I've never been this bloody close to losing a limb. But it won't heal if I can't get this gods-damned fucker off my leg."

A chain trailed from the metal maws of the bear trap, ending in a spike. Bugger, even he would have struggled to pull that from the ground *without* the damage that had been wrought. Somehow, he had done it. Her brows drew together.

What would have possessed him to force such a feat of strength?

Why wouldn't he stay put and wait for them to find him?

Anna met his gaze then. "Bait?"

He nodded his head, sweat pouring down his face and chest.

She couldn't imagine the pain he must be in. Maybe he had already gone into shock and that was where this resignation stemmed from. His face had paled considerably, his freckles standing out like drops of ink on paper. Maybe if she set it and wrapped it, it would heal correctly.

"Well, we won't know if we don't try," she said, crawling toward the pirate.

Anna settled back on her heels, pressing her hands against her thighs as she leaned forward and inspected the metal jaws around his leg. Trevor remained where he was, chest heaving as he stared at the mess of his leg.

No wonder his leg had been torn asunder; the teeth had been filed to sharp points.

"Already saw the abyss twice. Blood loss, I reckon," he murmured quietly. "Hasn't bled in a while."

Anna had never been squeamish, but the sight of bone sticking through blood and skin cracked from the trap's teeth had her fighting to keep Bodhi's soup in her stomach. Her stomach spasmed, and saliva accumulated in her mouth.

"It'll be okay," she told him and herself—because it would be. They would stop Cunningham and sail off into the sunset and live happily ever after. "We'll find a way to be okay, I just—first this. Help me pry this off you."

"I already tried, luv," he said kindly.

Did he honestly believe that would deter her?

"Splendid. *I* haven't."

Anna cut her fingers on the teeth, the blood smeared on the metal making it hard to grip. Lifting his head fully, resignation and exhaustion had made their home in his eyes. Anna growled obscenities under her breath as she breathed deep, knowing exactly what would come next. She'd have to press his leg into the trap in order to put enough pressure on the plate to release the jaws.

"'Tis fine, lovely."

She shook her head at him, wiping her shaking fingers off on her trousers. "It's not fine."

"Ye need to fucking leave before they come back."

"I hope they do. I hope they come back so I can gut every single one of them."

It seemed she needed to remind Cunningham she was a Savage, that she was her father's daughter. The snake had always been their sigil for a reason—they hit hard and they hit fast, leaving poison in one's veins to rot the limb from the inside out.

Consequences, her father had always said, *are far more memorable when one is left to live with them.*

Trevor ran a hand through his hair, smearing dirt in the sweat laden-strands. "*Please,* Anna."

"Why would I leave now?"

"Why wouldn't ye, lass?" he shot back, frustration clear in his tone and the way he set his jaw. "I can't keep ye safe if Cunningham finds us. I can't fucking do anything right now."

Her gaze met his slowly. The softness of his eyes reminded her of velvet or the sky on a moonless night. From this close, she could see each of his freckles, stark against his skin, and several paper-thin scratches against his cheek.

"You're not going anywhere either way," she told him, voice thick with emotion. "So neither am I. This...is going to hurt."

Before the pirate could say anything, she clenched her jaw and pressed his leg downward into the trap. Sweat coated her back, and blood slicked her hands. Trevor did his best to keep his pain unheard, but it slipped out every now and then in sharp intakes of breath or choked screams that churned her gut and made it hard for her to breathe. His chest rose and fell in heavy, ragged pants.

The beartrap groaned, quickly followed by a ghastly, wet, sucking noise. Trevor coughed, thigh shaking as he sat up farther. Finally, they were getting somewhere. The teeth still clenched his flesh tightly, but it was progress.

Leaning harder on his leg, she pressed his boot against the plate. She only needed enough room to carefully slide his leg out, she didn't need it to open all the way. Trevor's breathing increased, and his leg shook beneath her arms.

The soft click had her heart surging with hope as the teeth caught, open enough that they would be able to slide his leg from the trap. Anna turned to Trevor, quickly smothering the victorious grin that had pulled at her lips. His eyes were squeezed shut and he'd paled further, the relief likely more painful than the pressure had been.

Perhaps she should give him a minute to breathe before moving his leg again.

"Shite." He sighed as tears dropped from his chin onto his chest. "Can no' feel my foot, but I can feel my gods-damned leg."

"I need to find...something to splint it with, and to pack it too...I think," she muttered quietly, looking to see if any torches were nearby.

They had been as quiet as they could be, and though the wind had picked up, it was very likely someone had heard.

Bugger, she really should have paid more attention in anatomy.

Just in the distance, there were low-hanging branches that would work as splints, and she was more than prepared to rip her shirt to tatters if it meant keeping his leg in a better position for healing. Anna squinted at small bundles of thorny plants growing at the bases of the ghostly pines—*thornehallow*. She could use those to pack the wound; they had medicinal qualities—bugger, spending time with her father in the greenhouse had actually done her some good.

"Anna," he said quietly, "why don't ye ever leave?"

Her heart thumped painfully loud.

Because I love you, she nearly said.

Instead, she asked, "What kind of question is that?"

"Everyone else always leaves." He shrugged, brows pinched and gaze on the bleeding that had resumed now that the teeth had been pried out. "Ye should too. All I do is get people killed."

"I couldn't leave you to suffer on Cunningham's ship and I won't leave now," she said stubbornly, tears welling in her eyes. "Why do you think it would be so easy for me to leave you to torture and pain? Why is it so hard for you to believe I don't want to see you hurt?"

"As long as he doesn't have ye, he can't hurt me."

Anna went very still, listening for the words hidden in the spaces of his breath. Scooting nearer, she placed her hand on his cheek and shivered when he closed his eyes and leaned into her touch. So many words welled in her chest, every single one of them fighting to rise and speak their truth. There was power in words, in spoken or written language; they gave meaning to the world, painted with intention and influence.

Trevor might not be one for words, but Anna always had been.

"You want to know why I won't leave?"

He nodded softly, his short beard scraping against her palm.

"It's because I am so desperately in love with you that each breath feels a bit like flying." She paused. "How could I ever leave the man who has gifted me wings?"

"Ye love me." It wasn't a question. "I'm no' good for ye. It wouldn't be fair—I'm a wicked, broken thing, Anna. If we make it off this fucking island, ye deserve better. *More*."

"Who are you to tell me what I do or do not deserve?" she challenged, spine straightening. "I want a love and a life with a man who loves me for me. Don't tell me I don't deserve you, Trevor. Tell me every horrible or atrocious act you have committed, tell me what skeletons you keep in your closet. Tell me, and *I will love you anyway*."

Trevor was not one for words.

Instead, he sat up all the way, gaze dropping from her eyes to her lips as one of his hands curled around her neck. His thumb brushed her pulse, his skin rough but unbelievably warm. Heat rolled off the pirate, flooding her and unfurling the thing she kept locked away in her chest.

Please, God, feel the same.

His thumb brushed her jawline, fingers threading through her hair. She closed her eyes, leaning into the feel of his skin sliding against hers, into the knowing that Trevor Lovelace, the Pirate King, very well might return some of her feelings.

"Anna, I—" The pirate stopped, hand leaving her neck to reach for a weapon no longer at his side.

Bugger.

Body stiffening, his muscles coiled in anticipation of something, and she didn't need to guess at what had caused the reaction. Anna turned her head just so. Dread cooled her body, sending nervous flutters to her stomach and fingers. The knife in her boot wasn't far, she just needed—

Hands clamped around her, ripping her from Trevor as his head flew backward, blood streaming from his mouth. Anna memorized the print of the boot; she had plans to sever the damn thing from the rest of the leg. Several short bursts of movement later, the man who had grabbed her was bent over, bleeding from the nose, arm twisted at an odd level.

In her periphery, Cunningham walked into the clearing, clapping slowly.

Fingers pulled her hair as another set of hands wrapped around her bicep like iron, leaving bruises in their wake. Elbow exploding against one man's face, she reached for the rapier hovering near her hip. She swung it wildly, spinning and bringing it down through the arm wrapped around her bicep. Her eyes watered, hair ripping from her scalp as she planted a foot against the man's sternum before she sheathed the rapier in his gut.

"Drop your rapier, Miss Savage," Cunningham sighed, the sound of another blade drawing adding menace to his voice.

Attention drawn by the wicked sound, Anna stilled, her own rapier freezing mid swing. Her ex-suitor stood over Trevor, blade hanging loosely in one hand, his other casually in his pocket. What was he up to? Did he intend to kill her pirate here and now? Anna's brows knotted and she took one step in their direction.

"I said, *drop your rapier.*"

And then Cunningham kicked the bear trap.

It snapped closed.

Trevor's hoarse, cracking scream tore through the clearing, stopping her in her tracks.

Anna dropped the rapier and fell to her knees. "*Please,* don't—don't hurt him."

Cunningham said something in response, but she ignored him, far more distracted by his steps carving a path between her and the pirate. She didn't have a spare second for Cunningham, not unless it involved severing his head from his blasted body.

She laid her head against the carpet of pine needles, listening as Trevor emptied his stomach. Anna turned her head until she caught the pirate's gaze, his eyes red. Whatever healing had been accomplished had been decimated in that one act.

There had to be a way out of this.

There was always a way out of *this.*

Trevor pulled himself up, rolling over until he kneeled on his forearms and knees. A mad laugh echoed throughout the small clearing. His left leg remained twisted behind him, shrouded in shadow. Cunningham planted his boots right in front of her face, but she barely noticed them. Instead, she watched the vicious wind grasp at the curls in front of her face, her mind jumping from one thought to the next.

What could she say that would buy her more time to think?

Good God, she just needed the time for her head to settle.

Anna had counted four sailors and three marshals in her short-lived rebellion. Cunningham might as well as count as ten with those rapiers...but separate him from them and he was just another man. Anna tensed, a plan slowly forming in her mind. As long as no one tried to behead Trevor, he should heal from whatever retaliation she incited while disarming and killing the sailors and marshals.

Bugger, that meant she had to disarm Bryce.

She and Markus had only been able to best him two out of eight times, and only when they worked together. She let a calm focus settle her nerves like a weighted blanket. There was a first time for every-thing—Bryce Cunningham was only a man, even he could bleed and know defeat.

Cold steel tapped her beneath her chin, encouraging her to look upward, to rise to her knees and sit back on her heels. Cunningham stared down at her, brown hair slicked back and the utter image of perfection. He inhaled deep, brows pulling together in a line that could only be described as consternation.

Gritting her teeth, she glared up at him.

She was a Savage, and Savages didn't lose.

"Do whatever ye fucking like wi' me, boyo," Trevor growled as he drew himself to his knees despite the pain. "But ye leave her the fuck alone."

"I wish I could, Lovelace, but you listen best when she is in peril."

A bird whistled in the background, drawing Anna's attention. She searched the surrounding area for the fowl. A bird? *Now?* She hadn't seen evidence of any animal living on Calaveras beyond the ghoulish sharks swimming about like the monstrosities they were and the eerie flaps of leathery wings. The brush to their left rustled on a discreet breeze, the soft snaps of sticks just barely hiding beneath it.

Curious, yes, but not at all anything she had time for.

Cunningham dragged the cold steel precariously close to her jugular, opening the skin at her throat. She inhaled sharply through her nose at the swift sting, at how the cold air against the open wound ached maddeningly. Flowing like a fiery river down her neck, the blood followed the path that had been carved by another man's cutlass three years ago.

Trevor lunged forward, growling as he clutched the thigh of his useless leg.

"She'll die," he snarled, eyes darkening until they looked like pits in hell. Wind whipped around the clearing fiercely, creating an air tunnel that spiraled upwards and shook needles from the trees. "She'll fucking die, she's no' like me, ye gods-damned cunt!"

They made eye contact, his face hard and furious and something entirely *other*.

Cunningham stepped back, pivoting until he faced the Pirate King completely. The black reached from Trevor's pupils and irises in spindly webbing. All the old stories echoed in her head, all the ones that made him out to be an adventurer, a ruthless force on the seas.

Bugger, there had been stories claiming the Pirate King was closer to a devil than a man—and then those that whispered he was more akin to a god.

Anna thought she had seen the Pirate King before in the heart of Tiburon.

She had thought wrong.

"I'll go, ye fucking shite." He exhaled hard, chest heaving as he dropped his chin. "I'll go. But ye hurt her and I will rip every star from the gods-damned sky. I'll make sure ye never breathe wi'out tasting ash. The Kraken is a sweet dream compared to the bloody nightmare I could be. Ye would do well to remember that."

"The Senate requires your head," Bryce mused, the steel of his blade lightly scraping downward until it pressed against her breast, right above her heart.

"They can fucking have it."

For a moment, all Anna heard was the roar of a different storm. They had been on a ship and the pirate had been on his knees, beaten and bruised with blood dripping from his face. Good God, it was that night all over again—only worse because every drop of love she had for him stole her breath and kept her frozen in place.

Anna loved him.

She loved him and he thought he could do this to her—that she would *let* him?

Trevor refused to look at her, to acknowledge her gaze likely branding his skin.

"*Trevor*," she breathed, eyes stinging as she blinked back tears.

Still, he refused, gifting her with his devastating profile. Blood dripped from his chin and nose, the droplets either falling to his pecs or running down his neck in winding rivulets. Her jaw trembled in frustration with the corner Cunningham had backed her into.

Time—she just needed time.

"Then put these on."

The irons hit the ground in front of Trevor with all the finality of a death sentence.

"Please," she whispered, lip wobbling.

She bit the damn thing to steady it, aware of the marshals and sailors snickering cruelly around her. One carefully wrapped his hand around her bicep in a clear request to stand. He could just bugger off. Trevor clasped the manacles around one wrist and then the other. Anna would consider herself lucky if she ever forgot that sound, of the death toll it reminded her of.

His gaze shifted to something behind her before finally landing on Anna. Throat bobbing, he took all of her in; she felt dissected in front of him, like he pulled her apart layer by layer until he saw only the important things, the things that made her tick. He smiled at what he saw, eyes red and raw.

"I'm sorry, my wee luv, I'm so sorry."

It all happened incredibly fast.

Trevor lunged, propelling himself upward until his manacles wrapped around Cunningham's throat and dragged him to the forest floor. Trevor wrestled a knife from somewhere and then it sailed just shy of her head. Blood sprayed the back of her neck, and the hand that had been around her bicep fell away. Arms banded around her waist, someone heaving her up and off her feet as another arm tucked under her legs.

Trevor's voice broke as he screamed his brother's name, giving a single command: *run*.

CHAPTER FORTY-EIGHT

Trevor tried rolling to his stomach only to choke back a scream.

Fuck that shite.

Pinching his eyes shut, he breathed deep through his nose, letting his chest expand. Arms were fine, fingers sore. His chest ached fiercely, but he expected that wi' the beastie trying to take a bite of him. A slow chuckle shook his chest—damn straight, the Pirate King was a mouthful. He couldn't wait to tell Tate he'd choked a fucking guardian.

Shaking his head, he bent his elbows and rolled his wrists.

He wiggled his—

"What's this shite?" he whispered, lifting his head to glare at his legs.

The right one moved, sore from the climb up all those gods-damned steps—Trevor hated stairs, there was naught worse in the world than stairs. But his ankle rolled, and his knee bent, even his toes twitched. Turning his head, he narrowed his eyes at his left leg.

His heart thumped wildly in his chest, looking at the mess of his calf.

Ah, fuck, that's right.

The gods-damned bear trap.

Trevor squinted hard at his leg, forcing it to bend at the knee—it did it, stiff and swollen as it was. But his bloody ankle wouldn't move. If he could feel it, if it was pain stopping him, Trevor might have considered it a fine day, but as it was, he felt naught, and that concerned him rather greatly.

Shite, he needed to find Bodhi before they had to re-break his leg to fix the bloody damage.

But, bloody hell, where was he?

Trevor looked around the dark room; only three candles flickered in the strong breeze coming from beneath the canvas walls. The tent itself was surprisingly sparse for a Briland captain—and a marshal, at that. A twin bed boxed off the ground leaned in one corner, and the rug Trevor laid on was mediocre at best, naught like the ornate rugs in his quarters. In the corner, a brass brazier burned coolly, nearly reduced to embers. Silverware and plates littered the floor, a matching goblet of wine near the flap.

Someone was bloody pissed and throwing shite like a babe.

Good.

Trevor's gaze drifted from the room to what kept him anchored to where he was. A manacle had been clamped around his ankle; the other end was attached to a stake set at least two feet into the bloody ground. It seemed a wee bit of overkill. Trevor doubted he could walk. He'd likely need crutches to get anywhere, crawling on his knees was beneath a male like him—unless it was crawling toward the lass, he'd do that in a heartbeat.

Anna.

She'd changed his entire world wi' those three wee words. If no' for that, he'd happily roll to his death here if it meant she'd be safe from Cunningham. But wi' that knowledge tucked away like the coppers he'd save for Taylee and Tate, there was naught he wanted more than to find his way back to her.

Seeing his beastie meant getting up, and getting up meant putting up wi' his bloody leg. He'd lived a hard life, experienced more than he likely had any right to—a bum leg had naught on him. Trevor glared down at it. Fucker did no' even twitch.

"Gods—fucking—son—of a—*cunt*," he growled, forcing himself to his elbows and pulling his right leg up.

"Please, tell me you haven't kissed my sister with that vulgar mouth?"

"Her mouth isn't the only part of her I've—" Trevor stopped, whipping his head in the direction of the male's voice. "Fucking Markus Savage, is that ye?"

The blond frowned at him, shaking his head slowly, lips curled in disgust. "I knew I couldn't leave the two of you alone. Blast it all to hell, I *knew* it."

Trevor made it to his hands, sitting upright to get a better view of the lass's brother. He sat slumped in an old chair wi' his feet on a box, one hand placed over his gut. Anna'd said he'd been run through by Cunningham on the bastard's ship. His hair had grown, curling around his ears in matted strands—prick's whiskers were even blonder than the dirty mop on his head.

"Ye look like shite."

Markus snorted. "I'd offer you a mirror, wretch, but the captain broke them all."

"What the fuck are ye talking about, mate?" Trevor grinned. "I'm bloody delightful to look at."

"Have you seen your leg? I can smell the rotting thing from here."

Trevor shrugged. Fuck the leg.

Anna loved him.

"You're in far too good of a mood," Markus said suspiciously.

"Your sister loves me," Trevor replied proudly, grin forcing its way to his face.

"About time she realized it."

"The fuck? Ye knew?"

"Of course, I knew, she's my twin," he said, staring hard behind Trevor. Was the male watching the tent flap? "Now, listen, wretch— we have to get you out of here."

"Aye, mate. Can't marry your sister on a fucking cursed island," Trevor mumbled quietly, gaze skipping around the room.

He'd need something to lean on.

Markus laughed but naught was funny about the sound. "No, you don't understand. Cunningham needs you to control the Kraken. It's something about your blood."

Trevor waved him off. "Cuntingham can piss the fuck off. I have other plans."

"Oh, I'm sure you do." Markus lowered his feet from the crate and tucked a wee journal in the back pocket of his trousers. "But we really need to get you as far from here as possible. This isn't Cunningham's plan, it's my father's."

"No' wi'out Anna."

Markus pinched the bridge of his nose before dragging his hand down his face in a growl. "*Why* are you two like this? If you and I leave, she will have no choice except to follow."

Shite, he couldn't argue wi' that.

Trevor hissed through his nose as he rolled onto his forearms, forcing his right leg underneath him. Slowly, he stood, head swimming and visioning tunneling. He grasped the frame of the bed, using it to keep himself upright until his head calmed the hell down.

"Can you walk on that?" Markus frowned. "It looks like a pack of wild dogs went at it."

"Of course, I can fucking..." He clenched his jaw, slowly putting weight on his left leg. Trevor backed off as quickly as his aching body could move. "*Fuck.*"

It wouldn't even bear his weight.

The lass's brother groaned something fierce. "I suppose I can drag you if it means getting out of here and stopping my father."

"Ye no' dragging me anywhere, mate."

"Suit yourself, you can hobble."

Trevor's lip twitched.

Bodhi was going to cut his leg off as soon as he found him. No sense keeping something that was broken like this, and Trevor didn't think his surgeon would be able to fix it. Some things weren't worth fighting and fixing, and this might be one of them. At best, he'd walk with a bloody limp, and at worst, he'd need a peg for a leg.

What would his lass think of that?

Trevor didn't think she'd care but it didn't stop vulnerability from creeping up.

She deserved a male that was whole and—

Who are you to tell me what I do or do not deserve? her voice echoed in his head.

He stopped and whipped his head in Markus's direction. "Markus," he said, grin growing on his face as he used the frame of the bed to hop forward. "Can I marry your sister, if she'll have me?"

"Wh—*no.*" Markus stumbled to a stop, coughing and grasping at his abdomen. "Proper etiquette dictates you ask our father first, scoundrel."

"Aye, but your da is a gods-damned bastard and he'll say no."

"You're absolutely right." Markus grinned, something warm in his gaze. "Good thing Anna has never given a damn about what he thinks. I'm sure she'll say no, just to be contrary."

Trevor shot the male a vicious glare.

Bloody hell, he hoped the fuck no'.

"He really is a bastard, isn't he?"

"Aye, always has been," Trevor said. "Your da was a bloody pain in the Old Crow's ass as a lad too. The prick would yell up and down the bloody deck of the *Devil's Advocate,* cursing your da's name."

"Whatever for?" he asked, looking at papers on the desk. "My father was a captain in the Briland Navy, yes, but as he tells it, he hardly saw pirates during his service. If anything, he had more trouble with you wretches after marrying our mother and expanding the merchant empire he inherited from our grandfather."

What was the male looking for?

Trevor hesitantly sat on the bed, wincing at the pain echoing in his bloody leg. Sighing, he rubbed the back of his neck and stared at a lowly flickering gaslight on the desk. "It may have been a long time ago, but I am bloody positive your da made all sorts of trouble for the Old Crow. Mostly in stealing cargo."

Markus's brows pulled together, and he drummed his fingers on the tabletop. "What cargo could the Old Crow possibly have that interested my father?"

"Well, Stedd had the normal bounty you'd expect of a pirate raiding ships...priceless baubles, fancy clothing..." Trevor trailed off, leaning back on his hands. "The old bastard was the first in a bloody long time to start stealing fems from their beds."

"Does that mean William Stedd started the slave trade all those years ago?" Markus asked, surprise in his voice.

"No," he said, meeting Markus's eyes. "His gods-damned mark was a spider; the crew wore webs. If the slavers were working for him, they'd all have had that shite on their skin."

"What happened to yours?"

"My *what?*"

"Your spider web. You were a cabin boy on his ship and then later a wretch of worth—important and skilled enough that you eventually had your own ship." The blond frowned then, gods-damned displeased about one thing or another. "I watched Anna give you several sponge baths. I don't recall seeing any webs."

"It was on my arm, here," he said, pointing to his bicep. "Fucker bled from my skin as my tattoos crept up my arm."

"*Bled?* How positively atrocious," Markus said, finally turning toward him. "You...when we were on the *Contessa,* you said you found snake bites on slavers?"

Trevor forced himself to stand as Anna's brother took a bloody dainty step forward. Sighing, he said, "Aye."

Markus's eyes widened as the flap to the tent snapped open, thunder rumbling and lightning flashing. It drew both their gazes like moths to flame. Markus stepped backward until the backs of his legs touched the twin-size bed and he sat down, shoulders rounding out. Trevor focused on the door, brow raising curiously as Bryce Cunningham walked under the flap. An icy gust chilled Trevor to the bone.

Rather fitting that the cunt appeared wi' a storm like an omen.

He was no' impressed, though; he could create an entrance from a bloody nightmare and bad luck too. He grinned at the male, the split in his lip cracking as something full of spite curled in his gut. "Savage says ye broke all the bloody mirrors. I would too if I looked like ye."

Cunningham was soaked, rainwater running off his coat in long streams. He hardly looked at Trevor or the lass's brother. Wi'out stopping, the bastard kicked Trevor's bad leg, sending him straight into a fit that lived somewhere between laughter and wheezing on the ground. Clutching his leg, his eyes burned something fierce and his leg throbbed.

"Aye, fuck ye too," Trevor growled through his grin.

"I see you're both awake," Cunningham said, voice low. He removed his cloak, snapping it in a way that sprayed Trevor wi' the gods-damned rain. "How is your leg, Lovelace?"

He felt hot all over, sweat dripping down his spine and from his temples, sight growing dark at the corners. "No' much of a leg, bucko."

"Excellent. That means you won't be able to run away. The surgeon wanted to amputate it, you see, but I want to watch you walk to the gallows."

"Gallows?" Trevor laughed. "You've been busy if ye plan on hanging me here."

"Not here, wretch," Cunningham said, threading his arms through the sleeves of another coat. "In Bellcaster. You still have crimes to pay for."

Trevor opened his mouth, probably to fucking argue, but what was the gods-damned point?

Thunder cracked again, and Cunningham leaned forward, a grim smile on his face. "It appears it's time to begin."

Shite.

458

CHAPTER FORTY-NINE

"I'm not sorry for stabbing you," Anna whispered as she pressed herself against the outside of the temple. The foliage grew thick along its base. Flora groped at them, pulling at her arms and legs, smacking against her face and tearing small holes in her clothes.

"Fucking fantastic, lassie, 'cause I'm no' sorry ye stabbed me either," Tate snapped back, jabbing her with the pommel of his cutlass. "Care to take another go at me? Because I still feel like shite."

Anna rolled her eyes at the quartermaster's antics, choosing instead to focus on where she planted her feet and how far the next sentry was. They had only run into one so far—or at least only one that she could see.

Good God, she had never seen a storm quite like this.

The wind raged, ripping at her hair and clothing while the rain pelted them like softened bullets. She had to keep one hand up to keep the water from her eyes. The icy downpour had already soaked her clothes, and puddles were quickly developing in her boots. Dark had completely descended; the eerie green light cast off the circling guardians was all they had to see by. Torches stood watch along the path, long since put out by the strong gusts.

Tate's pommel tapped against her rump this time, drawing a quick glare from her. "So ye and my brother, huh?"

Anna sucked on her teeth, taking a deep breath. "I'm not talking about your brother with you, Tate."

"Fair, fair."

"I'm not," she said, stopping to squint at the quartermaster. "I mean it."

"If ye say so, lassie. Everyone talks to me about one thing or another, ye'll see."

Anna parted a sea of fronds from her face, peeking to check for marshals or sailors—or glowing great whites. The entrance into the temple was more akin to an abyss, a pillar of shadow that seemed to inhale as she stared at it, shadows warping at its edges. A giant beak protruded from the rest of the grey stone, making it look like the maw of the Kraken.

Splendid.

"He feels the same about ye, Anna," Tate said quietly, gaze on the temple. "I know my brother didn't say it when he should have."

Anna hadn't considered the alternative—not once.

"I know. He shows it," she said, patting the quartermaster on the shoulder. "Come on, Tate, let's go save our idjit brothers."

Striding forward, she ducked into the shadows, feeling her way along the wall. If Calaveras truly belonged to the khan, there might be pictographs carved into the wall—ones to tell her whether or not a hall was friendly or fiendish. The walls had been sanded smooth; a soft wobbling told her it was by hand over the course of a very long time. Pictographs didn't prick against her fingers, and so she followed the hall down into what felt like the literal belly of a beast.

Fear did not cool her nerves or quicken her thinking. It was not the emotion that tangled itself between her ribs and made her skin prickle with the need for physicality—fury was. The furious cold froze her from the inside out. Most assumed Markus had inherited their famous Savage temper growing up, the one that ran like ice in their father's veins.

The path wound around farther and farther into the ground. Algae slickened the stone tiles, and the churning sound of water echoed up at them from farther in.

Were they descending into whatever water source hid behind the temple?

Would they find the Kraken sleeping against the far wall, just waiting to be woken up?

How did one do that anyway? She frowned against the cold, slimy feeling of the walls brushing her fingertips. She didn't think the map told someone *how* to wake a mythical beast, only *where* to find it.

If a way to wake it had been written, did that mean someone had also penned a way to put it back to sleep?

Her brows drew together as she squinted into the nuanced dark of the tunnel. Good God, there had to be a book somewhere that contained that knowledge. There had been a book written about every subject known to man in the archives beneath the university in Bellcaster—even thousands-year-old smut.

A soft grin flickered against her lips as the crashing waves drowned everything else out. The erotica texts she had stumbled on while clearing out and cataloging a section had actually been quite good.

She blinked against the sudden brightness cast from the torches farther down the tunnel. Pulling her to a stop, Tate's hand tightened around the collar of her shirt. In one long-legged stride, he stepped around her, positioning himself in front. The quartermaster's arms stretched out in the dim light, careful to keep her behind him while they crept forward.

Where were the guards?

The spiraling tunnel opened in an arch of light, and the vague shapes moved back and forth. The sound of hustling and bustling men finally filtered over the sound of churning waves. Tate held his hand up, shifting forward, muscles of his shoulders and back bunched tight in anticipation.

"You're going to have to tell me how you do that when this is all said and done," she muttered, realizing his black-bladed cutlass had disappeared from sight.

Tate glanced over his shoulder, tucking some of his rain-soaked hair behind his ear. Despite the wind raging outside, his wine-red locks had remained tied back in their half bun, the other strands tangling around his collarbones.

"Do what?"

"However that works with your blades." Anna's gaze lowered to his forearms, which were covered in intricately designed blades of all sizes and shapes before dipping to the cutlasses tattooed against his sides.

"Anna, I'd luv to show ye how my blade works, but my brother'll want my fucking head afterward." He winked, slowly creeping around her shoulder.

She devoured every inch of the cavern, noting the sea monsters carved into the walls and the krakens draping from the top of every pillar. The craftsmanship was positively brilliant; every one of the beasties looked like it could have been real, simply frozen in time. Inhaling slowly, she looked beyond the stone columns that stretched high above. She couldn't make heads or tails of what laid beyond them except for constantly roiling shadows.

"What do ye think that is?" Tate asked, motioning to the swirling vortex of water that had been cut directly into the floor, five pillars surrounding it.

Bugger, that would have been quite a feat—tunneling through stone to create a pool of that size.

"Likely where the Kraken is sleeping," she muttered, more concerned with what encircled the pool.

Five groups of five men laid upon the ground between the pillars, throats slit and bleeding into grooves in the ground. She followed the blood flowing like gurgling brooks straight into the swirling waters at the center. Slowly, her attention moved from the piles of dead men, centering on a stone box directly in her line of sight, crude crowns patterned into its sides.

"If Trevor is anywhere, he's in that box," she told Tate.

"What makes ye think that?" he said, nearly growling.

"It's only an educated guess, but look at the pattern—"

"The crowns?"

"Aye." Anna grinned, gaze trailing the pillars. "Do you see those pillars?"

"They're rather hard to miss. Why?"

"Take them down and we should bring the entire temple down on Cunningham's head."

Tate grinned, skin prickling in the cold as his hand drifted to his hip and rested on one of his many tattoos. "The fucker only brought forty or so men; this'll be cake."

Black bled from his irises, swallowing the whites of his eyes like dye dropped into milk. A cold chill chased its way up her spine as the temperature dropped around her. Anna watched in cool curiosity as the tattooed knives seemed to ripple against his skin.

Good God.

The stories had always claimed the Pirate King manned a crew of the damned, that they had been cursed five times over, once by every sea. Looking at Tate now as his eyes darkened to black, she had a difficult time believing otherwise.

The chaos of the cavern drew her attention. The men Cunningham had brought with him looked forlorn and pale, a mad gleam to their eyes as they frantically completed tasks. Her attention shifted back to the strange box that likely contained the Pirate King before moving beyond it to—

"Markus," she breathed.

Trevor screamed, voice hoarse as the sound of grinding stone bounced off the cavern, quickly masked by a choked laugh. Swallowing hard, she stared at the stone box once more—bugger, sometimes she hated it when she was right. Her attention dropped back to the river of red filling the grooves in the floor and then to the swirling water inside the vortex.

That was her pirate's blood muddying the dark, chaotic waters.

Anna tasted bile, jaw clenching.

"Shite, we—*ANNA!*" Tate screamed as she took off.

An explosion rocked the temple, pillars trembling and ground shaking beneath her feet.

Juliana and Bodhi had brilliant timing.

Throwing her hands out to the side, she kept her gaze focused on Markus—*he* could die, that was a truth she couldn't deny. Trevor would live no matter what happened so long as his head remained attached to his neck. Skirting to the right, Anna rounded the pool. Marshals and sailors called after her, pulling pistols and rapiers from their belts.

Bugger.

The temple rumbled again, and stones the size of giants fell from the ceiling and crushed several of the Briland sailors in their evergreen uniforms. She slid to a stop, coughing past the grit coating her mouth. Silence fell over the cavern like the first blanket of snow in Bellcaster; even the water stilled. Motes of dust filtered down through screens of light created by flashes of lightning. Looking up, she saw a hole had been cracked in the ceiling. Water poured through it, brought by the raging storm.

A shot rang out, and a man on the far side of the temple slumped against the wall, leaving a smear of red in his wake.

She watched as another sailor's legs buckled beneath him as thunder echoed in the cavern. Blood dribbled from his frontal bone, showcasing the skill of whoever had the rifle. Brows drawing together, Anna wondered if it was Bodhi or Juliana who held the rifle. Which one of them was such an excellent shot?

Anna ran toward her brother, taking advantage of the sailors' distraction as a rope unfurled from the hole in the cavern and slapped against the ground. If the rifle poking through the ceiling hadn't grabbed everyone's attention, that single act had.

Her steps only stuttered a moment, neck craning to witness what would come next.

Juliana Gray plummeted from the hole, one hand on the rope as she repelled down at harrowing speeds. The air whipped her hair back, and lightning flashed, illuminating her lithe frame. Oh God— Anna squinted, it must have been one hundred feet between the cavern floor and the ceiling.

The woman was gloriously mad.

Juliana's boots cracked against the flooring, one of her knees just touching the stone tiles before she flicked her head up. Anna stumbled at the vicious smile splitting her face, at how the lightning reflected back off it and revealed a mouth full of too many razor-sharp teeth. But it was the Man-Eater's eyes that drew and held her attention like a rat caught in a trap.

They were black, a matching pair to Tate's.

Juliana stood, a pistol spinning in each hand and a rifle slung across her back.

Laughter broke from her chest at the sheer stupidity of their collective actions. Had there ever been a ragtag crew of so few to attempt such a feat as this? She gasped for breath as she ran—likely not, and there likely wouldn't ever be one again.

"Kill her!" Bryce screamed from somewhere in the cavern. "*Kill the Man-Eater!*"

Glancing over her shoulder, she found Bryce standing near the stone box Trevor lay entombed in. His gaze was focused on Juliana Gray. Had that been panic she heard twanging in the captain's voice? He was entirely in his right mind if the Man-Eater evoked even a weensy amount of fear. Sailors and marshals alike ran in a frenzy, revolvers and pistols pointing in Juliana's direction. She looked like an instrument of death, grinning with pistol smoke shrouding her gaze.

A glimmer of steel shined from the corner of her eye, drawing her attention back to the matter at hand. Ducking beneath the swing, Anna flinched as the man's face blew away in the echo of gunfire. She didn't have time to stop, didn't have time to blink. She dragged her arm down her face as she sprinted toward her brother, trying to ignore the blood warming her cheeks and neck.

"*Anna!*" Markus screamed, red-faced and struggling against the manacles around his wrists.

Bugger, they were connected to chains that were bolted to the damn floor.

She slid in next to him in a flurry of motion. Her gaze roved over the manacles as she procured her hammer and picks. The lock was in a tricky place, but it wasn't anything she and Markus hadn't worked with before. Glancing up, her fingers stilled as she met her brother's gaze.

Markus huddled over her, shirtless, his bronzed, bloodied skin on display. Shifting, his thin stomach pulled tight and drew her attention to a grisly scar. When she had thought of how his wound might heal, Anna had always thought of it like Trevor's most recent impalement —a white scar, thinner than the width of a blade.

But her brother's was angry and red, set just above and to the right of his belly button.

The cacophony of stone grinding against stone permeated the air, quickly followed by Trevor's scream. Anna's gaze bolted over her shoulder to where Cunningham stood next to the stone tomb, lightning flashing off his drawn swords. She had never wanted to kill a man before, not quite like this. It was a visceral burn in her veins, a haze tinting her vision. The only thing keeping her tethered to her brother was the knowledge that Trevor Lovelace could not die.

No matter the agony he experienced now, he would survive it.

He had to.

A harsh exhale escaped her lips as she snuck an aggrieved look at her brother, brow cocked. "Is anyone else feeling nostalgic, or is it just me?"

"Not *one* word, Anna." Markus flinched at the next burst of gunfire. "Not. One."

"At least you have trousers this time."

Her brother snorted, gaze scanning whatever fight went on behind her. If even half the stories were true about the *Pale Queen's* crew, they would be fine, but knowing and believing were two entirely separate entities. A scream rent the air, brutal and high-pitched, fear resonating in every echo as it cut through the din.

"I'm surprised to find you in such a joyous mood with your pirate being bled dry." Markus's throat bobbed in the corner of her eye.

She kept her attention on the lock, visualizing how the tumblers moved within. "My pirate?"

"Well, I sure as hell did not profess my undying love for him," Markus said quickly. Her gaze snapped up and met her brother's, heart thundering. "We talked about it very briefly earlier. I was there when he woke up. You love him?"

"I do."

Markus groaned dramatically, and, despite everything, it brought a smile to her face. Leave it to her brother to believe her love life was more perilous than the situation at hand. "I knew you couldn't be left unsupervised. What could you possibly see in the scoundrel?"

Shrugging, Anna ran her tongue over her teeth. "Have you seen him shirtless? He also has an incredibly large—"

"No." He inhaled, head snapping in her direction. "Do not speak it."

"I was going to say library. I know it is incredibly difficult for you, Markus, but do try to keep your mind from the gutter."

Markus stiffened, the action jostling her pick in the lock as his entire body twitched. Another cluster of gunfire echoed from above, dropping someone just behind them with a wet slap. Anna frowned, turning her attention away from the lock and over her shoulder. A black blade planted in a man's eye before bursting in a cloud of obsidian smoke on impact.

"They truly are monstrous," her brother muttered, jaw slack.

"Rather fortuitous, if you ask me," she said, squinting down at the manacles.

She ignored every single one of the splendid questions that leapt forth. There would be plenty of time to ask the quartermaster later; right now, she needed to pick this damnable lock and free her brother.

"Markus," she hissed, hand slipping as he tried to stand.

A growl ripped from his throat as his icy gaze narrowed on something just behind her. With the short chain, he didn't gain much height, back hunched and knees bent. The hair on the back of her neck prickled, stiffening her shoulders in anticipation. Anna turned as her brother's hand brushed her shoulder, either to turn her or move her, she wasn't sure.

Brilliant, she thought, staring down the barrel of a revolver.

Markus's attention darted from the man who might be about to murder her. Something close to betrayal tightened her stomach. What could possibly be more important than standing witness to his twin sister's death? Nothing. Nothing should be more important than that.

But then she saw the flash of red and cream, leather and steel.

Juliana Gray.

The master gunner rolled over her brother's back, foot smashing the man's face and sending him sprawling backward. As one boot touched down, she caved his face in with the stock of her rifle before lobbing it over her shoulder. Eyes widening, Anna watched the rifle sail through the air and straight into her brother's awaiting palm. Markus dropped to a knee and took careful aim—several shots fired out, leaving her ears ringing as Juliana snatched the pistols from her waistband.

How very interesting, she thought, squinting at the two.

If Anna hadn't known any better, she might have thought they'd rehearsed that splendid little number.

"Bodhi?"

"Finding that blasted dynamite," Juliana replied, a strange musical twang layered in her voice.

The lock clicked, and her brother rose to his feet, snatching a rapier from the nearest marshal as he strode toward the Man-Eater. Anna frowned from where she knelt on the ground, unsure of where he'd misplaced his gratitude. Another piece of the cavern crashed to the ground behind them, but that didn't draw her gaze away from her brother.

Anna was missing something, some integral part of the puzzle.

Bugger, she was sure of it.

Markus's hand drifted to his most recent wound, jaw clenched as the Man-Eater turned toward him. Hand flashing to his bicep, her eyes were full of concern as they darted to his stomach, brows drawn. Anna pulled herself to her feet, body angling toward where Trevor lay entombed. There truly was no time like the present, especially when one considered Cunningham had plans to raise a damn sea monster by draining the blood from her pirate.

But then Markus bent low, his fingers wrapping around Juliana's neck as he pulled her lips to his in a deep kiss. Her nose brushed his, eyes closed as he wiped a drop of blood from her cheek like one might a tear. He didn't seem at all put off by her glimmering teeth or the black of her eyes.

Oh no. Anna choked back bile.

Disgusting.

Absolutely and abhorrently disgusting.

"Good *God*, Markus," she snapped. "Is now really the time? Snogging in a collapsing temple while the Kraken is being woken from its watery tomb? Have some decorum, you bumbling oaf!"

Gagging quietly to herself, Anna put Bryce Cunningham in her sights. If she wanted something done, she'd have to do it herself—Bryce certainly wasn't going to keel over of his own accord. Oh no, she would find spectacular pleasure in administering his end.

Men littered the ground between them, dying or dead.

A tight circle had formed around the quartermaster; though she couldn't see him, she watched his black blades arc over heads before they were severed from necks. Tate's laugh carried above the thunder, the *shing* and *snick* of his weapons a near constant echo.

She had always believed his claim to quartermaster had something to do with nepotism, with being the baby brother of the Pirate King. But as he cut through sailor after sailor, cleaving limbs from bodies and separating men from their souls, Anna swallowed past a hard knot of understanding.

Tate Lovelace was not the quartermaster of the *Pale Queen* because he was Trevor Lovelace's younger brother. He was the quartermaster because he had earned it—by might and right, and likely a teensy bit of mischief.

Ripping a sword from the chest of a marshal at her feet, his blood puddling beneath her boots, she began cutting a path through Bryce's men. Most who remained were sailors, men who fought pirates from a distance and rarely on deck, let alone land. Even fewer marshals remained, small black blips in a sea of Bellcaster green, and the majority of them had clustered around Tate as others called to surround Juliana.

Anna frowned as she ran.

How had *that* even happened?

Her brother and the master gunner of the *Pale Queen*?

That would be a tale for the ages.

A monstrous groan reverberated through the cavern, amplifying until it was the only thing they heard. Several sailors doubled over, pressing their hands to their ears. Anna would have as well if not for her blade sinking into a man's gut, the cross guard pressed tight against his stomach. The ground shook beneath her feet and loose rockery fell from the ceiling. With a wince, she ripped her rapier back out, hands coated in blood.

Cunningham was ten feet away, his back to her as he showered orders upon his men's heads.

Trevor's stone tomb stood between them, a poor excuse as a wall to guard his back. Planting her foot, she vaulted over it, rapier poised to cut Cunningham in two. Lightning flashed off her blade before it bounced off his. Bryce turned in a fast swoop, and the ring of steel-on-steel reverberated through her ears and hummed in her arm. He swung his leg around, catching Anna on the side and launching her into Trevor's tomb.

The wind was knocked from her lungs and her back ached from where it connected with the sharp stone edge. Anna pressed one hand onto the stone even as she raised the other to block his incoming swing—

Markus appeared, steel clashing with Bryce's and driving him back.

Pushing herself from the stone coffin with a snarl, Anna shoved the way Trevor called her name from her mind and lunged at Bryce.

It was time the real fight began.

She loathed to think anything kind or complimentary of Bryce, but he was a poet with a rapier—any blade really—and this fact held true as Markus and Anna danced around him in spinning arcs. His rapier clashed and clanged off theirs. Spinning and twirling, he blocked and parried as if they were dancing to a song only he knew the footing to.

In minutes, her breathing came in ragged gasps, and sweat slicked her back and chest. Her arms shook from the effort of raising her rapier. Markus grunted after Bryce's fist thumped against his wound; dropping his sword, his arms collapsing to wrap around his torso. The only indication that Cunningham was tired as well was the sweat dripping from his temples and the flush of his cheeks.

Staggering, she batted his blade away as her chest heaved. He stared at her, rage plain in his features. Some other emotion lingered there, perhaps hurt or disappointment. Whatever it was, it was a petty emotion he had no right feeling, not anymore.

Bryce and Anna held like that, gazes narrowed at each other like generals across a killing field.

Another tremble shook the very core of the cavern, but this one was different than the others had been—this one felt like it came from below. Her gaze dropped to the detritus clogging the cavern floor, watching as small pebbles bounced with the deep rumble.

It stopped, and everything went inexplicably silent.

Anna stepped back, eyebrows drawing in concern at the water flowing past her boots. Swallowing hard, she looked over her shoulder to the previously swirling vortex in the middle of the cavern. Its waters had stilled, the top placid enough to look more akin to black glass. Dread pooled in her stomach and her heart started thumping painfully behind her ribcage.

Bugger.

Bugger it all to hell.

She scanned the room, looking for her allies. Juliana stood with a sword in one hand, her pistol raised to fire. She stared at the pit, nostrils flaring with her deep breaths. Bodhi froze, reaching into a crate that had been marked for explosives as Tate took deep gulps of air, bodies strewn about him like dropped dolls.

A splash pulled her attention back to the calm pool, rings of water echoing outward as if someone had dropped a rock at its center.

The temperature dropped drastically, tightening her exposed skin and sending a shiver up her sweat-slicked back. The cool air stung her lungs. As she exhaled, her breath plumed in front of her face. The water bubbling up from the pool became a steady stream.

"What's...what's that?" a man breathed from near the still pool.

Get away from the edge, she thought desperately.

A black, leathery tentacle erupted from the waters, pulling him into the air before dragging him beneath the surface. Good God, it happened so fast, all before she could blink. That poor man hardly had the chance to scream or draw a weapon.

Everyone's gaze froze on the sloshing waters.

Blood bloomed across the surface like an unfurling flower, and Anna remembered what fear was in that moment.

"We need to leave," Markus hissed from behind her, stepping back with a grimace.

Shaking her head, her grip tightened on her rapier. "Not...not without Trevor."

Markus shoved her to the cavern floor and she felt the *whuff* of wind, loose hair roaring to the side with the gust.

Another man screamed, followed by another dreadful splash.

"We're not done here, little bird," Bryce growled, bringing his rapier down.

Anna and Markus rolled in opposite directions as another tentacle shot from the water as quick as a bullet. It gripped a pillar on the opposite side. Two more followed and then the Kraken began pulling itself from the pool. Oh, bugger—that was not good. Mark her words, that was not an event they wanted to see the conclusion to.

Images of the maw at the entrance to this hellish temple flashed in her head—of the dark, wickedly sharp beak.

Her hand hardly found her rapier in time to block Cunningham's incoming swing. He rained down blow after blow like a vengeful god, but Anna couldn't find it in herself to focus on him. Not with *that* behind him. Not when she stared down its throat and at all the suckers and barbs just waiting to snatch her up.

The Kraken roared. It was like nothing she had ever heard, caught somewhere between a fairy tale and a nightmare.

"*Take it down!*" she screamed, voice cracking. "*The dynamite! Take It down!*""

Bugger, she didn't know how to stop the Kraken, but bringing the entire cavern down on top of it might at least slow it down.

Her brother's blade ricocheted off Bryce's, causing his arms to swing back above his head. Anna swept at Bryce's leg, bringing him to one knee as Markus's fist snapped his head to the side. Her heart thumped wildly at seeing Bryce wipe blood from the corner of his mouth. His rapier glanced off hers—once, twice, again, again, *again.*

Cunningham pressed forward at a relentless pace, driving Markus and Anna back one small step at a time. Despite working in tandem with her brother, a cut opened against her ribcage and then a second one on her thigh. Markus growled, blinking back the blood spilling into his right eye from a cut above his brow.

With a flick of Bryce's wrist, Anna's rapier clattered to the ground. Gritting her teeth, she glared at him, listening to the soft *tink* of her mother's ring as it ricocheted somewhere in this god-forsaken caver. Panic stiffened her breathing for a short moment; she'd never find her mother's ring here, not after they brought down the cavern.

Oh God, she *hated* him.

She hated him for the irreparable loss of her mother's ring. Hated him for putting her pirate in a box, hated him for this vendetta he wore like a badge on his breast. But most of all, Anna hated how she had let him make her feel small.

She looked down at her right hand to where her ring finger bent at an impossible angle.

"This won't be enough, Miss Savage. You are not enough to stop me," Bryce spat, rotating his blades.

"I am all I need to be," she growled back, picking up her rapier with her left hand.

Gunfire and small explosive bursts drew the Kraken's attention away from them. The cavern shook with his frustrated screams, the noise reverberating and echoing off every surface until her head felt like it would explode.

At least someone kept the beast busy.

Anna had a different monster to kill first.

Her brother flanked Bryce, rapier opening a red line along the captain's arm. From the corner of her eye, another tentacle rose from the water. Deceptively fast, it stretched and slammed against the ground just next to them. Bryce lost his footing, either slipping in the water or unprepared to avoid the tentacle. His knee bent just enough that her rapier missed his head; instead, it cleaved his clavicle with a snap before ripping through a sizable chunk of his shoulder and neck.

Surprise clouded his face as blood oozed from his wound.

He fell backward over the tentacle and did not move.

Anna stared for a moment.

Had they really—had they done it?

A wild grin split her face, and she turned to Markus who looked equally confused. His arm had wrapped around his stomach once more, a rapier in his opposite hand. He gripped the hilt loosely, the blade nearly touching the ground.

Wait.

What was her brother staring at?"

Anna's head whipped in the direction of his attention, every bit of victory running through her veins amplified. Bodhi lit sticks of dynamite and threw them at the Kraken as Juliana raced from pillar to pillar. The Kraken's tentacle crushed one of the columns, and it slipped a fraction into the water.

The Man-Eater lit a match on one of her leather bracers.

"Time to go, Markus!"

"*I* have been trying to leave, *you* have been trying to get killed!"

"Semantics, brother dear!"

Anna stepped back slowly before turning tail. Bodhi threw one more stick before sprinting in the opposite direction. Launching herself over the tomb, she dropped onto the other side and pressed her body against it with her hands over her head. Markus landed next to her, pulling her underneath his arms as well.

Good God, her brother needed a bath.

Three.

"What in the bloody fuck is going on out there?" Trevor growled, voice hoarse and crackling at its edges.

Two.

"Well—"

One.

A bright flash lit up the cavern in a blinding light. Anna closed her eyes tight, comforted by the strength of her brother's arms around her. The ground shook violently, and the Kraken screamed louder than the explosion. Dust and debris wafted over them in a thick wave as the ceiling of the cavern caved inward.

For several minutes, all she knew was a trembling earth and a cacophony of sound.

The downpour coming from the completely collapsed cavern ceiling weighted the dust down, making it more manageable to breathe. Anna slowly pulled away from Markus, blinking against the howling wind and pouring water.

Half of the cavern had collapsed. The far side that had a window to the sea beyond was not completely composed of rubble. Satisfied that the dark pool the Kraken had crawled from now lay beneath a layer of debris, she squinted into the dark, searching for the others.

Any torch that had been used to light the cavern had been put out, either in the gust from the blast or from the rain. The outline of one of the Kraken's tentacles laid upon the ground, and various men started groaning.

Bugger, she couldn't see anything in this dark and without her—

"Markus!" Juliana coughed, a shadow standing off in the distance.

"Here!" he called back, slowly making his way to his feet.

Her brother met Juliana across the way, just another overly large shadow in a decimated tomb. Lightning flashed, illuminating the entrance of the cavern. Anna did not want to climb more stairs, but *those* stairs would take her out of this fresh hell. She continued to scour what she could see of her surroundings while leaning her shoulder against the stone lid.

If Tate had died in that explosion, she would never forgive herself and Trevor likely wouldn't either. Anna called her pirate's name quietly several times, hoping to rouse him without alerting any of the remaining marshals or sailors of her intentions. In the next flash of lightning, she saw Tate jogging her way, a bright smile on his face and eyes alight with victory.

The only one left to find was Bodhi.

"Come on," she grunted, shoving the lid with both hands.

Heaving all her weight into the lid, it finally budged an inch to the side and then another. If there had been any light to see by, she might have been able to glimpse some of his face. But as it was, she had to settle for the sound of his deep, pained breaths carrying through the crack.

"Is that ye, luv? What the fuck are ye doing here?"

Anna gasped, throat tightening.

Her nose burned and tears streamed freely down her face. "I told you I could never leave you. I'll have you out of there in a minute, but we must move fast, pirate. I don't know if the Kraken survived but—"

A boulder shifted, toppling from the top of some pile.

Anna cocked her head, gaze narrowing and stomach flipping at the sound of stone cracking against stone. Another flash brightened the cavern for a harrowing second. Markus and Juliana were near the stairs now, and Tate was nearly to her. Splendid. The quartermaster could help her get this damnable lid off, and they could leave all the sooner.

Another bit of debris bounced its way from the top of a pile.

"What's going on?" he whispered, exhaustion in every sound he made.

She prayed to every god and goddess she could name. She begged for finality, for a closing of a chapter long overdue. Closing her eyes, she clenched her jaw and pushed against the stone top. It budged another few inches. There was nearly enough space to drag Trevor through it.

Lightning flashed again, and she wished she hadn't looked up.

A tentacle burst through the rubble, slamming into Tate and throwing him across the cavern like a rag doll. His body cracked against the far cavern wall. Another flash revealed a smear of blood and an actual imprint from where he had connected. He would be fine; he couldn't stay dead. Knowing that did little to alleviate her panic.

"Anna! *Watch out!*" Markus screamed.

Staggering forward, she felt like a fist had connected with her spine.

She looked down, eyes widening as a flash of lightning brightened against the steel protruding from her abdomen. Blood poured down her stomach and legs, warming her chilled flesh. Anna coughed as the Kraken screamed in the background, likely spraying blood on Trevor as she choked on it.

Tears tracked down her cheeks as she withheld the soul-deep sobs trying to escape.

"Anna, luv, what's wrong?"

Stupid question, she almost laughed to herself.

Good God, this pain was going to swallow her whole.

"I l—" she choked out, vision blurring as the steel in her stomach wrenched one way and twisted.

Trevor screamed, likely realizing what now covered him in the tomb.

"I told you, little bird," Cunningham whispered into her ear, lips dragging against her skin, "you aren't enough."

Damn every god and goddess she could name.

Why did Cunningham's voice and Trevor's broken cries have to be the last things she would ever hear?

CHAPTER FIFTY

Trevor's heart kicked against his ribs again, fresh air lingering on his tongue.

Fucking shite.

What had he done this time?

His chest expanded painfully, drawing deep wheezes from his lungs. Bloody hell, it was dark wherever he was. And what the fuck was the taste of blood doing in his mouth? He tried swallowing, but his throat ached, raw. His wrists burned something fierce too. No matter how many times he blinked, it was still dark. Was it night, or was he in a room wi' no windows? The ocean echoed in the distance, a churning meat grinder of a thing.

Where the hell was he?

Trevor breathed deep through his nose, smelling citrus and silk buried deep beneath the smell of blood.

Anna.

Sitting up fast, he cracked his skull against stone. Stars peppered his vision, but he cared naught for them. Shite, where was the lass? If he could smell her, she had to be close. Groping around revealed he sat in a box of some sort, pulling a tremor down his spine.

"Anna," he whispered hesitantly. "Anna, luv, please answer me."

She said naught.

478

Frustration pulled a growl from his chest. As his eyes adjusted to the dark, he noticed a slit in whatever bloody box he was in, the gap near enough to fit himself through. He called her name again and then Tate's; if anyone could tell him what the fuck was going on, it was his babe of a brother. But if Tate was here, why was Trevor still in the gods-damned box?

His chest tightened, skin tingling as it became harder to breathe.

Laughter murmured back, but he didn't recognize any of the gods-damned voices.

Would no' be the first time his ears played tricks on him.

He glanced up, feeling a drip against his chest as an outline formed in the shadows. Bringing his hands up, he felt the sharp bite of a sword—fuck. His breath whooshed out of him, dread lurking in his every bone. Hand trembling and eyes burning, he followed the blade upward until his hand pressed against soaked fabric.

Anna—gods, no.

He remembered—he fucking remembered, and he wanted no part of it.

The sound of the steel punching through her stomach and that of her last breath.

What had he done to deserve this?

The tears started slowly, and on his next inhale, they came all at once—burning tracks down his cheeks and stinging his eyes. Fucking hell, he couldn't breathe. There was no' enough air in this wee box Cunningham had stuffed him in, and what air had been left was rotten wi' the metallic smell of her blood.

Why? he thought, trembling.

Wheezing and near chokingly, he turned on his side to empty his fucking stomach, muscles clenching as bile crept like a bloody fire up his throat. Trevor shook his head and tried taking deep breaths, but bloody hell, he couldn't find an ounce of calm in him. Anna lay dead above him, and he was soaked in her gods-damned blood, unable to follow.

He loved her. He was so hopelessly and endlessly in love wi' her.

And he hadn't told her when he had the chance.

He saw it.

He fucking saw it all laid out before him.

In another life, another time, where they'd have met by chance, Trevor would've been a bloody baker and the lass would've come into his shop to buy those wee shell pastries.

The bell would've sung as she bumped the door, and he would've looked up, sun breaking through at the same time Anna did, making her pale hair shine bright. He'd have noticed her eyes first, and he'd have nodded and smiled politely, fingers brushing as he accepted her money. Trevor would no' have said shite, couldn't talk to save his fucking life, and she'd always be the loveliest thing he'd ever seen.

But she'd have come back the following bloody week and the one after that.

They'd have kissed and talked and whispered about dreams.

Would've asked her to marry him wi' a ring he'd saved up for all his own, and she'd have said yes immediately—if only because this was his fucking fantasy and she was a wee more agreeable in it.

They'd have married and there'd be babes, wee ones to fill a home wi' love and laughter. Bright red curls and eyes so blue they'd break ye. Lads and lasses, as many as she wanted, as many as she would let him have.

They would have been a family—*his* family.

But he would get naught now.

Naught but ash and what-ifs.

Trevor bit into his arm, gasps wet and ragged, and tried to keep his pain to himself.

Fuck, he was going to lose his damn mind.

CHAPTER FIFTY-ONE

"We'll go back for them," Juliana whispered against his hair again. "I promise we'll go back for them."

Her arms were wrapped tight around his shoulders as he laid against her torso on the ground, hand clutched against his chest and knees tucked against his stomach. His skin burned and his clothes were too tight. He pressed his face against Juliana's chest, the small swell of her breast beneath his cheek.

"What if he takes my sister with him? What if I n—" His voice broke. Juliana ran her fingers through his hair until his breathing evened out. Voice lowering, he stared out into the churning ocean from where they hid behind a stack of rubble. "What if I never see her again?"

Juliana sighed, her breath warm against him. "You will see her again. He won't take her."

Cunningham's remaining men had started creeping back into the ruins an hour ago. They had stuck to the walls at first, creeping from one stack of debris to the next. Markus wished they had something to worry about, that the Kraken would reach back up from that blasted pool and drag them all down. But it had slithered back beneath the water's dark surface hours ago.

"*Shh,*" one of them snapped, the sound echoing.

"Do you think it's gone?"

"I hope so; Captain is having us drag that sorry son of a bitch back to the ship whether it's gone or not."

Markus waited until a pair of dark shapes crept past. He blinked a few times at the growing light in the cavern. It wasn't much, but visibility increased minute by minute. The sun must have broken the horizon.

It was a new day.

Anna wasn't in it.

He swallowed hard, a stabbing pain ripping through his chest.

"How do you know?" he murmured.

Juliana tensed beneath him, her arms tightening. He listened as her heartbeat increased, his ear right over where the organ sat in her chest. "They won't take her."

"They're taking him."

"They won't take a corpse aboard," she said quickly before swearing and dropping a kiss to the crown of his head. "I'm—I'm sorry."

Shaking his head, Markus closed his eyes tight against the truth trying to suffocate him. She was a corpse, her soul long since having left the cage of her body. Did that matter, though? Did it matter to him that what made his sister herself was no longer there?

Markus didn't think it did.

He wanted to bury something, to have somewhere to go to pay his respects and tell all his secrets to. They hadn't had that with their mother. Father had had Sara Sommers cremated, her ashes spread into the ocean she so loved—or so he claimed. Markus would have emptied them out in the desert surrounding Heylik Toyer.

"We can't leave her here," he choked out.

"We won't," she whispered, rocking him slightly. "I promise you, we will not leave your sister here. She'll have a proper burial, a place to visit, a stone with her name that will stand the testament of time. I promise you that, Markus. And then when we have grieved and placed painted flowers and seashells upon her grave, I will promise you revenge."

Blast it all to hell.

Markus would not stop until he had Cunningham's head.

He would not stop until it sat upon a pike, rotting and fetid.

Juliana's hand slid against his forehead. "You feel warm."

"Do I?"

He couldn't tell—he couldn't...feel much of anything.

Exhaustion, maybe?

Crippling anger?

A seeping numbness that threatened to turn him to stone like some of the monsters of old?

"You should sleep."

He wished he could.

But when he closed his eyes, Markus saw the glint of steel pass through Anna's stomach.

LATER

"Lovelace, the sun has risen, it's a lovely day, and it's time for you to leave the box."

Trevor roared, making it clear he'd fucking kill anyone who came near him.

Had it only been hours?

Fucking hell, it had felt like years. The lid fell to the side, quickly followed by a noose. They dragged him from the tomb, his ruined leg giving out as soon as he put pressure on it.

That mattered naught.

He would no' be a king if he couldn't fight on his bloody knees.

Trevor killed more than half a dozen men before catching sight of her on the ground. The trembling started in his hands before it spread to the rest of his gods-damned body. The hope that she would come back, that maybe she'd drank from the chalice all those years ago, guttered out. If the lass had no' come back yet, chances were she would no'.

Bryce fucking Cunningham stepped over her body, ripping the rapier from her stomach. Trevor's own blade fell from his grasp, clanging against the stone flooring before his hands slapped against the cold ground, attention never leaving her. He laid his head upon the ground wi' another choked laugh, gaze stuck on his lovely female, on his Anna, looking like a gods-damned angel even in death.

He met her dead eyes, her lips parted and blood red, a lost curl caught at their corner in a smear of blood.

In the end, Cunningham's crew dragged him out of the temple wi'out a fight.

And he went willingly to their ship like he would go willingly to their gallows.

ACKNOWLEDGMENTS

Write a book, they said.

Then write *another* book.

And, eventually, *another.*

I'm not entirely sure if it ever ends and I'm okay with that. Story telling is just as much a journey for the author as it is the reader. Every book is a tangle of beginnings and endings, a multitude of possibilities, a tale of *there and back again.* The greatest part of every adventure is that the hero never embarks alone, and neither did I.

First and foremost, I lay my gratitude at RaeAnne's feet. *These Hollow Shores* wouldn't have been possible without her and her unending grace and flexibility. I have actual nightmares that she will retire from editing one day.

Thank you, Dane & the rest of the Ebook Launch for another amazing cover. Nothing will ever be quite as motivating as seeing the cover of my book.

Thank you to my wonderful *THS Hype Crew* for all your words of encouragement and feedback! Everyone needs a team of individuals who loves their work, and you're mine. I adore each of you! Thank you, Abigail and Aliss, Brittnie and Charity, thank you, CJ and Danielle, Heather and Jess, Kat and M'Kenzee, Sarah, Tiffany, thank you, Tricia and Kay!

My favorite part of publishing *This Savage Sea* was befriending other authors, most of which hold a special place in my heart now. Bilbo had his dwarves and Frodo had his fellowship. I had you while writing and editing *These Hollow Shores.* May oodles of adoration be showered upon you, I am so appreciative of your friendship. Thank you for walking this path with me, Miranda Joy, Lindsay Clement, L.L. Campbell, E.K.B, and T.M. Ledvina.

I will forever be grateful to my family, for fostering creativity, for my dad asking, *"why not you?"* He was right. Why not me, why not publish, why not publish *again?* Thank you, mom and dad for always being there for me and talking to your friends about my book. And thank you, Grandma for buying *This Savage Sea* and sending it to all my cousins, aunts, and uncles. I imagine you'll probably do it again with *These Hollow Shores*—I'm sorry in advance if any of you don't like explicit spice.

Glenn and Bella.

Thank you, thank you a thousand times. I'm crying as I write this, but I hope everyone can tell how much I love the both of you by the words I put on paper between Anna and Markus. I know I've said it before, and I'll say it again: the Savage siblings and their interactions wouldn't be possible without you.

When I married my husband, I was gifted a second set of parents who love and value me like my own. Thank you, Martha and Eric for being there for me as well. I have felt welcome and loved since I first met you when I was seventeen.

They always say, *save the best for last.* I have saved my greatest. If there ever was a reason *These Hollow Shores* wasn't pushed back, it's my husband. Thank you, babe, for all that you have done in the past year so I can finish my book. Thank you for being you. Thank you for being mine.

I love you.

ALSO BY A.P. WALSTON

TIDES OF FATE

This Savage Sea